MW00531955

THE GREATEST
URDU STORIES
EVER TOLD

Also by Muhammad Umar Memon

My Name is Radha: The Essential Manto
Naiyer Masud: Collected Stories
Naiyer Masud: The Occult
The HarperCollins Book of Urdu Short Stories
An Epic Unwritten: The Penguin Book of Partition Stories
The Colour of Nothingness: Modern Urdu Short Stories
Fear and Desire: An Anthology of Urdu Short Stories
Hasan Manzar: A Requiem for the Earth
Abdullah Hussein: Stories of Exile and Alienation
Intizar Husain: The Seventh Door and Other Stories
The Tale of the Old Fisherman: Contemporary Urdu Short Stories
Abdullah Hussein: Night and Other Stories

The
GREATEST
URDU
STORIES
EVER TOLD

selected & translated by

MUHAMMAD UMAR MEMON

ALEPH

ALEPH

ALEPH BOOK COMPANY
An independent publishing firm
promoted by *Rupa Publications India*

First published in India in 2017
by Aleph Book Company
7/16 Ansari Road, Daryaganj
New Delhi 110 002

ISBN: 978-93-83064-07-6

1 3 5 7 9 10 8 6 4 2

Printed at Repro Knowledgecast Limited, India

For Luca and Kai
with much affection

CONTENTS

INTRODUCTION

Fiction in its limited Western sense and in two of its major forms—the novel and short story—is only a recent and borrowed phenomenon in Urdu. Exceptionally rich in poetic creation, the pre-modern Urdu literary tradition offers few works of belles-lettres in prose that can compare favourably with modern notions of the short story or novel. It isn't exactly that Urdu lacked fiction of any kind. There was always the dastan, to be sure. But the dastan, until it was finally written down and printed in the nineteenth century, was an oral and anonymous composition, narrated by professional dastan-gos or story-tellers for the entertainment of feudal or metropolitan aristocracy, though it didn't preclude public recitals for the amusement of the masses. More significantly, the dastan, because of its flair for exuberant fantasy and the supernatural, used plot and character in fundamentally disparate ways from Western fiction. Here, the intent and design was to *prove* or *disprove*, rather than to reveal, some established or preordained truth about life. It referred all causality to supernatural rather than to human or natural agencies, offered a different notion of time, and its characters were unavoidably two-dimensional. Stripped of individuality, they were commissioned to personify abstract ideas. The dastan was thus a different—but by no means inferior—fictional possibility from the Western novel and short story.

Although artistically more refined works of fiction were still roughly a hundred years in the future, some transitional work had already begun to appear in the early nineteenth century, as in Mir Amman's *Baagh-o-Bahaar* (1801) and Rajab Ali Beg Surur's *Fasaana-ye 'Ajaa'ib* (1834). However, they did not depart in any significant way from the long-standing tradition of the dastan, except perhaps in length. And while its setting was contemporary, its contents in some respects new, and its dependence on supernatural incident practically non-existent, Pandit Ratan Nath Sarshar's *Fasaana-ye Aazaad* (serialized between 1878 and 1879 in *Avadh Akhbaar)* too, did not manage to break away entirely from the style of the dastan. Not until the novels of Deputy Nazir Ahmad (d. 1912) would the prolonged courtship with the dastan finally appear to break off, only to be resumed briefly in the works of his younger contemporary, Abdul Halim Sharar. Nazir Ahmad was motivated less by a creative impulse than by a concern for the moral education of his own children. For greater effect, he turned to the form of the novel: a story with a plot—but nonetheless a story to teach, yoked inexorably in the service of moral instruction. He wrote several novels. All shared his unfailing touch for realism. The idiom was unpretentious, crisp, and close to everyday speech. Often his prose managed to achieve great evocative power. But ultimately, Nazir Ahmad's transparent didacticism only managed to subvert the notion of fiction as an autonomous realm.

With Abdul Halim Sharar (d. 1926), a journalist and pioneer of historical romance in Urdu, the world of Urdu letters began to harken back to the dastan, or so it seems. He wrote out of a desire to rehabilitate Islam and sing its bygone glory at a time when Muslims were on the retreat in practically all areas of their political life. Their pride had been badly hurt in the 1857 War of Independence, which they had lost. Sharar's romances, of which he wrote many, flouted every law of probability and played fast and loose with history. But this didn't deter the Muslims from loving them, mostly for their balmy effect; their immense therapeutic potential.

It was this fictional background against which Mirza Muhammad Hadi Ruswa wrote his *Umraao Jaan Adaa* (1899)—the first true novel in Urdu, more in the sense of fundamentals than in refinements. For Ruswa hadn't fully managed to suppress the didactic element, yet this element was least intrusive or jarring. What Ruswa had managed to achieve was considerable: a sense of character with distinct selfhood; a keen understanding of the mechanics of good fiction. He told his story skilfully; he gave it a well-constructed and coherent plot which developed according to believable causality; and he also knew how to enliven the work with dialogue full of subtlety, wit and humour.

Although the short story had made its hesitant appearance during this period, its employment by the Urdu writer was both sporadic and tentative. Not until Munshi Premchand (1880–1936), the first professional short story writer in Urdu, did it develop into a discrete genre and a major landmark of literary topography. But even in Premchand, the notion of fiction as an autonomous realm was relentlessly subordinated to a notion of fiction as an instrument of protest, reform, and redress. As much was already clear in his very first short story, 'World's Priceless Gem' (1905). In the pervasive, gushy and oversweet romanticism of the period, it set the tone for a new kind of literature—at once socially more aware and aggressively patriotic.

However, there is enough evidence to suggest that in his later work, as in the short story, 'The Shroud' (1936)—a masterpiece of wry humour and clawing irony subsumed by a dispassionate, objective narrative style—he was slowly edging towards some notion of fiction's autonomy.

His limitations aside, Premchand's chief contribution lay in helping the short story emerge as a distinct, freestanding narrative genre. He was also able to give it a more expansive range of topics and, more importantly, finalize its inevitable and long-pending break with the cloying romanticism of his time, best exemplified by such writers as Sajjad Hyder Yildirum and Niaz Fatehpuri. Premchand's discovery of rural life and its conflicts as potential fictional subject matter opened new possibilities for many of his contemporaries. Under his influence, Pandit Sudershan, Ali Abbas Husaini, Akhtar Orainvi, Suhail Azimabadi, Lam Ahmad, Upendra Nath Ashk, and Hayatullah Ansari produced many short stories focusing on life in rural India.

The joint legacy of Ruswa and Premchand was enriched by the publication, in 1933, of *Angaare* (Embers), a collection of ten short stories by a group of four young writers: Ahmed Ali (d. 1994)—the future author of the celebrated English novel *Twilight in Delhi,* Sajjad Zaheer (d. 1973), Rashid Jahan (d. 1951), and Mahmuduzzafar (d. 1954)—all from the urban upper-middle class, and all highly educated. *Embers* strove for an alignment of literature with the contemporary socio-political reality of India. At a deeper level, however, because the writers were well read in Western fiction, the work introduced a more varied and relatively more complex treatment of the form of the short story, under what appeared to be unmistakable Marxist and Freudian influences.

Naive and simplistic from today's perspective, these stories nonetheless carried within them the embryo of some of the future developments in the form. They didn't renounce Premchand's socio-political concerns; rather, they expanded the thematic parameters of those concerns. For instance, sex was added as a valid subject for fiction. A corresponding expansion in the range of devices closely followed the widening of the thematic range.

Five years later, the foursome, along with a few like-minded intellectuals, launched the Progressive Writers' Movement in Urdu, as an offshoot of the Indian Progressive Writers' Association, founded two years earlier in London.

The Progressive Movement—a literary arm of the Communist Party of India—took over Premchand's legacy of socially aware writing and built on it further by incorporating literary assumptions drawn from several Russian writers, among them Leo Tolstoy and Maxim Gorky. It strove, on the one hand, to expose the plight and struggle of the economically depressed classes in rural and urban settings (such as the peasantry and the proletariat) and, on the other, to articulate the political and nationalistic aspirations of a disenfranchised people seeking liberation from the British Raj.

In its time, the Progressive Movement represented the single most formidable literary force throughout India. A whole generation of the brightest minds of the period had been attracted by it. What especially drew these people to the Progressive Movement was its passionate commitment to Indian independence and religious harmony. This aspect of the Progressive mandate—its 'anti-imperialist slant', in Rajinder Singh Bedi's (d. 1984) characterization—continued to fascinate even those writers who found little else to agree with in the literary mindset of the Progressives. It also kept them glued to the Movement. But not for long.

Ideological rigidity lurked just around the corner. As the Movement became dogmatic and doctrinaire, it arrogated to itself—and itself alone—the right to expound on the essence of 'progressivism' in literature. Sex, which even Sajjad Zaheer had earlier admitted as a valid fictional subject, came to be played down and was disowned as being downright reactionary. While writers such as Krishan Chandar (d. 1977) clung unquestioningly to the Movement's distinct Marxist rhetoric, a few bold and independent-minded spirits, including Ahmed Ali and Akhtar Husain Raepuri (d. 1992), who had been at the cutting edge of the Progressive Movement, eventually broke away from it. Not that they didn't believe in the socio-political reality of their times; rather they found it irrelevant or inadequate as the final arbiter of the value of their creative work.

The eleven years between the founding of the Progressive Movement in 1936 and the Partition of India in 1947 are remarkably intriguing from the perspective of Urdu literary history. The short story proper, born with Premchand, grew to relative maturity in that brief period, in both thematic range and technical skill. The bulk of the writing of the period, however—which was made up of the 'utilitarian' fiction of the Progressives—continued to be traditional in its main technical attributes. It was marked, above all, by a pronounced emphasis on linear development and sequential plot. The narrative mode was still largely naturalistic, hesitant to turn inward, unaware—or perhaps uncertain—of the potential of devices such as the deliberate scrambling of temporality, interior monologue, subtle interplay of consciousness and its free associations, exploited with such surety of touch by James Joyce and introduced by his forerunner, the French Symbolist, Edouard Dujardin. While incipient stream of consciousness and flashback could be detected even in some of the works of the writers of the *Angaare* group, a more skilful, though by no means widespread, treatment of these devices, as well as surrealism, was to be found in some of the short stories of Ahmed Ali, Saadat Hasan Manto (d. 1955), Muhammad Hasan Askari (d. 1978), and Qurratulain Hyder (d. 2007).

Major strides in the short story of this period were generally made by those writers who stood outside the Progressive fold or belonged to it only nominally or, as in some cases, had split from it. Among the so-called renegades, Akhtar Husain Raepuri, Saadat Hasan Manto, Muhammad Hasan Askari, Ahmed Ali, and Mumtaz Mufti (d. 1995) came in for the worst kind of verbal attacks by the Progressives, as their fiction was declared to be without any redeeming social value and therefore plainly decadent. In their patriotic and humanitarian zeal, the Progressives took a minimalist view of contemporary man: a victim of socio-economic forces. That such a man could also be a psychological being with memory, desire, and history, be a part of a cultural continuum, have an inner life, a distinct personality—these questions were ignored as irrelevant.

A part of the failure of the Progressives was inevitably due to their overbearing concern with society at the expense of the individual, but a part was also due to their relatively less secure grasp of the poetics of fiction. The treatment of the inner life cannot, almost of necessity, avoid a thorough familiarity with a wider range of narrative devices, especially suited to plumb the individual consciousness. These devices might place less emphasis on plot and even replace linear order with psychic associations. Eventually, all such discussions must be predicated upon a premise which recognizes the inherently autonomous status of literature, something the Progressives rejected out of hand.

Manto, working under Gorky and Guy de Maupassant's influences, Bedi and Askari under Anton Chekhov's, Ahmed Ali under Joyce and Kafka's, and Mumtaz Mufti under Freud's, were thus better equipped to map the inner topography of man. All of them dealt with the theme of human alienation, but the feeling produced a distinctive shade of colouration in each.

The Partition of India in 1947 amidst bloodshed and gross human misery generated by communal riots handed an unprecedented thematic boon to Progressive and non-Progressive writers alike. The former seized the opportunity to denounce the riots for their unmitigated violence. Most of their writing on the subject, however, tended to be rather facile and effusive, the worst offender being Krishan Chandar, one of the most ardent and die-hard Progressives of his time. Tragically he limited, as only he could, the scope of the meaning of Partition to inter-religious riots, a case, merely, of some Hindus killing Muslims, some Muslims killing Hindus, quite failing to exploit the event's tremendous potential for a fresh, if painful, exploration of human possibility, and its meaning against the wider backdrop of subcontinental history.

The best writing on the theme of Partition, again, came from the 'independents'. In a single brilliant piece, 'Laajwanti'—(written in the early 1950s)—for instance, Bedi portrayed the devastating effects of Partition on individual lives more powerfully than Krishan Chandar in his half-a-dozen pyrotechnical conflagrations, of which 'Peshawar Express' (1947), 'Amritsar before Independence' (1947), 'Amritsar after Independence' (1947) and 'The Blind' (1947) were by no means the only examples. However, according to common consensus, the most sustained and masterly treatment of Partition came from Manto, who dominated the literary scene as the master craftsman of the short story right up to his death in 1955 and continues to guide and inspire even such modernists as Balraj Manra (d. 2017). His unforgettable 'Toba Tek Singh' (1949), 'Cold Meat' (1949), and 'Khol Do' (1949) have lost none of their poignancy even today, more than six decades after the division of India.

The Progressives were a spent force by the mid-1950s, or at least had lost their earlier mesmerizing hold on the imagination of the writer. Half of their ideological battle had been won: the firangi had left, the country was free—even if the freedom had come in the wake of a traumatic division, killings, an exodus, and a massive dislocation. The other half, the dream of a just, equitable and secular society, however noble, properly belonged—as a generation of artistically better-informed writers was to soon find out—in the realm of political and social action. For this generation, brought up on Dostoyevsky and Joyce, existentialists Jean-Paul Sartre and Albert Camus, and such anti-novelists as Alain Robbe-Grillet and Michel Butor, sincerity and nobility and social usefulness had little place in a narrative art whose basic building block was 'fabrication'.

Partition was thus perhaps the only major theme which inspired a sizeable corpus of writing dealing starkly and unabashedly with a political issue. Few Urdu writers in India or Pakistan have since ventured to step into that domain so demonstratively and persistently. And where they have, such as the dismemberment of Pakistan in 1971 and the subsequent emergence of Bangladesh as a sovereign nation, their writing invariably suffered from overtness, but gained through indirection, suggestion, a sense of distance, and inwardness.

A few exceptions notwithstanding, the Urdu short story up to the mid-1950s was structurally quite simple. Causality, seriality, the tripartite formula of a beginning, a middle, and an end as popularized by E. M. Forster, an almost fanatical insistence on what is often termed 'unity of expression and effect', the twist at the end à la Maupassant or O. Henry—here the repertoire ended. Social reality, not the character's psychology, provided the inspiration for the writer and defined his calling. But in exposing contemporary social reality, the writer almost always overlaid the fictional event and character with his own prejudices. There was little evidence yet of a move towards either suppressing the writer's point of view, or cancelling the narrator altogether.

However, in at least one story by Manto, 'Tassels' (1954), the narrator was wholly suspended. Using absolutely incredible events and characterizations which relentlessly shunned the factual, 'Tassels' at no point allowed the writer to become the narrator. Thus, both the character and events remained free from the writer's intruding persona. The resulting reality existed in an eccentric and autonomous domain, and even though it drew its building components from social reality, it was not otherwise bound by it.

The next logical step was to develop further the expressive possibilities inherent in 'Tassels' and in a few other short stories by Askari and Ahmed Ali. This step was taken by what is called *jadeed afsaana* (the new short story).

Periodization has never proved satisfactory in either literary history or in literary taxonomies. While a precise date for the emergence of the new short story cannot be given, as some of its elements were already present in Manto and others, it can nonetheless be said that the new short story as a more pervasive genre is a phenomenon dating from the 1960s. Although Intizar Husain (d. 2016), Enver Sajjad (b. 1936), Surendra Prakash (d. 2003), and Balraj Manra are generally credited with ushering in the modernist phase of the Urdu short story, none except Manra started out with recognizably 'modernist' fiction. The other three came to it after a prolonged apprenticeship in the traditional mechanics of the short story.

The word 'modern' might be best understood in this context as a synonym for 'post-realism'. It undergirds a set of literary assumptions, viz., that there is an internal structure to reality beyond what meets the eye, and human nature is infinitely more complex than was assumed by Progressive writing. Realistic, mimetic paradigms employed hitherto were equipped to deal with external reality only. A more flexible and inclusive paradigm is called for, if it is man in his infinite mystery that one is after. This new paradigm cannot put its trust unquestioningly in the techniques of realism; rather it might freely revise old notions of linearity, plot and character.

In Dujardin's novel *Les lauriers sont coupées* (1887) Western fiction had found the narrative technique to plumb the depths of individual consciousness in the most spontaneous way yet—to let the consciousness narrate itself. The very first sentence lands the reader, directly and ineluctably, in the mind of Daniel Prince, the novel's dandy protagonist.

If Dujardin was unknown to the Urdu writer, James Joyce was not. Some of the Progressives themselves were influenced by him. Interior monologue and stream of consciousness had already been employed, though somewhat tentatively, by Sajjad Zaheer, Ahmed Ali, and Askari; however, in Urdu, the use of these techniques became closely associated with Qurratulain Hyder. Hyder, whose literary career dates from Partition or thereabouts, turned decisively towards a focused use of stream of consciousness only in the late 1950s, with her novel *River of Fire* (1959), which she wrote, as some Urdu critics believe, under influences absorbed from Joyce and Virginia Woolf.

Other narrative devices, too, made their appearance at about the same time. Intizar Husain, whose literary career coincided roughly with Hyder's, experimented in varying degrees of success with collapsing the seriality of time and staggering the linear chronology of events, to articulate, on the one hand, the powerful inner tensions of his protagonist; to capture, on the other, the precise ambience of the enchanted world of his childhood. His novel *Basti* (1979) offered a more refined treatment of this technique, already anticipated in numerous previous short stories of his, among them 'The Threshold' (1955), 'The Stairs' (1955), and 'A Stranded Railroad Car' (1954).

With Enver Sajjad, Balraj Manra, Surendra Prakash and Ahmad Hamesh (d. 2013), fictional narrative turned further inward. The traditional notion of causality gave way to an abstract principle of causality. Narrative foreground was deliberately muted or flattened, and the form was taxed with the entire burden of creating meaning.

Sajjad, for instance, in his story 'The Bird', did away with all but the most crucial particularizing detail, to penetrate, seemingly, down to the essence of experience with relentless immediacy and directness. The highly textured narrative surface of his work strove, quite self-consciously, for a fusion between fictional form and content. He expressed his subject through a medium—mostly the short story—stripped down to the bare minimum. The attenuated form inevitably packed his prose to breaking point, but gave it a brutal directness and poignancy. His subject—as he often delineated it for the reader—was essentially the same: the protest to fight against all forms of oppression. Preoccupation with tyranny and oppression might suggest topicality and even appear modish, reducing the piece to a mere tract for the times. Indeed, some ideological critics, and certainly the remnants of the Progressives, rushed to anoint Sajjad as the saviour of the Third World. But some astute critics, among them Shamsur Rahman Faruqi (b. 1935), have also noted that the expected reduction or degeneration just does not occur, precisely because the integrity of the objective distance between the writer and his subject is scrupulously maintained in the greater, and certainly the better, part of his work. The resulting elusiveness (in the best meaning of the word), heightened by the desire not to pin down, fix, determine or otherwise explain, left the experience intact, untrammelled by spatial or temporal specificity. His stories therefore refused to be read as social documents.[*]

Other writers mobilized similar modern techniques to achieve the effect of simultaneity through linguistic manipulation, juxtaposition, and superimposition—all in the effort to develop a model more organically suited to fathom the nature of experience. Their fiction was not one of verisimilitude or of real life; it studied, if anything at all, 'itself', its own processes. It was self-referential or non-referential. Which makes it more difficult to determine the fictional subject with precision.

Indeed, it is not easy to determine the fictional subject of Surendra Prakash—India's leading Urdu short story writer after Rajinder Singh Bedi. His stories, because they do not replicate familiar reality but create a new one, are essentially—to use Joseph Frank's term—experiments in 'spatial form'. In other words, their different constituent elements—rather units— do not 'unroll in time', but are 'juxtaposed in space'.[**] His characters often appear to be a pristine essence unlikely to receive palpable existence or personality—consciousnesses caught in the moment of self-reflection at a pre-verbal and pre-existential level—frozen in an instant of time, as in a snapshot; and if they move at all, they do so only within the confines of their minds.[***]

---

[*]Cf. Shamsur Rahman Faruqi, *Afsaane ki Himaayat Meñ* (Delhi: Maktaba-ye Jaami'a, 1982), p. 138.

[**]'Spatial Form in Modern Literature,' in his *The Widening Gyre: Crisis and Mystery in Modern Literature* (New Brunswick: Rutgers University Press, 1963), p. 10.

[***]Cf., Faruqi, Preface, in Surendra Prakash, *Doosre Aadmi ka Draa'ing Room* (Allahabad: Shab-Khoon Kitaabghar, 1968), penultimate page of the Preface.

'Jippizaañ' (Name of the Awaited Patriarch; 1969) and even more his nightmarish 'Wood Chopped in the Jungle' (1969), like a painting by Dali, bring forth characters and events that refuse location in familiar time and space. The surface unreality is reinforced by names that do not ring a bell. 'Jippizaañ' not only has no identifiable personal attributes, he is also non-existent as a personal name. When faces pale, they pale 'like the blossoms of zarfanki', and earlobes burn a flaming red 'like the tender new shoots of qartuni'. So how is one to imagine the precise shade of 'pale' and 'flaming red' when zarfanki and qartuni are names of no known plants and tend to have a purely imaginary existence? It is a fiction that compares itself to itself and stands familiar reality on its head. Debunks and defamiliarizes it! It depicts a city—as in 'Wood Chopped in the Jungle'—'where they sell melons halved like human heads'. And insists that even if we don't know who Jippizaañ is, or whether indeed he ever existed, we must still find his image—sprouting 'a khaitri (a mini grainfield) in his right palm and holding a shankh (conch-shell) in his left hand'—grippingly beautiful. The suppression of the familiar, of the temporal/causal coordinates could not be more relentless!

The unique incorporeality of Prakash's fiction, therefore, evokes shock and wonder, but authenticates, however dimly, some of the writer's own subliminal fears and anxieties. He achieves this effect, as Faruqi has so aptly observed, 'by keeping close to the quintessential experience, so that it could be exposed in all its stark horror, awesome beauty, and spellbinding freshness.'* Unlike Premchand and most of the Progressives, the writer in his work is—to borrow a phrase from James Joyce—'refined out of existence'.

The writer also disappears in some of Khalida Asghar's (b. 1938) work. Take, for instance, the all-time favourite 'The Wagon' (1963). Told in a straightforward linear manner by a first-person narrator, the writer-narrator is held hostage to a montage of insane, causally incomprehensible events, which he doesn't editorialize, but which, nonetheless, immediately take hold of the reader and draw him/her into the midst of a horrific experience, using the writer-narrator as little more than a conducting medium. Similar self-control and self-denial is evident in the narrator of her story, 'The Millipede' (1964). Never for a moment here, as elsewhere in some of her creative work, do we feel manipulated, nor is our sense of discovery undercut.

These stories can scarcely offer an apprehension of reality, though they

---

Ibid.

do invite the reader to reflect, meditate, and feel with the writer what must inevitably remain quite elusive—the experience not in retrospect or tamed or vanquished—vanquished, that is, by a mediating point of view—but unfolding, out there, before the eye in its pristine, unreferenced uniqueness. More importantly, being experiments in 'spatial form', they undermine in varying degrees of intensity 'the inherent consecutiveness of language' and thus 'place a greater burden on the reader's synthesizing power than do more conventional temporal narratives'.*

Yet the modernist artifice and the new poetics of fiction have not dislodged the traditional short story and its conventional architectonics. The traditional form continues, with greater subtlety, technical virtuosity, and artistic finesse in, among others, Abdullah Hussein (d. 2016), Hasan Manzar (b. 1934), Zamiruddin Ahmad (d. 1990), Muhammad Salim-ur-Rahman (b. 1934), and Iqbal Majeed (b. 1934).

Alienation as a fictional subject surfaced with Askari, Bedi and Manto and arose out of immediate material conditions. In Balraj Manra, working under Camus' influence, it assumed a different shade of colouration—metaphysical absurdity which drove man to radical estrangement, captured hauntingly and with rare economy of words in his memorable piece 'Vo' (He; 1964). With Abdullah Hussein, on the other hand, it shaded off into powerful feelings of guilt and exile. His characters experience, as I have written elsewhere:

> emotional disorientation resulting from a harrowing sense of some real or imagined inadequacy, the unbridgeable gulf between longing and becoming. The sources of man's dissatisfaction are many, and most are found in his environment. But for the substantial number of Hussein's characters, the malaise is produced, rather, in the interior landscape of the self, is inevitably pointed inward, and is, therefore, the more tragic. They cannot blame others for their condition; they are poised fatally against themselves.**

Practically all of Hussein's work takes the reader on a journey that explores the nature of alienation and exile. In 'Phool ka Badan' (1963), for instance,

---

*Jeffery R. Smitten, paraphrasing Joseph Frank, in *Spatial Form in Narrative*, ed., Jeffery R. Smitten and Ann Daghistani (Ithaca and London: Cornell University Press, 1981), p. 17.

**See Preface and Acknowledgement, in Abdullah Hussein *Downfall by Degrees and Other Stories*, ed. and trans. by Muhammad Umar Memon (Toronto: TSAR Publications, 1987), pp. 7–8.

Sarwat, after ten years of being married to a man she respected but did not love, and all her thirty-two years of pining for the man she did love, finally gets what she wanted: a night of uninterrupted intimacy with Naim, her childhood love. But is she the happier for it? Has she been set free, as she thought she would be, after the delayed encounter of bodies? Hardly. The morning after, she wakes up to the bitter truth: desires—fulfilled or thwarted—give us nothing; they only rob us. For once two hearts have lost their mutual rhythm, they drift apart, unlikely to ever come back together, even by a sacrifice of the flesh.

On the other hand, Naim is pleasantly surprised to discover that the woman he had all along ignored, considering her erotically flat, turns out to be so filled with passionate energy, 'so amazingly incandescent...so vibrant with life that she carried him to the summit of unimaginable bliss'. By her true giving and spontaneity, she has awakened him to a new reality: 'When passion has run its course, and the blood has chilled, love is what remains behind...like the fugitive scent of a rose' which, however intangible, 'is still more real than its bloom'.

But the knowledge comes—alas—too late to do either of them any good. As true exiles, both Sarwat and Naim must now drift inconsolably in their orbits of loneliness, equipped with a knowledge that does not redeem or soothe, but only picks at the scab to expose the raw, throbbing wound.

Like Hussein, Zamiruddin Ahmad, Hasan Manzar, and Salim-ur-Rahman too prefer a relatively simple and direct narrative style over one riddled with technical gyrations (although Rahman's style does subsume a measure of technical innovation). But the surface simplicity hides a more textured art, and one no less complex. Take, for instance, Rahman's futuristic 'Ashes' (1981) or the disarmingly simple 'Siberia' (1979). Neither story depends on rhetoric or outlandish technical experimentation for effect. Yet only with intense reflection could the reader hope to intuit, falteringly, some of their elusive wealth. Here, complexity results from introducing a more fantastic event (ashes falling from the sky and enveloping the entire landscape in one case; the illusion of snow, taken as real by the protagonist, in a city where it never snows, in the other) in the otherwise perfectly normal structure of the stories. In 'Siberia', the writer's point of view is so scrupulously witheld that the slightest clue to the meaning of the central event is denied to the reader, who nevertheless comes away with a visceral experience of the protagonist's ambivalence about the ultimate meaning of the events. In time, the experience generates in the reader his or her own confused responses vis-à-vis his or her own events. The truth—or, precisely therefore, the meaning—of the story lies in making palpable the atmosphere of troubled anticipation without resorting to any of the conventional methods of evoking fear and anxiety. 'The Night Time Melted Away' (1967), written two decades earlier than 'Ashes' and 'Siberia', on the other hand, does show a minor technical innovation. The narrative is temporally staggered, in perfect consonance with the mental state of the protagonist, for whom time has come to a standstill. The story is a stunning masterpiece of the unity of form and content.

A master of understatement, Zamiruddin Ahmad excels in squeezing out the last suggestion and nuance from the expressive powers of the language. In his earlier stories, he dealt masterfully with the themes of duplicity in interpersonal relationships, of moral death, and of the suppressed sexuality of middle-class women of eastern U.P., often married and Muslim. But 'The Easterly Wind' (1987) and 'Sukhe Saawan' (1987) remain unsurpassed for their controlled eroticism and sensuality in Urdu fiction.

The work of Naiyer Masud (b. 1936) defies any attempt at classification. His fictional world is, quite simply, unrivalled. It has the cushy softness of dreams, 'where the shadowy wistfulness', in the words of Salim-ur-Rahman, 'conveys a sense of queer foreboding',* where an otherwise artless surface hides a troubled and troubling vision. He reminds one of Kafka, whom he has creatively assimilated, not slavishly imitated. His theme, which can only be sensed dimly, is truly colossal: the entire problem of *being*.

'Nusrat' (Victory n.d.), although rather opaque, is according to Rahman:

> obviously about the loss of an old ethos, an old way of living, the
> disappearance of old values. The division is neat. An inner courtyard
> with an old surgeon who has given up his art but can still manage to
> be effective; a tree, almost of knowledge or wisdom, but seemingly of
> no use to anyone; Nusrat ('victory' rather ironical), the soul or the yin,
> unable to walk, i.e., to progress or proceed. The outer room is literally
> a dead end, probably the modern world encroaching on the old. But it
> is inorganic, with lifeless curios, and has to do with inquisition, trials,
> harshness, suffocation. Life-denying not life-enhancing. The old surgeon
> can affect a cure but once he has disappeared the narrator can do
> nothing. He runs around the house like a madman and although he
> bravely claims to remember it all, he is lying. And when he unwittingly

---

*'To Make Dreams Truth', in *The Pakistan Times* (Lahore) 13 January 1989).

causes Nusrat's feet to get injured again, he can of course do nothing about it. It is all over. The door is shut permanently. The final image of Nusrat beneath the tree with her face hidden by yellow leaves held together by cobwebs reminds one of Magritte's paintings... The story is definitely about a great loss.[*]

The legacy of the modernists such as Surendra Prakash and Enver Sajjad, on the other hand, still awaits fulfilment. There is no dearth of followers. Indeed, a whole generation of younger avant-garde writers in India and Pakistan has been experimenting most assiduously with deconstruction and metafiction. But its impatience with time, character, and plot, and its passionate human concern remain to be crystallized into a definite artistic expression. So far, Anwer Khan and Muhammad Mansha Yad (d. 2011) have consistently produced good modern fiction.

Altogether then, the short story is essentially a borrowed form in Urdu. The British domination of India and the questionable validity of traditional constructs prompted Indian intellectuals to look at the world in fresh ways. It also stimulated experimentation with Western fictional forms like the novel and short story. Two tendencies immediately stand out in the writing of the period: literature subordinated to societal regeneration (the didactic impulse) and literature as an autonomous realm (the individualist impulse). The didactic writing is socially oriented. It seeks to reform society, by ridding it of its own traditional ills (religious, economic, and gender exploitation), and by generating strong patriotic feelings to put an end to British colonial rule. The individualist strain offers two varieties: romantic and psychological. It is the latter that vehemently preserves the integrity of literature as an autonomous domain, bound only by its own laws and values. If it appears— until the mid-1950s, at any rate—somewhat overshadowed by the 'utilitarian' writing of the Progressives, it is because the latter's ideological commitment to Indian freedom exercised a hypnotic pull on the nationalistic aspirations of the people. But today, after the decline of the Progressives, it is the individualist impulse that has unmistakably moved to centre stage. The present volume is, by and large, concerned with this impulse.

Despite its technical and thematic wealth, the Urdu short story has remained less widely known among South Asians of different linguistic

---

[*]In a letter to Muhammad Umar Memon, 3 March 1989.

backgrounds. Since English alone enjoys the status of a shared language among these readers, it is inevitable that one reaches out to them through English. Hence this collection. But in doing so, I have, with a few exceptions, concentrated mainly on writing since Partition. I have also tried to discuss the short story as a development in form. It is because chronological, rather than formal, development has dominated the critical discourse where there has been any discourse at all. In Urdu criticism itself, if it's any consolation, an analysis of the short story as a discrete fictional form is a recent phenomenon, so far undertaken only by critics such as Shamsur Rahman Faruqi and Waris Alvi (d. 2014)—in a concerted and focused manner by the former, in a diffused though insightful manner by the latter. Sikandar Ahmad (d. 2013), a banker by profession, also produced a few penetrating articles about the art of the short story. The present selection hopes to achieve two objectives: to present the texture and flavour of the modern Urdu short story, both as a daring experiment and as a more refined heir to the traditional form; and to eschew all pronouncements about literature's alleged social relevance. To the extent narrative fiction is bound up with character and event, it cannot avoid a certain social reference; characters do, after all, eat, talk, and appear clothed—elements that give them away. Then again, prose, by its very nature cannot transcend time. To reduce literature to its social usefulness, or to read it as history, is to do violence to its nature. Ali Imam Naqvi's (b. 1945) 'The Vultures of the Parsi Cemetery' (1984), Syed Muhammad Ashraf's (b. 1957) 'The Man' and Salam Bin Razzaq's (b. 1941) 'A Sheet' are first and foremost successful stories, and only later astute observations on the nature of communal strife which still plagues secular India seven decades after Independence. The message—if there is one—the observation, the indictment alone could not have made them into works of art. Conversely, Naiyer Masud's 'Obscure Domains of Fear and Desire' continues to glow long after one has miserably failed to make it yield up even an ounce of social usefulness.

And yes, there has been a deliberate attempt throughout not to talk of women writers as a distinct group. In this age of rampant discussions, partisan or otherwise, of divisions and subdivisions, of cultures and subcultures, of liberation and identity, the only decent way to show respect to half of humankind seemed to lie in not identifying it as a marked species. Woman and man are part of a single continuum, and to think otherwise is downright vulgar. Urdu literature is an act of imagination. And who ever heard that man imagines better than woman, or the other way round?

xxiv   *The Greatest Urdu Stories Ever Told*

More in the nature of daydreaming, there is also the fervent hope that this collection might prove useful to the comparativist who may wish to assess the nature of the Urdu short story against its counterpart in other major subcontinental languages, specifically Hindi.

The stories offered here are, quite simply, the stories I personally have enjoyed reading. I can offer no better criteria for their inclusion than my own passion and prejudice. Nor is the selection intended to be exhaustive. The exclusion of some writers, however, is not meant to belittle their importance. In addition to those included in the present work, Aziz Ahmed, Razia Fasih Ahmad, Hijab Imtiaz Ali, Rashid Anwar, Masud Ashar, Saleem Asimi, Mirza Hamid Beg, Muhammad Ahsan Faruqi, Akhtar Jamal, Farkhunda Lodhi, Hajira Masrur, Khadija Mastur, Masud Mufti, Banu Qudsiya, Shafiqur Rahman, Anwer Sen Roy, Qudratullah Shahab, Mumtaz Shirin, Shaukat Siddiqui (Pakistan), Khwaja Ahmad Abbas, Qamar Ahsan, Anwar Azeem, Jilani Banu, Satish Batra, Prem Nath Dar, Ghayas Ahmad Gaddi, Devindar Issar, Balraj Komal, Ram Lall, Iqbal Matin, Kumar Pashi, Joginder Paul, Qazi Abdus Sattar, Balwant Singh, Wajida Tabassum, Mohsin Khan (India), Sham Barakpuri, Hyder Safi, Gholam Mohammad (Bangladesh), and still others, have all contributed to the richness of Urdu fiction with truly impressive work. But to sample even one-half of them would have required an investment in time and space quite beyond the ability of the present editor or his publisher.

I have tried to achieve a balance between the realist, traditional type of short story and its more daring modern counterpart. This has led me to discuss some stories and authors who are not part of the present work but are crucial to the understanding of the development of the Urdu short story.

Since the anthology is intended, primarily, for the South Asian reader who, presumably, knows little or no Urdu, I have cited Urdu titles sparingly, often using, where possible, only their English approximations. I have also tried to save the work from becoming—rather, degenerating into—a textbook by eschewing annotations or glosses, except in two or three instances.

I'm grateful to Javaid Qazi, Caroline J. Beeson, and my late friend, Faruq Hassan, who participated with me in translating the short stories by Naiyer Masud, Intizar Husain, and Zakia Mashhadi and to my former student, G. A. Chaussée, for translating Ghulam Abbas's 'Aanandi'.

Boundless thanks are also due to Aienla Ozukum and Rosemary Sebastian

Tharakan for their careful editing, but most of all to Simar Puneet for her unflagging interest in this book which, eventually, made it possible for me to undertake it. I shall never be able to thank her enough for her generous help and consideration.

Muhammad Umar Memon
12 June 2017
Madison-Wisconsin

OBSCURE DOMAINS OF FEAR AND DESIRE

NAIYER MASUD

Ba kuja sar niham keh chun zanjir
Har dare halqa-e dare digar-ast
(Hide—but where?
Each door I close opens another.)
—Anonymous
(found in a ghazal by Mir Taqi Mir)

Thou holdest mine eyes waking;
I am so troubled that I cannot speak.
I have considered the days of old,
the years of ancient times.
—Psalm 77

We kept looking at each other, in silence, for the longest time ever. Our faces didn't betray any kind of curiosity. His eyes had an intensity, a brightness, but throughout this time, never for a moment did they seem to be devoid of feeling. I could not tell if his eyes were trying to say something or were merely observing me, but I felt we were coming to some silent understanding. All of a sudden a terrible feeling of despair came over me. I was experiencing it for the first time since I'd come to this house. Just then, his nurse placed her hand on my arm and led me out of the room.

Outside, as I spoke with his nurse, I realized that my speech was a shortcoming and that the patient was travelling far ahead of me on a road I knew nothing about.

I have given up talking, not looking. It isn't easy to stop looking if one happens to possess a pair of eyes. Keeping quiet, even though one has a tongue, is relatively easy. At times I do get an urge to close my eyes. But so far they are still open. This may be due to the presence of the person who is looking after me. She is my last link with that old house where I opened my eyes for the first time and learned to talk. When I lived in that house, she was just a cute little doll, only a year-and-a-half old. And so affectionate towards me. I would call for her as soon as I entered the house and then she would cling to me all the time I was there.

Now she has no memory of those days. All she's been told is that I am the last representative of her family. She does not know much else about me. In spite of this, she is very fond of me. She thinks this is the very first time she has seen me. She does not remember that I used to call her my 'Little Bride'. Actually, I started calling her that because she would refer to me as her bridegroom whenever someone in the family asked her who I was. This amused everyone. They would all laugh and then, just to tease her, someone would claim me as a 'bridegroom'. When she heard this she would throw a regular little tantrum. Among those who teased her were several older relatives, both male and female. In those days, her small world was crowded with rivals. But even then, the ranks of her rivals did not include the person for whom she had the warmest feelings, not counting her mother or myself. And in return, this woman cared more deeply for the little girl than anyone else.

1

She was at least two years older than me. Twelve years prior to the time I'm talking about, I had seen her at my older brother's wedding. She was the younger sister of my brother's wife. But due to a complicated pattern of kinship, she also happened to be my aunt.

At the time of my brother's marriage, she was a mature young woman and I was a mere boy—a shy, awkward youngster. She adopted towards me the attitude of someone much older than myself. Of course, we often chatted, shared jokes and teased each other. But despite all this informality, she maintained the air of an elder. However, I never detected any affectation in that attitude, which perhaps would have irritated me. She treated me not as though she were much older than I, but as though I were quite a bit younger than she. And I liked that.

There were times, however, when I got the distinct impression that I was, after all, just her young nephew. This happened when she compared her hometown with mine and insisted that hers was a much better place. I would immediately leap to the defence of my town and argue with her endlessly in a rather childish manner. During those years, she visited us once in a while and stayed with us for long periods of time. And during this particular visit she had been with us for three or four days.

I came into the house and, as usual, called out to my 'Little Bride' as soon as I'd stepped into the courtyard. But the house was silent. No one seemed to be home. However, Aunt was there. She had just emerged from the bathroom after her bath and had sat down in a sunlit spot to dry her hair. I asked her where all the others were and she said they had all gone to a wedding somewhere. Not knowing what else to say, I asked her about my 'Little Bride' even though I had a hunch that she might have gone to the wedding with the others. I went and sat next to Aunt and we started talking about this and that. Most of the time we talked about my 'Little Bride' and chuckled over her antics. After a while Aunt's hair was dry and she stood up to tie it in a bun. In an effort to arrange her hair, she raised both arms, with her hands at the back of her head. Her bare waist arched slightly backwards, her bust rose and then fell back a little, causing her hair to fall away from her. I saw this in a fraction of a second but it had no particular effect on me. She continued to tie her hair in a chignon and we went on talking. Suddenly one of her earrings fell off and landed near her foot. I quickly bent down to retrieve it for her. As I knelt at her feet, my eyes fell upon the pale curve of her instep and I was reminded once again that she had just taken a bath. I picked up the earring and tried to put it back in her ear while I kept up a rapid flow of conversation. I could smell the musky odour which rose from her moist body. She continued to fiddle with her hair and I kept on trying to put her earring back in. But for some reason I couldn't get it to stay and her earlobe began to turn red. I must have jabbed her with the post of the earring. A little cry came from her throat and she scolded me mildly. She then took the earring from me with a smile and quickly put it in herself. Soon afterwards, she went up to her room and I to mine.

A little later, I went upstairs looking for a book. On the way back, I glanced at Aunt's room. She stood in front of the bamboo screen. Her hair hung loosely about her shoulders and her eyes looked as though she had just woken up. I went into her room and again we started talking about the same sort of trifles. She started to tie up her hair all over again and once more I saw what I had seen earlier. Seeing her waist bend backwards once again, I felt a bit uneasy. We talked about the wedding that my entire family had gone to attend and I told her that there was a great difference in height between the bride and bridegroom. Exaggerating rather wildly, I insisted that the bride barely came up to the waist of the bridegroom.

Aunt laughed at this and said, 'Anyway, at least she's a little taller than your bride.'

We started talking about my 'Little Bride' whose absence made the house seem quite empty. I was about to introduce some other topic when Aunt stood up from the bed and came towards me.

'Let's see if you're taller than I am,' she said with a smile.

Grinning, we came and stood facing each other. She moved closer to me. Once again I became aware of the fragrance that rose from her body, a warm, moist odour that reminded me that she had just bathed. We drew still closer and her forehead almost touched my lips.

'You're much shorter than me,' I told her.

'I am not,' she retorted and stood up on her toes. Then she giggled, 'How about now?'

I grabbed her waist with both hands and tried to push her downwards.

'You're cheating,' I told her. And bending, I grabbed both her ankles and tried to plant them back on the floor. When I stood up after some time, she wasn't laughing any more. I clasped her waist firmly with both hands once again.

'You're being unfair,' I said to her as the grip of my hands tightened on her waist.

Her arms rose, moved towards my neck, but then stopped. I felt as though I were standing in a vast pool of silence that stretched all around us. My hold on her waist tightened still more.

'The door,' she said in a faint whisper.

I pulled her close to the door without letting go of her waist. Then I released her slowly, bolted the door and returned to her. I remembered how she had always behaved like an older relative towards me and I felt angry at her for the first time, but just as suddenly, the anger melted into an awareness of her tremendous physical appeal. I bent over and held her legs. I was still in that position with my grip around her legs progressively tightening when I felt her fingers twist in my hair. She pulled me up with a violent intensity and my head bumped her chest. Then, with her fingers still locked in my hair, she moved back towards the bed. When we got to its edge, I eased her onto it, helping her feet up with my hands. But she suddenly broke free and stood up. I looked at her.

She murmured, 'The door that leads up the stairs…it's open.'

'But there's no one in the house.'

'Someone will come.'

Silently we went down the stairs and bolted the door at the bottom. Then we came back up together, went into her room and bolted the door from the inside. Apart from the tremors running through our bodies, we seemed fairly calm, exactly the way we were when we talked to each other under everyday circumstances. She paused near the bed, adjusted her hair once again and, taking off her earrings, put them next to the pillow. In a flash of recollection, I remembered all those stories I'd heard about love affairs that started after the lovers stood together and compared their heights. But I decided at once that these stories were all imaginary, wishful tales and the only true reality was this experience I was having with this woman, who was a distant aunt—but an aunt who also happened to be the younger sister of my brother's wife. I picked her up gently and made her lie down on the bed, reflecting that just a short time earlier I had entered the house calling for my 'Little Bride'. It's possible that the same thought may have crossed her mind. A light tremor ran through our bodies. I had just begun to lean towards her when she suddenly sat up straight. Fear flickered in her eyes.

'Someone is watching,' she said softly and pointed at the door. I turned my head to look and got the impression that someone was peeking through the crack between the double doors. The person appeared to move away and then return to look again. This went on for a few minutes. Both of us continued to stare in silence. Finally, I got up and opened the door. The bamboo screen which hung in front was swaying back and forth gently. I pushed at it with my hands and then closed the door once again. The sunlight streaming in through the crack in the door created a pattern of shifting light and shade as the bamboo screen moved in the breeze. I turned back towards Aunt. A weak smile flickered around her lips, but I could hear her heart throbbing loudly in her chest, and her hands and feet were cold as ice. I sat down in a chair next to her bed and began telling her tall tales of strange optical illusions. She told me a few similar stories and pretty soon we were chatting away as we always did. Not one word was exchanged about anything that had transpired only a few minutes earlier. At length she said to me, 'The others should be coming home soon.'

At that moment it occurred to me that the door leading up the stairs had been bolted from the inside. Just then we began to hear the voices of family members. I got up, opened the door of the room wide and went out. Aunt was right behind me. I unbolted the door that led up the stairs and then we came back to her room and continued to make small talk.

After a while, I heard a noise and saw my 'Little Bride' standing at the door. She really did look like a bride. Aunt uttered a joyful shout, grabbed the little girl, pulled her into her lap and started to kiss her over and over again with a passionate intensity. The little girl shrieked with laughter and struggled to escape from her embrace. Apparently, in the house where the wedding had taken place, some overly enthusiastic girls had painted her up like a bride and decked her up with garlands. A few minutes later her mother came up to the room along with some other children. By this time the little girl was sitting on my lap and I was asking her about the delicious food she'd eaten at the wedding. She could only pronounce the names of a few dishes and kept repeating them over and over. Her mother tried to pick her up but she refused to budge from my lap.

'Oh, she is such a shameless bride,' Aunt said and everyone burst out laughing.

At some point we all came down to the veranda where the other members of the family had gathered. Aunt kept showing my 'Little Bride' how to act shy, and every now and then bursts of laughter rose up from the small group.

2

By the time the sun had gone down, I'd made many attempts to catch Aunt alone. But she sat imprisoned in a circle of women, listening to anecdotes about the wedding. During the night, I tried three times to open the door that led up the stairs but it appeared to be bolted from the other side. I knew that a couple of women—themselves never married and perpetual hangers-on in the household—also slept in her room, but even so I wanted to go upstairs. Next day, from morning till noon, I saw her sitting with the other ladies of the family. I never did like spending much time with women so I uttered some casual remarks to her and did my best to stay away. By late afternoon all my family members had retired to their rooms and most of the doors that opened onto the courtyard were now bolted from within. I went up the stairs and lifted the bamboo screen from Aunt's door. She lay on the bed fast asleep. I looked at her for the longest time. I had a feeling that she was merely pretending to be asleep. She lay with her head tilted back on the pillow and her hands clenched tightly into fists. She had removed her earrings and placed them next to her pillow. Scenes that had taken place in this very room just the day before flashed through

my mind, but I drew a complete blank when I tried to remember what
had happened during the moments that followed. It seemed to me that I
had just picked her up in my arms and placed her on the bed. I stepped
inside the room and turned to close the door but noticed one of those
extraneous women sitting with her back against the balcony, winding some
woollen yarn into a ball. She gave me an enthusiastic greeting and made
the utterly superfluous remark that Aunt was sleeping. I pretended to be
looking for a book and then, complaining about not being able to find it,
I left the room. But while I was searching, I looked over at Aunt several
times. She seemed to be fast asleep after all.

Late in the afternoon, I saw the extraneous woman come downstairs
and once again I went up and peered into Aunt's room. She was standing
in front of a mirror combing her hair with her back towards me, while
another extraneous woman recited a tale of woe about the first time she
was beaten by her husband. I'd heard this story many times before; in
fact, it had been a source of entertainment in our house for quite some
time. Aunt laughed and then, noticing me in the mirror, asked me to sit
down. But I questioned her about the imaginary book which I had been
searching for and went back downstairs.

I was away from the house for most of that evening. I had been sent
to take care of some family matter, but I botched the whole business and
returned home late at night. The doors of all the rooms were closed from
within, including the one that led up the stairs. I went into my room and
closed the door. For a while I tried to summon the image of Aunt, but
I failed. I did manage to evoke her scent very briefly. As I slipped into
sleep, I felt sure I would see her in my dreams. But the first phase of my
sleep remained blank. Then, towards midnight, I dreamt that the extraneous
women were dressed up as brides and were making obscene gestures at each
other. Soon after that I woke up and only managed to get back to sleep
closer to dawn. At daybreak I woke up from a dreamless sleep. My head
felt foggy and confused. I decided to take a shower. In the bathroom I got
the feeling that Aunt had just been there and I shook my head again and
again to clear my senses. When I emerged from the bathroom I saw Aunt
sitting in the sun drying her hair. One of my elders went up to her and
began a lengthy discourse on the various ancient branches of our family.
On the veranda, the same two extraneous women I had seen yesterday were
quarrelling over something, but the presence of the old gentleman forced
them to keep their voices low. Three other women in the same category

soon joined the fray and contributed their halfwitted views to reconcile the two or perhaps add fuel to the fire. Aunt was listening to the elderly relative very attentively and had covered her head as a sign of respect. I left her talking to this gentleman and went upstairs. But I came to a dead stop outside Aunt's room. Another extraneous woman was standing outside the bamboo screen. She asked me if Aunt had taken her bath. I told the old hag that I wasn't responsible for bathing Aunt and went downstairs again. Until now I'd had no idea we had so many extraneous women crawling about our house. Their only practical use seemed to be to help with domestic chores, whether exacting or easy. Downstairs, the elderly gentleman was still pacing in front of Aunt. He had dealt with the past history of the family and was starting on the present.

Late in the afternoon I was sent out once again. But the situation that I'd been trying to deal with since yesterday deteriorated even more and I returned without accomplishing anything. That night I woke up many times. It occurred to me that the customary visit of Aunt as our house guest was almost at an end and the hour of her departure was drawing near. In the morning I felt as though my head was full of fog once again and in spite of a cold shower, I couldn't get rid of this heavy-headedness. I felt sure that if I found Aunt alone somewhere, I would kill her. I didn't much care how I would do this either. I decided that I'd better stay away from her that day.

Much later, just as I emerged from my room, I saw her. She sat talking with some other women of the family and motioned with her hand for me to come over. The veranda was unusually quiet. The Little Bride slept in her mother's lap. Clearly, she was ill. I took her into my lap and questioned her mother about her condition. Then the old gentleman, one of my elders, came into the veranda and the atmosphere became even more sombre. He made an effort to lower his loud voice and asked about the child. But the little girl woke up. She looked as though she had almost recovered. The old gentleman began to tease her about her bridegroom. From the way the child responded, it became clear to us that she had not realized she was in my lap. The old gentleman then queried her regarding my whereabouts. Her response made everyone laugh. Finally, I tickled her lightly. She realized who I was and began to giggle in embarrassment. The elderly relative picked her up and took her away. She was quite fond of him too and had woken up several times during the night calling for him.

As soon as the old gentleman left, the atmosphere of the room changed and peals of laughter rang out again and again. While they were all talking, Aunt and I began to argue about what the date was that day. As we debated back and forth, the others looked on with keen interest. Aunt simply couldn't be convinced. From where we sat, I could see the corner of a calendar that hung in a room next to the veranda. Long ago, a relative had drawn it up for us. With it, one could tell the date of any day in any year. But this took a long time and one had to do several lengthy calculations. Eager to prove our cases, we got up to examine this calendar. Both of us entered the room together. But as soon as we were behind the door we clung to each other convulsively and almost sank to the floor. Then, just as abruptly, we got up and went out. The little girl's mother asked us if we had decided who was right, but just then there was some laughter, and then some more. Aunt was looking pale. Anyone coming in on us at that moment would undoubtedly have assumed that we had just come out of the room after spending quite a long time together.

That day I successfully finished the task I had mishandled twice earlier and returned home even later than the previous night. Everybody was in bed, so I also went in and lay down. From the moment that Aunt had gotten up from the bed and come towards me to compare heights, to the time we had entered the room with the millennium calendar, I hadn't given much thought to how she might be feeling. I hadn't even considered that she might be totally unaffected by it all. Even so, I thought about killing her. All night long I was assaulted in turn by remorse, the allure of her physical charms and the longing to meet her alone again.

In the morning, when I came out of my room after a sleepless night, I was in the throes of remorse. So when an extraneous woman, the first one to rise, told me that Aunt's brother had arrived late at night with some bad news and that they had both left together, the only thought that came to my foggy mind was that I wished I'd been able to apologize to her.

None of the elders in my family could believe it when I told them that I had grown tired of my sheltered life and wanted to be on my own. And when they expressed reluctance, I was quite unable to assuage their doubts and concerns. Nevertheless, I succeeded in making them give in to my demands, mainly because they cared a great deal for me. Upon seeing all the elaborate arrangements they had made for my journey, I realized how comfortable and secure I had been in that house and felt rather fed up with myself. A few days before my departure, they gave me a small stone amulet inscribed with sacred names to wear around my neck. It was an heirloom which had been in our family for many generations. This increased my annoyance. Quietly, I took the amulet off and put it back in the chest full of old clothes where it had always been kept.

My elders said goodbye to me in a subdued way and, as I walked away from my home, the voices I could hear for the longest time were those of all the extraneous women. They were praying for my safe return.

3

I faced great hardships as I struggled to make myself independent. And in the end it was the good name of the family elders that helped me along. Thus, without moving a finger, indeed without even being aware of it, they helped me stand on my own two feet. The work that I had undertaken involved inspecting houses. Initially, I had the feeling that I would fail in this profession because back then, apart from my own house, all other houses looked to me like heaps of inorganic matter or half-dead vegetation. Sometimes I felt a vague hostility towards them, sometimes they looked like cheerless toys to me, and sometimes I stared at them for a long time as though they were foolish children, trying to hide something from me. Perhaps this is why, though I cannot seem to recall exactly when, houses began to assume a life of their own right before my eyes.

In the beginning I had no interest in the humanity that existed in these houses, though by merely looking at one I could make an estimate of how old it was, how and when certain improvements had been made over the years, as well as the speed with which Time passed inside these structures. I was sure that the speed of Time within these houses was not the same as it was on the outside. I also believed that the speed of Time could vary from one part of a house to the next. Therefore, when I calculated the rate of a home's deterioration and the years still left in the structure, the estimate usually bore no relationship with the outward appearance of the place. Still, none of my calculations ever proved to be right or wrong because even the smallest estimate of the years left in the life of a house was always larger than the years remaining in mine.

One day, as I was standing in front of a house, something about its closed front door gave me the impression that it had covered its face, either out of fear or to shield itself from something, or perhaps out of a sense of shame. I was unable to assess this house. Therefore, when I went in I examined every nook and cranny, every ceiling, wall and floor very carefully. I wasted the entire day there without coming to any conclusion and at length came home only to spend most of the night thinking about this place. I reconsidered my assessment strategy and tried to remember all the details. At some point, it finally occurred to me that there was one part of the house which aroused fear and another part where one felt that some unknown desire was about to be fulfilled.

The next day I found myself standing in front of another house. The front door was closed but it seemed to me that the house was staring at me with fearless, wide-open eyes. A short while later I was wandering inside it. When I entered a certain part of the house I became very apprehensive. Now I awaited the second sensation, and sure enough, in another part of the house, I got the feeling that some significant but unexpressed wish of mine was about to come true.

I was surprised at myself for having overlooked this fact until now. I returned to the houses I had seen many times and located these domains of fear and desire. No house, whether old or new, nor one among many of the same basic design, was without these domains. Looking for these domains of fear and desire became a vocation with me and, ultimately, this vocation proved harmful to my business. Because I was becoming convinced, without the least bit of proof, that it was impossible to assess the life span of homes when they contained these domains of fear and desire. After suffering tremendous losses, I felt I had turned into an idiot or was losing my mind altogether and I decided to give up this vocation. But inspecting houses was my work and even if I did not look for these domains of fear and desire consciously, I would instinctively come to know where they were. All the same, I made an effort to cut down on my interest in them.

Then one day I discovered a house where fear and desire existed in the same domain.

I stood there for a while, trying to decide whether I was experiencing fear or desire but I could not separate the two feelings. In this house, fear was desire and desire, fear. I stood there for the longest time. The lady who owned the house wondered if I was having some kind of fit. She was a young woman and at the time there was no one else in the house except the two of us. She came close to me to examine me carefully and

I realized that this domain of fear and desire was affecting her as well. She grabbed both my hands and then with a strange, cautious boldness, she advised me to rest for a short while in the front room. I told her that I was quite well and, after a few minutes of conversation with her about business matters, I left the house. Perhaps it was after this day that I started taking an interest in the humanity that lived in these houses.

Eventually, I could not imagine one without the other. In fact, at times I felt as though both were one and the same, because both intrigued me equally.

This interest increased my involvement with houses. Now I could look at a house in the most cursory manner and yet discover passageways that were secret or wide open, in use or abandoned. I could tell whether voices rising from one part of the house could reach other parts of the house. I'd examine each room very carefully to ascertain which parts of the room were visible from the crack between the door panels, or from the windows, or the skylights, and which parts could not be seen. In every room, I found a part that was not visible from the crack between the door panels nor from any window, nor from any skylight. In order to isolate this part, I would stand in the middle of the room and paint the whole place black in my imagination. Then, using only my eyes, I would spread white paint on all those parts that could be seen from the cracks or windows. In this manner, the parts which remained black were found to be the truly invisible parts of the room. Apart from certain rooms that were meant for children, I never did find a room in which the invisible part could not provide a hiding place for at least one man and one woman. Around this time, I began to concentrate on the shapes of these invisible parts. They made up the outlines of different images and at times had a truly amazing resemblance to certain objects. But I never did find a complete picture of anything. Everything appeared to be incomplete or broken, even though I examined countless such 'invisible' parts. Some of these images had familiar shapes—of a lion, for instance, or a crab, or a pair of scales—but they all seemed like fragments. Other images resembled unknown objects and they looked incomplete although unfamiliar. They left a strange effect on the mind which was impossible to articulate.

One day I was in the outer room of a new house looking at the image of the invisible part of the room. The image had an unfamiliar shape. As I examined this shape it occurred to me that long, long ago I had seen a decrepit old house in which the domain of desire had had exactly the same shape.

Until now I had only ascertained the boundaries of the domains of fear and desire in these houses. I had not thought about the shapes which could be formed from these outlines. But now I began to recall many—or, perhaps, all—shapes, and it occurred to me once again that either I was turning into an idiot or I was losing my mind altogether. Anyway, I became convinced that no one else could look at houses the way I did. I was also quite overwhelmed by the thought that no one else had the kind of rights that I had over the humanity that lived in these houses.

4

I didn't stay in any one place. I wandered through many cities and moved in and out of many homes. To me, at least, it began to look as though the cities were crowded with houses and the houses were filled with women. And every woman seemed to be within easy reach. Many women made advances towards me and I made advances towards many. In this, I also committed many blunders. For instance, some women whom I thought to be empty of, or unfamiliar with, or even full of hate for desires, turned out to be saturated with them and more than willing to do the utmost to fulfil them. In fact, at times they made advances so boldly that they frightened me. Other women who seemed to me to be oozing with desire and just waiting for the slightest sign from me, turned out to be so naïve that when I did make a gesture towards them they were unable to understand my intentions altogether. Some were overcome by depression, others were terrified. In fact, one got so worked up that she abandoned her calm and tranquil domestic life and actually left her home. She had a habit of arranging and rearranging her lustrous black hair. And I thought she wanted to draw my attention to it. Then she went away. That was totally unexpected. So I set out looking for her. I just wanted to tell her that her black hair had misled me, but she kept running away from me. Perhaps she thought that I was pursuing her like some sex-crazed animal. I never found her and I suspect that the fear I induced in her might have been the cause of her death. But I often console myself with the thought that she might have accidentally fallen into the river and resurfaced somewhere and been rescued.

5

After this, I gave up making advances towards women. Instead, I took to waiting, wanting them to come after me. At times these waiting periods became rather protracted. During one such lengthy interval, I went to a new city where no one knew me. One morning, as I was wandering around the main bazaar of the city, a woman standing in front of some shops smiled at me and made a sign with her hand. She wanted me to come close to her. At first, I thought she might be a professional and kept on walking. But then she called out my name. I stopped and turned towards her and she hurried over to me.

'Don't you know who I am?' she asked with a smile.

I finally recognized her. Many years ago, she and I had been very close. She hadn't changed much except for the fact that she looked a little older. I was surprised that I had not been able to recognize her. But I was also pleased to run into someone who actually knew me in a strange town.

'What are you doing here?' I asked her.

'I live here,' she said.

In a few minutes we were chatting with the greatest informality. Again and again I got the feeling that she had become a prostitute. I had no experience with professionals. I couldn't even tell them apart from ordinary women. Then why did I suspect she was one? As I talked to her I kept staring at her and my suspicion deepened. She noticed that I was examining her and a smug sort of look came over her face, which made the reason of my suspicion clear to me. For quite some time she had been making a play for me with her eyes, her words and her body. In the past, I had been the one who made advances. Several years earlier, during the period when I'd known her, she was already a woman of some maturity. And now she stood there acting coy like a teenage girl. This saddened me. I examined her closely once again. Even now she was quite attractive. But she had also changed a great deal. As I stood there talking to this woman, I felt as though Time were speeding up, there, in that bazaar.

'Where do you live?' I asked her.

She pointed towards a neighbourhood behind the shops.

'Come, I'll show you my house,' she said. 'If you have the time.'

I had time. In the past, our relationship had begun pretty much in the same manner. She had shown me the house where she lived by herself in those days. Now we started walking side by side through the busy street. She stopped at a shop and bought a big padlock. She placed the lock and one key that went with it in her bag, and dangled the other key casually between her thumb and forefinger as she discussed the merits of a certain type of lock with the locksmith. Then, in an absent-minded way she handed me the key she had in her hand and we walked on.

She wants everything the way it used to be, I thought to myself, and once again it seemed to me that Time was speeding up in that bazaar.

'How much further?' I asked her.

'We're almost there,' she said and turned into a broad side-street.

Presently we found ourselves standing in front of an ancient wooden door that had just been given a fresh coat of paint. She removed the padlock that hung on the door, put it in her bag and went inside. I stayed where I was. Then a smaller side door adjacent to the main door opened and she stepped out. She now had the new lock in her hand.

'You haven't forgotten, have you?' she asked and flashed a bold smile at me.

'I remember,' I said.

I took the lock from her and she went back into the house through the small side door. I bolted the main door and locked it with my key and went into the house through the small side door, bolting it from inside. Now I found myself in a large room that contained many niches and alcoves but nothing by way of furniture. I stepped out of the room into a spacious courtyard which had been enclosed by a wall. I noticed that a tall window made of weathered wood had been built into this wall. I started walking towards it when I heard a voice to my right, 'No, not there. Over here.'

I turned and saw that adjacent to one corner of the wall and behind several small trees there was a veranda. The woman stood there under an arch. I went and sat down on a divan which had been placed there. Behind me there was a door. She opened the door and we went into a room. The room contained a bed and other domestic odds and ends which had been arranged neatly. She fell on the bed heavily as though she were very tired and I took a chair.

'So do you live here alone?' I asked her.

'Alone…well, you could think of it as living alone. Actually, I live here with an old acquaintance—an elderly woman.'

'Where is she now?'

'I don't really know. A few days ago she abruptly burst into tears and cried quietly all night long. In the morning she said, with the greatest reluctance, that she missed a certain house. All of a sudden she longed to be in the house where she'd spent her childhood. Soon afterwards she packed up all her things and went away. I'll introduce you to her when she returns.'

'Why should I want to meet a melancholy old crone?'

'No, no. You don't understand. She can be very amusing. One minute she'll be telling you what a marvellous man her husband was. And the very next, she'll launch into a story about how he used to beat her up. She can be murderously funny.'

'I have no desire to be killed by the anecdotes of some old hag,' I said and left the room.

She came after me.

'What's the matter?' she asked.

'I'd like to see the house,' I responded and went down into the courtyard.

'There isn't much to see,' she said. 'There's this veranda and this room, and that outer room. The rest of the structure has collapsed.'

We were standing some distance away from the window that had been built into the courtyard wall. I examined the wall carefully. It was apparent that the house had been one large structure and the wall had been put up to divide it into two halves.

'Who lives on the other side?' I asked her.

'I don't know,' she said. 'Perhaps no one.'

Now we were standing near the window. The window had been poorly constructed out of rough planks. A board had been nailed diagonally across the two panels in order to seal it permanently. I was drumming softly on this board when I felt the ground under my feet shift. I placed my hands around the woman's waist and pulled her close to me. She looked a little surprised. I too was amazed at myself. I took a few steps back and then let her go. So the domain of desire is right here, I said to myself and then, stepping close to the window, I turned towards the woman again. She looked up at me and smiled.

'You've become rather aggressive,' she said.

Once more the ground shifted under my feet and I shuddered.

And also the domain of fear, I thought, with a causeless melancholy.

The woman stood in front of me, smiling. Somehow, she had succeeded in simulating a look of arousal. I lingered near the window for quite a while. It was a strip of ground barely two feet wide adjoining the window. The rest of the domain lay on the other side of that window.

'Who lives on the other side?' I asked.

'I told you, Mr Impatient, no one.'

'Come on, let's go,' I said, moving close to her. We proceeded towards the veranda. Now she had really begun to feel aroused and put her arms around my shoulders.

'It's very close and oppressive in there,' she said in a whisper and we stopped where we were. I recollected our old encounters when passion used to sweep her off her feet like a wind storm, and now, here in this house, she was either being overwhelmed by a storm of desire once again or leading me to believe that she was. In this house, or at least in this particular part of the house, Time moved faster than it did in the bazaar. A kind of affection began to stir in me for this woman who happened to be the only person I knew in this strange city.

'You haven't changed at all,' she said softly.

'Well, along with Time…' I began and then suddenly, glancing upwards at the window, I saw something shiny in the crack between the frame and the upper edge of the panels. At exactly this time, the woman started to slip away from my grasp. She had closed her eyes, the way she used to. I took her in my arms and looked at the window once again. A pair of dark eyes was looking at us through the crack at the top. As I bent over the woman in my arms, I caught a fleeting glimpse of a red dress through the chinks between the boards. Slyly I looked up once again. The bright black eyes were locked on us. They were not looking into my eyes. They were focusing on our bodies. The idea that we were being watched by an unknown woman who was under the impression that I was unaware of her presence excited me and I averted my face.

At this point we were standing very close to the window. Slowly, very slowly, I bent over this strip of ground until my head reached the bottom of the window. I had only the vaguest sensation that there was a woman with me and that I was holding on to her with both my hands. I fixed my eyes on the lowest chink in the window. Looking down through the aperture, I saw a bare foot. Had the toe of this bare foot not twitched again and again, I would have thought that it had been moulded in pure white wax. Behind the foot, at a distance which I could not determine, I saw an ancient arch of dark wood and the lower portion of a column. The foot took on a red glow from the shade of the dress and I sensed the fragrance of a body in which another, more ancient, odour was also implicated.

The toe rose from the ground and I saw that a long black string had been tied around it. I couldn't tell where the string led. If I'd wanted to, I could have reached in and grabbed the string, and perhaps I had decided to do just that. But the woman with me gripped my hands. Then she opened her eyes briefly and closed them tight again. She may have suspected that I wasn't focusing on her. So I became attentive to her. After a while, she rearranged her hair and said, 'You haven't changed at all.'

I looked at the window once again. There was no one on the other side. It was then that a question welled up inside me. Had this woman wanted to stage a show for a girlfriend? I kept on staring at the window for the longest time and then suddenly I turned towards the woman again and examined her face intently.

But a vacant look of satiation had settled over her expressionless face.

'You haven't changed either,' I said to her and went on to the veranda.

6

I went to see this woman nearly every day.

'Until the old lady returns,' she had told me the very first day, 'this house is yours.'

And, frankly, I did begin to think of it as my own house, and went there whenever I felt the urge. If the main door happened to be closed from the inside, I would knock and she would come and open it. I would sit and talk with her for a little while and then I'd go away. If the main door had a lock on it, I would produce my key, open the lock and enter the house. Then I'd come back out through the side door, put the lock on the main door, re-enter the house through the side door and bolt it from inside. She would meet me either on the veranda or in the room and I would end up returning late that day. But lately it seemed that almost every time I went to see her, I found the main door locked from the inside. I'd have to knock to be let in. She'd open the door and we would spend some time laughing and joking and then I would leave.

One day I knocked on the door for a long time before realizing that it was locked from outside. It dawned on me that I had become used to knocking. I unlocked the door and went in. Then I came back out from the side door, put the lock on the main door, re-entered the house through the side door, bolted it from inside and walked towards the veranda. The woman was not in the veranda and the door to her room was closed from the outside. A couple of times in the past, she'd come home some time after my arrival. I opened the door to her room and lay down on her bed. I must have stayed there for a long time, neither sleeping nor awake. Eventually, I left the room and went out on to the veranda. The afternoon was fading into evening. I was somewhat surprised at myself for having waited so long for her. Anyway, I waited a little longer and then went out through the side door, unlocked the main door and went into the house again. I bolted the side door from the inside and was about to go out the main door when I stopped suddenly and turned back towards the veranda. I walked across the veranda into her room and changed the position of the bed.

She should know, I thought, and came back out on to the courtyard. I was going towards the main door when something made me stop in my tracks. I turned around slowly and looked at the window in the wall. A pair of dark eyes was looking straight into mine through the chink between the top of the window and the frame. I turned back towards the main door.

I should have known, I thought with groundless melancholy, and slowly turned and walked back towards the veranda. I went into the woman's room once again and pushed the bed back to its original position. Then I came out into the courtyard and crept along the wall that ran at an angle to the veranda. Staying close to the wall, I slowly inched forward in the direction of the window. When I got close to it, I bent down so far that my head almost touched the ground. Through the aperture at the bottom I could see the waxen foot with the black string still attached to the big toe. At first it remained perfectly still, but then it looked as though it had started to pull back. I reached under the crack suddenly, grabbed the black string and wound it around two of my fingers. The foot struggled to retreat, but I pulled it back with equal force. Now, between my eyes and this foot, there was my intervening hand with the black string wrapped around the fingers. The string, apparently of silk, was very strong and clearly my fingers were about to be sliced off. I gave it several more turns around my fingers and then suddenly my hand came in contact with the toe.

The pull of the string was making it impossible for me to think clearly. When I had moved from the veranda towards the window, I had decided to make a play for her, but now I couldn't figure out what to do and my fingers were just about ready to drop off. The evening gloom fell over my eyes like a heavy blanket of darkness. I felt a cutting pain but at the same time it became possible for me to think. The very first thing that occurred to me was that I was not the only one in pain. In contrast to my tough and masculine hand, the delicate feminine foot was very soft and the thread that was cutting into my fingers was also tied to that foot. I pressed the toe gently and caressed the foot with two fingers that were free. It felt even softer than what I had imagined it to be, but it was also cold as ice. Yet I could feel the warm current of blood surging under the delicate skin.

By now the blackness of night had spread everywhere and I could barely see the silhouettes of the small trees. I'm hurting her, I thought. Suddenly, it occurred to me that until now I had only pulled the string towards me once. I loosened the string around my fingers by a few turns and groped about the window with my other hand. I grasped the board that had been nailed obliquely across the window and tried to get up. But the board came loose and, precisely at that moment, the string unwound from my fingers. I placed both hands on the window to keep my balance but the window fell open since there was nothing to keep it closed now. In an instant, I found myself on the other side of the window. In the darkness, I could barely see the dim outline of the dark wooden arch and a shadow moving slowly towards it.

I followed the shadow into a region of dense gloom beneath the arch and soon lost sight of myself.

This was my first experience with total darkness. I passed through the arch and went forward for a short distance. But then I found myself stopping. I tried to move north, east, south, west—in all four directions—but the darkness made it impossible for me to advance. I lost all sense of my whereabouts. Nor could I determine the position of the arch any more. All I knew was that I was with an unknown woman in an unknown house and that—I was sure of this—we were alone. My long association with women and houses had given me the keen instincts of an animal. And now as I stood in the darkness, I peered about keenly as an animal does. I took a deep breath. I was certain that the characteristic perfume emitted by ancient houses, which I'd begun to smell outside the door, would soon assail my nostrils. But this did not happen. And even though I knew it to be futile, I squinted into the darkness with such intensity that my features must have surely looked frightening. In spite of this, I could not cut through the darkness. As far as the sounds of voices were concerned, I had ceased to be conscious of them the moment I gave the very first turn of the black string around my fingers. Still, I made an unsuccessful effort to listen. It felt as though I had been standing there straining my senses for a very long time. Then again, it seemed like I had just passed under the arch. Soon afterwards,

I felt two soft hands brush up against mine. I grasped them firmly and pulled them towards me.

After a long interval, I relaxed my grip, and my hands, exploring the elbows, arms and shoulders, began to move towards the face. I tried to get a sense of individual features. But apart from a hint of long, thick eyelashes, I could not get an idea of how anything else looked. My hands wandered across her body, along her legs and down to her feet until my head touched the ground. I tugged at the string gently and then stood up. Now, once again, I felt soft hands clutching my own. Her palms pressed against my palms. And then in the darkness my hands became aware of colour for the first time. Two white palms, upon which a pattern had been traced with red henna, moved from my palms to my wrists, then to my elbows, and from there to my shoulders and then further up until they cupped my face. Her fingers, which had red rings around them, passed over my cheeks and came to a stop at my neck. She tapped my neck three times and then her palms came to rest on my shoulders and stayed there for a long while. Groping slowly across my clothes, they reached down to my feet; then they vanished from that darkened scene for a few seconds and came to rest on my shoulders again. I remembered that ancient scent which had wafted towards me once, mingled with the odour of femininity. This odour is among those smells that are as old as the earth and were around long before flowers came into existence. It was an odour that brought to mind half-forgotten memories. However, at this moment it did not remind me of anything. In fact, I was fast forgetting what little I did remember.

The pressure of the hands on my shoulders increased and then relaxed. And now, all at once, I became aware of the fulsome, palpable presence of a female body. It occurred to me that I was with a woman who had seen me with another woman—at least once—in broad daylight. I also realized that it was useless to try and see in the dark. I closed my eyes. I knew that closing them would not change anything. And, truthfully, there was no difference, not for a while at least. But just when I'd forgotten the physical limitations of my eyes, I saw that I was slowly sinking into a lake of clear water. At the bottom of this lake I could see the ruins of ancient temples. I opened my eyes and was relieved to see only darkness all around. I recalled that there was a woman with me in this gloom. My breath felt the heat that was rising from her body. She is being swept along by a storm, I thought. Once more my eyes began to close and I could not keep them open no matter how hard I tried. Once again I saw the same clear-water lake. The ruins of ancient temples drifted up towards me until they hit my feet. But I couldn't feel them. Then, even as I was watching, the clear water of the lake became very dark and the ruins disappeared.

I don't know how long it was before I woke up. It was still pitch dark all around me. But on one side I saw the outline of the arch and beyond it the beginnings of dawn. I turned to the body lying motionless in the dark and let my hands wander all over it, touching everything. I placed my palms on hers, waiting for a long while for them to become moist with warmth. But they remained cold and dry. However, my hands did feel once again the bright red pattern on one of the palms. The shape of this pattern represented something unfamiliar. I stared hard at this shape and it became clear to me that the shape resembled at once the domain of fear in a certain house, the domain of desire in another house, and the invisible part of yet another room. I tried to remember all the places where I had seen this shape and then it occurred to me that even though the shape was unfamiliar, it was, nevertheless, quite complete. For this reason, I had to struggle to convince myself that I had never seen this shape anywhere before. I made a futile attempt to pick up this shape from the palm of her hand. Then I touched it with my forehead, walked through the wooden arch and went outside. The window resembled a dark stain. I went through it and emerged on the other side.

When I crossed the courtyard and made my way towards the main door, the morning birds were chirping in the small trees directly across from the veranda and some old woman there was coughing away.

7

I did not suddenly stop speaking. First of all, it never even dawned on me that I had given up speech. This is because I never have been very talkative in the first place. The fact is, I just started devoting more time to thinking. After I came away from that house, I slept for two days straight. I caught myself thinking even in my dreams and I continued to think after I woke up. The first thing that occurred to me was that I had got through that night with only the sense of touch to guide me. I had experienced everything by touch alone; rather, all that I had experienced was merely a transformed reflection of my sense of touch. Even so, I had missed nothing and, except for the first few minutes, I imagined that all five of my senses were being fully satisfied.

I never felt any curiosity about that woman. This reaction surprised me and I tried to force myself to think about her. But my mind rejected every image of her that I conjured up. I struggled with myself for many days but I was eventually forced to accept defeat. In the entire fierce encounter with my mind, I came to a realization: I wouldn't be able to recognize her even if I saw her from very close by. But she would recognize me instantly, whenever and wherever she saw me. This thought didn't disturb me very much, but then it didn't make me feel at ease either. I accepted it like some worn-out and exhausted truth and gave up thinking about it. At about this time I realized that I had, more or less, also given up talking.

I have not sworn an oath of silence. It's just that I do not need to speak. This has been made possible for me by the kind people who live in this house. They spotted me somewhere, recognized me, and told me that for many generations our families had been very close. They brought me to this spacious house and graciously urged me to pick out whatever place I would like to live in. I looked over the whole house and chose for myself—who knows, this might have pleased them—a section which had been unoccupied for a long time.

My bed is positioned exactly on top of the domain of fear. I have not been able to discover the domain of desire in this house. But that cannot be. So I have now become convinced that fear and desire converge here in exactly the same spot and that I have dominion over it.

Once I was walking about my room in the middle of the night when I happened to see this spot. It had assumed a black shape. This shape had an unfamiliar but complete outline. I kept on staring at this image for a long time. Then I examined the entire room carefully, peeking into each and every crevice, every window, every skylight. I stained the room white with my eyes, but the black shape remained untouched by this whiteness.

The shape of the invisible part—I thought... At exactly this moment, I began to hear the chirping of the morning birds outside. I felt very strongly that if I tried even a little I would remember where I had seen this shape before. But I made something of a pact with myself never to make this effort. From that moment on I gave up talking.

The same day that I was introduced to my nurse, I moved a part of my bed a little distance away from the domain of fear and desire. She sits on this part of my bed and I just look at her. I believe that in this way I'm protecting her and also protecting myself.

Co-translated by Javaid Qazi

THE SHEPHERD

ASHFAQ AHMAD

It was a long, cold winter night. I was sound asleep in my warm bed, with the quilt pulled all the way over my head, when somebody rudely shook me awake.

'Who is it?!' I screamed.

A large hand bumped against my head and a voice shot forth from the darkness, 'The police have arrested Ranu.'

'What?' I said, as I tried to push the trembling hand away from me. 'What is it?'

The ghost of darkness repeated, 'The police have arrested Ranu—now, translate it into Farsi.'

'Damn you, Dauji,' I moaned, on the verge of tears. 'No peace even at midnight! Get out of here! I won't stay in your house any more. And I won't study either. Damn you, Dauji! You're a dog!' I broke down in tears.

Dauji made a kissing sound to calm me and said, 'How will you pass your exams if you won't study? And if you don't pass your exams you won't become a great man. Well then, how will people come to know about your Dauji?'

'May God just make everyone die...you...people you know...even me. Especially me.' The thought of dying so young made me weep so much that I choked.

Meanwhile Dauji caressed my head with great affection and said, 'Enough. That's enough. Be a brave boy, my darling son. Come on now, just translate this sentence, and I won't bother you any more.'

The stream of tears was beginning to subside. I said in a huff, 'The bastards have got Ranu today, tomorrow they'll whisk away somebody else. But your translations...'

'No, no,' he interrupted, 'I'll never wake you up at night again and ask questions. I promise. Now come on, be good and translate: "The police have arrested Ranu."'

'I can't,' I said, still sulking.

'Always quick to say "No,"' he said, removing his hand from my head. 'At least try.'

'I won't,' I said in a huff.

He laughed a little and translated the sentence himself: 'Kaarkunaan-e gazma-Khaana Ranu-ra tauqeef kardand. There. "Kaarkunaan-e gazma-Khaana" stands for thanewale. Okay? It's a new word for you, a new construction. Now repeat it ten times.'

I knew he wasn't about to get off my back. Helpless, I started the litany of 'gazma-khaanas'. After I'd finished my ten repetitions, Dauji said, practically entreating me, 'Well now, repeat the whole sentence five times.' When the five-fold affliction, too, was over, he helped me back into my bed. Pulling the comforter over me he said, 'Don't forget it. I'll ask you first thing in the morning.'

And then he left the room.

Every evening I would return home via the miller's lane after my Quranic lesson at Mullaji's. All sorts of people lived in that lane, but I was familiar only with the portly water-carrier whom we had nicknamed 'Kaddu Karela Dhaa'i Aane'. There was an enclosure for goats right next to his house. It was bordered on three sides by mud houses, and had a high fence in the front made up of thorny bramble and slap-dash pieces of wood nailed together. On the other side of the enclosure was an open square field, and beyond it the dingy one-room house of the crippled potter. Next to that was another small—but real brick—house with red ochre-framed windows and a door covered with ornamental brass nails. The lane slowly curved at this point and narrowed, and the further one walked down it, the more its two sides seemed to draw together. It was, perhaps, the longest lane in our qasba. It was certainly the loneliest. Walking down it alone I was always overwhelmed by the feeling of walking down the barrel of a gun—the moment I'd come out of it, a deafening bang would go off and I'd fall dead. But in the evening I usually found someone or the other passing by and felt my life had been spared.

One of the pedestrians I occasionally ran into was a tallish man with a snow-white moustache. He bore a strong resemblance to Mulkhi, who sang baarah-maasas. He sported a large turban of fine muslin, a long khaki coat which hung loosely from his slightly bent back, narrow-legged pyjamas of coarse cotton, and a pair of flat boots. A boy about my age, and outfitted every bit like the older man, often appeared in tow. The older man talked to him in soft tones, his head bent, his hands stuffed into his coat pockets. As they came up to me, the boy looked at me and I at him. We each turned our heads ever so slightly and moved along without stopping for a moment.

One day, after some unsuccessful fishing at Thathiyan's pond, as my brother and I were returning to our qasba, we saw the same man sitting on the bridge over the river. His turban lying in his lap, and his white chutiya looking as though it had been pasted on his head like a soiled chicken feather. When we came up to him, my brother raised his hand to his forehead and said loudly, 'Salaam, Dauji.'

The man nodded and replied, 'May you live long.'

I was delighted that my brother knew the man. A little later I too squeaked, 'Dauji, salaam!'

'May you live long, may you live long,' the man acknowledged the greeting, raising both his hands in blessing.

My brother, however, whacked me hard on the face and thundered, 'You show-off! Dog! Why did you have to greet him after I did? Why do you have to poke your nose into everything? You wretch! Do you even know who he is?'

'Dauji,' I said, putting on a crying face.

'Dauji who?' my brother asked, flaring up.

'The man sitting over there,' I replied, fighting back my tears. 'He's Dauji.'

'Don't talk nonsense,' my brother said glaring at me. 'Imitates me in everything. Copycat! Dog! Show-off!'

I said nothing in response and followed my brother in silence. Actually, I was happy for having been finally introduced to Dauji. I couldn't care less about the abuse I had received. I was used to my brother hitting me. He was older and liked to show off.

Now that I had made my acquaintance with Dauji, I started timing my own passage through the lane to coincide with his. Greeting him pleased me, and receiving his greeting pleased me even more. He said 'May you live long' with such deep affection that I felt a strange exhilaration wash over me, and I had the sensation of walking slightly above the ground.

The exchange of greetings continued for about a year. During this time, all I could find out about Dauji was that he lived in the house with red ochre-framed windows, and the little boy who accompanied him on his walks was his son. I tried to tease more information about him out of my brother, but he was mean to me and always took exception to every little thing I said or did. Whatever I asked, he fired back his two routine answers: 'None of your business!' or 'Stop this nonsense!' But thank God, I didn't have to wait long to satisfy my curiosity.

When I passed my class four at Islamia Primary School and entered the fifth in M. B. High School, Dauji's son turned out to be my classmate. Through him, and without owing my brother anything, I learnt that Dauji was a Khatri by caste and worked as a petition writer outside our qasba's courthouse. The boy's name was Amichand. He was the smartest boy in class. He sported a turban larger than anyone else's and had a small face like a cat's, which prompted some boys to call him 'Meow', and others, 'Mongoose'. I, however, called him by his real name, in deference to Dauji, I guess. Maybe that's why we became friends. We exchanged secret mementos and took an oath to remain close friends through thick and thin.

It must have been a week before the summer vacation when I visited Amichand's house for the very first time. The day was a scorcher, but the desire to acquire Shaikh Chilli's stories had so possessed me that I gave no thought to heat or hunger and accompanied him right after school. Amichand's house was small but sparkling clean and well lit. A small dyorhi immediately inside the door with the brass nails led into a rectangular inner courtyard, at the edge of which was a red veranda. Behind this was a room of similar length. One side of the courtyard was occupied by a single pomegranate tree, a few canna plants, and a small patch of coriander. On the other side was a fairly wide staircase, with a tiny kitchen situated under its arch. The red ochre-framed windows opened into the sitting room adjacent to the dyorhi. The door of the sitting room was blue.

As soon as we stepped into the dyorhi, Amichand shouted, 'Bébé namaste!' Leaving me alone in the middle of the courtyard, he slipped into the sitting room. Bébé had spread out a large gunny sack in the veranda and was sitting on it, working her sewing machine. A girl sat next to her, cutting fabric with a pair of large scissors. Bébé mumbled something by way of response and continued to work her machine. The girl, though, lifted her face and looked at me, and then turned around and said, 'Bébé, looks like Doctor Sahib's boy.'

The machine stopped.

'So he does,' Bébé said, smiling, and made a sign with her hand for me to approach her.

Twisting the strap of my satchel and taking uneven steps, I walked timidly over and stood flat against a pillar.

'What is your name?' Bébé asked me affectionately.

I lowered my eyes and told her my name very softly.

'He resembles Aftab quite a bit, doesn't he, Bébé?' the girl said as she laid the scissors down on the floor.

'Of course he does. He's his brother, after all.'

'What about Aftab?' a voice came from inside the room. 'What was that about Aftab, my child?'

'Aftab's brother is here, Dauji,' the girl replied after a pause. 'He's come with Amichand.'

Dauji emerged from the room, shirtless, the legs of his pyjamas pulled up to his knees, his turban still lodged securely on his head. He walked into the veranda carrying a small bucket of water. He looked at me closely and remarked, 'Yes, indeed, he does resemble Aftab quite a bit. But my Aftab is very skinny, while he is quite gol-mol.'

He put the bucket down on the floor, patted me on the head, pulled over a wooden stool and sat down beside me. He lifted his feet a bit, dusted them off, and then plunged them into the bucket. 'Does Aftab write home?' he asked, as he scooped handfuls of water and splashed them on his legs.

'He does,' I replied slowly. 'We got a letter from him just the day before yesterday.'

'What does he say?'

'I don't know. Abbaji would know.'

'I see,' he said, wagging his head. 'Well, you should ask Abbaji. One who doesn't ask, doesn't learn anything.'

I remained silent.

After some time, still splashing water onto his legs, he asked, 'Which sipaara of the Quran are you learning these days?'

'The fourth,' I replied, confidently.

'What is the third one called?' he quizzed me.

'I don't know,' my voice sank.

'Tilka 'r-Rusul,' he said, pulling his hand out of the bucket.

For a while Dauji shook his hand dry in the air. Meanwhile Bébé continued to work on her machine, and the girl laid out food on the low wooden chauki in the veranda, while I continued to twist and turn the strap of my satchel. Amichand was still inside the sitting room, and I, pasted to the pillar, was sinking progressively deeper into my embarrassment. Abruptly Dauji turned towards me and said, 'Recite the Sura Fatiha for me!'

'I don't know it,' I said, utterly ashamed.

He looked at me with surprise and asked, 'Not even al-Hamdu li'l-lah?'

'That I do know,' I said quickly.

He smiled a bit and said, as if to himself, 'It's the same thing, the same thing.' Then with a nod of his head he said, 'Recite it for me.'

As soon as I began, he pulled the legs of his pyjamas down and spread the loose end of his turban over his shoulders. After I had said 'ad-dalleen', he joined in to say 'aameen' with me. The thought occurred to me that he would now get up and give me a reward, because the first time I had recited the al-Hamdu li'l-lah before my Taya, he too had repeated the word aameen with me and had given me a rupee reward. But Dauji didn't budge. If anything, he seemed to have turned into stone.

Meanwhile Amichand appeared with the Shaikh Chilli book. As I was leaving, I said, somewhat less ardently than was my habit, 'Dauji salaam', and still immersed in his thoughts, he responded softly, as was his wont, 'May you live long.' Bébé briefly interrupted her work and said, 'Come over and play with Amichand sometime.'

'Yes, yes, do come sometime,' Dauji chimed in, as if reminded of something suddenly, 'Aftab used to come too.' Then, bending himself over the bucket he added, 'Our Aftab—how we miss him!' and recited a couplet in Farsi.

Such was my first, formal meeting with Dauji. I concluded from it that he was a skinflint, too quiet for anyone's good, and, perhaps, a bit deaf as well.

That evening I told my mother about my visit to Dauji's and how he missed Aftab Bhai. She said with a note of bitterness in her voice, 'You should have asked me first. It's true Aftab took lessons from him and respected him a lot, but your father doesn't speak to Dauji. They had a quarrel some time ago and have been upset with each other ever since. If your father finds out that you've been to Dauji's, he'll be angry.' Then, feeling sorry for me, she added, 'Don't breathe a word about it to your Abbaji.'

I was not about to. But, I kept visiting Dauji, and heartily enjoyed discussing all sorts of grown-up things with him. I would find him sitting on a mat reading some book or another. I'd go and stand quietly behind him. Sensing my presence he'd close the book and say, 'Ah, Golu, you've come. Good!' Then looking over his shoulder at me, he'd smile and say, 'Let's hear the latest gossip.' I'd dig deep inside, and with my limited ability and understanding would find something or the other to say. He laughed hard—to please me, I guess, for, as I now think about it, the things I said were hardly interesting. Then, tearing a sheet of paper from his register, he'd have me do a question. I hated it. But the deal he proposed I found too seductive to resist: after one question I could shoot the breeze with him for the next fifteen minutes, then another question, then fifteen more minutes of talk. Invariably I'd give in. I'd take the sheet of paper and work on the question. But his made-up question turned out to be so frustratingly complicated that it ate up not only the gossip session but the next round as well. If, as luck would have it, I answered it quickly enough, he would point to the mat and ask, 'What is it?'

'Mat,' I'd shout.

'No, no,' he shook his head, 'I mean in Farsi.'

Irritated, I snapped, 'What, you think we're taught Farsi at school?'

'But I teach you, Golu, don't I?' he tried to calm me down. 'Here, listen: boriya in Farsi, hasir in Arabi.'

Mischievously I folded my hands before him and said, 'Mercy—please! Spare me your Farsi and your Arabi. I don't want to learn either. Please, I beg you!'

He pretended not to hear me and kept repeating: 'Boriya in Farsi, hasir in Arabi.'

There was no stopping him after that, even if one poured lead into one's ears to block it out.

Amichand was a bookworm. Perched in the sitting room he studied all day long. Dauji rarely interrupted him, but that doesn't mean he escaped Dauji's assaults either, which were quick to come whenever the opportunity offered itself. When he emerged from the room for a drink of water, then and there Dauji, looking up from his book, fired off the question: 'Tell me the noun form of the verb "to do".'

'Deed,' Amichand answered, his lips still stuck to the tumbler. He tossed the tumbler under the pitcher-stand and slipped back into his room. Dauji resumed his reading.

Of all his family, Dauji was most fond of his daughter. To all of us she was Bibi; Dauji alone had christened her Qurrat. Now and then he called out to her and said, 'Qurrat Bitiya, when are you going to get rid of those scissors?' In reply, she merely smiled, but Bébé, who simply hated this 'Qurrat'-business, retorted loudly, 'By calling her "Qurrat," you've doomed her to stitching kurtas all her life. Even if one may not be pleasant, one should still say nice things.' And Dauji, taking a long, cold breath, remarked, 'How could the ignorant ever know what "Qurrat" means!'

This provoked Bébé's anger, and she spat out whatever came to her mind—first name-calling, then curses, finally descending to galis. If Bibi tried to stop her, Dauji told her not to: 'Daughter, the wind has to blow, and galis have to rain down. Don't even try to stop her.' He would then gather his books, pick up his favourite hasir and quietly go upstairs.

Right at the beginning of the ninth class I fell into a particularly bad habit, which brought me great grief. The late Hakim Ali Ahmad was the only physician who practiced traditional Unani medicine in our qasba. Only moderately interested in his practice, he was, rather, a fantastic storyteller. Stories of Sufi saints, of genies and ghosts, of the domestic life of King Solomon and Queen Sheba—these were his surefire remedies. A few tins of confected drugs, a dozen or so bottles of different syrups, and a pair of magnifying glasses was all his dingy, dark clinic had for medical wherewithal. In addition to medicine, he treated his patients with his magical orations and special charms, handed down orally from Prophet Solomon. So patients even from far-flung villages flocked to him for treatment, and returned cured.

Within a couple of weeks of our acquaintance Hakim Sahib and I worked out a deal: I'd swipe empty bottles and vials from my father's dispensary for him, and he'd lend me volumes of *Dastan-e Amir Hamza* to read. These books were so full of wonder that I read them on the sly in my bed all night long, with the result that I invariably overslept in the morning. This annoyed Amma a lot, and made my father worry about my health. But I assured them that I'd risk my life to clear the tenth class, and clear it well enough to secure a scholarship. Nights I spent roaming the magical palaces of *Tilism-e Hosh-Ruba*, and days standing on the classroom bench in punishment. I nearly flunked my quarterly examination. By the time the second quarterly exam rolled along, I fell ill. The finals I passed, but only through the influence that Hakim Sahib was able to use on my schoolteachers.

Sandalinaama, Fasaana-e-Aazaad, and *Alf Laila* were my constant companions in the tenth class. I kept the first two books at home and *Alf Laila* at school, locked up in my desk. Sitting at my desk in the very last row, under my geography book, I'd strike out with Sindbad and roam the world over.

Around ten in the morning of 22 May the examination result arrived from the university to which M. B. High School was accredited. Amichand was ranked first not only in the school but in the entire district. Twenty-two boys had been successful, and six had flunked. Hakimji's magic was ineffectual against Punjab University, which had heartlessly included me among the failures. That very evening His Reverence—my honourable father—thrashed me with a cane and threw me out of the house.

I went and sat on top of the Persian wheel, thinking well into the night about what I might do next and where I might go. The land of God was by no means narrow, and I too was well equipped with the stratagems of Amar Ayyaar—Amar the Trickster—and the devices of Sindbad the Sailor. Yet I couldn't figure out a way. For some three hours I sat right there thinking hard of a way that might enable me to live on. Right about then, Amma, wrapped in her white chadar and frantically looking for me everywhere, wandered into the area. She asked me to return home, promising that she would persuade Abbaji to forgive me. I wasn't interested in any forgiveness; I had only one more night to spend at my parents'. Come morning, I'd be on my way. So I followed her back to the house without even a hint of regret and stretched out on my bed as usual.

Next day I ran into two of my fellow flunkies, Khushya Kodu and Desu Yabyab, sitting near the lumber store behind the mosque. They were cooking up a plan to go to Lahore and set up some kind of business. Desu Yabyab told me that Lahore was full of business opportunities, because he had often heard his uncle mention a friend of his, Fatehchand, who had done so well there that he bought two cars in just one year. When I asked him about the nature of Fatehchand's business, Yabyab said Lahore offered all kinds of business. All you needed was an office with a big signboard. People saw the signboard and they came of their own and gave you more business than you could handle. By 'business' he meant, at that time, 'currency notes'. When I asked him once more to explain the business we'd get, Kodu flared up and said, 'Yaar, Desu knows everything. What we want to know is this: are you with us or not?'

He then turned towards Desu and asked, 'We'll set up our office in Anarkali, right?'

Desu thought for a bit and then replied, 'Either there, or outside Shah Almi—both places are equally good.'

'Anarkali would be better,' I said. 'It's more famous. All the newspaper ads give Anarkali as their address.'

And so we decided to leave for Lahore the next day by the 2 p.m. train.

I returned home and started to prepare for the trip. As I was polishing my shoes our servant walked in and told me with a mischievous grin on his face, 'Come, Doctor Sahib is asking for you.'

'Where is he?' I got up, putting the brush back down.

'At the dispensary,' he said, still grinning widely, since he, too, was present at the scene of my humiliation the other day.

I climbed the stairs full of fear, slowly opened the screen door and entered into Abbaji's room. Dauji was there with him. Still cringing from fear I greeted Dauji and heard, after a long silence, his familiar blessing, 'May you live long.'

'Do you recognize him?' Abbaji asked me sternly.

'Of course,' I replied in the manner of a polished salesman.

'Damn you, you bastard! I'll—'

'No, please, no, Doctor Sahib,' Dauji pleaded, raising his hand. 'He is a good child, he—'

But Abbaji rudely cut him short and said, 'Munshiji, you have no idea how this miserable wretch has sullied my honour.'

'Please don't worry,' Dauji replied, his head lowered. 'He is even brighter than Aftab, and one day...'

This really made my father fly into a rage. He banged his fist on the table and said, 'What kind of talk is that, Munshiji? He doesn't even measure up to the dust on Aftab's shoes!'

'He will, Doctor Sahib, one day he will,' Dauji nodded his head in affirmation. 'Please don't worry about him.'

Dauji got up from his chair, placed his hand on my shoulder and said, 'Look, I'm going for a walk. You come along too. We'll talk on the way.'

My father continued to sit and fume as he nervously turned the pages of his register, muttering all the while. Slowly I walked over to the screen door and as I was opening it, Dauji turned around and said to my father, 'Doctor Sahib, please don't forget. Have it delivered right away.'

'Yes, yes,' Abbaji said amidst all his banging.

Dauji said 'Khuda hafiz' and left the room with me.

Taking me along through the town, and telling the names of different trees in Farsi, Dauji brought me to the same bridge where I'd first met him. He took his favourite spot on the bridge, removed his turban and put it in his lap, rubbed his head and beckoned me to sit opposite him. He closed his eyes and said, 'I shall be your teacher from this day forward. And even if you don't come out at the top of your class, you certainly will pass with a first division. This I assure you. I'm backed by *Khudavand-e Ta'ala* in whatever I resolve to do, and thanks to His mercy, I've never been disappointed.'

'I don't want to study,' I interrupted rudely.

'Well then, what will you do, Golu?' he asked with a smile.

'I'll go into business,' I replied. 'I'll make money. And when I come back here in my own car, you'll see.'

This time around it was Dauji who interrupted. 'May Allah give you not one, but ten cars,' he said with exceeding kindness. 'But I shall not ride in the car of an illiterate person, and neither will Doctor Sahib.'

'Who cares?' I retorted, flaring up. 'Doctor Sahib can live happily in his house, and let me be happy in mine.'

'You don't care even about me?' he asked, surprised.

I was about to say something when he sadly repeated, 'You don't care even about me? Golu, not even me—really?'

I was moved by the tone of his voice and said softly, 'I do care about you, but...'

But he didn't let me finish. 'Could such a word, such a word of kufr have ever escaped from my lips before my hazrat, my ustad?' He quickly put his turban back on his head and, joining his hands in reverential humility, added, 'I, the lowliest of creatures in the durbar of the Prophet? Humbler than the dust under the feet of Hazrat Maulana? A mere servant, how could I have ever said such a thing to my Master? Wouldn't I have merited the collar of reproach, of opprobrium?'

He then folded his hands on his chest, and, lowering his head all the way to his thighs, continued, 'I, a goatherd by caste, my father a milkman from Mundasi. I, a child of ignorance, my family the family of Abu Jahl. But how a single glance of kindness, a single gesture of the Master, transformed Chintu into Munshi Chinta Ram. People call me Munshiji, but I say I'm merely a lowly servant of the Master—may God's mercy be on him! Fit only to carry his slippers... People think...'

Dauji carried on, sometimes joining his hands in humility, sometimes bowing his head low, sometimes kissing his fingers and then touching his eyes, and punctuating it all with the recitation of Farsi couplets. Perplexed and a bit regretful, I found myself touching his knees and pleading with him softly, 'Dauji, Dauji.' But Dauji was on with his own litany. 'My Master, my Hazrat Maulana, my Murshid.'

When finally he emerged from his mystical absorption, he raised his eyes and said, 'What nice weather! When it's hot during the day, the evenings are always cool and very pleasant.'

He got down from the bridge wall and said, 'Let's go. I have to buy some things from the bazaar.'

Insolent and haughty as I had been when I set out with him, I was a good deal more ashamed and sorry when I returned with him. He bought a few items from the shop of Ghume Pansari (who was none other than Desu Yabyab's father), picked up the bags and started walking. Many times I wanted to take the bags from him and carry them myself, but I lacked the courage to ask. A strange shyness, an unfamiliar diffidence got in my way. Such was my inner state when we arrived at his house.

It was only then that I found out that henceforward I was to sleep and study at Dauji's, my bedding, with a hurricane lantern lying beside it, having preceded me.

It was not my fate to become a businessman and honk my way through the streets in a Packard car. And, it would appear, neither was it the fate of my friends who had fled to Lahore. Within three days of their departure, their parents hauled them back home. But who knows, had I been with them, what glorious year of success our office in Anarkali would be enjoying today.

Dauji made life a living hell for me. He practically destroyed it. I spent the day at school, listening to all that garbage, and the night—the incredibly short night of summer—answering all the questions he threw at me. His cot right next to my bed on the flat rooftop, he busily quizzed me about the rivers Moong, Rasool, and Marala. And although I'd given him the correct answer, he'd still ask me the same question. I gave him the correct answer once again, and once again he asked about the same rivers. I flared up and snapped at him, 'I don't know! I don't want to answer!' which made him fall silent and hold his breath. I closed my eyes and tried to fall asleep, but felt the sting of remorse in my eyes, like grit. So I called him softly, 'Dauji?'

'Yes,' he said in a grave voice.

'Ask me another question?'

'Bahut be-abroo ho-kar tere kooche se ham nikle—describe its syntactic structure!'

'It's a very long sentence. I'll write it down in the morning and do it then. For now, give me another.'

He lifted his eyes to the sky and said, 'Mera Golu bahut achchha hai—there.'

After thinking a bit I started, '"Achchha" is an adjective; "hai" a copula; together they make up the predicate...'

Dauji sat up erect on the cot, raised his hand and said, 'Jaan-e Pidar, haven't I told you to identify the subject first?'

To save myself from the torture of syntactical description I asked him, 'Why do you call me Jaan-e Pidar? Why don't you call me Jaan-e Dau?'

'Bravo!' he exclaimed with delight. 'Now that's an excellent question. "Jaan" is a Farsi word, and "dau" comes from Bhasha. You cannot join the two with a Farsi genitive. Those who write or say din-ba-din commit a terrible mistake. One should either say roz-ba-roz or din par din. Likewise…'

Obviously the trick had backfired, I was dragged into a problem more daunting than syntactical description. And so I yawned and tried to say sweetly, 'Dauji, I'm very sleepy.'

'But the syntactical description?' he asked abruptly.

No matter what excuses I now used, or the things I said to deflect his attention, he remained unyielding, sitting rigid and expectant on his cot. And if my response didn't come quickly enough, he picked up the turban lying on the chair and replaced it on his head. There was no getting away from his questions.

After Amichand went away to college, I moved into the sitting room previously occupied by him, and gradually also replaced him in Dauji's affections. The fact is, I too had grown exceedingly fond of Dauji. Which doesn't mean I liked the way he treated me. I found it atrocious, and I still do. Even more atrocious today. Perhaps because I'm now a psychology student, a rather bright student, and Dauji had been schooled in the rigid environment of maktabs. Two of his worst sins were: to assault you with questions without letting up, and to stop you from any kind of play or diversion. Study, study and study—he'd settle on nothing less, and when your time was up, you'd die hunched over a pile of books. He had only one prescription to keep yourself bodily fit: long walks, and early in the morning at that. Two hours before sunup he walked into the sitting room and woke me up. He shook me by the shoulder and said, 'Get up, Golu! See, you've grown fat.'

Every other parent woke their child with a sweet, 'Come on son, wake up, it's morning' or 'the sun's risen'. But his humiliating catchphrase was 'You've grown fat.'

If I whined, he'd try to sweet-talk me, 'If you become too fat, how will you tour your district mounted on a horse?'

Unwilling to stir from my warm bed, I'd join my hands and plead with him, 'Dauji, please, not so early in the morning. Kill me, take my life, but for heaven's sake don't wake me up! Please!'

This never failed to get to him. He quickly pulled the comforter back over my face and walked out of the room.

Bébé, it would appear, bore some old grudge against Dauji. And he feared her very much. She stitched clothes for the neighbourhood women all day long and kept up a steady barrage of curses against him. Her name calling and invective infuriated me, but living in the river I couldn't very well get on the wrong side of the crocodile. Now and then, when her abuses became particularly nasty, Dauji sought refuge in my room. He sat himself down in the chair and put his hands over his ears to block out the relentless stream of maledictions. After some time he remarked, 'I know it is a great sin to speak behind someone's back, and God forgive me for that, but your Bébé is a perfect bhatyaaran, and the three of us—my Qurratulain, I, and to a degree even you—are merely hapless sojourners in her inn.'

Bébé did, in fact, look something like a bhatyaaran. Very dark, with intensely white teeth, she had an arched forehead and narrow eyes. She padded her way around stealthily like a cat, sniffing out gossip like a go-between. She targeted poor Bibi for such name calling that it sent her weeping for days. She got along well only with Amichand, perhaps because the two resembled each other quite a bit, or perhaps because, unlike Bibi, he didn't love his Dauji all that much. I liked Bibi all right, but getting along with her was something else again. I'd be upstairs in the barsati doing a math problem, while Dauji sat downstairs. If Bibi came upstairs to pick up some firewood, she stopped briefly to look at me and then peered down the short wall and shouted, 'Dauji, he isn't studying; he's playing instead—making cots out of sticks.'

I made a face at her like an angry child and snapped, 'None of your business! Okay, I'm not studying—what's it to you anyway? Behaving like some thanedaarni?' Whereupon Dauji called out to me from below, 'No, Golu, no. One doesn't fight with sisters.'

I yelled, 'She's plain lying! I am studying!'

Meanwhile he came softly up the stairs. Seeing the cot I was fashioning out of sticks half concealed under my notebook, he said to Bibi, 'Qurrat, my child, you shouldn't tease him. I've had quite a time bringing this genie under control. If he slips out again, there is no way I can bring him back in line.'

Unmoved, Bibi said, 'Just pick up the notebook, Dauji, and see for yourself.'

I glared at Bibi, but she gathered the firewood and went back downstairs, leaving Dauji to reason with me. 'All this that Bibi says, it is for your own good. Why else would she bother to tell me? Whether you pass or fail, it makes no difference to her. But she has your best interests at heart. She wants you to succeed.'

I just couldn't understand Dauji's logic: how could she have my best interests at heart by complaining about me? By squealing on me? Back then, my routine went something like this: I'd leave Dauji's at about ten in the morning for home, eat my breakfast and then go to school. My lunch would arrive from home during the midday recess. After school I'd return home, fill my lantern with kerosene and come over to Dauji's, where in time my dinner would arrive from home.

When the courts weren't in session, Dauji came and sat in the school's playground waiting for me. On the way home I had to face a gale of questions. He would ask me the details of what all I had been taught at school that day. He would escort me to my house and then take off for his evening stroll. The judge set up his court in our qasba for ten days a month; the other twenty days he presided at the district court. Those ten days Dauji regularly sat outside the courthouse. Now and then somebody came along, Dauji wrote out the petition for him, and thus earned a couple of rupees. The rest of the time he spent reading books—even there.

Bébé's work, on the other hand, was rather more steady, and her stitching and socializing with the neighbourhood women produced a more profitable result. For some years now the major part of the house's expenses was covered by the money she earned from stitching. As a result, she had come to dominate Dauji even more.

One day, contrary to the routine, I went to the courthouse to meet Dauji. Court was over for the day and Dauji was lounging on a bench inside the thatched shed of the baker's shop sipping tea sweetened with raw sugar. I quietly reached down and picked up his mat and bag, and then, throwing my arms around his neck, said, 'I've come to fetch you today. Let's go.'

He downed the remaining tea in a few big gulps, took an anna coin out of his pocket and gave it to the baker, and quietly walked out with me. A streak of mischief danced through me and I said, 'Just wait until we get back. I'll tell Bébé how you help yourself to tea on the sly.'

To evade his embarrassment, Dauji smiled some and said, 'He really fixes excellent tea. Besides, raw sugar tea relaxes the nerves. And he gives a full glass for just an anna—not bad! But please don't tell your Bébé. She'll kick up a huge fuss. She'll become more violent with me.' And then, somewhat fearful and somewhat sad, he added, 'She can't go against her nature.'

I felt a surge of tenderness well up in me for Dauji that day. I felt I wanted to do something for him, indeed, I wanted to do a whole lot. But at that time, the promise that I wouldn't tell on him was already a whole lot. When I told Mother about the incident, she began to have me or the servant carry gifts of milk, fruits, sugar, etc., over to Dauji's now and then. But poor Dauji, he never saw any of these provisions himself. But it did catapult me in Bébé's regard, and she started treating me somewhat more preferentially.

I vividly remember walking into Dauji's with a pitcher of milk one morning. Bébé had gone away with her friends to bathe in Baaba Saawan's pond, and only Dauji and Bibi were at home. Spotting the pitcher of milk Dauji chuckled, 'Let's make some tea. I'll go and get some raw sugar from the shop. Meantime you put the kettle on.' Right away Bibi started to get the fire going. I went and brought water in a pan. The two of us sat down on the chauka and started chatting. Dauji promptly returned with some raw sugar and said to us, 'You go and do your work. I'll fix the tea.'

So Bibi started working the sewing machine and I busied myself with the direct and indirect speech exercises. Meanwhile, Dauji kept blowing into the fire and, after his habit, kept instructing me loudly, 'Galileo said that the earth moves around the sun. It was Galileo who discovered that the earth revolves around the sun. Make sure that you don't write, "revolved around the sun".'

The water had come to a boil. Dauji was happy, joyously swaying his head back and forth and repeating the song he'd just improvised, 'O Golu! O Golu! Don't forget what Galileo said, what Galileo said, O Golu.' He added the tea leaves to the boiling water. The pan was still on the fire and Dauji, like a small child, was trying to synchronize his 'Golu Galileo, Golu Galileo' with the 'gul-bul, gul-bul' of the boiling water. I was laughing as I did my grammar exercises, and Bibi quietly smiled as she worked the sewing machine. The three of us were very happy in our small home, it was as if the joys of the whole neighbourhood, indeed, of the entire qasba, had alighted on our house like fairies with large, colourful wings.

Just then the door opened and in walked Bébé. Dauji turned around to see and, instantaneously, his face turned pale. Steam was rising from the boiling pan, in which small bubbles were furiously chasing each other. The old man was caught red-handed at his forbidden game. Bébé took a few steps towards the hearth, and Dauji, rising from the chauka, intoned apologetically, 'It's just tea.'

Bébé gave him a whack and thundered, 'Have you lost all your shame? May you be damned! May death take you away! What, you really think you can drink tea at your age? I wasn't home, so you thought you could take advantage. You couldn't care less if I died, indeed, you'd rather I died today, so that you could be happy, make all your wishes come true. Damn the woman who brought you into this world! Damn the fate that's stuck me to you. Why don't you die? Why would you…'

Frothing and foaming away, Bébé jumped over the chauka like a she-wolf, picked up the pan with a piece of cloth, and threw it on the floor. Boiling tea splashed over Dauji's legs and feet, who fled like a child, screaming, 'May God help you, may God help you!' and sought refuge in the sitting room.

Bibi and I couldn't help but break into a laugh at his departure, rather at the manner in which he had fled. We laughed so loudly that, for a second, the whole house resounded with it. I somehow escaped Bébé's wrath, but Bibi had to bear the full brunt of her assault. She pounced on her, grabbed her by the hair, and screamed, 'My saut, tell me what you think you're doing with this old coot? Come on, out with it, or I'll strangle you this minute! Why did you give him the key to the pantry?'

Poor Bibi started to sob. I got up and slinked into the sitting room. Dauji was ensconced in his favourite chair and was slowly rubbing his scalded feet to soothe the pain. He looked so comic that I again started to laugh, but I stuck my head into the closet to muffle the sound. He beckoned me to come over and said, 'Shukr-e kirdgaar kunam keh griftaaram ba musibati na keh ma'siyati!' (Thank the Creator that though I'm in trouble, I haven't sinned.) After a brief pause he added, 'I'm lowlier than the lowest slaves of him on whose blessed head the old hag of Mecca used to dump her garbage.'

When I gave him a perplexed look, he explained: 'Should I, the meanest slave of Aaqaa-e Naamdaar, complain about a few splashes of hot water, then may my life be cursed. May God save me from the fires of hell through His love of the Prophet Muhammad. May the God of Ibrahim grant me strength. May the God of Ayyub bless me with the gift of patience.'

I asked, 'Aaqaa-e Naamdaar—who's he, Dauji?' This pained him, but he said with his usual affection, 'Jaan-e Pidar, that's no way to ask. Don't make the spirit of my ustad, my hazrat, angry with me. He was not only my 'Aaqaa, he was also my father and my teacher. In fact, he stands in the relationship of a grandfather to you. Your grandfather teacher…' He quickly folded his hands over his chest in extreme reverence.

I owed my very first exposure to the phrase 'Aaqaa-e Naamdaar' and the compound 'kotah qismat mujawwizah' to Dauji. He took his sweet time in relating the incident in which these occurred, following up every sentence with Farsi couplets extolling the Prophet of Islam, again and again sending the reward for them to the soul of his dear departed ustad.

After he was done narrating, I asked him with great politeness, 'Dauji, why do you love your ustad so much? Why do you always join your hands when you say his name, and why do you call yourself his servant?'

Dauji smiled and said, 'A man who can transform an ordinary donkey like me into one addressed as Munshi Chinta Ram, as Munshiji, what would you call such a man if not a Messiah, an 'Aaqaa?'

Slowly I inched my way from the edge to the centre of the cot, wrapped the quilt securely around myself, and fixed my gaze on Dauji. He sat with a drooping head, now looking at his foot, now gently rubbing his calves, laughing some and then slipping back into silence. Finally he said:

'It's amazing. What I started out as, what I became!...The first words Hazrat Maulana uttered to me! Lifting his blessed face to me he said, "Shepherd boy, come here." I walked over to him, leaning upon my staff. Boys from Chhatta Pathhar and other villages were sitting in front of him in a semi-circle memorizing their lessons. It seemed I'd walked straight into a durbar: no one dared even look up at me. When I approached the Huzoor, he said, "My dear, aren't you the one I see herding goats around here everyday? Maybe you should let the animals graze on their own and come over here and study with me a bit." He didn't wait for my answer and instead asked, "What's your name?" "Chintu," I replied, in the coarse manner of a country boy, which prompted His Eminence to smile, even laugh a bit. And then he asked, "What is your full name?" Again, without waiting for my response, he proceeded to say, "Must be Chinta Ram." I nodded my head. His students were now stealing glances at me. I was wearing a long khaddar shirt and a loincloth in place of a proper pyjama. On my feet I had a pair of coarse half-hide shoes; my head-covering improvised from an old pair of red shorts. "My goats..."'

I interrupted him and asked, 'You used to be a shepherd? Really, Dauji?'

'Yes, yes indeed I was,' he said with pride, 'I was a shepherd. My father owned a dozen goats.'

My mouth fell open in surprise. In an attempt to get to the bottom of it all I rushed to ask, 'And you used to graze them near the school?'

Dauji pulled his chair over to my cot and said, stretching out and resting his feet on the edge of the bed-frame, 'Jaan-e Pidar, back in those days, even the cities didn't boast schools, and I'm talking about just a village. Who'd heard of your M. B. High School seventy-four years ago? It's just that my 'aaqaa was fond of teaching. So people living in the neighbourhood sent their boys over to him to learn their ABCs. His entire family was adorned with the jewel of knowledge and enjoyed a surfeit of spiritual blessings. His father had the rare distinction of being the only hakim in the entire district, and a top-notch preacher to boot. And his grandfather was the Mir Munshi in the employ of the Maharaja of Kashmir. A veritable river of learning flowed in their home. Farsi, Arabi, algebra, Euclidean geometry, medicine, astronomy—they were the maids they employed in their house. I never had the good fortune of meeting Huzoor's father, but I was fortunate enough to hear the stories of his great erudition. He was good friends with the poet Sheftah and the poet-physician Momin Khan Momin, while he, Hazrat Maulana himself, had been educated in Delhi under the close supervision of the late Mufti Azurdah.'

Afraid that Dauji might be tempted to leave his main story and strike out on some tangent, I quickly asked him, 'So you started to study with Hazrat Maulana?'

'Yes,' Dauji began, as if reminiscing to himself. 'What a wonder he was! What a discriminating eye he had! Whoever he singled out for his attention, he transformed him from a humble servant into a master and lord. He could infuse a speck of lowly dirt with the most astounding power of cure...

'Then and there I laid down my club and took a seat near him on the bare ground. But he commanded, "Go and sit with your brothers on the mat." To which I replied, "All my eighteen years I've spent on the bare earth. What difference would it make now?" He smiled again, took out a scroll of abjad letters from a wooden chest, and said, "Repeat after me: Alif, be, pe, te..." What a lovely voice he had—God be praised! With what affection, what tenderness he spoke: "Alif, be, pe, te..."' Chanting the alphabet Dauji lapsed into his past.

A while later he raised his right hand and said, 'Over here was a Persian wheel, and a pond of fish right beside it.' He waved his left hand in the air and added, 'And over there, the brick houses of peasants who worked the fields. The space in between was occupied by Huzoor's garden, and facing it was his magnificent haveli. He set up his school in this very garden. The gate of munificence was open; everyone was welcome. Religion offered no barrier; difference in creed was of no consequence.'

After thinking for some time and fashioning a sentence which would do justice to the decorum imposed by the lofty memory of his revered teacher, I enquired, 'What was the ism-e girami sharif (honourable and noble name) of Hazrat Maulana?' Whereupon Dauji first corrected my construction and then said, 'Hazrat Ismail Chishti, may God's mercy be upon him. He used to say that his father always called him "Jaan-e Jaanaan", but sometimes "Mazhar Jaan-e Jaanaan" too, because of the correspondence of the two.'

I was eager to hear more of this fascinating story when Dauji abruptly stopped and said, 'Explain the Subsidiary System to me.'

Damn these British! Whether they came in the guise of the East India Company or as bearers of the royal edicts of Queen Victoria, they always managed to spoil things for us. Anyway, I explained the whole structure of the Subsidiary System to Dauji, like the multiplication table of one-and-a-quarter. Subsequently, he picked up the grammar book from the table and said, 'Go and see if your Bébé's anger has subsided.'

I stepped out into the veranda, pretending to add some water to my inkwell, and found Bébé busy at her sewing machine and Bibi cleaning the chauka.

The greatest sore spot of Dauji's life was Bébé. Whenever he perceived relative calm inside the house, whenever Bébé looked to be in a better mood, he would call out to us, 'Come, all of you, and recite a she'r each.' Invariably, I was asked to go first, and I almost always obliged with these lines:

Laazim tha keh dekho mera rastah ko'i din aur
Tanha ga'e kiyun ab raho tanha ko'i din aur

(You should have waited for me a while longer
You wanted to go alone—well then, stay alone a while longer.)

He would break into applause and then lay down his terms, 'Good. But give me a fresh couplet, and make sure it isn't in Urdu, nor from a longer poem.'

'Okay, but give me time to think,' I said. 'Meanwhile, Bibi can recite hers.' Bibi too had a favourite couplet she usually began with:

Shunidam keh Shapour dam dar kasheed
Chu Khusrau bar ismash qalam dar kasheed

(I've heard that as Shapur breathed his last
Khusrau struck out his name.)

Once again Dauji shouted 'Order! Order!' And Bibi, putting down her scissors, recited a different one:

Shori shud wa az khvaab-e adam chashm kashodim
Didim keh baaqist shab-e fitnah ghunudim

(A tumult awakened us from our sleep of non-existence
We dozed off again seeing that the night of commotion had not ended.)

Even as Dauji complimented Bibi, he would still point out, 'Daughter, you've already recited that one several times before.' Then, looking at Bébé, he said to us, 'Well, today, even your Bébé will recite a couplet.'

But Bébé had only one answer, a stale one at that: 'I don't know any she'r-geet.'

'Well then, sing some ghoriyan instead,' Dauji tried again. 'The ones you sang at your sons' weddings.'

Bébé's lips made as if to smile, but somehow couldn't. Instead, Dauji himself started singing ghoriyan, exactly mimicking the manner of women, inserting sometimes Amichand's and sometimes my name into the festive verses. Then he declared, 'When my Golu Molu gets married, I'll flaunt a bright red turban. I'll walk with the Doctor Sahib in the wedding procession, and I will sign my name as a witness on the papers.'

At this I would lower my eyes with the customary shyness of a young boy. He would continue: 'Who knows, my little bahu must be in the fifth or sixth class somewhere in the country today. Girls are taught housekeeping one day a week, so she must've already learnt to cook quite a few dishes. She'll be very bright, not like this blockhead who can't even remember whether madiyan means mare or hen. She, of course, will have all this at the tip of her tongue. Far-far, just like that. I'll teach her Farsi. I'll start with basic calligraphy, and then I'll teach her the shakistah style. Our women usually don't know how to write shakistah. But my bahu will, I'll teach it to her. Which means—listen Golu—that I'll be living with you. My bahu and I will speak to each other in Farsi, and while she will elegantly say "Befarma'id, Befarma'id" all the time, you'll just stand there like an idiot and gawk at us.'

Dauji would then fold his hands on his chest, bow slightly in a gesture of deference and respect, and rain down a torrent of 'Khele khub, khele khub, Jaan-e Pidar, chira in-qadr zehmat mi-kashi,…khub…yad daaram' and God knows what else. Poor Dauji! He'd set up his little world on his little mat, and he kept it going by issuing edicts in ornate Farsi.

Sitting one day sunning himself on the rooftop, after he had ordered just such an imaginary world into being, he said to me softly, 'God has granted you a virtuous wife and me a dutiful bahu. May He, by His generosity, also grant just as good a wife to my Amichand. His ideas don't sit well with me. All this Seva Sangh, this Muslim League, this Belcha Party—I don't like them at all. You know, he's learning how to use lathis and clubs these days. He's not likely to listen to me. But if the Venerable and Sublime God could grant him a pious and momin wife, she'd surely talk some sense into him.'

The word momin bothered me quite a bit, but I decided to remain silent. Anything I would have said would only have hurt Dauji. While Amichand's and my marriages were mere talk at his point, Bibi actually did get married, on 12 January. Dauji had already filled me in about jijaji Ram Partab: what a fine boy he was, how he measured up to Dauji's prior consultation with the Quran, so on and so forth. But what pleased him the most was that his samdhi was a teacher of Farsi and belonged to the Kabir Panthi sect.

That evening, when the time came for Bibi to leave her parental home for good, the whole house was thrown into a commotion: Bébé wept inconsolably, Amichand shed his tears quietly, and the women from the neighbourhood whispered among themselves. I stood leaning against the wall, and Dauji stood right beside me with his hand on my shoulder, repeating now and again, 'Why do I feel so wobbly today? Seems I can't keep my balance.'

When the bridegroom's father came over to Dauji and asked for permission to leave, Bibi suddenly fell backward and fainted. She had to be moved to a cot, and the women dutifully started fanning her. Just then, still leaning on me for support, Dauji walked over to her cot. He helped Bibi sit up and said, 'This is no way to behave, my child. Get up now! Isn't this, after all, the very first hour of your new and independent life? Come on, don't make it inauspicious!'

Bibi hugged him, still crying loudly. He stroked her head gently, lovingly, and said, 'Qurratulain, I'm a sinner, for I couldn't give you the education you deserved. I'm ashamed that I'm unable to send you off with knowledge as your dowry. I know you'll forgive me for this, and perhaps even barkhurdar Ram Partab will too. But I'll never be able to forgive myself. I'm at fault and I stand before you with my head bowed in shame.'

This made Bibi cry even harder, and copious, fat tears rolled out of

Dauji's eyes and fell on the ground. The groom's father quickly moved forward and reassured him, 'Munshiji, please don't worry. I'll teach her the Karima myself.'

Dauji hurriedly turned around and said as he joined his hands deferentially, 'That I've taught her already, as well as *Gulistaan* and *Bostaan*. But, to my deep regret, that's not nearly all I wanted to teach her.'

Whereupon the other man laughed and said, 'Well, well—even I haven't studied the whole *Gulistaan*. Whenever I came to a passage in Arabic, I just skipped it.'

Dauji stood quietly for some time, his hands folded as before. Bibi thrust her hands out of her embroidered red silk shawl and patted first Amichand and then me on the head, and, supported by her girlfriends, picked her way slowly toward the dyorhi. As Dauji, still leaning over me, also made to move, he hugged me tightly and said, 'What, are you crying too? Were you not supposed to give me support?! O, Golu...the apple of my eye... what's the matter with you?...Jaan-e Pidar, why are you...?'

His voice choked and my tears too came fast. The groom's party were riding in tongas and ikkas, followed by Bibi seated in a rath, while Amichand and myself, with Dauji between us, walked along behind them. If a cry escaped from Bibi's lips, Dauji quickly moved forward, lifted the screen of the chariot, and advised her, 'Say Laa-haul, daughter, say Laa-haul.' The loose end of his turban that he had placed over his eyes had by now become completely wet.

Ranu was the coarsest individual who lived in our neighbourhood. Evil and meanness seemed to have been pounded right into his bones. The enclosure I referred to earlier actually belonged to him. He kept a couple of dozen goats and a pair of cows there, and sold their milk in the mornings and evenings in the open field right next to the enclosure. Just about everyone in the neighbourhood bought their milk from him and, because of his propensity for making mischief, sort of yielded to him. As he walked past our house, just for the fun of it he'd rap his lathi on the ground and greet Dauji with 'Pundata, jai Ramji ki!' Time and again Dauji told him that he was not a pundit but only an ordinary man. As Dauji saw it, a learned man alone was entitled to be called a pundit. But Ranu wouldn't buy it. He'd chew on his moustache and say, 'Listen to this! Whoever sports a bodi on his head has got to be a pundit.'

Anyway, Ranu was friends with all the petty thieves and playboys of the area, who came together in the evening at his enclosure for gambling and poetry full of sexual innuendo. One day, after Bibi had been married, when I went to buy milk from him, he winked at me and remarked, 'Still living there, eh? But the morni's already flown away.'

When I didn't react to it, he stirred the frothy milk with the tin measuring cup and said, 'The Ganga was flowing right inside the house— tell me, did you take a dip?'

Anger flared up inside me. I swung the pitcher I'd brought along for milk and brought it down on his head with all my strength. The tremendous blow, even if it failed to produce any blood, almost knocked him out. As he collapsed on the takht, I ran back home. After recounting the incident to Dauji, I hurried to my own home and told Abbaji what all had happened. Thanks to my father's intervention, Ranu was immediately summoned to the police station, where, after a mild rebuke and a stern warning, he was released by the Havaldar Sahib. From thereon, Ranu, whenever he ran into Dauji, made him the butt of his biting taunts, the nastiest ones reserved for the small tuft of hair, the bodi, that Dauji wore on his head. And truth be told, that flattened width of hair really didn't look at all good on Dauji's learned head. But he used to say, 'This is a memento of my deceased mother, and it's as dear to me as life itself. She'd put my head in her lap and shampoo it with yogurt, then massage it to a sparkling shine with a bit of mustard oil. Although I never dared remove my turban before my Hazrat Maulana, he knew that I had a bodi. When I returned home for vacation after working for a year at Dayal Chand Memorial High School, His Excellence asked me, "I hope the city didn't make you get rid of it." I shook my head "no" which made him very happy. "Few mothers can boast a more dutiful son than you," he complemented me, "and few teachers can have the good fortune, as I have, of teaching a student like you." I touched his feet and said, "Huzoor, please don't put me to shame. Whatever I may be, it's all due to the grace of your feet." He laughed and said, "Chinta Ram, please don't ever touch my feet. What good is the touch which I can't even feel?" Tears surged in my eyes. I said, "If only someone could tell me where to find it, I'd spare nothing to bring you the remedy. I'd offer even my own life, if its vitality, its warmth would return life to Your Honour's legs, but I'm helpless."

'He fell silent. After some time, he looked up at the heavens and said, "If such is God's will, then let it be. May you live long. Thanks to your sturdy shoulders I've managed to see the whole village once again after ten years."'

Dauji, going further back into his memory, down to the farthest reaches of days past, resumed: 'Every day at the crack of dawn I'd arrive in the dyorhi of his grand mansion and call out, "Your servant's here!" After the ladies had withdrawn to one side, His Honour would call me from the courtyard to come in, and I'd approach him, my hands joined in obeisance, complimenting myself over my good fortune. After touching his feet I waited for his command. He'd bless me and enquire after my parents' health and the affairs of the village, after which he'd say, "All right then, Chinta Ram, you may now lift this bundle of sins." I'd take him onto my back, as though he were a basket of flowers, and exit the mansion. Sometimes he asked, "Give me a tour of the garden!" Another time he commanded, "Take me straight to the Persian wheel!" And still other times, with touching tenderness, he'd request, "If it won't tire you, would you please take me to the mosque?" I told him repeatedly that I could take him to the mosque every day, but he always declined, saying, "Whenever I feel like going there I ask you, don't I?" Anyway, I'd sit him down on the ablution platform, remove his delicate shoes and, after securing them in my sack, sit snug against the wall. From the platform His Reverence would drag himself to the prayer rows. Only once could I endure seeing him labour in this fashion. Never again. My courage wouldn't hold. After I'd removed his shoes I'd quickly cover my face with the bottom of my shirt, raising it only after he called out for me.

'On the way back, I took him home through some of the longer lanes of our qasba. At this he never failed to remark, "You take a meandering route, Chinta Ram, only to please me. I suppose you don't think that I notice. But it pains me to see how you have to lug me around like this, to waste your time."'

'How could anyone have told him, "But, Aaqaa, this period is the high point of my life; this inconvenience, the very purpose of my being. You say I have to lug you around. Hardly! I feel I'm carrying the phoenix, whose auspicious shadow falls on me alone."

'The day I learnt the *Sikandarnama* and recited it from memory, he became so overjoyed it seemed as though the sovereignty of the seven climes had been bestowed upon him. He showered me with his blessings, for this world and the next, patted my head affectionately, and then rewarded me with a rupee. I considered it as precious as the Black Stone of the Kaaba, kissed it, touched it to my eyes, and tucked it into my turban as if it were Sikandar's very own diadem. Meanwhile he went on blessing me, raising both his hands and saying, "You've accomplished what even I couldn't. You are a pious man, and God has granted you this distinction. You may be a shepherd, but you're like Moses. You're a true follower of the Lord of Batha. That's why God has blessed you. And He will bless you even more. You will see much, much prosperity."'

Dauji put his head on his knees and fell silent.

Exams were approaching and Dauji was getting stricter with me. He made sure that I'd be occupied with one thing or another even in my free time. After I'd finished work on one subject, he'd be ready to assault me with the books of the next. Even if I got up to have a drink of water, he pursued me like a shadow, using the time to quiz me about important historical dates. He had made it his routine to be present at the school gate in the afternoon. One day I slipped out through the boarding house door, so he now started to take his perch right in front of my classroom. Not only had I grown irritable and stubborn, but also foul-mouthed as well. 'Dauji ke bachche!'—had become my catchphrase. I wouldn't even hesitate to call him a dog when I felt put out by the relentless manner in which he tossed his questions at me. If this made him unhappy, he never said anything more than 'Watch it, Domni. Is this any way to talk? When I find you a wife, the first thing I'm going to tell her is: "Jaan-e Pidar, he used to call your father-in-law a dog".'

'Domni!'—that's as far as he went in retaliation to all my insults and name calling. Or, if he felt slightly more hurt, he'd call me 'Munhcarhi Domni'. That was the limit of his anger and distress. He never called me by my real name. Whenever my older brother was mentioned, he referred to him as 'Son Aftab' or 'Barkhurdar Aftab'. But he coined a new name for me every day. Among these 'Golu' was his favourite, with 'Tanbura' a close second, followed by 'Mister Hawannaq' and 'Akhfash Square'. 'Domni' was reserved for times when his anger got the better of him. At times I really gave him a hard time. He'd be sitting on his mat reading something, having already served me with an algebra problem, which had taxed my patience to its limit. I'd kick the pile of books and notebooks lying in front of me and start singing loudly:

Tere samne baith ke rona te dukh tenun naiyyun dasna.

(I'll sit in front of you and cry but I'll never tell you the reason why.)

Dauji would look at me mystified, and I'd promptly start singing a qawwali, clapping out the time:

Naiyyun, naiyyun, naiyyun dasna te dukh tenun naiyyun dasna dasna,
dasna, dasna, dasna tenun, tenun, tenun, tenun...

He'd peer at me over his eyeglasses, smiling, then walk over to me, pick up my notebook, open it to a fresh page, stick his big hand between my clapping palms, and say with great tenderness, 'Look, son, this isn't really a difficult problem.'

But as soon as he removed his hand to explain the problem, I'd start clapping again.

'Look, son, am I not your Dauji?' he'd ask with great pride.

'No, you're not,' I'd say curtly.

'Then who's your Dauji?' he'd ask, disappointed.

'Voh sachchi sarkar,' I'd point towards the sky and say mischievously. 'He's the true Master, He's the true Provider of everybody... Come, come goat, tell me now, who's the Provider of everybody?'

He'd get up and start to leave. Just then I'd curl my arms around his waist. 'Dauji, you're not angry, are you?'

He'd break into a smile. 'Let go of me, Tanbure! Let go of me, son! I was just going to get a drink of water. I'll be right back.'

I'd pretend to be hurt and say, 'Just when the time came to explain the equation, Dauji suddenly remembers that he's thirsty.'

He'd promptly sit down and open the notebook. 'Akhfash Square, when you could see very well that it was a 4x2, why didn't you apply the third formula? And even if...'

After all this, God alone knows how long Dauji went without a drink of water.

It was the second week in February. Only a month and a half remained before the final exams. The fear of doomsday had taken hold of me like a ghost. Without any urging from anybody, I had stepped up my studies and had become quite serious. But I just couldn't get the geometry problems. Try as hard as Dauji might, nothing seemed to work. So, in exasperation, one day he told me, 'There are fifty-two propositions in all. Just memorize them. There's no other way.' So I started cramming. But any proposition I'd memorize the night before would be forgotten the next morning. I became disheartened, and felt beaten. One evening, after he had finished making me draw an assortment of geometrical diagrams and had drilled me in a number of exercises, Dauji too became anxious. I'd faltered many times, and he felt quite crushed. When he had left, after ordering me to bed right away, I took out my notebook and pencil and wrote like mad, cramming until one-thirty in the morning. But whenever I'd try to write down a proposition without looking at the book, I'd get stuck after only a few words. I nearly cried, imagining Dauji's crestfallen face and my own hopeless condition. I went out into the courtyard and sat on the stairs and actually broke into tears. Huddled, with my head on my knees, I cried and shivered from the cold at the same time. An hour or so later it struck me that the only way to save Dauji's honour was to open the door and leave for good. Having made my decision, I raised my head to begin acting on it, and who did I see but Dauji, standing in front of me wrapped up in a blanket. He pulled me to himself and hugged me with great affection, and I broke into sobs which resounded throughout the courtyard. He gently kissed me on the forehead and said, 'Well now, Tanbure, what's this? I didn't think you'd give up so easily.'

He then wrapped the blanket around both of us and led me back to my room. He sat me on the bed, carefully wrapped the blanket around me, and himself sat down in a chair, tucking his legs underneath himself.

'Euclidean geometry,' he remarked, 'is a hard nut to crack. It's made you miserable. Well, it used to make me miserable too. But in a different way. I had already gone through and taken notes from all the algebra and geometry books I could find at my Hazrat Maulana's. Nothing in them seemed inaccessible. I thought I'd mastered mathematics. One night as I lay in my bed thinking about a certain problem that had to do with isosceles triangles, I got confused. I lit my oil lamp and drew the diagram and thought about it deeply. The "given" seemed okay from an algebraic point of view, but I couldn't come up with a geometric proof. The whole night I kept working on the problem, but I didn't cry like you. Early in the morning, when I appeared before the Hazrat, he drew the problem on paper and started explaining it to me. But the point where I'd got stuck was precisely the point where his otherwise penetrating intelligence also felt some resistance. And he said, "Chinta Ram, we can no longer teach you. At the point where a student's and a teacher's learning coincide, the student is well advised to look for another teacher."

'I gathered my courage and said, "If anyone else had suggested it, I'd have considered it out-and-out kufr. But, Huzoor, since you say it, your smallest word is like a divine command unto me. How can Ayaz, a mere slave, dare say a word before Mahmud, his Ghaznavi master?! I accept what you say, but I feel terrible."

'He said, "Come now. Don't be so sentimental. Hear me out."

'I bowed my head and said, "Please go on."

' "In Delhi," he said, "Hakim Nasir Ali Sistani is considered a great expert in geometry. Since you like geometry so much, maybe you should go and study with him. I'd be happy to write him a recommendation for you."

'I expressed my willingness. But he said, "Go and ask your mother first. If she agrees, then come back to me."

'Ask Mother to let me go? There was no chance of this ever happening, so I didn't ask her. When the Huzoor enquired about the matter, I told him some lie, like I was busy whitewashing the house and would ask her when I was done.

'The next few days I spent in great nervous tension. Day and night I struggled with myself to find a way out of the problem, but it proved quite intractable. Its unyielding severity made me more confused and flustered. I wanted to go to Delhi, but I couldn't hope to get either the Huzoor's permission or his reference letter, at least not without proof of my mother's consent. Which she, at such an advanced age, was not likely to give.

'One night, when the entire village was asleep, and I was feeling as despondent as you feel today, I took half the money, a total of two rupees, from the savings my mother kept in a small basket, and slipped out of the village. May God forgive me for this, and may He keep the souls of those two elders forever pleased with me. Really, I'd committed a great sin. My head will remain bowed before them with shame and guilt until the end of time.

'I came to the place behind the haveli where the Huzoor used to sit and teach. I fell to my knees, kissed the ground, and said in my heart, "I'm indeed an unfortunate man. I'm leaving without your permission, but I'll forever need your blessings. And if you don't forgive me, I'll die at your feet."

'With these words, I picked up my staff, laid it on my shoulder, and set out... Are you listening?' Dauji looked at me intently. Huddled inside my blanket I sat still as a porcupine. I blinked my eyes quickly a few times and said in a hushed voice, 'Yes.'

Dauji resumed: 'Providence really was on my side. They were laying the railroad tracks for the Jakhul-Junaid-Saras-Hisar line in those days. This was the most direct route to Delhi, and one could also get work along the way. So I'd work one day and walk the next two. Thus, with the assistance of the Invisible, I made it to Delhi in sixteen days. But while I had reached the place of my desire, the object of my desire still eluded me. I was unable to locate the house of Hakim Nasir Ali Sistani. Nobody seemed to know where he lived. I searched for two days, without any success. Luck, however, still hadn't abandoned me. New houses were being built for the British. I found work there. In the evening, I'd look for Hakim Sahib's quarters, and at night spread out my khes in a dharmashala and sleep soundly upon it. Finally one day—as the saying goes, "He who seeks, finds"—I found out where Hakim Sahib lived. His house was in one of the dingy, dark alleys of the stone-workers' neighbourhood. I presented myself to him that evening. He was sitting in a small room talking to some friends in a loud voice. I removed my shoes and stood at the threshold. One of the gentlemen asked, "Who is it?"

'I greeted them and said, "I've come to see Hakim Sahib."

'Hakim Sahib sat surrounded by his friends, his head bowed and his back towards me. Without altering his posture he asked, "Ism-e girami?" (Your respected name, sir?)'

'I joined my hands and replied, "I've come from Punjab, and…"

'Before I could finish he said in a loud voice, "Oh, so you are Chinta Ram!"

'I didn't know what to say. But he went on. "I got a letter from Ismail. He writes: 'Chinta Ram might visit you. He's run away from home, without telling us. Help him.'"

'I remained standing in silence. This prompted him to say in his sweet, strong voice, "Miyan, come on in. What's this—have you sworn not to speak?"

'Even when I took a few steps towards him, he didn't bother to look at me and continued to sit huddled like a new bride. Then, in a commanding voice, he said, "Barkhurdar, sit down."

'I promptly sat down where I was. He said to his friends, "Give me a minute. Let me settle with him first." He then asked me, again in a commanding voice, "All right, what's the geometry problem you don't get?"

'Timidly I told him. Without changing his posture he reached for his shoulders, pulled his shirt up so that his back was completely exposed, and said, "Come on, use your finger and draw the isosceles triangle on my back."

'I went into a daze, unable to move. After a minute, he said. "Come on, Miyan, hurry up. I'm blind, so this is my paper and pen."

'I took a timid step towards him and, shaking all over, started to trace the triangle on his broad back. After I'd drawn the invisible figure, he said, "Now draw a perpendicular line *b* from point *s* to point *j*."

'I was completely flustered to begin with. And on top of this, there was nothing there to see. So I took a guess, placed my finger on a spot, and just as I was about to draw the perpendicular, he said sharply, "What're you doing? That isn't point *s*!" And then, "Well, you'll get used to it, in time. Six finger-widths below the left shoulder is point *s*, draw the line from there."

'Allahu Akbar! Allahu Akbar! I can't even begin to tell you how learned he was! What an incredible voice he had! What sharp intelligence! He was explaining while I sat wonderstruck. It seemed that right then, with this last sentence of his, the isosceles triangle was about to appear on his back in lines of pure light.'

By now Dauji had drifted off into a recollection of his time in Delhi. His eyes were wide open. He was looking at me. Then again, he was not. I asked impatiently, 'What happened then, Dauji?'

Getting up from the chair he said, 'It's late. Go to sleep. I'll tell you some other time.'

But, like an unruly child, I wouldn't leave him alone. So he said, 'All right, but you must first promise not to let despair get the better of you. That you will consider these trifling geometrical propositions to be just like so many batasha sugar drops.'

'I'll consider them pure halva, don't worry.'

Still standing, he draped the blanket around himself and said, 'The long and short of it is this: I remained in Hakim Sahib's attendance for a year and washed my blind eyes with the few drops I could gather from that Ocean of Knowledge and Learning. When I got back, I went straight to the presence of my Aaqaa and placed my head at his feet. Whereupon he said, "Chinta Ram, I'd pull back my feet if I had the strength to do so." I broke into tears at this, and he said, passing his hand lovingly over my head, "I'm not angry with you, but one year is an unbearably long time. Next time when you decide to go away, don't forget to take me along".'

Tears surged into Dauji's eyes as he repeated these words. He slipped out of the room, leaving me stupefied and still.

The exams were just around the corner now. The very thought gave me the shivers. But, strangely, my body was getting fatter, which became a source of great consternation for Dauji. He'd often grab my chubby hands and retort, 'Be a thoroughbred Arabian charger, don't just sit around like a tethered donkey!'

I'd take great umbrage at this remark and in protest I'd stop speaking to him. Even my constant threats of fast-unto-death failed to move him and his worry turned into full-fledged anxiety. One day he woke me up before his morning stroll and, despite my kicks and screams, my pleas and curses, pulled me out of bed and stuffed me into my coat. Grabbing me by the arm he practically dragged me out of the house. It was a winter morning, around four o'clock, not a soul anywhere in sight throughout the alley, completely dark all around, and Dauji was taking me for a stroll! I was talking nonsense. To which he responded, 'He's still groggy! The Tanbura's still tuning up.' Adding, now and then, 'Come on, Tanbure, play in tune! What's this strumming offbeat!'

Dauji let go of my arm only after we'd gotten far outside the village and the icy gales of the morning had forced my eyes open. We passed the Persian wheel belonging to the Sardars and left it behind, then the river, then even the cemetery, but Dauji kept walking on as if possessed, reciting what sounded like verses from the Quran. When we reached the rubble mound, I practically dropped dead from fright. People avoided walking through that area even in broad daylight, because it was believed to be the site of a city buried long ago, haunted by the victims' ghosts who ate the heart of anyone who happened to wander through. When I began to tremble with fear, Dauji carefully wrapped a warm muffler around my neck and ordered, pointing to the two acacia trees up ahead, 'Run around them as fast as you can. Ten times. Then breathe deeply a hundred times, and then come back. I'll wait for you here.'

To get away from the haunted hill, I took off towards the trees. First I sat down on a rock to catch my breath, and figured I had sat long enough to have run six of the ten rounds. I got up and ran the last four laps around the trees at the slow pace of a camel and then sat down on the same rock again, taking deep breaths. Meanwhile, strange animals started howling near the trees, and an excruciating pain shot through my ribs. I thought it best to return to the hill, wake up the drowsing Dauji, and after we had returned home, to let him have it. Filled with anger and shaking with fear, I picked my way to the hill. And what did I see but Dauji kneeling on the rubble, as he thrashed his head like a mad man, loudly reciting his favourite couplet:

Jafa kam kun keh farda roz-e mehshar
bah pesh-e ashiqan sharmindah baashi

(Don't be so cruel, lest tomorrow at Resurrection
you may come to feel small in the company of lovers.)

He'd strike the ground with his palms, look up and wave his index finger in the air, as if saying to somebody who stood before him, 'Come, think it over. I'm telling you...I'm telling you...' Then he'd lunge and throw himself on the rubble, repeating over and over again, on the verge of tears, 'Jafa kam kun, jafa kam kun.'

For a while I stood frozen. Then I screamed and, instead of the qasba, ran back toward the acacias, as the realization hit me that Dauji—there can be absolutely no doubt about it—knew the ism-e a'zam, the sovereign charm, and was presently trying to bring a genie under control. What I'd seen with my own eyes standing before him was none other than a genie—exactly like the one in the illustrated edition of the *One Thousand and One Nights*. But Dauji, unable to subdue him with the charm, had himself fallen before him, screaming again and again, 'Jafa kam kun, jafa kam kun.' The genie, however, wouldn't let go of him.

I sat down on the same rock and started to cry. After some time Dauji appeared, back to his normal self, and said, 'Come, Tanbure, let's go,' and I, smitten with fear, meekly followed him. On the way, he seized the two loose ends of his turban, now come undone and hanging from his neck, and started to sing, rocking his head to and fro:

Tere lamme lamme vaal Farida turya turya ja.

(Walk along briskly, Farida, your long hair streaming behind.)

As I was walking behind this magician, with my own eyes I saw his head change its shape: his serpentine curls began to hang down past his shoulders, his entire body became covered with long, matted hair. Past that day no amount of threat, not even being hacked to pieces, could induce me to go out with him for a walk again.

Just a few days after this, big clods of earth and pieces of brick began to fall into our courtyard. Bébé raised hell with her yelling and screaming. She stuck to Dauji like a bitch with pups. She pounced on him, hitting him so hard that he fell to the ground. She was screaming hysterically all the while, 'You old warlock, look what your spells have done, your Farsi, your black magic! It's all backfired! The evil spirits you've let loose are throwing bricks at my house! They want to destroy it! They want death!'

She started to scream even harder. 'He's killing me! He's burnt me alive, people! This old fool has cooked up a plan to take my Amichand's life! He's cast a spell on me! He's broken every bone in my body!'

Amichand was as dear to Dauji as his very own life. How could he be out to kill him? But it is also true that all that ghostly brick-throwing had been set in motion entirely on account of Dauji.

When I backed Bébé up on this, Dauji, for the first time in his life, spoke harshly to me: 'You're an idiot. And your Bébé, Umm-e Jaahileen—What, you've started believing in jinn-bhoots? After I've been teaching you for a whole year? Oh, how you disappoint me! What a pity, instead of placing your trust in knowledge, you've come to believe in women's superstitions. What a pity!'

Leaving Bébé to her screams and Dauji to his moans of regret, I climbed up to the rooftop and sat down in the sun. That very evening, as I was returning to Dauji's from my house, Ranu, squinting as usual, asked me, 'I hear rocks are coming down at your Pundit's house. Hope you didn't get hurt—did you, Babu?' I didn't want to tangle with the low-life, so I quietly stepped into the dyorhi. That evening, as Dauji listened to me go over the geometry propositions, he suddenly asked, 'Son, do you really think that jinn-bhoots and pari-churails are real?' When I said that I did think so, he chuckled and said, 'You really are very naïve. I'm sorry I snapped at you today. Why didn't you tell me before that jinns existed, that they could throw bricks? I wouldn't have gone through the trouble and expense of having Wali, the mason, and Phatte, the labourer, build the rain portico for us; I could have just as easily asked one of your jinns to do the work—and for free, to boot. But tell me this, do the jinns only throw bricks? Or do they also know how to lay them?'

'Laugh as much as you want, Dau, but the day a brick cracks your head open, you will know.'

'Not in a million years, and certainly not by a brick one of your jinns hurls. You know why? Because a jinn just doesn't exist. He can't pick up a brick, so there's no question of it hitting my head, or for that matter yours, or your Bébé's.'

After a pause he added: 'Listen. It is a basic law of physics that a material object just can't be moved by something non-material. You follow me?'

'I understand,' I said hotly.

While our qasba did have a high school, it had no facility for taking the high school exams. For that we had to go to the district centre. So, when the day arrived for our class to leave for the exams, parents and such like gathered around our lorry. Dauji was not one to stay away. While the parents and relatives of other boys were sending them off with blessings and prayers, Dauji, having jotted down the summary of the main points of a year's worth of instruction, was bombarding me with one question after another, answering them himself along with me. From a question on the reforms introduced by Akbar, the Mughal emperor, he'd next jump to a question about the causes of weather changes, and thereon to: 'Then came along another king who, by his comportment, resembled a Hindu. He was dead drunk, and a woman...'

'Jahangir,' I answered.

'And the woman?'

'Nur Jahan,' both of us answered together.

'What's the difference between sifat-e mushabbah and ism faa'il?'

I dutifully explained the difference.

'Examples?'

I gave him a few examples.

The rest of the boys had by then already boarded the lorry. Somehow I pried myself free from Dauji and darted into the vehicle. But he was not about to let me off the hook so easily. He swung around and walked over to the window and threw yet another question at me: 'Make sentences using "break in" and "break into".'

I made the sentences.

The engine started and the lorry began to move. Dauji kept coming along and shouted, 'Tanbure, maadiyaan means ghori and maakiyaan means murgi. Remember: maadiyaan—ghori, maakiyaan—murghi, maadiyaan—ghori, maakiyaan—murghi...'

It took me a whole year to get this drum-beat repetition out of my head and begin to breathe freely. The first day, I did well in the history exam. Still better the next day in the geography exam. The third day was a Sunday. The math exam was scheduled for the following day. On Sunday morning I received a page-long letter from Dauji crammed full of nothing but algebraic formulas and mathematical laws.

After the exam I came out to the veranda and compared my answers with some of the other boys. I'd done well enough to score 80 out of a total of 100 points. I went wild with joy. My feet scarcely touched the ground, exclamations of joy pouring out of my mouth. As soon as I stepped out of the veranda, I saw Dauji. He was standing with his khes thrown around him, looking intently at the math exam he had borrowed from one of the students. I hugged him, screaming '*Eighty points! Eighty points!*' He grabbed the paper from my hands and asked with bitterness in his voice, 'Show me, which ones did you get wrong?'

'The one about the four walls,' I said, still swaying with exhilaration.

He become irritated and said, 'You must have forgotten to subtract the area of the windows and doors.'

I hugged his waist and shook him like a tree. 'Yes, yes! To hell with the windows!'

'You've ruined me, Tanbure,' Dauji said in a sinking voice. 'All those three hundred and sixty-five days—how I cried myself hoarse warning you to be extra careful when you attempted the question about surfaces. But you weren't careful. You just let yourself forget it. You wasted twenty points...an entire twenty points!'

And looking at his face, my eighty per cent success was so overshadowed by my twenty per cent failure that it seemed to have no reality at all. On the way back, he kept muttering to himself the entire time, 'If the examiner turns out to be a charitable man, he'll at least allow for one point. The rest of your exam is correct.'

Dauji remained with me there till the end of exams. He'd stay in the serai where our entire class was housed and instruct me clear up to midnight, after which he would leave, as he said, for a friend's. He'd be back at eight in the morning to accompany me to the exam hall.

The exams over, I dropped Dauji from my life as if I never knew him. I'd spend the entire day roaming around with my friends, and my evenings reading novels. In between, if I had the time and inclination, I'd drop in to say 'Hello' to Dauji. He was insistent that I spend at least an hour with him every day so that he could prepare me for college. But I was not about to walk into his trap. Flunking a hundred times in college was infinitely more agreeable to me than studying—or even talking—with him. It still is. Even if I only casually asked him something, he'd tell me to translate it into Farsi. When I did so, he'd tell me to break it up syntactically. Somehow, as we were talking, the Havaldar's cow barged into the house; I tried to drive it out with a stick, but Dauji could only think to ask me, 'Is "cow" a noun or a verb?' Even an idiot with a fifth class education knew that it is a noun. But Dauji's verdict: it's both. A noun as well as a verb. 'To cow' means to harass, to threaten.

All this went on after I'd taken my exams and was waiting for the results. One day some of my friends and I decided to go hunting. I begged my friends not to go by way of the courthouse, because Dauji was sure to be there. He'd stop me and start asking about all those idioms that have to do with hunting, guns, and cartridges.

If I spotted him in the bazaar, I'd quickly slink into a side alley. And on those rare occasions when I did go to greet him, out of courtesy to be sure, I'd spend more time with Bébé than with Dauji. He'd often say, 'You're abandoning us just as Aftab did.' And out of pure mischief, I'd respond, 'Khele khub, khele khub' and start laughing.

The day my results were announced, Abbaji and I visited Dauji with a small basket of laddoos. We found him sitting on his hasir, with his head bent low. But he got up the minute he saw Abbaji, went inside the room and promptly returned with a chair, which he placed next to his gunny sack mat. 'Doctor Sahib,' he began, 'I'm genuinely ashamed. Fate works in strange ways. I was expecting a first division for him. Unfortunately it couldn't be. He started with a weak foundation...'

'But I missed it by only a single point!' I chimed in.

He looked at me and said, 'You have no idea how that one point has broken my heart. But, I must consider it God's will.'

Abbaji and he began to talk and I went over to Bébé and started to chat with her.

In my first days at college, I always wrote back to Dauji promptly; later, only sporadically. Gradually, our correspondence practically ceased.

Back home on vacations I went to greet Dauji just as I would any other of my former schoolteachers. Now, though, he no longer threw questions at me. He felt happy seeing me all dressed up in 'kot', 'patloon', and 'tai'.

He wouldn't let me sit on the cot. 'If you won't let me grab a chair for you,' he'd say, 'then at least bring it yourself.'

I'd pull a chair up beside him and sit down. He'd express his desire to look at the books I'd checked out from our college library, and in spite of my promise to bring them over to him, he'd show up at our house the very next day to have a look.

Amichand, for reasons best known to himself, had meanwhile dropped out of college and left for Delhi to work in a bank. Bébé still stitched clothes for her neighbourhood customers, and Dauji still sat outside the courthouse, though he brought hardly any money home. Bibi wrote home now and then. She was living a happy, contented life. A year's worth of college life had managed to put a lot of distance between Dauji and myself.

The girls, who until a couple of years ago freely played all sorts of games with us boys, had now become self-conscious and shy. Throughout my second year at college I tried, and to a degree even succeeded, in spending my vacations away from home. The long journey to Abbotabad seemed considerably more appealing and satisfying than the short trip home.

It was during this time that I bought myself a lovely pink writing pad with matching envelopes—my first ever. Obviously not the kind on which one wrote to Abbaji or Dauji. Dussehra vacations came and went, as did the Christmas break, and Easter afterwards. The days just rolled on.

As the time for the country's independence drew near, a series of clashes broke out and fast deteriorated into violent attacks and bloodshed. News of communal riots started to pour in from all over. So Amma promptly had all of us return home. This was still the safest place for us. Banias and rich merchants began to flee, leaving their property behind. But other Hindus and Sikhs had not yet made a move. Shortly thereafter refugees from across the border started to stream in, bearing the news that the country had finally become independent.

One day a few houses were torched in our qasba, too, and on at least two street corners fierce battles took place. The police and military declared a curfew. When it was lifted, all the Hindu and Sikh residents of our qasba fled.

In the afternoon when Amma sent me to find out about Dauji, I saw all kinds of strange faces in that familiar lane. An ox stood tethered in the dyorhi of Dauji's house, with a gunny sack curtain hanging behind it. I rushed home with the news that Dauji and Bébé too had fled, and choked as I said the words. I felt as though Dauji had left us for good, that he was not going to come back. Ever.

But Dauji was not as faithless as that.

Three days later at the local mosque, long after sundown, after I had taken down the names of the freshly arrived refugees and promised to have blankets sent to them, as I was walking through that same alley, I saw a crowd of perhaps two hundred men gathered in the open field. Muhajir boys, brandishing lathis, were shouting slogans and abuses all at once. I made an attempt to tear through the throng and penetrate to its centre, but the ominous, bloody look in the eyes of the Muhajirs held me back. A boy was telling an older man:

'He'd gone away to the neighbouring village. When he returned, he just went straight into his house.'

'Which house?'

'The one the refugees from Rohtak have claimed,' answered the boy.

'So?' the elderly man asked.

'So nothing. They seized him. Found out he was a Hindu.'

Just then someone from the crowd yelled, 'Oye Ranu, run! Come quickly! This one's yours. The Pundit. Just the one for you!'

Ranu, at the time, was driving his goats back to the enclosure. He halted them, asked a lathi-wielding boy to keep an eye on them, and himself lunged into the crowd.

My heart skipped a beat: was it Dauji they had grabbed? Without even looking at the accused man, I pleaded with the people nearest me, 'He is a good man. A pious man. Don't hurt him, please! He is…'

Several pairs of hate-filled eyes glowered at me, and a young man, brandishing his chopper, threatened me, 'Maybe I should let you have it too! Supporting him like the devil's own advocate! You weren't there, that's why!'

Others in the crowd heaped abuse on me and concluded, 'Must be an Ansar.'

Scared, I ran to the other side of the crowd and tried to blend in. Ranu, along with a contingent of his friends, stood surrounding Dauji. He was tugging at Dauji's chin and mocking him, 'Come, son, what do you have to say?'

Dauji just stood there in silent immobility. Suddenly a youngster snatched the turban from Dauji's head and yelled, 'His bodi! First, clip off the bodi!' And Ranu dutifully obliged, clipping it off with the sickle he used for pruning twigs and branches.

'Should we let him have it now? What do you say?' the same youngster asked.

Ranu replied, 'Nah! Let him go. He's far too old. Maybe I can use him to tend my goats.'

Seizing Dauji by the chin and lifting his face up, Ranu ordered, 'All right, Pandata, let's hear you recite the kalima!'

'Which one?' Dauji asked, softly.

Ranu struck Dauji's now bare head so hard that he nearly fell down. He fumed, 'Saale, bastard, you make fun of me? You think there are five, six, seven kalimas or what?'

After he was finished reciting the kalima, Ranu shoved his lathi into Dauji's hands and said, 'Get going, you coot, the goats are waiting for you.'

Bareheaded, Dauji started off behind the goats, as though he were Farida, the one with the long flowing hair.

THE SHROUD

MUNSHI PREMCHAND

Outside the hut, father and son sat in silence in front of the firepit already gone cold. Inside, Budhya, the son's young wife, kept thrashing about in labour, intermittently sending forth piercing cries of pain that momentarily froze the hearts of the two men. It was a cold wintry night. Stillness pervaded all around. The entire village was engulfed in darkness.

'Doesn't look like she'll make it,' said Ghisu. 'She's been writhing in agony all day long. Perhaps you should go in and have a look at her.'

Madhu replied in a mournful voice, 'If die she must, why linger on. What's there for me to look at, anyway?'

'You are a heartless man... So unfeeling towards the woman who gave you every comfort of life for an entire year!'

'I just can't bear the sight of her flailing about in utter agony.'

Theirs was a family of chamars, and none too liked for its ways throughout the village. Ghisu worked one day and took rest for the next three. Madhu shirked work if he could help it. And even if he did work for an hour, he spent an equal amount smoking his chillum. That's why no one felt like hiring these layabouts. If the house had a fistful of grain, well, that was as good a reason as any not to work at all. When, however, they had to go without food for a couple of times, Ghisu climbed on trees and broke some branches, which Madhu then took to the bazaar to sell. For the time the money lasted, the two idled away without a care, until the next bout of starvation overtook them, and the earlier routine of gathering firewood or looking for work kicked in again. It wasn't like there was shortage of work in this village of farmers. Hundreds of jobs were ready for the taking for any hardworking man. People took them on only when necessity drove them to hire two men to do the job of one. Had the two been only sadhus, there would be absolutely no need to seek contentment and trust in God through ascetic self-denial, for these were their innate attributes. It was a strange life; they owned nothing beyond a few clay pots, torn rags to clothe their nakedness—free of wordly deceptions, weighed down by heavy debts, the butt of people's insults and scorn, and yet not a worry to speak of. Despite their abject poverty, people still lent them something, fully aware that none of it was ever coming back. At harvest time, they would steal green peas or dig up potatoes from other people's fields, bake them and have their fill, or pick a few stalks of sugarcane to suck at night. Ghisu had lived through all his sixty years in such ascetic frugality, and Madhu, every bit his father's son, was following in his footsteps; if anything, he had put a gloss on his old man's fame. Ghisu's wife had died a while back. Madhu had married just a year ago. Ever since her arrival, this woman had put a measure of order and civility in their family. She would do chores for others; grind grain or cut grass to earn a little and buy some flour to fill the stomachs of these shameless bums. Her presence had made them even more indolent and slothful. If anyone offered a job, they audaciously asked for double wages, as if they couldn't care less. And now the same woman was writhing in deathly labour since the morning, while the two men were perhaps waiting for her to kick the bucket so that they could finally get some peaceful sleep.

Ghisu yanked out the potatoes from the ashes, started peeling them and told Madhu, 'Come on now, go inside and see how she's doing. Looks like some evil spirit has possessed her—yes, evil spirit, a witch. Here, even an exorcist asks for a rupee. Who's going to give it to us?'

Afraid that if he went inside Ghisu would polish off most of the potatoes himself, Madhu said, 'I'm scared.'

'Scared—scared of what? I'm right here.'

'Well then, go yourself and see.'

'When my woman lay dying, I didn't leave her side for three days. Wouldn't Budhya be embarrassed seeing me? I've never seen her face without her veil on. If she sees me in her senseless state, she wouldn't be able to thrash freely out of modesty.'

'Say, what if she did give birth to a child? Ginger, raw sugar, oil—we have got nothing in the house.'

'Oh, we'll get everything. First, let Bhagwan give us a child. The very people who are averse to giving us a penny now will rush in to provide. Nine boys were born to us and we were flat broke, but each time things worked out swimmingly.'

The emergence of such a mindset was not surprising, indeed it was inevitable in a social milieu where the general condition of those toiling away day and night was not much better than that of Ghisu and Madhu and where carefree existence was the privilege of only those who took advantage of the dismal circumstances of the peasantry. One would even venture to say that Ghisu reflected a keener sense of reality and discernment than the peasants in joining the ranks of the rogues and the rabble-rousers rather than those of the dim-witted community of the farm workers. What he sorely lacked, though, was the ability to stick to the rules and the ways of the rogues. So, while others of his ilk became wielders of power and authority in the village, he remained the object of everyone's scorn. But there was comfort in the thought that as bad as his situation was at least he didn't have to work his backside off like farmers, that his simplemindedness and unassuming manner were his greatest assets against anyone taking advantage of him.

Both men pulled out searing hot potatoes and started eating ravenously. They hadn't had a morsel to eat since the day before and could hardly wait for the potatoes to cool. As a result, they repeatedly singed their tongues. The outer part of a peeled potatoe didn't feel overly hot, but the instant the teeth dug into its inside, the burning pulp scalded their tongues, their palates, and their throats. It was better to quickly swallow the live ember than chew on it. It would be cooled once it had plopped into their stomachs anyway. They hurriedly swallowed the embers; however, the effort caused their eyes to water profusely.

As they gobbled the potatoes, Ghisu remembered the day when, twenty years ago, he was part of the Thakur's wedding procession. He had eaten so much and so well at the banquet that day that it became the most memorable event of his life. Its memory was still vividly alive in his mind. He said, 'Would I ever forget that fabulous meal! I haven't had anything quite like it ever since. It was out of this world. I could eat as much as I wanted. The bride's family served fried puris. Bigshots and nobodys, all—and I mean all—ate puris and satpanis made from pure ghee, raita, three types of dried leaf vegetable dishes, another kind of vegetable dish, yogurt, chutney, and sweetmeats! I cannot begin to tell you how fantastic the food tasted. You could eat as much as you wanted, ask for anything, and eat until you could no more. People ate so much, so much they had no room left for a drink of water. But those serving the food kept piling up our plates with piping hot and perfectly round fragrant kachoris, regardless of how much we asked them not to or shielded our plates with hands. They just wouldn't know how to stop. When the guests had rinsed their mouths and washed their hands, they were each offered a cone of paan. But I had no mind to chew paan. I could hardly stand up. I made it to my blanket and splayed out on it as fast as I could. Such was the generosity of the Thakur! It knew no bounds!'

Madhu, savouring these flavourful delicacies in his imagination, exclaimed,

'If only someone served us such a meal now!'

'Who will? Not a chance. That was a different time. Now people tend to be tightfisted. They say, "Don't spend too much on weddings! Don't spend too much on funerals!" Just ask them, "So what are you going to do with what all you have been squeezing out of the poor?" Squeezing never stops, frugality kicks in only when it comes to spending.'

'You must have eaten twenty puris, I guess?'

'More than twenty.'

'I would have gobbled fifty.'

'I wouldn't have eaten less than fifty. I was a strapping youth back then. You are not even half as strong.'

After eating potatoes, they drank some water, covered themselves with their dhotis, and dozed off near the firepit, curling their legs in foetal position, like two enormous coiled snakes. Meanwhile, Budhya kept groaning in labour.

Come morning, Madhu went inside the hut and found that his wife's body had turned cold. Flies were buzzing around her mouth. Her stony eyes were turned upward in a frozen stare and her body was smeared with dirt and grime. The child had died in her womb.

He rushed out to Ghisu. Both men broke out into loud wailing and started beating their chests. The neighbours came running when they heard their doleful cries. According to the age-old custom, they expressed their sympathy and tried to console them.

However, there wasn't time for much wailing and chest-beating. They had to worry about a shroud for the dead body and wood for the pyre. The money in the house had disappeared like carrion in a buzzard's nest.

Father and son went wailing and crying to the village landlords, who hated the very sight of the two and often had occasion to beat them up for pilfering, for not showing up for work despite promising to. Anyway, they asked, 'What is the matter, Ghisu? Why are you crying? You've become so scarce these days. You aren't thinking of leaving the village, are you?'

Ghisu put down his forehead on the ground and, with tears in his eyes, said, 'Sarkar, a terrible calamity has struck me. Madhu's wife passed away last night. She kept writhing in pain all day long. Both of us stayed by her side half the night. Medicine, drugs, you name it—we tried everything, but she left us all the same. Who would feed us now? Master, we are ruined. The house is desolate. I am your slave. There is only you to help with her cremation. Whatever little we had was spent on medicine and drugs. Her funeral rites will be performed only through your benevolence. At whose door should I go begging if not yours?'

Zamindar Sahib was a gentle soul, but showing mercy to Ghisu was like trying to dye a jet-black fabric a varied colour. He felt like telling him off: 'Get the hell out of here! Keep the corpse in the house and let it rot! When I call you for work, you put on airs and don't show up. Today, when you're in need, you come flattering me—you freeloading son of a bitch! Rascal!'

But this was hardly the time to get angry or seek revenge. Zamindar Sahib took out two rupees and disdainfully threw them at him, without a word of commiseration. He didn't bother to even look at him, as if he just wanted to get this weight off his chest, and get it off pretty damn quick.

Once the Zamindar had dished out two rupees, how dare the banias and monylenders of the village refuse him? He went around announcing loudly that the Zamindar had donated two rupees. People gave, some two annas, some four. Within an hour Ghisu had bagged a tidy sum of five rupees. Some offered grain, some others wood. Around noon both men set out for the bazaar to buy a shroud, and others started to chop bamboo stalks to fashion a bier for the corpse.

The tender-hearted womenfolk of the village came to look at Budhya's dead body, shed a few tears at the hapless woman and left.

After they had made it to the bazaar, Ghisu said, 'We've got enough wood for the pyre, Madhu, what do you say?'

'Oh yes, plenty,' Madhu replied. 'All we need now is the shroud.'

'Well then, let's get a cheap one.'

'Of course, a cheap one. By the time the corpse is carried off for cremation, it will be night. No one would care to look at the shroud in the dark.'

'What a lousy custom! Someone who could not get a tattered rag to cover her body while living must have a new shroud now when she dies.'

'A shroud burns up with the corpse.'

'What else! If we had the same five rupees earlier, we could have spent the money on her treatment.'

Both understood the implied meaning of the other. They meandered through the bazaar until evening shadows began to deepen. Whether by accident or by design they found themselves standing right across from a tavern. They walked in, as though driven by some tacit agreement, and stood there hesitating for a bit. Then Ghisu bought a bottle of country liquor and some flats of gajak to go with the drink. They sat on the veranda and began drinking.

A few glasses down their throats in quick succession and both men's heads began to swim.

'What good is a shroud for? It would have burnt to ashes anyway. Bahu wouldn't have carried it with her.'

Madhu looked at the sky, as if trying to prove his innocence to the angels, and said, 'Such are the ways of the world. Why do these moneybags give away thousands of rupees to the Brahmins? Who can tell whether they would get any recompense for it in the next world.'

'The bigshots have plenty to burn, so let them. What have we got to burn.'

'But what will we say to the people? Wouldn't they ask, "Where is the shroud?"'

Ghisu cackled. 'We'll say the money slipped off our waists. We looked and looked but couldn't find it.'

Madhu cackled too. At this unexpected good fortune and on outsmarting fate, he said, 'Poor woman, she was so good to us. Even in death she's made sure that we are well fed.'

By now they had been through more than half the bottle. Ghisu sent Madhu for two sers of puris, a dish of curried meat, spicy roasted liver, and fried fish. The shop was straight across from the tavern. Madhu returned in no time at all, bringing everything on two leaf platters. It cost them one rupee and a half. They were left with a little bit of change now.

They sat eating with the majestic air of a tiger feasting on his prey, without a care about having to answer for their actions, or haunted by any thought of the coming disgrace. They had overcome such scruples a long time ago. Ghisu said philosophically, 'If our souls are content, wouldn't she get some reward for it!'

Madhu bowed his head with overabundant reverence and agreed, 'Of course she will, no doubt about it. Bhagwan, You are all-knowing! Give her a place in heaven. We pray for her with all our hearts. Never in our life did we taste such delicious food as we did today.'

A split second later Madhu was assailed by doubt. 'Well, Dada, we too will have to go there some day.'

Ghisu brushed aside this childish question and looked at Madhu reproachfully.

'What if she asks us up there, "Why did you people not give my body a shroud?" What will you say?'

'Pipe down.'

'But she will be sure to ask us.'

'How do you know that she won't get her shroud? You think I'm an arsehole or something? I haven't been dawdling all my sixty years. She will get her shroud all right, and she will get a very nice one, much better than what we could have ever given her.'

Madhu, who didn't believe him, said, 'Who is going to give it? You've blown up all the money.'

'I said that she will get a shroud,' Ghisu said in a huff. 'Why don't you believe me?'

'But why won't you tell me who'll give it?'

'The same people who gave this time, except the money won't come into our hands. And if somehow it did, we will again be sitting here drinking away. And we will get a shroud for the third time.'

As the darkness spread and the stars began to shine brightly, the tavern took on an air of exuberance. People broke into song, made merry, hugged their companions, raised wine cups to their friends' lips. The atmosphere was shot through with inebriated gaiety, the air gently intoxicating. It took just a few sips for many to get drunk. People came here for a taste of forgetfulness. Their enjoyment came more from the tavern's ambience than from liquor. Wordly cares had dragged them here—a place where they could forget for a while whether they were alive or dead, or living-dead.

And here they were, father and son, sipping their drinks with a feeling of immense light-heartedness. Everyone's gaze was glued on them: lucky guys, an entire bottle to share between them!

After they were done eating, Madhu picked up the platter of the leftover puris and gave it to the beggar who had been standing nearby, casting greedy looks at them. For the first time in his life Madhu felt the swagger, the elation, the joy that comes from giving.

'Here...take it. Eat your fill,' said Ghisu. 'Give your blessings. The woman who earned this is no more, but your blessings will certainly reach her. Let every pore of your body bless her. It was hard-earned money.'

Madhu looked at the sky again and said, 'Dada, she will surely go to heaven, won't she? She'll become the Queen of Heaven.'

Ghisu stood up and, as if awash in the tide of happiness, said, 'Yes son, she *will*. She will go to heaven. She troubled no one, harmed no one, and even as she lay dying fulfilled the most ardent wish of our life. If she doesn't go to heaven, then will these moneybags who rob the poor folk with both hands and make offerings of holy water at temples and take a dip in the Ganga to wash out their sins?'

The aura of joyful trust in Providence brought on by their inebriated state soon gave way to a bout of despair and sorrow.

'But Dada,' Madhu said, 'she suffered a lot in her life, and not least even when she lay dying.' He covered his eyes with his hands and broke into sobs.

Ghisu tried to comfort him. 'Son, why do you cry? Be glad instead. At least she is rid of the web of earthly illusions, free of wordly cares and anxieties. She was lucky to break free of the bonds of moh and maya so soon.'

Both stood up and started singing at the spot:

> *Enchantress, why do you entice us with your flashing eyes,*
> *Enchantress!*

The entire tavern watched the two tipplers in breathless amazement, who were singing away with abandon, oblivious of everything. Then they started dancing. They skipped and hopped. They stumbled and fell. Swayed their hips seductively. At last, overcome by the stupor brought on by alcohol, they crumbled.

TOBA TEK SINGH

SAADAT HASAN MANTO

A few years after Partition, the thought occurred to the governments of Pakistan and Hindustan that, as with ordinary prisoners, an exchange of lunatics was in order. Muslim madmen in Indian asylums should be sent over to Pakistan and the Hindu and Sikh lunatics languishing in Pakistani madhouses should be handed over to Hindustan.

Whether the proposition was smart or stupid only God knows. Anyway, following the decision of some wise men, a bunch of high-level conferences were convened on either side and concluded with the fixing of a date for the transfer. A thorough scrutiny was mounted. Muslim lunatics with relatives still living in Hindustan could stay there; others were shepherded to the border. In Pakistan, the question of keeping anyone didn't even arise since nearly all Hindus and Sikhs had already migrated to Hindustan. The remaining Hindu and Sikh lunatics were rounded up and brought over to the border under police escort.

Regardless of what did or didn't happen across the border, in the Lahore asylum the news of the imminent exchange stirred up rather interesting speculation among the inmates. There was one Muslim lunatic who had never missed reading the newspaper *Zamindaar* during the last twelve years. When a friend asked him, 'Molbi Sab, what is this thing called Pakistan?' he gave the matter prolonged, deep thought and said, 'It's a place in India where they make straight razors.'

The explanation satisfied his friend.

Likewise, one Sikh inmate asked another Sikh, 'Sardarji, why are we being sent to Hindustan? We don't know their language.'

The latter smiled. 'But I know the Hindustoras' language. They are absolute rascals—these Hindustanis. They strut around.'

One day, as he was bathing, a Muslim lunatic shouted '*Pakistan Zindabad!*' so loudly that he slipped, fell to the floor and knocked himself out.

There were some inmates who weren't mad. Most of them were murderers. Their relatives had had them committed after bribing the officers so that they would be spared the hangman's noose. They did seem to have some inkling of why Hindustan was partitioned and what this Pakistan was, but even they didn't understand the matter clearly enough. Newspapers weren't much help and the watchmen were morons, total illiterates; nothing definite could be gleaned from conversations with them. All they knew was that there was this man Muhammad Ali Jinnah whom everyone called Qaid-e Azam. He had made a separate country for Muslims called Pakistan. But they knew nothing about where it was located. So, these inmates, whose minds hadn't muddled entirely, were continually in a fix about whether they were in Pakistan or Hindustan. If they were in Hindustan, then where was Pakistan?

One inmate got so mixed up about this business of Pakistan–Hindustan, Hindustan–Pakistan that he became even crazier. One day, while sweeping the floor, he suddenly climbed a tree, installed himself on a limb, and for the next two hours held forth non-stop on the delicate matter of Pakistan and Hindustan. When the guards tried to coax him down, he climbed even higher. When he was threatened, he told them in no uncertain terms, 'I don't want to live in Hindustan and I don't want to live in Pakistan; I'll live here in this tree.'

Finally, when the bout of madness subsided, he decided to come down, whereupon he started hugging his Hindu and Sikh friends deliriously, crying all the while because he was overcome by the thought that they would leave him here and go to Hindustan.

A Muslim radio engineer with a Master of Science degree always kept himself aloof from other inmates and walked quietly on a certain path of the asylum's garden all day long. Suddenly, one day, he took off all his clothes, gave them to an officer and started frolicking in the garden stark naked.

A plump Muslim lunatic from Chiniot, once a very active worker for the Muslim League, bathed fifteen or sixteen times a day. He abruptly gave up bathing altogether. His name was Muhammad Ali, and one day he announced from his cubicle that he was Muhammad Ali Jinnah. A Sikh followed suit and declared himself Master Tara Singh. This nearly led to a bloodbath, but designating both men as highly dangerous and confining them to separate quarters averted the crisis.

A young Lahori Hindu lawyer who had lost his mind after failing in love was terribly hurt upon hearing that Amritsar had now been moved to Hindustan. His beloved was a native of that city. Although she had snubbed him, even in his madness her memory was fresh in his mind. He constantly hurled obscenities at the Hindu and Muslim leaders who had conspired to eviscerate Hindustan, making him a Pakistani and his beloved a Hindustani. When talk of the exchange began, many of the other lunatics tried to bolster his sagging spirits. They told him not to despair; he would be packed off to the Hindustan where his love lived. But he didn't want to abandon Lahore. He was afraid he wouldn't be able to set up a successful law practice in Amritsar.

There were two Anglo-Indian inmates in the European ward. They literally went into shock hearing that the English had freed India and gone back home. For hours, they quietly discussed the grave matter of their status in the asylum now that the English had left. Would the European ward be kept or liquidated? Would they get a 'real breakfast'? Or would they be obliged to force the bloody Indian chapatti down their gullets in place of the double-roti?

A Sikh inmate had arrived in the asylum fifteen years ago. He could be heard uttering strange gibberish all the time: 'Upar de gurgur de aiynks de be-dhyaana de mung de daal aaf de laaltain.' Day or night, he never slept. The watchmen could swear that the fellow hadn't slept even a wink in fifteen years. Whenever he heard talk in the asylum of the coming exchange, he always listened to it intently. If someone asked him his opinion, he would answer with complete seriousness: 'Upar de gurgur de aiynks de be-dhyaana de mung de daal aaf de Pakistan government.'

Later, though, he changed aaf de Pakistan government to aaf de Toba Tek Singh government, and started asking the other loonies where Toba Tek Singh, the place he came from, was. But no one knew whether Toba Tek Singh was in Pakistan or Hindustan. And if someone tried to explain, he inevitably got confused, thinking that Sialkot, which used to be in Hindustan, was now said to be in Pakistan. Who knew, perhaps Lahore, currently in Pakistan, would move over to Hindustan tomorrow, or maybe all of Hindustan would become Pakistan. And who could say with any surety that both Hindustan and Pakistan would not disappear altogether.

Over time this lunatic's kes had become so scraggly that it almost seemed to have disappeared. He hardly ever bathed, so the hair of his beard and head had become matted and stuck together, giving his features a frighteningly grotesque look. However, he was a harmless man. During his fifteen years in the asylum he had never had a brawl with anyone. The old staff knew that he had owned quite a bit of land in Toba Tek Singh. He had been a prosperous landowner until one day, suddenly, he went berserk. His relatives brought him to the asylum in heavy chains and had him admitted. They came to visit him once a month, enquired after him and then went back. Their visits continued for a long time, but stopped when the Pakistan–Hindustan garbar started.

His name was Bishan Singh, but everyone called him Toba Tek Singh. Although he had no awareness of the day or month or how many years had passed, somehow, he always knew the day his relatives were expected. He would tell the officer that his 'visit' was coming that day. He would take a long bath, scrub his body vigorously with soap, oil and comb his hair, have his clothes, which he hardly ever wore, brought out and slip into them, and meet his visitors thus, looking all prim and proper. If they asked him something, he remained quiet or mumbled his incomprehensible 'Upar de gurgur de aiynks de be-dhyaana de mung de daal aaf de laaltain' now and then.

He had a daughter who, growing a little at a time, had become a young woman in fifteen years. Bishan Singh never recognized her. As a little girl, she would cry when she saw her father, and now, as a young woman, tears still welled up in her eyes at the sight of him.

When this confusing business of Pakistan and Hindustan began, he started asking his fellow lunatics where Toba Tek Singh was located. His curiosity grew by the day when he didn't get a satisfactory answer. Now the 'visits' had also stopped. Where before he would instinctively know when his relatives were coming to see him, now that inner voice no longer intimated such a visit to him.

He fervently wished those people who talked with him with such kindness and warmth and who brought him gifts of fruits, sweets and clothes would visit him. If he were to ask them, they would surely have told him whether Toba Tek Singh was in Pakistan or Hindustan because he thought they themselves came from Toba Tek Singh.

One lunatic called himself 'God'. One day Bishan Singh asked him about Toba Tek Singh: Was it in Pakistan or Hindustan?

As usual, 'God' burst out laughing and said, 'Neither in Pakistan nor Hindustan because we haven't yet given the orders.'

Bishan Singh begged 'God' many times to give the order so the dilemma could be laid to rest, but he said he was too damn busy because he had many other orders to give first. So, one day, fed up with 'God's' dilly-dallying, Bishan Singh let him have a piece of his mind: 'Upar de gurgur de aiynks de be-dhyaana de mung de daal aaf Wahe Guruji da Khalsa and Wahe Guruji ki Fateh—jo bole so nihal, sat siri akaal!' Perhaps he meant to say: You're the Muslims' God, had you been the God of the Sikhs you would surely have heard my plea.

Some days before the scheduled exchange of lunatics, a Muslim friend of Bishan Singh came to see him. He had never visited him before in all these years. Bishan Singh saw him but shrugged and started to turn back. The guards stopped him and said, 'He's come to visit you. He's your old friend Fazl Din.' Bishan Singh hardly glanced at the man and started to mumble something. Fazl Din drew closer and put his hand on Bishan Singh's shoulder. 'I've been thinking of visiting you for quite a while now but was pressed for time. All your relatives have safely left for Hindustan. I helped them as much as I could. Your daughter, Roop Kaur...' He suddenly held back.

Bishan Singh looked as though he was trying to remember something and then mumbled, 'Daughter Roop Kaur.'

Fazl Din said falteringly, 'Yes...She...she's all right...she went with them.'

Bishan Singh remained quiet. Fazl Din continued, 'Your family asked me to keep enquiring after your well-being. Now I hear that you're also leaving for Hindustan. Give my salaams to brother Balbeer Singh and brother Vadhwa Singh...and, yes, to sister Amrit Kaur as well. Tell brother Balbeer Singh that Fazl Din is doing well. The two brown buffaloes they had left behind—one of them gave birth to a male calf. The other also had a calf, a female, but it died after six days... And if there's anything more he'd like me to do, tell him I'm always ready. And this, here, a little morandas for you.'

Bishan Singh took the small sack of sweets and handed it to the guard standing nearby. He then asked Fazl Din, 'Where is Toba Tek Singh?'

Fazl Din was a bit bewildered. 'Where...where it's always been.'

Bishan Singh asked him again, 'In Pakistan or in Hindustan?'

'In Hindustan...No, no, it's in Pakistan.' Fazl Din was flummoxed. Bishan Singh left, mumbling, 'Upar de gurgur de aiynks de be-dhyaana de mung de daal aaf de Pakistan and Hindustan aaf de durfatte munh.'

Preparations for the exchange had been completed. The list of lunatics who would be swapped had been sent over to the country receiving them and the day when the exchange would take place had been fixed.

On a freezing morning, lorries packed with Hindu and Sikh lunatics started out from the Lahore asylum under police escort along with the officials overseeing the exchange. At the Wagah border, the superintendents of both sides met, concluded the preliminary formalities, and the exchange began, continuing well into the night.

Getting the lunatics out of the lorries and handing them over to the officials on the other side turned out to be a gruelling job indeed. Some resisted getting out, others who were willing to come out became impossible to control because they took off in different directions. As fast as the stark-naked ones were clothed, they tore the clothes right off again. One rolled out a torrent of obscenities, another broke into song. Some got into fisticuffs, while others cried their hearts out, sobbing inconsolably. The hullabaloo was deafening. The female lunatics were raising their own separate hell. And all this in a cold so punishing that it made one's teeth chatter non-stop.

The majority of lunatics were against the exchange. They couldn't understand why they were being uprooted. Those who still had some sanity left were shouting *Pakistan Zindabad!* or *Pakistan Murdabad!*—which so enraged some Muslim and Sikh lunatics that they nearly came to blows.

When Bishan Singh's turn came and the official across the Wagah border began to enter his name in the register, he asked, 'Where is Toba Tek Singh—in Pakistan or in Hindustan?'

The official laughed. 'In Pakistan.'

Bishan Singh jumped, withdrew to one side and ran to his fellow inmates. Pakistani guards grabbed him and started pushing him towards the other side of the border. He dug his heels in, refusing to budge. 'Toba Tek Singh is here!' and then he started to spew out loudly: 'Upar de gurgur de aiynks de be-dhyaana de mung de daal aaf Toba Tek Singh and Pakistan.'

They did their best to coax him into believing by saying 'Look, Toba Tek Singh has now moved to Hindustan, and if it hasn't yet, it will be sent there right away,' but he stubbornly refused to accept that. When they attempted to drag him forcibly across the border, he dug in with his swollen legs with such determination on the patch of earth that lay in the middle that no force in the world could move him from it.

Since he was entirely harmless, the guards didn't force him and let him stand where he was while the rest of the exchange continued.

Just before sunrise an ear-splitting cry shot out of Bishan Singh's throat. Officials from both sides of the border rushed over to him, only to find that the man who had stood on his feet day and night for the past fifteen years was lying face down. There, behind the barbed wires, was Hindustan, and here, behind the same barbed wires, was Pakistan. In between, on the thin strip of no man's land, lay Toba Tek Singh.

LAAJWANTI

RAJINDER SINGH BEDI

Touch the leaves of the laajwanti,
they curl and wither away.

After Partition, when countless wounded people had finally cleaned the gore from their bodies, they turned their attention to those who had not suffered bodily but had been wounded in their hearts.

Rehabilitation committees were formed in every neighbourhood and side street and the campaign to help the victims acquire business, land, and homes for themselves got underway with much enthusiasm. There was one programme, though, which seemed to have escaped notice. It concerned the rehabilitation of abducted women. Its rallying cry was 'Rehabilitate them in your hearts!' It was bitterly opposed by Narain Bawa's temple and the conservatives who lived in and around it.

A committee was formed in the Mulla Shakur neighbourhood near the temple to get the programme off the ground. Babu Sundar Lal was elected its secretary by a majority of eleven votes and the Vakil Sahib its president. It was the opinion of the old petition writer of the Chauki Kalan district—in which other well-regarded individuals of the neighbourhood concurred with him—that no one could be expected to work more passionately for the cause than Sundar Lal, because his own wife, Laaju—Laajwanti—too had been abducted.

Early in the morning when Babu Sundar Lal and his companions Rasaloo and Neki Ram used to make their rounds through the streets singing in unison, *Touch the leaves of the laajwanti,/they curl and wither away!* Sundar Lal's voice would fade. Walking along in silence he would think about Laajwanti—who knows where she might be? In what condition? What would she be thinking of him? Would she ever come back?—and his feet would falter on the cobblestone pavement.

But by now things had reached a point where he had stopped even thinking about Laajwanti. His pain was no longer just his; it had become part of the world's anguish. And to spare himself its devastation he had thrown himself headlong into serving the people. All the same, every time he joined his companions in that song, he couldn't help wondering at how delicate the human heart is. The slightest thing could hurt it. Exactly like the laajwanti plant, whose leaves curl up at the barest touch. Well, that may be. But for his own part, he had never spared any effort in treating his own Laajwanti as badly as possible. He would beat her on the flimsiest pretext, taking exception to the way she got up, the way she sat down, the way she cooked food—anything and everything.

Laaju was a slender and agile village girl. Too much sun had turned her skin quite dark, and a nervous energy informed her movements, which brought to mind the fluid grace of a dewdrop rolling like mercury on a leaf: now to one side, now to the other. Her slim build, which was more a sign of health than its absence, worried Sundar Lal at first, but when he observed how well she could take all manner of adversity, including even physical abuse, he progressively increased his mistreatment of her, quite forgetting that past a certain limit anyone's patience is sure to run out. Laajwanti, too, had contributed her share in obscuring the perception of such a limit. She wasn't, by nature, one to dwell on her anguish for too long. A simple smile from Sundar Lal following the worst fight, and she was unable to stop her giggles: 'If you beat me ever again, I'll never speak to you!'

It was obvious she had already forgotten all about the fights and beatings. That's how husbands treat their wives—she knew this truth as well as any other village girl. If a woman showed the slightest independence, the girls themselves would be the first to disapprove. 'Ha, what kind of man is he? Can't even keep his little woman in line!' The physical abuse men subjected their wives to had even made it into the women's songs. Laaju herself used to sing:

Marry a city boy?—No sir, not me.
Look at his boots, and my waist is so narrow.

Nonetheless, at the very first opportunity she had fallen in love with just such a city boy, Sundar Lal, who had first come to her village as part of a wedding party and had whispered into the groom's ear, 'Your sister-in-law is pretty hot stuff, yaar! Your wife must be quite a dish too!'

Laajwanti had overheard him. She took no notice at all of his large, heavy boots, and forgot all about her own narrow waist.

Such were the memories that Sundar Lal recalled during his early morning rounds with his companions. He would say to himself, 'If I could get another chance, just one more chance, I'd rehabilitate Laaju in my heart. I'd show the people that these poor women are hardly to blame for their abduction, their victimization by lecherous rioters. A society which is unable to accept and rehabilitate these innocent women is rotten to the core, fit only to be destroyed.'

Sundar Lal would plead with the people to take these women under their roof and give them the same status which any woman, any mother, daughter, sister, or wife enjoyed. He would urge the families never to mention, even to hint at the things the poor women had to suffer, because their hearts were already wounded, already fragile, like the leaves of the touch-me-not plant, ready to curl up at the merest touch.

The Mulla Shakur Rehabilitation of Hearts Committee took out many early morning processions to put its programme into effect. The wee hours of the morning were the most feasible time for their activity: no human noise, no traffic snarls. Even the dogs, after an exhausting night-long watch, would be asleep at this hour, as they lay curled up inside the tandoors long since gone cold. And people, huddled in their beds, would wake up to mumble drowsily, 'Oh, that group again!'

People listened to Sundar Lal Babu's propaganda, sometimes with patience, sometimes with irritation. Women who had made it safely to this side of the border lay loosely in their beds, while their husbands, lying stiff beside them, mumbled protests against the noise kicked up by the morning rally, or a child somewhere opened its eyes for a moment and fell back to sleep, taking the doleful petition of 'Rehabilitate them in your hearts' for a lullaby.

Words which enter the ear so early in the morning rarely fail to produce an effect. They reverberate in the mind the entire day, and even if their underlying meaning is not plain, one nonetheless finds oneself repeating them. So, thanks to this effect, when Miss Mridula Sara Bai secured the exchange of abducted women between India and Pakistan, some people in the Mulla Shakur neighbourhood willingly took their women back. They went to receive them outside the city at Chauki Kalan. For a while the abducted women and their relatives faced each other in awkward silence. Then, with their heads bent low, they returned to pick up the pieces of their lives and rebuild their homes. Meanwhile Rasaloo, Neki Ram and Sundar Lal rooted for them with cries, now of 'Long Live Mahendar Singh!' now of 'Long Live Sohan Lal!' They kept it up until their throats went dry.

But there were some abducted women whose husbands, parents, or siblings refused even to recognize them. As far as their families were concerned, they should have killed themselves. They should have taken poison to save their virtue. Or jumped into a well. Cowards—to cling to life so tenaciously!

Hundreds, indeed thousands of women had in fact killed themselves to save their honour. But what could they know of the courage it took just to live on? What could they know of the icy stares it took for the survivors to look death in the face, in a world where even their husbands refused to recognize them? One or another of the abducted repeats her name to herself: 'Suhagwanti'—she who has suhag, the affection of her husband. She spots her brother in the crowd and says only this one final time, 'Even you, Bihari, refuse to recognize me! I took you in my lap and fed you when you were small.' Bihari wants to slip away, but he looks at his parents and freezes, who steel their hearts and look expectantly at Narain Bawa, who in turn looks in utter helplessness at the sky—which has no reality, which is merely an optical illusion, the limit beyond which our eyes do not reach.

Laaju, however, was not among the abducted women Miss Sara Bai brought back in the exchange. Sundar Lal, balanced precariously between hope and despair, saw the last girl come down from the military truck. Subsequently, with quiet determination, he redoubled his efforts in advancing the work of his Committee. No longer only in the mornings, the Committee took out an evening rally as well, and now and then also held meetings at which the old barrister Kalka Parshad Sufi, the Committee's president, held forth in his raspy, asthmatic voice, with Rasaloo always tending his duties beside him, holding the spittoon. Strange sounds would pour out from the loudspeaker: 'kha-ba-ba-ba, kha-kha...' Next, Neki Ram, the petition writer of the Chauki, would get up to say something. But whatever he said or quoted from the Shastras or Puranas served only to contradict his point. Just then Sundar Lal would move in to salvage the situation. But he couldn't manage more than a couple of sentences. His voice would become progressively hoarser and tears would roll down his cheeks. He would give up and sit down. A strange silence would sweep over the audience. Sundar Lal Babu's two sentences, which sprang from the depths of his heart, affected them more than all the oratory eloquence of the old barrister Kalka Parshad Sufi. But the people shed a few tears then and there, which eased their hearts, and returned home, as empty-headed as ever.

One day the Committee-wallahs started out on their preaching mission early in the evening and ended up in an area long known to be a conservative stronghold. Seated on a cement platform around a peepul tree outside the temple, the faithful were listening to stories from the Ramayana. Narain Bawa was narrating the episode in which a washerman had thrown his wife out of the house saying, 'I'm no Raja Ramchandar, who would take Sita back after she had spent so many years with Ravan.' Which led Ramchandarji to order the virtuous Sita out of the house even though she was with child.

'Can you find a better example of Ram Raj?' asked Narain Bawa. 'True Ram Raj is one in which a washerman's words too receive the utmost consideration.'

The rally had by now reached the temple and it stopped to listen to the Ramayana story and pious hymns. Sundar Lal caught the last few words and retorted, 'We don't want Ram Raj, Bawa.'

Angry voices shot up from the throng of the faithful:

'Be quiet!'

'Who do you think you are?'

'Shut up!'

But Sundar Lal, undaunted, moved forward. 'Nobody can stop me from speaking!' he shouted back.

To which he received a fresh volley of equally angry words—'Quiet!' 'We won't let you speak!'—and from a corner, even the threat, 'We'll kill you!'

Narain Bawa said to him gently, 'Sundar Lal, my dear, you don't understand the rules and regulations of the Shastras.'

'But I do understand one thing, Bawa. And it is that even a washerman could be heard in Ram Raj, while its champions today won't even listen to Sundar Lal.'

The very people who a minute ago had gotten up determined to put him in his place quickly sat down, sweeping away the peepul fruit which had meanwhile fallen on their seats, and said, 'All right, let's hear him out.'

Both Rasaloo and Neki Ram spurred Sundar Lal on, who said, 'No doubt Shri Ram was our great leader. But why is it, Bawaji, that he believed the washerman but not his own wife, the greatest Maharani ever?'

Narain Bawa explained, putting a novel spin on it. 'Sita was his own wife. It would appear, Sundar Lal, that you have not realized the importance of this fact.'

'Yes, Bawa,' Sundar Lal Babu said, 'there are many things in this world that I don't understand. But as I look at it, under true Ram Raj, man wouldn't be able to oppress even himself. Injustice against oneself is as great a sin as injustice against another. Today, Lord Ram has again thrown Sita out of his house, just because she was compelled to live with Ravan for some time. But was she to blame for it? Wasn't she a victim of deceit and trickery, like our numberless mothers and sisters today? Was it a question of Sita's truth or falsehood? Or of the stark beastliness of the demon Ravan, who has ten human heads, but also has another, bigger one, that of a donkey. Today our Sita has been expelled once again, totally without fault, our Sita...Laajwanti...' He broke down and wept.

Rasaloo and Neki Ram raised the red banners on which the school children had that very day skilfully cut out and pasted different slogans for them, and the procession got going once again, all shouting 'Long Live Sundar Lal Babu!' in unison. Then someone yelled 'Long Live Sita—the Queen of Virtue!' and someone else 'Shri Ramchandar...'

'Silence! Silence!' a joint cry went up. Within seconds, months of Narain Bawa's labour went down the drain, as a good portion of his congregation got up and joined the procession, led by barrister Kalka Parshad and Hukm Singh, the petition writer at Chauki Kalan, both triumphantly tapping their old walking sticks on the ground. Sundar Lal walked along with them. Tears were still streaming down his cheeks. His heart had been hurt very badly today. The people were shouting with great gusto:

> Touch the leaves of the laajwanti,
> they curl and wither away.

The song was still reverberating in the ears of the people. The sun had not yet risen and the widow in house number 414 in Mulla Shakur was still tossing restlessly in her bed. Just then Lal Chand, who was from Sundar Lal's village and whom the latter and Kalka Parshad, using their influence, had helped to set up a ration shop, rushed over to Sundar Lal's. He offered his hand from under his thick, coarse shawl and said, 'Congratulations, Sundar Lal!'

'Congratulations for what, Lal Chand?' Sundar Lal asked, putting some molasses-sweetened tobacco in his chillum.

'I just saw Laaju Bhabhi.'

The chillum fell from Sundar Lal's hand and the tobacco scattered on the floor. 'Where!?' he asked, grabbing Lal Chand by the shoulder, and shaking him hard when he didn't answer quickly enough.

'At the Wagah border.'

He abruptly let go of Lal Chand's shoulder. 'Must be someone else.'

'No, Bhaiya, it really was Laaju,' Lal Chand tried to convince him. 'She was Laaju all right.'

'Do you even know her?' Sundar Lal asked as he gathered the tobacco and ground it between his palms. 'Well then,' he said, removing the chillum from Rasaloo's hookah, 'tell me, what are her distinguishing marks?'

'A tattoo on her chin, another on her cheek.'

'Yes, yes, yes!' Sundar Lal himself completed the description. 'And a third one on her forehead.' He didn't want there to be any doubt.

Suddenly he recalled all those tattoos on Laajwanti's body he had known so well, tattoos she had gotten as a little girl, which resembled the light green spots on the touch-me-not plant and caused it to curl up its leaves at the slightest hint of an approaching hand. Exactly the same way, Laajwanti would curl up from modesty the instant anyone pointed at her tattoos. She would withdraw into herself and disappear, afraid that all her secrets had been let out, that she had been made poor by the plunder of a hidden treasure. And Sundar Lal's entire body began to burn with an unknown fear, with an unknown spirit and its purified fire. He grabbed Lal Chand by the shoulder once again and asked, 'How did Laaju get to Wagah?'

'There was an exchange of abducted women between India and Pakistan,' Lal Chand said.

'What happened then?' Sundar Lal asked, as he squatted down on the floor. 'Tell me, what happened then?'

Rasaloo too sat up in his cot and asked, coughing as only smokers do, 'Is it really true? Laajwanti Bhabhi's returned?'

Lal Chand continued. 'At the Wagah border, Pakistan handed over sixteen women and received sixteen in exchange. But an altercation developed. Our volunteers objected that there were too many middle-aged, old, and useless women in the contingent Pakistan was handing over. A crowd quickly gathered on the scene. Just then, volunteers from the other side pointed at Laaju Bhabhi and said, "Here, you call her old? Have a look. None of the girls you have returned can match her." Meanwhile Laaju Bhabhi was frantically trying to hide her tattoos from the people's probing eyes. The argument got more heated. Each side decided to take back their 'goods'. I cried out, "Laaju! Laaju Bhabhi!" But our own military guards beat us up and drove us away for making a racket.'

Lal Chand bared his elbow to show where he had been struck by a lathi. Rasaloo and Neki Ram remained silent, while Sundar Lal gazed far away into space. Perhaps he was thinking about Laaju, who had returned, but then again had not. He looked like someone who had just crossed the scorching sands of Bikaner and now sat panting under the shade of a tree, his parched tongue hanging out, too exhausted even to ask for water.

The realization struck him that the violence of the pre-Partition days still continued even after Partition, only in a different form. Today, people didn't even feel sympathy for the victims. If you asked someone about, say, Lahna Singh and his sister-in-law Bantu, who used to live in Sambharwala, quick and curt would come the answer: 'Dead!' and the fellow would move on, unaware of death and the difference it made.

Worse still, there were cold-blooded people who traded in human merchandise, in human flesh. Just as at cattle fairs prospective buyers pull back the snout of a cow or a water buffalo to assess its age by examining its teeth, these human traders now put up for public display the beauty of a young woman, her blossoming charm, her most intimate secrets, her beauty spots, her tattoos. This sort of violence had sunk right down to their very bones. In former times, at least, deals were struck at fairs under the protective cover of a handkerchief. Fingers met, negotiated, and concluded in secrecy. Today, however, even that screen had been lifted. Everybody was bargaining shamelessly in the open, with no regard for decorum. This transaction, this peddling, recalled an episode straight out of Boccaccio—a narrative depicting the uninhibited trafficking of women: countless women stand lined up, baring themselves before the Uzbek procurer, who pokes and prods them with his finger. It leaves a pink indentation where it touches the body, a pale circle forms around it, and the pink and the pale rush to meet. The Uzbek moves on, and the rejected woman, crushed by humiliation and shame, sobs uncontrollably, holding the waistcord of her loosened lower garment with one hand, hiding her face from the public's gaze with the other. Later, even the feeling of shame departs. Thus she walks nude through the bazaars of Alexandria. [...]

Sundar Lal was getting ready to go to the border town of Amritsar when the news of Laaju's arrival overtook him. Its suddenness unnerved him. He hurriedly took a step towards the door but, just as swiftly, stepped back. A sudden feeling to give in to his unhappiness overwhelmed him. He felt he wanted to spread all the placards, all the banners of his Rehabilitation Committee out on the floor, and sit on them and cry his heart out. But the situation was hardly proper for such an expression of emotion. He bravely fought back the turmoil raging inside him and picked his way slowly towards Chauki Kalan, the venue for the delivery of the abducted women.

Laaju stood straight in front of him, shaking with fear. If anyone knew Sundar Lal, it was she. She had forgotten none of how badly he had treated her before, and now that she was returning after living with another man, there was no telling what he might do. Sundar Lal looked at Laaju. She had draped the upper half of her body in a black dupatta, one of its ends thrown over her left shoulder in the typical Muslim fashion, but only out of habit. Perhaps it made it easier to socialize with the Muslim ladies and finally to make her escape from her captor. Then again, she had been thinking of Sundar Lal so much and was so mortally afraid of him that she scarcely had the mind to change into different clothes or even to worry about draping herself with the dupatta in the right fashion. As it was, she was unable to distinguish the basic difference between Hindu and Muslim cultures—whether the dupatta went over the right or left shoulder. Right now, she stood before Sundar Lal, trembling, balanced between hope and fear.

Sundar Lal was shocked. He noticed that Laajwanti looked fairer and healthier than before; indeed she looked plump. Whatever he had imagined about her turned out to be wrong. He had thought that grief would have wasted her, that she'd be too weak even to speak. The thought that she had been happy in Pakistan wounded him, but he said nothing to her, for he had sworn not to quiz her about such matters. All the same, he couldn't help wondering: why had she chosen to return if she lived a happier life there? Perhaps the Indian government had forced her to, against her wishes.

But he was quite unable to see the pallor on Laajwanti's tawny face, or to fathom that it was suffering, and suffering alone, that made her firm flesh loosen and sag from her bones, making her look heavy. She had become heavy with an excess of grief, though superficially she appeared healthy. Hers was the kind of plumpness which made one pant for breath after taking only a few steps.

Sundar Lal's initial gaze at the abducted wife unsettled him. But he fought all his thoughts back with great manliness. Many other people were also present and one of them shouted, 'We're not about to take back these Muslim leavings!'

But the slogans of Rasaloo, Neki Ram, the old petition writer of Chauki Kalan drowned out the man's voice. Above them all rose the loud, cracking voice of Kalka Parshad, who somehow managed to speak and cough at the same time. He was absolutely convinced of this new reality, this new purity. It seemed he had learnt a new Veda, a new Purana, a new Shastra, which he desperately wanted to share with others. And surrounded by all these people and voices, Laaju and Sundar Lal returned home. It seemed that after a protracted moral exile, the Ramchandar and Sita of an age long past were entering Ayodhya, while the people both celebrated their return by lighting lamps of joy and, at the same time, showed regret for having put the couple through such incredible misery.

Sundar Lal continued his 'Rehabilitation of Hearts' campaign with the same ardour even after Laajwanti's return. He had lived up to it both in word and deed. People who had earlier taken his involvement for just so much sentimental idealism were now convinced of his sincerity. Some were truly happy at this, but most felt disappointed and sad, and many women of the Mulla Shakur neighbourhood, except for the widow, still felt uncomfortable crossing Sundar Lal's threshold.

To Sundar Lal, however, it made no difference at all whether people recognized or ignored his work. The queen of his heart had returned and the yawning emptiness in his chest had been filled. He had installed the golden image of Laaju in the temple of his heart and diligently stood guard at its doorway. Laaju, who used to be so afraid of him, now began slowly to relax under his unexpectedly gentle and caring regard.

Sundar Lal no longer called her Laaju, but 'Devi', which made her go mad with indescribable joy. How much she wanted to tell him what she had been through, and cry so profusely that the tears would wash away all her 'sins', but Sundar Lal deftly avoided listening to her. And so she still carried a trace of apprehension in her new-found ease. After he had fallen asleep, she would simply gaze at him. If he caught her watching him and asked for a reason, she wouldn't know what to say beyond 'Nothing' or 'I don't know'. Sundar Lal, exhausted from the day's gruelling work, would go back to sleep. Once, though, in the beginning, he did ask Laajwanti about her 'dark days'. 'Who was he?'

'His name was Jumma,' she said, with downcast eyes. Then, fixing her eyes on his face, she wanted to say something more, but faltered. He was looking at her in a strange way, as his hands caressed her hair. She lowered her eyes again. Sundar Lal asked, 'Was he good to you?'

'Yes.'

'He didn't beat you?'

'No,' Laajwanti said, dropping her head on Sundar Lal's chest. 'He never hurt me. And yet I was very afraid of him. You used to beat me, but I never felt scared of you. You won't beat me again, ever, will you?'

Tears welled up in Sundar Lal's eyes. He said, feeling deep shame and regret, 'No, never again, Devi.'

'Devi!' Laajwanti thought, and she too broke down in tears.

She felt overwhelmed by a desire to tell him all, holding back nothing, but Sundar Lal stopped her saying, 'Let's just forget the past. You were hardly to blame for what happened. Society is at fault for its lack of respect for goddesses like you. In that it doesn't harm you a bit, only itself.'

And Laajwanti couldn't get it all out. It remained buried inside her. She withdrew into herself and stared at her body for the longest time, a body which, after the Partition of the country, was no longer hers, but that of a goddess. Yes, she was happy, indeed very happy, but it was a happiness marred by a nagging doubt, a misgiving. She would sit up in bed with a start, like someone surrounded by a surfeit of happiness who suddenly hears an approaching sound and looks apprehensively in its direction, waiting.

Ultimately, the nagging doubt replaced happiness with a chilling finality. And not because Sundar Lal Babu had again started mistreating her, but because he had started treating her with exceeding gentleness. She didn't expect that from him. She wanted to be the same old Laaju once again, the one who would quarrel over trifles and then make up in no time at all. Now, though, there was no possibility of even a quarrel. Sundar Lal had convinced her that she was in fact a laajwanti, a glass object too fragile to withstand the merest touch. Laaju would look at herself in the mirror, and after thinking long and hard would feel that she could be many things, but could never hope to be the old Laaju ever again. Yes, she had been rehabilitated, but she had also been ruined. Sundar Lal, on his part, had neither the eyes to see her tears, nor the ears to hear her painful groans. How fragile the human heart can be—this escaped even the most ardent reformer of the Mulla Shakur neighbourhood. The early morning processions continued and, like a robot, he joined in the refrain with Rasaloo and Neki Ram:

> *Touch the leaves of the laajwanti,*
> *They curl and wither away.*

AANANDI

GHULAM ABBAS

The meeting of the Municipal Council was at full boil. The assembly hall was packed nearly to bursting, and contrary to normal, not a single member was absent. The issue under debate in the Council was the expulsion from the city of the zanaan-e baazaari, the 'women of the marketplace', for their very presence had become an unsightly and intolerable stain on the skirt of humanity, nobility, and culture.

One Council member, an imposing man, generally considered a true and sympathetic benefactor of the nation, was holding forth with great eloquence:

'...And gentlemen! Let us also not forget that their place of residence is located in a portion of the city which is not merely a primary thoroughfare, but indeed also constitutes the city's greatest commercial centre. Consequently, every honourable man is compelled perforce to pass through that bazaar. Furthermore, the chaste daughters of our noble citizenry are forced, by dint of that bazaar's commercial significance, to come and transact their purchases there. My colleagues! When our noble daughters see the finery and embellishments of these ill-reputed, half-naked seductresses, it is only natural that there arise in their hearts as well newfound desires for the trappings of ornamentation and allure. They then begin to demand of their poor husbands all manner of rouges, lavenders, gold-embroidered saris, and costly jewellery, resulting in their tranquil homes, their abodes of comfort and ease, being reduced to the very model of hell on earth!

'And my colleagues! Let us also not forget the budding youth of the nation who are now obtaining their education in our schools, and upon whose future advancement are pinned the very hopes of the nation! Reason dictates that it will be their collective head on which one day the garland wreath of this country's salvation will be placed. They too are compelled perforce each morning and evening to commute by way of that bazaar. These strumpets, done up in their myriad jewels and ornaments, ceaselessly rain down on each innocent wayfarer the arrows and spears of their provocative glances, issuing open invitations to the worship of their beauty. Seeing these harlots, can our simple, inexperienced adolescents, steeped in the intoxication of youth, unconcerned with profit and loss, keep their emotions and thoughts, their noble pedigree safe from the venomous effects of disobedience and sin? Mustn't the ascetic-seducing beauty of these fallen women lead our budding entrepreneurs to stray from their path of righteousness? Mustn't they stir in these young men's hearts the temptation to sin's innermost delights, produce in them a restlessness, an agitation, a *passion?!*'

At this a member of the Council who had earlier in his life been a teacher and who held a keen interest in statistics spoke up:

'Friends, may it be clear: the proportion of students failing their exams is twice of what it was five years ago.'

A bespectacled member of the Council, the honorary editor of a weekly newspaper, rose to give his speech: 'Gentlemen! Our city is daily witnessing the flight of honour, nobility, masculinity, beneficence, and abstinence, and in their place dishonour, effeminacy, cowardice, villainy, theft, and extortion are gaining dominion. The use of intoxicants has increased greatly, and instances of murder, suicide, and bankruptcy continue to rise. The simple cause for this is the polluting presence of those women of the marketplace. Becoming ensnared in their tangled tresses, our innocent citizens simply lose all sense and judgement, and proceed, by any means legal or otherwise, to procure the exorbitant funds necessary to gain access to these pleasure palaces. Occasionally, these efforts lead them so far as to cast off the garb of humanity altogether and to commit exceedingly vile and disgraceful deeds. The inevitable result is that they wash their hands of their precious lives, or indeed, they lie rotting in jail.'

Another member of the Council, an aged pensioner who was the patron of an extensive family and who had by now already seen the hot and cold of the world, who now had become weary of life's struggles and who desired only to relax for his remaining years and to see his family prosper under his benevolent shadow, rose to speak. His voice was tremulous and tinged with lamentation.

'Gentlemen, all night every night, the banging of these people's tablas, their caterwauling, the fist fights of their amorous customers, their swearing, their cursing, their noise, their uproar, their ha ha ha, their hoo hoo hoo—I tell you, the ears of the gentle people living nearby have *cooked!* Life has become pure vexation. If sleep at night is ruined, then what hope is there for peace of mind by day? Furthermore, the evil effect wrought by their proximity on the morals of our daughters—this every gentleman with children can estimate for himself...'

Uttering this last sentence the elderly man became choked up and could say no more. All the members of the Council felt the deepest sympathy for him, for by a cruel twist of fate his ancestral home was situated precisely in the middle of that beauty market.

After the elderly gentleman came a Council member who was a standard-bearing advocate for the antiquities of civilization, a man who held archaeological remains dearer than his own offspring. He too rose to speak:

'Gentlemen! When travellers from outside, or indeed our own friends, come to see this famous and historical city of ours, when they pass through this bazaar and enquire about it, then you can be assured, we almost die of shame.'

The President of the Municipal Council now rose to give his speech. Though he was small of limb and stature, his head was nonetheless quite large, which made him seem gentle and forbearing. There was a degree of sombreness in his tone. 'Gentlemen, I am in complete agreement with you in this, that the very presence of this social stratum is for our city and for our civil existence the source of a hundred disgraces. The problem remains, however: how is the situation to be remedied? If these people are forced to abandon this despicable profession of theirs, then the question arises: how will they eat?'

One gentleman spoke up: 'Why don't these women get married?'

At this there was an extended outburst of laughter, and the mournful atmosphere of the hall was suddenly infused with mirth. When the assembly had quieted down, the President again spoke. 'Gentlemen, this suggestion has been presented before these people time and time again, and their answer is always the same: our well-off and respectable citizens, out of concern for the dignity and reputation of their families, won't let them through their doors. And as for the poor and lower classes, well, these women won't give them the time of day, since they're out to marry them only for their money.'

One of the members spoke up: 'There's no need for the Municipal Council to get mixed up in the personal affairs of these women. They can go to hell for all we care. The sole issue for the Council is that they vacate the city.'

The President said, 'Even this is no simple task. There are not just ten or twenty of them; they now number in the hundreds. And on top of this, there are many women among them who own their own private houses.'

The issue remained under debate in the Council for nearly a month; in the end it was settled by consensus of all the members that the personal houses owned by the women of the marketplace should be bought up, and that they should be given a separate and discrete area far away from the city in which to live. The women protested strenuously against the Council's decision. Some women simply refused and endured heavy fines; some even went to jail. But ultimately there was no gainsaying the will of the Council, and the women were left helplessly to forebear.

For a time after this, lists were made of the houses owned by the women, floor plans were drawn up, and potential buyers were looked for. It was decided that most of the houses would be sold at auction. The women were permitted to remain in their houses for a period of six months, so that during this time they might have new houses built in the area that was set aside for them.

The area selected for the women was six kos from the city. A properly paved road extended for the first five kos, and beyond that there was an unpaved, rough, dirt path. There had apparently been a settlement there in an earlier age, but now nothing remained but ruins, which served as a home for snakes and bats, and where owls hooted in broad daylight. In the environs surrounding the area there were several small villages that comprised small mud huts, but none of these villages was less than several miles from the site. The peasant farmers inhabiting those villages tilled their fields by day, or they just knocked about, turning up occasionally at the ruins. But for the most part the place remained a desolate ghost town, where never so much as a human face was seen. Sometimes even jackals wandered about the area in the bright light of the day.

Among the more than five hundred prostitutes, there were only fourteen who, either out of obligation to their lovers, or out of their own hearts' attachment, or impelled by something else entirely, had in any event found cause to live openly near the city. Now, however, relying on their wealthy lovers' continual material patronage, they had readied themselves and their unwilling hearts to settle in this new area. The remaining majority of women had decided that they would either make the city's hotels their homes, or that they would take on the outward garb of chastity and abstinence and dwell in the obscure corners of the city's noble neighbourhoods, or indeed that they would give up the city altogether and set out for parts unknown.

These fourteen prostitutes had already been particularly well off. On top of this, they received handsome prices for the houses they owned in the city; the cost of land in this new area was nominal, and more than anything else, their lovers were only too prepared to provide them with financial assistance. And so, putting their trepidations aside and throwing themselves fully into their new situation, they firmly resolved to splurge and have great, grand houses built for themselves. Just a short distance from some broken-down, ramshackle gravesites, they selected an elevated and even parcel of land. They had the individual plots cleared away, they had nimble-fingered draftsmen draw up blueprints, and in just a few days the actual construction work began.

All day long bricks, mortar, lime, beams, girders, and other construction materials were hauled into the settlement in lorries, on bullock carts, on the backs of mules and donkeys, and on the backs of men. The munshis, with account books tucked under their arms, had them all counted and duly recorded the figures. The foremen called out orders to the builders, the builders harassed the petty labourers, and the petty labourers ran from pillar to post, shrieking at the female labourers to come give them a hand. In short, the entire day consisted of one single commotion, one single tumult; all day the neighbouring farmers in their fields and their wives in their homes listened to the faint sounds of distant construction borne to them on the gusts of wind.

In one place amid the ruins of the settlement were the remains of a mosque, and nearby was a well that lay sealed. Partly out of the desire to find some water and relax a bit, and partly with a mind to facilitate the worship of their prayer-reciting brethren (and thereby earning some spiritual reward), the master masons first repaired this mosque and well. Since the work was both humanly beneficial and spiritually meritorious, no one objected, and so in just a few days the mosque was ready.

At noon, as soon as it was time for lunch a couple hundred masons, labourers, foremen, munshis, and those relatives or representatives of the prostitutes who were entrusted with overseeing the construction would gather at the mosque, making it look to the entire world as though they were having a regular fair.

One day a rustic old woman who lived in one of the nearby villages showed up having heard news of the settlement. She was accompanied by a small boy. Under a tree near the mosque, the two of them set out a tray laden with cheap cigarettes and beeris, and sweets made of chickpeas and gur. It hadn't been even two days since the old woman arrived when a similarly old farmer brought a large earthen water pot from somewhere, constructed a small brick platform near the well, and began selling two glasses of sweet sherbet for a paisa. A greengrocer who had heard the news brought a large basket full of melons and setting out his wares near the old woman with the tray began to call out, 'Get yer melons here! Sweeter than honey, get yer melons here!' And another, what did he do?—he went home, cooked up a dish of brains and feet, put it in a pan, got some rotis, a few earthen bowls, and a tin drinking glass, loaded it all on a tray, brought it all to the settlement, and began to give the workers, out in the middle of nowhere, a taste of some good home cookin'.

When it came time for the noon and afternoon prayers, the foremen, the builders, and the rest could be seen making their ritual ablutions, with bucket after bucket of water drawn by the labourers. One person would enter the mosque and issue the call to prayer, another would be made the prayer leader, and the rest would stand behind him and perform their namaz. One day, a mullah from one of the surrounding villages heard that a certain mosque needed an imam, and so the very next day, wrapping the Holy Quran in its green protective cover, and gathering his panj-sura, his Quran stand, and a few theological pamphlets, he too appeared at the settlement and was officially installed as the imam of the mosque.

Every day late in the afternoon, a kebab seller from one of the villages would arrive bearing on top of his head a basket filled with his wares. On the ground, next to the old lady with the tray he would build a small brick stove and would then put on the skewers bits of kebab—liver, heart and kidney—which he then proceeded to sell to the settlement-wallahs. The wife of a tandoor-wallah saw all this going on and came with her husband in tow; in a field in front of the mosque she set up a rough thatched roof to protect her from the sun, and began to fire up her tandoor. From time to time one could see a young rustic barber as well making his rounds, carrying the tools of his trade in a beat-up old belt around his neck, kicking rocks and other debris from the unpaved dirt roadway.

Of course, the prostitutes' relatives or their business representatives were overseeing the construction of the houses, but on occasion, having finished their lunch, the women themselves would come accompanied by their lovers to see their houses being built, and they wouldn't leave before the sun set. On such occasions band upon band of wandering mendicants, male and female, would show up from God knows where, and until they were given their alms they would go on with their calls and cries, raising such a ruckus that the women couldn't even carry on a conversation. On occasion, the idle, dissolute, good-for-nothing hoodlums of the city made their way on foot to see what was happening in this new prostitutes' settlement. And if by chance on such a day the prostitutes too should show up, well, then it turned out to be a regular holiday for the hoodlums. Taking a step or two back they would encircle the women and walk around them, hurling jibes, laughing uproariously, making faces at them, and moving their bodies in lewd, crazy ways. On such days, the kebab seller did tremendous business.

An area where just a few days earlier there had existed nothing but wasteland was now bustling with activity. The dread the prostitutes felt at the idea of coming to live in such desolation had, to a substantial extent, vanished; the women now gleefully took every opportunity to press upon the builders their ideas about the decorations and colour schemes of their new houses.

At one place in the settlement there was a decrepit old tomb which, from all indications, appeared to be that of some revered holy man from long ago. One morning, when the construction of the houses was more than half completed, the masons saw a peculiar sight—smoke was rising into the air near the tomb. A large, tall, intoxicated fakir, wearing only a loincloth, his eyes blood red and his face and eyebrows shaven clean, was walking round and round the tomb, picking up rocks and stones and casting them aside. In the afternoon, the fakir brought a water pot to the well; filling it again and again he headed back to the tomb and washed it properly. As it happened, there was one occasion when a few of the masons were standing around the well. In a state of equal parts madness and sagacity, the fakir began to address the men: 'Do you know whose tomb that is? It belongs to Karak Shah Pir Badshah, that's who! My father and grandfather were the attendants at his shrine.' At which point, unable to suppress either his laughter or the tears welling up in his eyes, he began regaling the masons with tales of Pir Karak Shah's awe-inspiring miracles.

By evening the fakir had somehow managed to beg two earthen oil lamps and some mustard oil to fuel them; placing one at the head and the other at the foot of Pir Karak Shah's grave, he lit them both. On occasion late at night, intoxicated mystical chants of 'Allah-hu!' rang out from the tomb.

Even before the six-month period had elapsed, all fourteen houses were completed and ready to go. They consisted of two storeys each, and they all were essentially of the same design. There were seven on one side and seven on the other, with a broad street down the middle. The lower level of each house consisted of four shops, and on the upper floor facing the street there was a wide veranda on each floor. The front part of the verandas had been constructed with a kind of bench, boat-like in appearance and fit for a king, at the ends of which were depicted either marble peacocks in mid-dance or carved statues of water nymphs, their bodies half fish and half human. Inside each house in the sitting room behind the veranda were delicate pillars of marble, and the walls were done in beautiful mosaic. The floors were made of brilliant green stone, and when the marble pillars reflected their emerald sheen it seemed as though luminous white-winged swans were dipping their slender necks in some magical lake.

The auspicious day of Wednesday had been fixed for moving into the new settlement. All the prostitutes gathered together and performed a solemn consecration ceremony. The ground of the settlement's open field was cleared of debris and a large pavilion tent was erected there. The clanging of pots and pans and the aroma of meat and ghee drew fakirs and dogs from miles around. The charitable distribution of food was to take place at Pir Karak Shah's tomb, and by the time noon rolled around there was a larger throng of fakirs gathered there than one might witness even on Eid at the congregational mosque of a large city. Pir Karak Shah's shrine had been scrubbed spotless, and a sheet of flowers had been laid over his grave. A new suit of clothes had been stitched for the intoxicated tomb attendant, which he ecstatically tore from his body as soon as it was put on him.

In the evening, a bright milk-white sheet was spread out on the ground under the main pavilion tent, cushions and bolsters were neatly arranged, paan daans, spittoons, hookahs, and rosewater sprinklers were set out for the guests' convenience, and the assembly of song and dance got underway. Many other prostitutes too were invited from far away, being either friends or relatives of the ladies of the settlement. They brought along with them many of their patrons and customers, for whom seating had been arranged in a separate pavilion where bamboo screens had been hung for their privacy. Countless gaslights had transformed the place into an abode of pure brilliance. The prostitutes' dark-skinned, pot-bellied musicians were strolling about, twisting their moustaches, dressed in fine brocade sherwanis, fragrance-soaked wads of cotton tucked discreetly behind their ears. Alluring women too were coquettishly strolling about, immaculately made up, and dressed in sparkling gold-embroidered finery and saris more delicate than butterfly wings. All through the night it was a convocation of music and dance, an improbable island of revelry out in the wilds of nowhere.

A few days later, after the inevitable fatigue that follows such celebrations wore off, the prostitutes began busying themselves in the procurement of all their houses' furnishings and decorations. All manner of household items were brought in—chandeliers, lamps, crystalware, full-length mirrors, cotton tape-strung beds, gilt-framed paintings and calligraphy—all of which were then neatly arranged in their proper rooms. In a matter of some eight days the houses were ready to go, right down to the last nail in the wall. The women passed the greater part of their days taking music and dance instruction from their venerable teachers, memorizing love poetry and songs, studying their lessons, practising calligraphy, sewing and embroidering, listening to the gramophone, playing cards or carom with their teachers, amusing themselves with clever word games, or simply sleeping. In the late afternoon, they proceeded to the bathrooms to take their baths, where full tubs awaited them, their servants having already hauled bucket upon bucket of water from the hand pump. After their baths, they busied themselves at their toilette.

Upon nightfall, the houses shone with the illumination of gaslights adroitly concealed in half-open lotus blossoms carved from marble, and from a distance the tiny glimmering rainbows of light, refracted in the floral etchings of the windows and door panels, made for a wondrous sight to behold. The perfectly made up prostitutes sauntered back and forth on their balconies, giggling and carrying on with others nearby, and when they tired of standing they headed back into the houses where they took their seats on the moon-white sheets spread out upon the floor, regally reclining on bolsters and cushions. Their musicians went on tuning their instruments, while the women cut betel nut into fine pieces. As the night wore on their patrons would show up, arriving with their friends in cars and two-wheeled horse carriages, bearing baskets filled with fruit, snacks and bottles of liquor. A special sort of commotion and bustle commenced as soon as these men set foot in the settlement. The melodious singing, the dulcet notes of the instruments, the jingling of the tiny bells strapped to the ankles of the ravishing dancers—all mingled with the gurgling of decanting wine flasks to produce an atmosphere of delicious, exquisite delight. People lost themselves in these assemblies of revelry and intoxication, and the night passed on, unnoticed.

The prostitutes had been living in the settlement for only a few days when tenants for the shops beneath their homes began to appear. With a mind to populating the new settlement, the rent had been set very low. The first of the new shopkeepers was that same old woman who had earlier set up her tray under the tree in front of the mosque. To complete the look of her new shop she and her boy gathered up many empty cigarette packs and carefully arranged them in all the niches of the platform on which she would sit and transact her sales. She filled bottles with coloured water so that they would appear to be bottles of sherbet, and to the best of her ability she spruced up the shop with hanging streamers she had made from paper flowers and empty cigarette packs. She cut out photographs of actors and actresses from old movie magazines and pasted them on to the walls. The actual inventory of the shop, however, consisted of no more than three or four packets each of a few brands of cigarettes, eight or ten bundles of beeris, a half-dozen boxes of matches, a small bundle of paan leaves, three or four cakes of smoking tobacco, and half a bundle of candles.

In the second shop, there came a petty merchant, in the third a sweetmaker and a milk seller, in the fourth a butcher, in the fifth a kebab seller, and in the sixth a greengrocer. The greengrocer would buy up several kinds of vegetables from the neighbouring villages and sell them in his shop at a tidy profit. He also kept half a basket of fresh fruit for sale. Because there was no dearth of room in his shop, he took on a flower vendor as his partner. Throughout the day he sat making garlands, bracelets and all manner of flower ornaments, and in the evenings, he put them all in a basket and visited each house in turn, stopping not just to sell his flowers but to sit for a few minutes, chatting with the musicians there and taking a few pulls on their hookahs. If, as happened some days, a group of libertines arrived to take in the prostitutes' show and ascended the stairs while he was still there, then, as soon as the music started up, and despite the musicians' turning up their noses at him, he would stay for hours on end planted right where he was, joyfully beating his head in time to the music, staring like a fool at each of the musicians. And if, as also happened some days, the night passed and he had a garland left over, then he would put it around his own neck and wander about outside the settlement, singing at the top of his lungs.

The father and brother of one of the prostitutes, both of whom knew the tailoring business, brought a sewing machine and set themselves up in another of the shops. Soon a barber too arrived, and he brought along a cloth dyer. The brightly coloured, fancifully dyed dupattas waving in the wind on the clothesline outside his shop made for a wonderful sight.

With the passing of just a few more days there arrived a huckster as well, down on his luck and nearly bankrupt. It had become nearly impossible for him to extract enough from his meagre profits to pay the rent on his shop in the city. And so, unable to make a go of it there he turned his attention to this new settlement, where he was welcomed with open arms and where he found a brisk market for his assorted lavenders, his various powders, his soaps, combs, buttons, needles, threads, his laces, ribbons, aromatic oils, his handkerchiefs, and his tooth powders.

The thriving patronage of the settlement dwellers spurred a procession of other similarly down-on-their-luck shopkeepers—a cloth merchant, a vendor of spices and herbal remedies, a hookah-maker, a bread-maker— troubled by the depressed market and high rents of the city, they all sought refuge in this new settlement.

Having become fed up both with the dense population and with the excess of pharmacies in the city, a venerable old master apothecary, who was also proficient in the traditional Greek arts of healing, gathered his apprentices, left the city for the new settlement, and rented a shop there. All day long the apothecary and his apprentices arranged packets of medicine, bottles of sherbet, fruit confections, and jars of chutney and pickle, setting them all in their proper places on the shelves and in the cabinets. They placed the *Tibb-e Akbar,* the *Qaraabaadiin-e Qaadirii,* and other medical books on a shelf. They wrote large, clear advertisements in heavy black ink for their most excellent proprietary medicines, stuck them to pasteboards, and hung them on the insides of the cabinets' door panels and on the empty spaces on the walls. Every morning the prostitutes' servants showed up, drinking glasses in hand, and would take back home sherbet made of seeds, sherbet made of violet flowers, sherbet made of pomegranate, and other such pleasure-giving and spirit-enhancing concoctions, in addition to herbal pastes and special strength-producing confections covered with silver leaf.

The prostitutes' musicians and hangers-on brought their charpoys and set them up in the shops that remained unrented. All day long these people played cards, chausar, and chess; they had themselves rubbed down with oil; they held quail and partridge fights in a ring; watching the birds fight they'd call out 'Praise be to God's power!'; and improvising a beat on an earthen pot they'd sing to their hearts' content.

One of the prostitute's musicians saw an empty shop and set up his brother there, who was skilled in the construction and repair of musical instruments. He pounded nails into the walls of the shop and hung all the sarangis, sitars, tanburas, dilrubaas, and other instruments that were broken and in need of repair. This man was himself also very skilled at playing the sitar. He would play in his shop in the evenings; hearing the sitar's sweet sound all the neighbouring shopkeepers would leave their shops one by one, and sit around him still as statues, listening to his music. This master sitarist had a student, too, who was a clerk in the railway office, and who possessed an eager and zealous desire to learn the instrument. The moment he finished work at the office he'd fly on his bicycle to the settlement, sit down inside the sitar master's shop, and practise his exercises for an hour or two. In short, thanks to the sitar master, a delightful kind of vitality was sparked throughout the settlement.

While all the construction was going on, the mullah of the mosque would head home in the evenings to his village. But now, since he had begun to receive more rich, savoury food than he could eat for his two meals a day, he began spending his nights, too, right there in the settlement. Gradually children from the homes of the prostitutes began coming to the mosque for their schooling, and the mullah began earning a modest income from the small fees they paid.

When, due to both excessive land rents and their own insignificance, an old-fashioned, third-rate, itinerant theatrical company could find no venue in which to perform in the city, it turned its attention to the settlement and, in a field some distance from the prostitutes' houses, it erected its big-top pavilion and set up camp there. The company's actors knew nothing of the art of theatrical performance. Their costumes were old and worn out, missing many of the ornaments that once had adorned them, and the shows they put on were old and worn out as well. But despite everything this company caught on, the reason being that the tickets to their shows were very cheap. The menial labourers of the city, the factory workers, and the poor and destitute, wanting to compensate some for the daily rigours of their strenuous toiling with a bit of raucousness, lasciviousness, and debauchery, would band together in groups of five or six, hang festive garlands around their necks, and would make their way on foot from the city to see the company's show, laughing and joking with each other, playing impromptu songs on their flutes, taunting and jeering at their fellow travellers, swearing and cursing and carrying on all along the way. And if they were there anyway, why shouldn't they take a stroll through the prostitutes' beauty market as well? Until the show started, a clown stood on a stool outside the pavilion, by turns gyrating his hips provocatively, blowing exaggerated kisses, and winking lewdly at the passers-by. Seeing his strange and wholly immodest gestures the people laughed uproariously and showed their approval in the form of the filthiest curses.

Gradually other people too began coming to the settlement. The drivers of the two-wheeled horse carriages began calling out at the city's largest and busiest intersections, 'New settlement, new settlement, come see the new settlement!' Arriving at the paved road that extended five kos out of the city the carriage drivers, at the request of their passengers or out of greed for tips they might receive, began to race each other. They'd make honking horn sounds with their mouths, and when one carriage overtook another its passengers raised an ear-splitting uproar of taunts and encouraging cries. The racing took its toll on the horses, and instead of any fragrance coming from the flower garlands around their necks, there was only the odour of perspiration.

And the rickshaw drivers were hardly lagging behind the carriage drivers. Taking passengers at rates cheaper than the carriage drivers, they too began to head out to the settlement, going full tilt and ringing their bells all the way. Every Saturday night high school and college students, loaded two to a bicycle, would band together and also come to take a tour of that secret marketplace—something which, to their minds, their elders had unreasonably forbidden them from doing.

Over time the settlement's celebrity spread far and wide, and there developed a large demand for houses and shops there. Witnessing its prodigious growth, the prostitutes, who earlier dreaded the very idea of moving there, now began to regret their foolishness. Several women immediately bought land and started having houses of precisely the same model built right next to the prostitutes'. Further, some of the city's financiers too bought up much of the land around the settlement and quickly had many small houses built from which they could collect the rent. It followed that those harlots who earlier had disappeared into the city's hotels and noble neighbourhoods now emerged from their hideouts, swarming like ants and locusts to inhabit these new houses. And some were occupied by those shopkeepers of the settlement who themselves had families and who could not, therefore, spend their nights in their shops.

The settlement had become quite populous indeed, but still there was no electricity. So, a petition was sent to the government on behalf of the prostitutes and all the other residents of the settlement, which was approved in just a few days. Right on the heels of electricity a post office was opened as well, and very soon an elderly scribe appeared outside it with a small trunk full of envelopes, postcards, pens, and inkpots, and began writing letters for the people of the settlement.

It so happened one time that two groups of drunkards in the settlement came to blows, during which incident soda-water bottles, knives and bricks were freely employed, and several people were badly injured. It occurred to the government that perhaps a police station too should be opened. The theatrical company stayed for two months, and when they left they took with themselves a healthy profit. Upon their departure, the proprietor of a cinema hall in the city wondered why he shouldn't open a cinema in the settlement as well. No sooner did the idea occur to him than he bought up a parcel of land and had the construction work started immediately. The cinema hall was ready in just a few months, replete with a small garden outside. Should the cinemagoers arrive before the show began, they'd be able to sit in comfort in the garden. Of course, the people of the settlement too began to come, just to sit and relax a bit, or to take a leisurely stroll. Indeed, the garden became *the* place to come and take a stroll. Eventually water bearers showed up in the garden as well, banging their metal cups to announce their presence to any parched person who might want a drink of water. Men trained in the art of oiled head massage came as well to offer their services to any headache sufferers they might chance upon, calling out 'Massages! Massages! Get yer relaxing, invigorating massages here!', their waistcoat pockets stuffed with small bottles of exceedingly cheap and caustic aromatic oil, their grimy, tattered towels draped over their shoulders.

The cinema owner had a couple of houses and several shops built outside his cinema hall. A hotel was opened in one of the houses where rooms were available for the night, and the shops were occupied one after another by the owner of a soda-water factory, a photographer, a bicycle mechanic, an owner of a laundry, two paan sellers, a boot shop owner, and a doctor with his own pharmacy. And soon, permission was granted to open a tavern in another shop nearby. A watchmaker gathered all his equipment in a corner outside the photographer's shop, and with his jeweller's loupe permanently glued to his eye, remained absorbed in the minute components of his trade.

A few days later, official arrangements were made for the settlement's sewage, public lighting, and trash removal. Government surveyors arrived with their red flags, their measuring tapes, and their transits; they took their readings and did their calculations, they marked out the boundaries of the streets and lanes, and a steamroller began to level the unpaved streets of the settlement.

It's been twenty years now since this all took place. The settlement has since become a thriving city, with its own railway station and its own town hall, its own courthouse and its own jail. It's home now to some 250,000 people. There's a college in the city; two high schools, one for girls and one for boys; and eight primary schools, where the municipality provides free education. There are six cinemas and four banks, including branches of two of the world's largest banks.

Two daily, three weekly, and ten monthly periodicals and newspapers are published in the city, among which are four literary journals, two spiritual and ethical journals, one industrial journal, one medical journal, one women's magazine, and one children's magazine. There are twenty mosques in the various parts of the city, fifteen Hindu temples, six orphanages for Muslims, five for Hindus, and three large government hospitals, one of which is reserved especially for women.

In the beginning, for several years, in keeping with the people who lived there, the city went by the name 'Husnabad', that is, the City of Beauty. But later this was considered inappropriate, and so the name was modified slightly; instead of 'Husnabad' people started calling it 'Hasanabad', that is, the city named in honour of Hasan, the Prophet Muhammad's grandson. But this name didn't catch on, because the people just didn't distinguish between 'Husn' and 'Hasan'. Finally, after going through many thick, decaying old books, and after investigating many old manuscripts, the city's original name was discovered, the name by which the settlement was known hundreds of years earlier, before it was ruined. This name was Aanandi, the City of Bliss.

And so now the entire city is thriving, clean, and attractive. But the most beautiful, most vital, most commercially crucial point in the city is that very same market in which the zanaan-e bazaari live—the women of the marketplace.

The meeting of Aanandi's Municipal Council is at full boil, the hall is packed nearly to bursting, and contrary to normal not a single member is absent. The issue under debate in the Council is the expulsion from the city of the women of the marketplace, for their very presence has become an unsightly and intolerable stain on the skirt of humanity, nobility, and culture. One eloquent scion of society is holding forth: 'It is simply not known what the policy might have been on the basis of which this polluting class of people was given permission to live in the precise centre of this ancient and historical city of ours...'

This time, the area selected for the women to live in was twelve kos from the city.

—Translated by G. A. Chaussée

THE SAGA OF JAANKI RAMAN PANDEY

ZAKIA MASHHADI

Somebody should have gone and enquired from this Jaanki Raman Pandey, Advocate, why in the name of God did he have to go to Rasoolpur and die there when he was doing so well in Allahabad? And die, not just figuratively, but literally. The common belief is that the time and place of a person's death are preordained (and also the time and place of some events more important than death, for example, marriage). So why the fuss if one believes it has to be so? Well, what can one do? There are many wisecracks around, each smarter than the next. They say, of course, the Lord above has predetermined the time and place of death, but wouldn't you say something must be left for us humans to do too? So whether we dump nine tons of soil on the dead body or douse it with kerosene—by the way, this practice of pouring kerosene on the living and incinerating them has also become quite fashionable these days—or feed it to buzzards and crows, well, that's our business. But brother, the crux of the matter is that a person only likes beliefs that accord with his own proclivities and convenience, otherwise he usually picks up a cudgel and goes after the offending ones. At least that's our belief. If you don't want to take my word, just look at how Pandeyji fared.

Pandeyji's whole story was told by K. K. Mama—the K. K. stood for Krishan Kaant, but he was mostly known by just those two initials. He'd given up appending his surname long ago. He used to say that in this kalyug, the period of crass inhumanity and unmitigated evil, everyone has thrown all laws of proximity and abstinence overboard. Why, they have even started eating and drinking together. Be it high-caste Brahmin or someone as lowly as a sweeper or tanner, they are all mixing freely. So why should he drag the name of his worthy ancestors through the mud? But Krishan Kaant's disciples knew that all this posturing was merely a façade to hide the real K. K. He was hell-bent against caste differences. So purposely omitting his surname was really a sign of protest.

K. K. had perhaps no nephew of his own to call him Mama. But some wag had added the word Mama to his name. That stuck and he became everyone's Mama. He had spent quite some time in Lucknow, spoke fine Urdu, and was fond of telling stories. It was as though the spirit of some bazaar raconteur had been breathed into him—one time Jaanki Raman

Pandey had himself expressed some such idea. Shifting the glob of paan from one cheek to the other with his tongue, and lifting his face up so the messy spittle didn't splatter on his audience, he'd talk in a peculiar, rounded, rolling tone. But what an enchanting storyteller he was! Not one person would even think of getting up to leave while he pulled yarn after yarn from his inexhaustible stock.

His chief audience consisted of the young men from his extended family, one or two neighbours, including Mirza Anwar Beg's wife Nayyara Beg, and perhaps a visitor or two who happened to be around. It seemed like Anwar Beg was the only person who was always pissed off by K. K. Mama. Calling him 'a damned sissy', he would say, 'talks like gossiping women—someone in the family is like this; another one is like that...'

Regardless of what Anwar Beg said, it never made the slightest dent in K. K.'s popularity. A crowd gathered around him the minute he arrived, especially in winter when a heap of peanuts and steaming cups of tea would be on hand, a brazier of coals would be lighted, and K. K. Mama would sit in front wrapped in a quilt looking every bit the clown. And thereafter, a cornucopia of delights, a paradise of absolute fun!

During one such winter session, he told the story of Jaanki Raman Pandey, the Advocate, who went to Rasoolpur and croaked there, creating quite a crisis. This is how the story went:

'When Pandey was small—and it was a long, long time ago that Pandey was small—his mother, known as Punditayin, passed away. She was the first cousin of my mother's first cousin's sister-in-law's elder brother-in-law. There was, of course, the kinship, but there was also a close bond between the two families.'

'Was the bond just as close as the kinship, or more, or less?' Bipin Bhaiya had a habit of butting in, whether during a story or in real life.

'Well now, brother, I haven't invented any gadget for measuring closeness of relations. I can only tell you that we were quite close and the kinship was not inconsiderable either. And miyan, back in the old days people used to end their letters with the PS "Regard my brief note as a full letter..." And not just brief notes, they even regarded distant kinships as close kinships, and they steadfastly maintained those relationships. We're like them too,' K. K. said, striking his chest with his hand. Quite a bit of paan-spittle flew about and dissolved in the air. He wiped the edges of his mouth.

'I'm warning you, if you ever interrupt again in the middle—,' Nayyara Beg scolded Bipin Bhaiya. She seemed to have acquired the right to scold everyone, including Anwar Beg.

'So, bitiya, when Pandey's mother passed away, his father didn't take long to find himself another wife. Well, that's what people did in those days, if they felt the need they didn't even wait for the first wife to die. They went ahead and married again just like that. So if he did, it wasn't like he had committed some grave sin. And especially when the old ladies in the family kept goading, "Oh dear! Pundit, the poor motherless child is wasting away. Why don't you remarry? How in the world are you going to raise a five-year-old child by yourself?"'

A moment ago, Nayyara Beg had scolded Bipin Bihari for butting in; now she couldn't hold back and blurted out, 'What if the Pundit had somehow died? Would anyone have suggested to Punditayin that she get herself a new groom? Wouldn't that have easily taken care of all the looking-after Pandey needed? Perhaps nobody gave a moment's thought to how Pandey would be raised if his widowed mother stayed unmarried…'

'But it wasn't like Pandey was raised by his mother. His father had remarried all right, but the Punditayin he brought home this time was only about a year younger than Pandey's older married sister Uma.'

'Oh come on, Mama! A year older or younger?' Nayyara Beg nudged him again.

'Now, Nayyara Bibi, the fact is that she was a year younger, but if you would rather, then call her a year older,' Mama again pushed the paan from one side of his cheek to the other.

'Mama, next time someone interrupts, you give him a good whack,' Kaanti said. She was getting irritated by these constant interruptions of the story.

'Well, brother,' Mama took out another pinch of flavoured tobacco from the paan box and stuffed it in one of his cheeks, 'I'm too old for whacking. Just listen to what happened later. So, the daughter of Punditji, who had been married in Allahabad, was his eldest child. Actually she was named after the goddess Uma, but all the young men around called her Didda. She was about eighteen. She saw what was happening at her father's place: how the new wife, with a tika emblazoned on her forehead, moved about everywhere in the house jingling her anklet bells, while her own father either stayed in the men's quarters of the house or hung around the new mother rubbing his hands in anticipation of coming pleasures. So, no sooner had she returned home when she took to bed feigning illness and told her husband in no uncertain terms that she was going to have her little brother there with her, no matter what. A brother born after the death of three sisters, and the treatment he was getting from the stepmother! He craved a cup of milk and she wouldn't give him any even though two cows were tethered in the yard.

'"When did I ever stop you from bringing him here?" her husband said. "You could just as well have asked in a simple, straightforward way. Why become a second Queen Kaikeyi when you're my only wife?" And so on.

'A beaming Didda went back the very next day and brought Pandey with her to her in-laws' place. The stepmother thought it was better that way; the less junk, the cleaner the place. Her anklet bells began to jingle a bit more.

'Didda called Pandey "Bhaiyan" out of sheer love but treated him like a son, not a brother. Even after her own children came along, Bhaiyan's status didn't diminish. Those who didn't know the family well thought Bhaiyan was her firstborn. Her husband, Onkaar Nath Mishra, also regarded him equally. He considered himself lucky to have found a wife such as Didda: in appearance fair and lustrous like a Brahmin; in honesty and fidelity a Rajput; in maintaining the household accounts and looking after the land and property a Vaishya, and in being ever ready to serve, a veritable Sudra. Onkaar doted on her. He took great care of her brother. Bhaiyan got an absolutely first-rate education.

'Bhaiyan was in his graduating year when, to gratify her own desires, Didda went ahead and arranged his marriage.'

K. K. Mama shifted in his seat and rolled the paan in his mouth over to the other cheek, giving his narration a theatrical air. A respectful audience waited in hushed silence for the denouement to unfold.

'Now, brothers, understand that just after Didda arranged for the wedding, someone came and laid on Bhaiyan that the girl was as dark as one could imagine. Bhaiyan's heart sank. Summoning up his sagging courage, he approached Didda. She was sitting on the takht trying to figure out how much she needed to pay the washerman. That's when Bhaiyan, his eyes downcast, twisting the edges of his shirt, walking on tiptoe, stole behind her—behind, so that he might not have to look straight into her eyes and yet say his piece.

'"Didda," he said in a timid voice that was barely audible.

'"Heavens, that cursed man broke the buttons again."

'Bhaiyan was confused. Surely, when he was little, he did chew on the buttons of his shirt and shorts and was scolded by Didda, but now, had he broken off another button?'

"'No, Didda. Where, show me?" He quickly began checking his buttons.

"'Oh, it's you? What are you doing standing there? I was talking about that blasted washerman." She resumed counting, "Four dhotis, two sheets, one jacket..."

"'Didda," Bhaiyan breathed a sigh of relief as he scratched his head.

"'Yeah, what? Doesn't even worry about time; descends on you whether it's morning or evening."

'Bhaiyan was nervous again.'

"'All right Didda. I'll talk to you some other time."

"'Not you, Bhaiyan, I was talking about that accursed washerman. Come sit. Come on. Why are you standing behind me?" She pushed aside the load the washerman had just delivered and made room for Bhaiyan. "Just look at his audacity. It's breakfast time and he shows up. Then just dumps the washing and disappears." She mimicked the washerman, 'Get the account ready; I'll be back after I'm done with my round of the neighbourhood.' Anyway, tell me, what do you want?'

"'Didda..."

'Pandey again summoned up his courage and dropped what he thought was a bombshell.

"'That girl from Mirjapur, well, people say she's very dark, yet you went ahead and gave the word?"

"'What!" The pencil and notebook fell from Didda's hands. She had never in her wildest thoughts expected such shamelessness from Bhaiyan. She stared unbelievingly at him, the one she had treated like a child from her own womb. Hadn't she brought him here when he was hardly five years old? Hadn't she looked after him? Given him an education? How dare he talk like that?

'Actually Pandey would have never had enough courage to say what he really wanted to. Ever since he'd heard talk of his marriage, a face as bewitching in its beauty as the moon had started flashing before his eyes, but then someone spilled black ink all over this image with the news. The prospect of waking up in the morning to an ugly dark face right in front of him was truly soul crushing. Of course he couldn't say all this. He could only bring himself to utter just one brief sentence, and even that hid more than it revealed.

"'Listen, Bhaiya," Didda said, slapping the pile of clean laundry, "It's a courtesan whose appearance one worries about; if it's a wife you want to bring into the house, you look at her family. And her family is one in a thousand. No one even eats onions or garlic in their house, let alone meat or fish. They're nobler than the noblest. Add to this the fact that the young lady has also graduated from high school. Next Tuesday the girl's people are coming for barichha; the ceremony seals the alliance. But come to think of it, you have an exam coming up so you'd better go and concentrate on your studies. These matters are better left to your elders."

'Meanwhile Onkaar Nath Mishra, alias Bhaiya's brother-in-law, wandered in calling for his breakfast. He had overheard all the qualities of Bhaiya's bride-to-be. Solemnly he advised him, "Listen, young man. Go for the family now. Later on, when you get the chance, bring in one with a pretty face."

'Didda immediately drove her large, beautiful, questioning eyes right into her husband's. All the same, Pandey took his brother-in-law's advice to heart and happily, without any further ado, agreed to bring the Black Beauty home.

'A daughter-in-law, jingling her anklet bells, alighted in Didda's courtyard even before her own first-born had wed.

'Pandey loved Didda, as he ought to have, but he did not care any less for his kind brother-in-law. And rightly so. The man who had sired Pandey had never even once looked back to enquire after him. Whatever he had came from this brother-in-law alone. And because he was a lawyer, he was now giving Pandey a legal education. Bhaiyan would get good training in his own house, he would say. Apprenticeship under an established lawyer would give Pandey's own practice a head start. There was no way he could possibly ignore the word of such a godlike brother-in-law, was there? So, a few years after his law education, when his practice was flourishing and he had become completely independent, he brought home one with a pretty face.'

At this point in the story, K. K. Mama paused, heaving a deep sigh, and asked again for some hot tea. He'd made a dramatic pause in the narration, which only caused his audience's interest to soar.

During the pause Bipin Bhai Sahib laughed uproariously, enough to rattle the roof, and said, 'Why, we all know that the one with the pretty face was a musalmanti. But how and where he had met her, that only Mama will be able to say.'

Mama once again rolled the betel glob from one cheek to the other and carefully held up the spittle in his mouth.

'Mama, why don't you go and spit it out?' one listener objected.

'Quiet, you!' he got the answer from another one. 'Let the tea come and let Mama freshen up a bit.'

It didn't take long for tea to arrive. Nayyara Bibi poured tea in all the cups, scowled at Bipin and said to him, 'For this musalmanti bit, I'll deal with you a little later. For now let me hear Mama's story.'

'How many times have I heard that before, Nayyara Bhabi? So forget about your threats of dealing with me,' Bipin challenged. 'Haven't I asked you a hundred times to find me a ravishing musalmanti like you? But why would you bother! Now I'm going to fall in love with you. Damn the luck of that son of a gun Anwar! As some old master has said: a houri in the lap of a black-faced monkey...'

Nayyara sloshed a bit of hot tea on Bipin's neck, 'You wretched hinduchchey, you!'

After spitting out the glob of paan and rinsing his mouth Mama once again picked up the thread of the story as he slurped his tea. The listeners were sipping their tea too.

'Was there anything the people shied away from saying about her? Even called her a slut. But that wasn't the case, nor was the Pretty's family mediocre or lowly. As for musalmanta or musalmanti, just look at our Nayyara Bibi now and tell me for sure whether she's a Hindu or a Muslim. Just try. No one goes around wearing his or her religion or caste on their sleeves. And, folks, if it were up to me, I would have all the religions in the world banned. Nothing has created so much dissension and discord among people as...'

The intensity of passion and anger in his last sentence left everyone stunned for a moment.

Then he calmed down again, as people often do after a flare up.

'Pandey's brother-in-law Pundit Onkaar Nath Mishra, Advocate, had a faithful and loyal old scribe named Munshi Rajab Ali, just slightly older than Onkaar Nath. Rajab Ali's father, Imtiaz Ali, had been affiliated with Onkaar Nath's household ever since his father's time. He was responsible for looking after their entire property. As a manager, he was scrupulously honest. He got his son educated and so Onkaar Nath took him in his employ as scribe. Didda used to call him Brother Rajab Ali Sahib. Whenever Imtiaz Ali came to visit, she would draw her mantle over her face and touch his feet in a gesture of respect, but she wouldn't eat at his house. This was the time, folks, when people showed warm affection regardless of whether they ate at the other's place or not. Nowadays, it's the opposite: people eat together but their hearts are far apart, devoid of goodwill and affection.

What a shame!' Mama took out another folded paan from the betel box. 'The dietary prohibition applied only to cooked foods and liquids. It didn't extend to uncooked or dry stuff, such as paan, tobacco or fruit, etc. So at Eid, when the gift tray arrived from Rajab Ali's, it only contained uncooked vermicelli, spiralling dry vermicelli, dry fruit, sugar, and lo and behold, some crisp bank notes to buy milk along with Eidi money in small individual envelopes for all the young ones in the family. Everything was placed on a new round copper salver. The food, including the salver, was presented to Didda, prompting her to say every time, "What, Brother Rajab Ali Sahib, a brand new platter again? We have no prohibition about dishes in which food is neither cooked nor eaten. Go bring an old platter and take this one back." But Rajab Ali wouldn't even hear of that. After he passed away, Didda often heaved a deep sigh and said wistfully, "All the platters are lying in the storeroom. Go count them and you'll know how many Eids we spent together."

'The same Rajab Ali had a much older, widowed sister. Her own daughter had died while still young, leaving a little girl behind. The girl's father remarried. Rajab Ali brought the widowed sister and her granddaughter home. As he had no daughter of his own, he loved the girl very much and married her off with much fanfare. Didda too had sent a gift of clothes and such for the bride. Later it became known that the girl's husband suffered from some mental disorder. Eventually, the grief of having to seek divorce for his dear granddaughter killed Rajab Ali prematurely. The girl returned home. A silence had swept over her.

'The minute Pandey set eyes on her, he went berserk. He felt as if the sun was shining right above his head, melting away his brain. He had gone to Rajab Ali's to offer condolences and the girl had somehow walked straight into his presence—the portrait of a forlorn face, with red-streaked eyes. He was getting along in years: many lovely faces had passed by him, but never before had he lost his heart like that.

'Well, Pandey started visiting the house frequently, apparently out of regard for Rajab Ali and his unflinching loyalty. He showered them with gifts of all kinds. Poor Rajab Ali's wife was a simple, naïve woman. The trauma of her husband's untimely demise combined with the misery the poor girl was going through made her almost witless. For some time she had no idea what was happening. And as for Didda, she wouldn't even notice what season of the year it was. By the time she woke up, the water was already well above her head. Bhagwan, hai Bhagwan!

'"What is all this that I'm hearing, Bhaiya?" She confronted him.

'Bhaiya was dead silent, unable to say a word.

'"Why don't you open your mouth? In the whole wide world you could only find this one—a Muslim, and a divorcée to boot?"

'And when no response was forthcoming, "Am I talking to a stone or something?" Didda began to cry now.

'Love is known to turn even the smartest people into perfect idiots. When Didda kicked up more fuss, Pandey, who some years ago had very quietly succumbed to his sister's choice and gone through the seven rounds of the holy fire, was provoked to say—though he spoke very respectfully—"Didda, you're like a mother to me. If she were alive today, I couldn't have given her as much respect as I give you. I saved your face and your good name when you went and made a decision about my life without asking me. I honoured it with my heart and soul. My first one is the principal wife; that will not change. But this one is my love; that will also not change."

'Didda was speechless. Yes indeed, Bhaiya had answered back to her. That left no room at all for further discussion.'

'Bravo Bhaiya Sahib! You turned out to be quite gutsy!' clamoured someone in the audience. 'And what do we have here? Our Bipin Bhaiya. The girl didn't even belong to another religion; just a different caste. His mother gives a slight rebuke and there he goes running to hide under her mantle.'

'Shame, shame!' a collective cry shot up.

'Go smear dung on the faces of those who talk about the generation gap. Why must anyone malign today's people? Those older ones weren't any different.'

Bipin Bhaiya went completely numb, as if a serpent had sniffed him. Observing the doleful look on his face, someone came to his rescue: 'Okay, Mama. Something more must have happened afterwards, eh?'

'Whatever happened afterwards was all the handiwork of the heavens above. Didda or Pandey or the one from Mirjapur had nothing to do with it. Before he married his Pretty Face, Pandey already had two daughters, about five or six years old. But within a year of his second marriage, he had a son, followed by another son, while his first wife again gave birth to a girl, their third. Didda couldn't hold herself back any more. She went to congratulate her sister-in-law with traditional fanfare, gave her a pair of priceless earrings, a family heirloom, as a gift, and was overjoyed to see the faces of the nephews glowing like the sun and the moon. When their beautiful young mother bowed slightly and raised her hand to greet her,

Didda responded with words like "May you be blessed with many children and prosper", and accepted a roll of betel leaf from her hands—the betel box was always kept ready because of Pandey.

'After Didda returned home she arranged for a puja in honour of Lord Sat Narayan, customarily held to mark auspicious occasions such as this one. Then, taking along a share of the propitiatory offering, the prasad, she went back to the house of the same sister-in-law who belonged to another religion. She didn't explain anything, just offered it to her. The young lady smiled and accepted it gracefully in her two cupped hands, the way prasad is taken. ("Oh, the wretch! How pretty she is! Her hands look like they're made from silver," Didda thought to herself.) Then she raised her cupped hands to touch her forehead in a gesture of respect and gratitude and consumed what was in them. (Didda thought, Lord, what a dutiful and respectful girl!) Then after a pause Didda said, "With Bhaiyan by your side, the two of you look like Ram and Sita. From today, I shall call you Jaanki. You do know, don't you, that Sita's other name was Jaanki? And besides, it is also part of your husband's name."

'Pretty Face, whose name was Raushan Aara, smiled. ("What's in a name?" Shakespeare declaimed centuries ago. But then some bright spirits subjected his own name to their ingenuity and came up with "Sheikh Peer".)

'The couple had named their boys Aamir and Saabir. Didda changed them to Amar and Subir and, after incorporating everyone into her family by giving them Hindu names, returned home. Thus she filled up the entire yawning gulf in one minute flat. Even the Lord Hanuman's army wouldn't have built a bridge between Lanka and India in such a short time. However, the fallout from all this activity didn't turn out to be entirely propitious. The "one with the big family name" whom Didda had brought home with such eagerness felt offended and started to distance herself from her. Now, folks, such mother- and daughter-in-law tiffs are fairly common in every family, though they're kept somewhat hushed in respectable homes.'

'Yes, fellows, take the case of Princess Anne and Lady Diana. They never could get along well.'

'Bravo! There you go rushing straight off to England! Why forget our native Safdar Jung Road?'

From Pandey, the conversation had drifted to political figures and their relatives. Tea with peanuts and a session of backbiting lasted a long time. (Both give a lot of pleasure in winter, as famously said by Mushtaq Yusufi.) The fun lasted quite some time.

Such sessions still took place, but they had somehow lost their earlier zing. K. K. Mama, at fifty-five (in his own view, the prime of his life) was struck with cancer and two years later was no more. The protagonist of his story hadn't aged much either. Likely he was sixty, or just a little older, but he still had a muscular body. There was no sign that he would croak any time soon. It didn't look as if a single brick in that stout frame would come loose before he was eighty or eighty-five, let alone the whole edifice crashing down. But yes, Didda had passed away and the girls had grown, so the pressure of Pandey's first wife had increased on him. Even when he went to the Pretty Face's, he didn't stay long and came running back. But this time when he went to her he made up for all the lost time; settled all his past and future accounts. He died there. Just like that, suddenly. K. K. Mama was no longer around or he would have pontificated, 'Now, folks, you never can tell when someone will fall in love, nor is there a fixed time for a dust storm, a wedding or a death. Sometimes all these happen so suddenly it's hard to believe. Here, try to figure it out: Pandeyji was perfectly fine at home; why the heck did he have to go to Rasoolpur to die? Granted, *she* lived there, his favourite wife. But if he hadn't gone there at that time, he might not have died. Or he might have died but at least not there.'

When Pandey was making Raushan's life miserable by insisting that she marry him, she told him one day, 'But Pundit (that's how she addressed him, always), you and I belong to different religions. On top of that, you're married and the father of two daughters. You may well claim a thousand times to be ready to die for me but...'

'Oh, religion...yes,' Pandey took a deep breath and scratched his head. 'Granted, about that there's no doubt: you're a Muslim, I'm a Hindu. But why drag my being married into it? Your religion allows four wives, doesn't it?'

Raushan Aara smiled, 'And yours puts no ceiling at all. Four or forty.'

Pandey became irritated, 'The damned government does now. There was this ancestor of mine who, when there was no such law, married four real sisters, one after another. And when the stock ran out in that family he got himself a courtesan. But there's no restriction on you.'

Raushan Aara glowered menacingly, 'Of course, there is. On me, that is. Not on men of our community. By the way, Pundit, what do you take me to be?'

'Jaan-e Pundit, the love of my life.'

'The Persian genitive, that "-e" does not go well with a typical Hindi word. Like the two of us together. Looks downright awkward, odd.'

'Raushan Aara, keep it up and one of these days you'll get a fine beating.'

Raushan Aara suddenly tensed and her face became grim, 'Oh yes, I've been beaten all right, like a poor pawn on life's chessboard. What do I do now, Pundit?' Without thinking, she began rubbing her hands together. Her voice betrayed a feeling of utter helplessness.

'You don't have to do anything. Just marry me, without fussing.'

'In that case, you'll have to change your faith. No court marriage for me. No sir.'

'There will be no court marriage anyway. The one from Mirjapur is at home, isn't she? How would I deny having married her?'

'So, you're going to have me as a "keep"? Is that it?'

Now it was Pandey's turn to become deadly serious. Could one possibly pile such disgrace upon the woman he loved so dearly, so helplessly? For a moment he was speechless.

'Come on, Pundit. Speak up.' Her tone insisted on a categorical answer.

'I will go through the nikah,' he said with certainty.

'You'll have to change your religion. You know that, eh?'

'So now you're going to teach a lawyer, Raushan Aara Begum? You, a woman, whose intelligence, as the elders say, resides in her ankle?'

'We'll decide later whose intelligence resides in the ankle. First, you'd better be aware that the path is pretty rocky. To abandon the religion of one's ancestors…'

'To hell with it,' Pandey bit his lips.

'What are you sending to hell—religion or the ancestors?'

'The society that created the religion. But, of course, your religion is descended from the heavens.'

'Right now you're a Hindu so you may say whatever you like. Once you accept Islam, you'll not be allowed to show any disrespect.'

That night when he went home and lay down next to his wife, Pandey couldn't fall asleep. He lit a cigarette and went to sit on the veranda. Didda hadn't let him move away from her house even after he started making his own money. She only moved him to a newly built, cottage like bungalow in the empty lot—an extension of her own house—just so that her brother's ego wouldn't be wounded and he wouldn't become the object of people's gossip on account of living in his sister's house. The two houses had a joint compound. A trained gardener under Didda's own supervision made improvements to the garden. Some trees were so beautiful their leaves looked prettier than their blossoms. The breeze filtering through them felt a bit more refreshing. The moon hung like a chandelier in the middle of a clear blue sky. Pandey just sat there smoking cigarettes. The fragrance of maulsari hung about him like some magic spell overpowering the odour of tobacco.

There was still some time before dawn. He got up and started walking towards Didda's house. Huge white musandas stood lining one edge of the lawn. The story is told how in one of his incarnations Gautama Buddha was wandering in the forests of Sri Lanka. It was a moonless night and he was groping his way forward when suddenly row upon row of flowers opened and a glow spread through the musandas. The whole forest was bathed in a cool luminescence. A milky white light spread all over—light not of the moon, but of the flowers. Then Gautama Buddha blessed the musanda plant. The blessing is still effective: the shrub flowers year round. God knows whether it is a psychological effect of the story or whether the flowers themselves have some innate quality, but somehow calm descends upon one's mind and heart when looking at them. Could it be the result of Gautama Buddha's blessing? And did the Buddha not pray for the human race to be blessed with common sense? That the dross be eliminated from man's heart? And man cleansed of his innate evil? Spared old age, sickness and the cycle of deaths and rebirths? They all continue to afflict mankind and are still filling man's heart with terror. Mother...my dear mother.

Pandey's eyes welled up with tears as the thought of his beautiful mother who had died so young came sailing into his mind. An excruciating sigh rose from his heart at this hour of the waning night. Where would Mother have gone after dying? Would she really have to cross the river Vaitarni as the scriptures say? Were there any other worlds beyond this one? Would Pandey ever be able to see her again after his own death? The mother who always carried her little Jaanki Raman close to her heart when she was alive—would she be yearning for him now? Would the pind daan, the ritual charity and puja offered for the peace of the departed souls, really bring peace to them? Yes, soul? What is this soul?

(Raushan Aara, too, when she said the fatiha for Munshi Rajab Ali, said his soul received peace and reward from this.) What are gunaah and sawaab, the sin and the reward for virtue? Raushan had never let him kiss her, only allowed him to touch her fingers. 'This is sinful' was her favourite expression, which she used time and time again. ('But then, Raushan Bibi, according to your beliefs, meeting me, to even make this attraction between a man and a woman possible, is sinful.') Who had made these standards for sin and for reward? Restless, he had begun walking fast. If he recited the kalima and claimed he was a Muslim, would he still remain Jaanki Raman Pandey or would he become someone else? He decided, no, he would remain the same, with all his knowledge, his awareness, his legal hairsplitting, his body, shape, appearance, his feelings and sensations, his thoughts, his wickedness, his defects, all his loves... The name Jaanki Raman Pandey had everything and then again, nothing.

His loves...? He had two daughters and a wife. He had never felt the kind of attachment or stormy feelings for his wife as he did for Raushan Aara. What about Didda and his daughters...? Would his love for them diminish or disappear entirely just because he stuck a new label on himself? 'How could that be Jaanki Raman Pandey?' he reproached himself. Then, what was all the fuss about? And whose fuss was it?

The following week he went to Raushan Aara and told her he was ready to recite the kalima, to convert.

'But Raushan,' he said to this quiet, bright-faced woman with droopy eyelids, 'I am Vishnu's devotee; I may not be able to pluck him out of my heart. You might as well know that all these names, these conceptions—people have devised them at different times just to answer their own basic questions: Who made this world? Why do people die? Where do they go after dying? What awaits them there? Is there any recompense for all the injustice and suffering in the world? Those whom no law can prosecute, will they get their just deserts somewhere? Is there any reward for those who do good? As it is, Raushan Begum, the world is rife with sin and oppression. If there were no religion, it would be flooded by them. Religion at least sets limits around the devils residing within us; it gives human beings strength and courage during their suffering and crises; it keeps hope alive.

'And this "inshallah" you keep repeating so often...and "mashallah" to protect yourself from evil—that Allah of yours Who is merciful and forgiving, Who preserves and cherishes, Who condones sins as well as punishes for them, Who sustains life and promises death—well, my Vishnu has all those attributes too. It's just that we view Him in three separate forms—Creator, Sustainer, and Destroyer. They're all facets of the same supreme Being.'

He smiled. 'Your Allah is the Lord of all the worlds, not merely the Lord of Muslims. So...in that sense, He is mine as well. He was mine even before, but now I will declare Him openly as mine. And it is through His good offices that I shall be holding your hand. But the manner in which I have been worshipping Him in the past is not going to change. It will remain the same.'

He remained quiet for a short while. Then lowering his eyes a bit he said, 'And Raushan Begum…one other thing: I cannot give up my wife, or daughters, or Didda. My wife, such as she is, I have married her with all the proper rituals. My entire society is behind her. None of them can be made to sacrifice for one relationship.'

He paused again, and this time smiled a little. 'And don't you give me the example of King Edward of Mrs Simpson fame. He was a king, and a king of England at that. I'm just a common man, a member of the hoi polloi, victim of the most complicated caste-driven landscape of India.'

Holding her beautiful face in the cup of her hands, listening attentively to Pandey's lecture, Raushan smiled—a painful, troubled smile.

'Pundit, when I was handing over my heart to you, I hadn't considered that you were Jaanki Raman Pandey and I was Raushan Aara. By the time I discerned the difference between the names, it was already too late. You may do whatever you like. Only lift your finger and say the kalima. I cannot accept any other manner of being with you except after nikah. I won't even ask you to become a non-vegetarian.'

Then she spoke with a trace of anger, 'Whenever you come here, I'll feed you the fodder for the cows and oxen. And, may I eat pig's meat if I ever contemplate encroaching upon the rights of your wife. About coming here, you may do so whenever you want, and stay only as long as it does not upset your peace of mind.'

They were married the next week. Before the nikah, Jaanki Raman Pandey converted to Islam in the presence of a meek-faced, frightened-looking maulvi. At the time of the nikah, Raushan's maternal grandmother, that is, Rajab Ali's wife, was terribly sad and upset. Her concern wasn't that Raushan was marrying a Hindu. What pained her more was how she would now face Onkaar Nath's wife. How she would send the Eid vermicelli to her house. The relationship between the families went back a long way. Was theirs the only house left to burglarize? In any case, Jaanki Raman Pandey was a man, no one was going to say anything to him. And even though it wasn't love at first sight for Raushan, nor did she try to find excuses for him to make repeated visits or try to contact him—as a matter of fact in the beginning she was quite suspicious of his comings and goings—at that time she was passing through a delicate and very painful period. Caution escaped her when she found attention and love. But who would even stop to notice or listen to all of this, or ask for explanations. And, indeed, no one said anything to Jaanki Raman. They all pounced on Raushan.

A harlot. A dissolute woman. Abandoned her first husband. Does anyone ever hit a pretty woman like her? Must be a tramp, that's why she got beaten. And then blamed it all on him for being crazy. She'd never let him come near her, that's why she couldn't even beget a mouse in three years of marriage. And then, as soon as she marries Pandey, out comes a son. Who knows, she might have been carrying on with Pandey the whole time. (Pandey wasn't even remotely aware of her existence in those days.) A whore. Didn't even worry about what is permitted and what is not. She's corrupting a Brahmin's faith; she'll go straight to hell. Who knows, even hell may not find a place for her. Lord knows what she feeds him. Then one day, tired of people's jibes and what she herself thought, the first wife told Pandey, 'You eat *there*; separate your pots, pans and dishes from ours. Don't eat here in ours.'

Pandey always treated his first wife very courteously. Who knows how he had defended himself in other matters or what shrewd counselling he had given her, but on this issue of eating, he brought out the Holy Gita, put his hand on it and swore, 'When I stay there, my food is cooked in separate pots, on a separate stove. During those days, she herself does not eat meat, fish, onion or garlic. It's a purely vegetarian fare.'

The Mirjapur woman would burn hearing him use the plural, respectful form of 'she' for Raushan. But Pandey, swearing with his hand on the Gita, looked so pitiful, so innocent, so disarmingly truthful that afterward she gave up squabbling about what was lawful to eat and what wasn't.

Pandey did swear at that time, but ever since that day, he began feeling troubled in his mind. This was the first time he'd had to go to that extent to prove his honesty. He felt as if he was no longer the lawyer, but the culprit standing in the dock. He was reminded of the episode in the Ramayana in which Sita has to go through the trial by fire. He would sit brooding long hours over what this business of halal, haram, khadiya, akhadiya, lawful to eat, or unlawful to eat was. One could eat meat, the other couldn't. One could eat meat, but not pig's meat or cow's. Even in vegetarian food, there was a prohibition about onions and garlic, as there was in Pandey's own house. On the other hand, Didda's sons had started having onion pakoras fried in their house. Because of the same issue among

Didda's in-laws, they had to separate their cooking. A family that had held together for generations was now split apart.

A melancholy feeling had settled over Didda's elder brother-in-law because one of his sons had fallen in with bad company and had started eating meat. His wife was the daughter of some naval officer and so, quite upbeat and outgoing. Not only did she not reprimand her husband, she encouraged him. The food already had an excess of onions and garlic in it. At first the matter remained limited to restaurants. Later, as restraint relaxed a little, biryani and chicken started arriving in the lunch boxes. Such indignity in the house of a high-ranking Brahmin! Ram! Ram! The two brothers fought openly. The older one was a little orthodox in his views and loved his father dearly. If all of this hadn't happened while he was alive it might not have mattered that much. So the older one made his younger brother live separately. A huge two-storeyed home was divided into two households. The parents moved in with the older son and daughter-in-law. After the hearths were separated, all the issues that had been ignored earlier suddenly became contentious. One day, a lighthearted joke turned into a serious argument. 'Bhabi,' the younger brother said to the older sister-in-law, 'try a chicken drumstick sometime and you'll start eating whole men, not just chicken.' She screamed so hard that the entire household promptly gathered. The spat became so heated that the division of the estate and property was dragged in. (Actually, the older brother's wife had been contemplating the matter of the division of property for some time already. The fight provided a handy excuse to bring it up.)

How stupid man is! How long will he stay that way?

Wasn't Raushan Aara herself saying the other day that her mother never mentioned the word pig? She referred to it as 'the bad one' or 'haram-faced'. Her logic was that if one mentioned the word 'pig', the angels that brought blessings wouldn't enter one's house.

'And Bibi Raushan Aara, you're the people who eat chicken, goat, cow, buffalo, even camel and horse. Why so much fuss over a poor pig?'

'I never eat camels or horses,' Raushan fidgeted a bit. 'And beef—that you made me give up.'

'But they are considered halal at any rate. Aren't they? Baddan Miyan, remember, that distant relation of yours? Didn't he slaughter a camel to celebrate the birth of a son born after six daughters? And didn't he send a share of the meat to your house? Poor daughters! No one sacrifices even a measly goat when they're born, much less a whole camel.' And Pandey added, 'You may go on claiming that a woman's status is very high in Islam, but there's a clash everywhere between the beliefs of religion and society.'

'When did I eat camel meat?'

'The same silly argument! It's halal, isn't it? Your co-religionists eat it, don't they, whether you personally do or don't?'

'Right now you're the one making silly arguments. You sound like a broken record.'

'It's stuck because you never told me why you people fret so much about the pig. Remember, once you even swore that if you ever think of usurping the rights of my wife, you'll eat pig's meat.'

'Maybe because it looks so dirty and nauseating.'

'It looks the same to me as well. Maybe it does even to others. But why does it occupy such a negative place in your psyche? It's stupid to shy away from it so much. It is haram, just as a donkey or a dog is. Maybe because nobody eats a donkey or a dog, but people do eat pigs, that's why the idea has somehow stuck in your brains. What a shame! But when you people are angry, why do you swear by saying "Eat a pig!" not "Eat a donkey" or "Eat a dog"?'

'I've never thought about the logic. You go ahead if you wish.' Raushan Aara scowled, 'Seems as if you want to kick up a riot inside the house, eh? Haven't you done enough outside?'

Pandey laughed heartily.

Recently, they had escaped a riot by a hair's breadth. Some mischief-maker had thrown a sack of meat into the mosque. No one had it tested in a lab to find out what kind it was, everyone just assumed it had to be from a pig because it was thrown inside a mosque. Pandey was ahead of everybody in reasoning with the enraged youth and calming them down. He had come to Raushan and was present in Rasoolpur at that time.

'Look, you can't win over the majority by fighting. An ordinary mistake will cause great harm to your people. Have some patience and don't let such small things get to you.'

'You call it a small thing?' Raushan had snapped.

'Small in the sense that a person could easily pick up the sack and throw it out, fill up buckets of water and cleanse the floor. End of story. The ones who wanted to benefit by inciting you would then be left to wallow in total embarrassment.'

But it took all his powers of persuasion and a lot of time to make them understand this small thing. Picking up the sack himself, Pandey dumped it in the garbage and made entreaties to the imam of the mosque with folded hands. The situation had become quite volatile. Finally, with tremendous difficulty, he was able to avert a major incident. (How could there be a major incident anyway? Have Muslims got the spunk for it? If they so much as even make a peep, you guys beat them up and knock some sense into their heads. You confiscate their graveyards and threaten to send them to their graves too.) 'But we're not about to pack up and go to Pakistan,' Raushan had commented. The Babri Mosque issue was also pretty hot at the time. Somebody had also scribbled a slur on Raushan's wall: two places left for Mussalmans—Kabristaan [graveyard] or Pakistan.

Raushan was in a daze. Her face looked as if she was oblivious to everything around her. And indeed she was. Her long hair, which Pandey had undone the night before and spread over his shoulders, was still in the same dishevelled state, now even a bit tangled. Dark circles had appeared under her eyes. It seemed as if someone had filled those eyes, which even now had lost none of their brilliance, with bewilderment—bewilderment at the unexpected that had struck her. Her mind refused to accept it. In one corner of her mind, the scorpion of an idea had been stinging her: why did Pandey have to be with her when death came? (And if he had been at that other place perhaps she would have been jolted by a different shock, the inability to see his face as he lay dying.) God knows what everyone in that other house must be thinking... And then again, both of his sons were here. All the people of the area had gathered too.

Pandey was well liked in the area. Raushan did not know quite how to tell them that her husband was not a Muslim, that his last rites should be performed according to the Hindu faith. (The whole village was a Muslim settlement. There was just a smattering of Brahmin and Rajput households and a few tanners' huts at the edge of the village.) But could Pandey fit easily into a single category? Which one? And whose?

Once, a long time ago, when he had let Raushan's head rest against his chest while he leaned back moving his fingers through her long curls, she had said, 'Pundit, you're such a hypocrite! You even said the Jumma prayer in the mosque. Tell me truthfully, what did you actually recite, the Gayatri Mantra or the Hanuman Chalisa?'

Pandey laughed, 'I've memorized all seven kalimas, and even the Al-Hamd. I just recited those, switching them around a few times, and did the standing up and sitting down as the others were doing.' Then suddenly he became serious. 'Have you ever seen the chicken being spoiled when too many cooks butt in?'

'What makes you think of chicken all of a sudden, Pundit? Like to eat some?'

'Raushan,' Pandey was still serious, 'I used to be a simple, unpretentious Hindu. I got mixed up with you and became a fake Muslim. Then I didn't even stay a true Hindu. I have become a complete heretic, what you might call an atheist.'

Raushan jerked her hair away suddenly and sat up. 'Don't talk nonsense. I'm going to serve the food now.' She moved towards the kitchen and saw Pandey following her. He came over and stood leaning against the stove.

'Raushan, before, I never felt the need to think much about God and religion. I just figured there was someone who nourished us, so I did my duty towards Him by going through the evening prayer. I'd heard a lot of criticism about the other religions around and I also believed my religion was the best. Then I looked at the world carefully. After meeting you, I tried to understand your faith. I was just a lawyer in the beginning. All I ever knew was the law. Then I developed an interest in religion and studied a lot of subjects—history, sociology, anthropology, religion, and so on. And now Raushan, I've gone beyond all the boundaries, whether overt or covert.'

'Listen Pundit,' Raushan said as she emptied gourds filled with gram lentils from the pan into a beautiful deep dish, 'Don't take my jokes seriously. By God I haven't let your religion bother me at all. You mean everything to me just as you are, a human being who has given me all his love and security.'

'I know that Raushan. And I haven't loved you just for your looks either. It's also because of your intelligence, your wit, your deep understanding, and your innate nobility. I looked for all these qualities in my wife but couldn't find them. That's what drew me to you.

'But right now I'm in the mood to tell you something. I have a deep sense that in every epoch or age, all the secrets and mysteries of the universe, all the ups and downs of life, like old age, death, suffering and the like, have produced in humans of all races and colours, the conception of a Being that controls the whole of this intricate puzzle we call life. That Being is someone affectionate like a father, above every need. Someone we expect to support truth and oppose falsehood, someone always awake, watching over every creature. Someone from whom we can ask anything and everything. To please him, to avoid his wrath, we also formulate the concepts of sawaab and gunaah. Basically, sawaab are deeds that benefit others and gunaah are those that cause them harm.'

For a short while he stared at the gas flames flickering on the stove. Then he continued:

'But while doing all this, what we forgot was that it is quite natural for people's conceptions to vary in different regions, in different times, and according to their different ways of life, even though the basic objective is still the same. All religious systems ultimately take a person in the same direction—towards the Omnipotent Being Who created the universe and has control over life and death. But we only consider the system we ourselves follow as correct. We declare everyone who falls outside our own system as fit for beheading. And then we split up the basic gunaah and sawaab into a hundred different categories that make no sense at all.'

Raushan placed the rice dish on the tray with deep sorrow and said, 'Among those sins is also the one I have committed: marrying the follower of another religion. Pundit, I know, you agreed to embrace Islam only to make the nikah legally permissible.'

'That's correct, Raushan, but I too believe in one God. My ancient Hindu faith tells me the same thing. And I also respect your Prophet immensely. He was a great revolutionary reformer. No person has been born since who could win over such large numbers of people and bring about such tremendous, positive changes in His community.'

'And you're still not a Muslim?'

'I just told you, didn't I? I'm not even a Hindu any longer. I'm just a human being who sees God's glory in everything—in the chirping of the sparrows, the fragrance of the flowers, the open spaces, the scattered stars of the galaxy, in the waters of the rivers and the beauty of the rising and setting sun. Perhaps that's why our thinkers and philosophers started to worship the sun and the trees and the rivers. These are all manifestations of God's divine power.

'And I also concede every individual's right to his own religion and personal beliefs. How he wants to reach his God is his business alone. But it's also true that no other issue besides religion has resulted in the creation of so many walls and so much iniquity among mankind. After the discovery of America, when the Spaniards arrived in the New World, they didn't just bring gunpowder and smallpox for the natives, they also brought a new God. Surely, it must have been hard for the natives to adjust to this new God; it must have taken some time for them to forget the souls of their ancestors, whom they had worshipped, and not to grieve over the mass slaughter of their sacred buffaloes. The German tribes used to worship oak trees; the Catholic missionaries had them chopped down.

'And forgive me for saying that there's a lot of emphasis on missionary work in your religion too. From what I know about Islam, although it wasn't spread by the sword alone, the Islamic conquests did play an important role. The vanquished have always found safety in adopting the faith of the victor. The cultural and religious influences of the conquerors gradually supplant those of the confused or at least usher in a lot of change.'

'And you Hindus beat up the Buddhists and drove them away, didn't you? You razed their temples to the ground and gobbled up Mahatma Buddha by assimilating him in the Hindu pantheon of gods as the ninth incarnation of Lord Vishnu. Nice trick to put an end to the Buddhist faith,' Raushan said in a huff. Then she laughed and added, 'But I, a Muslim, have a great reverence for Gautama Buddha. All right, weed-eater, enough sermonizing. Come, your meal is served.'

'Raushan Begum, your Mahatma Buddha vigorously opposed idol worship, and not just that, *he* also opposed the entire gamut of Hindu ceremonial acts and sacrificial rites. And what did his followers do? They installed idols of him everywhere in the world; they started doing all the things he had opposed. The fact is, mankind needs a God, especially one they can see. It's very difficult to worship an unseen God like the one you have. That requires a profound metaphysical understanding rarely found in human beings. But of course, with a cudgel in hand a person quickly learns how to smash it hard on another's head and beliefs. To overcome the nasty devil hiding inside man...now take those magnificent statues at Bamiyan, your Taliban—'

Now Raushan really got angry, 'Why are the Taliban mine? Because they share my religion, is that it? My head sinks in shame when I think of it. No conqueror in Afghanistan ever touched those Buddhas, not even Mahmud, the one famous for being an "iconoclast". There's been so much progress, but man hasn't learned to be human. Why should someone who is wrong, narrow-minded, an enemy of history be called *mine*?' Sadness mingled with indignation in her voice.

'All religions were originally different than what their followers subsequently made them into. All right, tell me something,' Pandey asked, laughing, 'when I die, which religion will you follow for my last rites? Oh brother, I'm truly terrified of being buried under the dirt. Those angels of yours, the Munkar-Nakir duo, will come and torment me in the grave. *You* can take whatever nonsense I say, but they would pick up their maces and start their drubbing right on, dana dan.'

Raushan's lips formed into a smile and she looked away. Pandey's tongue continued wagging.

'And I'm not even Kabir so that when I die in place of my body flowers will appear, which the two of you might divide among yourselves, half you and the other half my first queen.'

Raushan scowled at Pandey. The narrow line of the smile had disappeared.

He laughed again. 'Okay, Raushan, tell me one other thing. Why do miracles always happen to people in the past, people we haven't seen or known? Why don't they happen to us? Today? Now? By the way, there is one good thing in all this. I'll earn double credit after dying. There will of course be pind daan; and in addition to that, you'll also recite the fatiha over me, as you did for your mother and for Uncle Rajab Ali.'

Raushan banged the plate down, 'Don't talk such gloomy nonsense with food in front of you.'

'Raushan, I'm much older than you, so it's almost certain that I'll go first. I added "almost" just in case you get tired of me and think of ending your life. But you wouldn't do that, would you? You wouldn't go away leaving me alone.' He grabbed a handful of her thick tresses and tugged. 'Tell me truthfully: what will you do if I die before you? Tell me.'

'What *can* I do?' Raushan pushed away the sudden gush of tears. 'I'd be resigned to the will of God, as I'm resigned now.'

'Resigned to His will,' Pandey repeated the words separately and forcefully. "Wherever Ram keeps me; that's where I'll stay." The Hindus say Ram is the same, the same Elevated Being to Whom we attribute everything and become free of our responsibilities, the One Who enables us to bear our miseries with patience. This is not Ram, the son of Dasaratha. This is the Brahma of the Vedas. Kabir had the same Ram, so did Gandhi. No matter what religion we adopt, what label we attach, we'll remain the same and perform our duties as humans.'

He suddenly became quiet. Then, as if he had remembered something, he added, 'I bequeathed half of my property to you and the boys, and the other half to the daughters. I've given the house where I live to my wife.'

'Pundit, I don't need anything. It's enough that you have arranged for us to live here in Rasoolpur. Both boys are well educated. They'll earn enough by themselves. You've given them the greatest wealth they can have.

You got them out of here and had them educated in the best schools and colleges. You looked after them very well. What more can you possibly give us now? My head seems ready to burst when I think that man is basically so mean and selfish. And I too have committed a selfish act: I've taken a poor woman's husband from her.'

'That woman isn't as poor as you might think, Raushan Begum. I've always been there for her, and I've been there completely. Society has given her much more than I could ever give you. It's terribly lonely living all by yourself, cut off from your people. So, if you ask me honestly, I've actually sinned more against you than her. I wouldn't like to add to it by dying and leaving you helpless. My heartfelt wish really is that when I die, I am with you.'

Raushan put her soft palm on Pandey's mouth.

If K. K. Mama were alive he would have said, 'He always had a black tongue. Whatever evil he uttered came to pass.' But K. K. had passed away a long time ago. Those stories of his, those memorable gatherings, were a thing of the past. God's name alone abides—God Who has no beginning or end, Who is invisible beyond comprehension, beyond life and death. (We humans only wish to be beyond death and keep forging other worlds in our imagination.)

The noise at the door was getting louder by the minute. People were carrying wooden clubs in their hands, some capped with burnished blades. They were all local residents. Pandey's three sons-in-law, one of their relatives, and people from the family of Didda's older brother-in-law had all come rushing from Allahabad, but two of Didda's own sons had remained aloof from this trouble. Upon hearing the filthy abuses hurled at their mother, Raushan's two sons had opened the door and come out unarmed. Inside, in the courtyard, Raushan stood holding up the Quran in her hands with every one of her limbs trembling.

History was repeating itself again so soon. When Raushan was a young girl, a contest between wrestlers had suddenly acquired communal overtones. Shopkeepers had quickly dropped their shutters. The noise of running feet had shaken Raushan's street. At that time, Raushan's grandmother, hoisting the Quran in her hands in the same way, had come and stood in the courtyard reciting it loudly. And the maid had covered her head with her mantle and raised her hands to pray: 'O Master Ali! Remove this hardship from our lives.'

(At the time of his martyrdom, Hazrat Uthman was reciting the Quran. His blood had spattered on the Word of God and made it colourful.) What had to happen happened. Raushan's grandfather, who had gone to the village to have the harvest brought home and was on his way back, was murdered along the way. Nothing happened in the city itself.

A distraught Raushan came straight out of the house and stood in front of her boys, shielding them.

'These are your own relatives, Jaanki Raman Pandey's children,' she screamed loudly.

'Let's start with the slut. Kill her,' someone shouted back from the crowd.

'Please bring the necessary papers and sit with us peacefully. We are willing to relinquish the property that the Pundit had given over to us.' Raushan remembered well the argument that had started at Didda's elder brother-in-law's house. What had been a squabble over eating or not eating meat had ultimately led to the division of ancestral property. Pushing the boys behind her, she uttered those few sentences very loudly.

With a premonition that something awful might happen, Onkaar Nath Mishra, over seventy now and practically a recluse after his wife's death, rushed to the scene in his jeep just in time. Having lived through the world's ups and downs, and being well aware of people's ways and dispositions, the thought of the world's impermanence had become etched on his heart. He had heard that Pandey's three sons-in-law had already left for Rasoolpur with the armies of their cronies in tow, all because Pandey had died there. It was confirmed that the proper funeral prayer had been performed for Pandey and he was then interred in the Muslim cemetery there. Onkaar Nath also had some perfunctory knowledge that Pandey had bequeathed half of his property to Raushan and the boys before his death. And rumour had it that because of the national elections just around the corner, ISI agents' activities had moved into high gear in the Rasoolpur area. Considering all that, the situation didn't look at all promising. Holding on to his back with his hands, he got up.

Pandey's first wife pulled her mantle over her forehead and came to him. 'Brother,' she said, 'don't let the boys and their mother come to any harm. Raushan Aara never snatched him away from me, and the boys of course are his own flesh and blood. A change of faith does not change the relationship.' Her voice became hoarse. 'I couldn't stop the sons-in-law.'

Even Onkaar Nath felt his eyes becoming moist. It was the first time he had felt like crying since his wife's death. He stood up. After a short pause he said, 'Pray to Bhagwan that nothing untoward happens before I get there.'

His deceased wife was devoted to her brother. It was because of that connection that he had accepted Raushan and the boys, but his own children were siding with Jaanki Raman's sons-in-law. True, they hadn't accompanied them, but they hadn't said anything either. And Onkaar Nath's nephews had even gone along with the crowd. They had suddenly remembered the kinship that existed between their two families.

The prayers of Jaanki Raman's dark, gold-hearted wife were answered. Onkaar Nath reached there in the nick of time, otherwise who knows what might have happened. Everything was settled peacefully. Raushan agreed to give up her share of the estate and property—with this promise, and upon some other conditions, the crowd returned home with Pandey's exhumed body.

This was Onkaar Nath's first encounter with Raushan. 'Chhoti Bahu, please give them your permission,' he had said very gently. 'There are only three of you here, but there are many innocents in the village who might lose their lives even though they have nothing to do with this dispute. The atmosphere is not good. Tell them yourself: fine, take it. There's grace in that. And besides, it will preserve the goodwill. We cannot fight with them all.'

Such disrespect for the Pundit's body! Raushan almost fell over, overcome by the shame. How much had she begged her village folk and her own sons to have his body taken to his house in Allahabad? But no one had listened to her.

'Chhoti Bahu, a dead body is never left to rot, neither at home, nor on the road. Everyone knows that.'

After the body was taken away, Onkaar Nath stayed there for some time. 'Whether you cremate him or bury him, what does it matter?' he said. 'He is gone from this world. The five elements have returned to the five elements: earth to earth, sky to sky, fire to fire, water to water, and air to air. The same process occurs in either case, it just takes longer if the body is interred, but people don't understand it. The rituals observed after death are all for the solace of the living. I'm an ordinary person; I'm not in a position to say much, but the thinkers and philosophers have called the body clothing for the soul which it keeps changing. The soul itself does not decay. It is immortal. If we accept that, daughter, exhumation of a body already interred makes no sense, but what can I do? Seems Bhagwan has a special love for the ignorant. For they abound in His kingdom. Practise patience.'

'Brother Onkaar Sahib,' Raushan lifted her tear-filled eyes and looked at him, 'the earth stands firm only because there are pious people like you around. Please do me this small favour: take us to Allahabad. Find me a place anywhere there. I have some relatives in Allahabad, though they have all severed contact with me. Grandfather Rajab Ali died a long time ago. Now even Grandmother is gone.' She began crying inconsolably again.

A funeral pyre burning away at the edge of the Ganga, lapped by its gentle waters. Orange flames leaping in the murky darkness. A few stray, spotty clouds sailing through the sky. The raucous sound of crickets hiding in the vegetation. The people are all gone. An awesome, eerie silence—eternal, unending, unaffected by the crackling fire, the noise of the frogs and crickets, or the waves—pervades the landscape. There are several other funeral pyres as well, devouring human bodies. Five elements returning to five elements.

River, O river! How many have you seen ablaze? On this edge and on the other? From here to there, where you begin and where you end?

Emerging from behind a clump of trees, she comes forward. The land is a little elevated on one side, hiding a row of eternal, lush green trees. She stands on this elevated ground—a fair woman, tall and slight (and at this time as blanched as white paper). The edge of her fine, white, lace-bordered sari flutters in the wind. She seems to have suddenly overpowered the whole scene.

This man who was offered up to the flames, whose abundant, gorgeous hair was consumed by the blaze in an instant, whose skull, sturdy despite his age, was cracked open with the ritual blow of the cudgel—what was this man to her? Why had she come to the cremation ground where women are not permitted? Who was she? And these people who, forgetting the maggots in the grave and the flames of the pyre, were ready to kill and be killed—who were they?

'Don't let anything deceive you, Raushan Aara Begum! This concept of the other world...it is nothing more than a childish fantasy to live forever. Our togetherness will last only as long as we live. And so far as the next world is concerned, well, if it pleases you, say the fatiha for me as well.' Then he had laughed mischievously, 'But would your fatiha reach me, since I'm...'

Uneasiness, like the smoke from the waning pyre, swirled inside Raushan's whole being.

'All the heavens, all the hells, we go through them in this world itself. They're all creations of our own making, the consequences of our own actions.'

'Oh, you talk so much nonsense, Pundit. Be quiet now.'

Raushan Aara wiped away her tears with her little finger.

'One of the mantras recited at pind daan says: go and never ever return to this world. I too would like to recite it. Jaanki Raman Pandey, you go now. And don't you come back. The world isn't ready for you, not just yet.'

Raushan Aara wrapped the fluttering hem of her sari tightly around her frail shoulders and, her heart heavy, started slowly retreating backwards— forty steps.

—*Co-translated by Faruq Hassan*

SUNLIGHT

ABDULLAH HUSSEIN

The bridge was perched so high across the ravine that the steep climb left him breathless. He halted. The city ended here and the grain fields began, interspersed with stretches of open, uncultivated land. He put his hands on his hips to catch his breath a little and squinted far into the shimmering distance, taking in the gorgeous colours of the bright afternoon. The spring weather was the same as ever.

'It's March,' he thought, joy stirring in his heart, and strained his memory, 'but what day in March is it?'

After a few minutes he gave up. 'Oh, well, it's been twenty years!' he thought, and felt the passage of time in a rush of saliva under his tongue.

He pulled his felt hat lower over his eyes, turned around and looked back. His seven-year-old son was trudging up the steep road, kicking a smooth, round grey rock as though it were a football, stopping now and then to catch his breath. The city was behind them, the sun behind the city, and in between lay the fort built by Emperor Akbar splayed out across a hilltop—the tallest object in the panorama, but terribly dreary inside. On either side of the fort the jagged skyline of rooftops and houses built one against the other gave the city the appearance of a massive hill, dark and cone-shaped, stirring with life, silhouetted against a bright sky, dotted here and there with small, low-hanging spring clouds—rough-hewn, bristly, round clusters, weighty frozen boulders of fluffed cotton that could spill forth a writhing fury of rain... Oh yes, he knew this peculiar shape of spring cloud very well, as well as he knew the shimmering pale blue sky of early March that flooded the eyes. Indeed, he had been familiar with them since he was a small child. He had been born here, after all. And although he was returning today after twenty long years, the minute he stepped on to the bridge he knew that the spring weather was exactly as he had known it then.

His son had now caught up with him. He too was looking at the city, squinting into the sun with his hands resting on his hips.

'Rest awhile,' he said to the boy.

The boy kicked the rock again and walked over to the bridge's far end. His back to the sun, he peered at the road sloping down the bridge.

'Baaba!' the boy abruptly turned back and shouted.

The man removed his hat and wiped the sweat off his forehead with his finger, then lowered his collar, strode over to his son and stood beside him, his hand on the boy's shoulder.

'Baaba!' the boy said, 'the earth is round, isn't it?'

'Yes, it is,' he replied. He too looked at the precipitous path of the road as it dived down the bridge and smiled. 'Everything is round, son. Everything.'

'Everything?'

He started to climb down the slope, his hand still on his son's shoulder. The sun was behind them now and their shadows crept ahead of them, hugging the road. 'Come on!' he cried, 'Come!' And tapping the boy's shoulder, he sprinted off. The boy laughed soundlessly and followed his father down the slope at a run. The road was nearly deserted. A single tonga-carriage, crammed with peasants, sped down the road some distance away. The early morning chill still hung in the air, and the leaves felled by the winter frost scudded along on both sides of the road. As he jogged along he noticed a single thread of a spider web dangling inches away from his eyes. He quickly ducked, stepping out of its path. When they reached level ground again, the older man stopped abruptly. The boy, still running, bumped into him and was thrown off balance, but he quickly grabbed his father's arm and swung from it. They stood for a while laughing and catching their breath. The man threw his arms around the boy's shoulders and led him off the paved country road to the fields running along one side of it.

'Have you seen a razor's edge, son?' he asked.

'Yes.'

'Can you describe it for me?'

'It's very sharp.'

'And round.'

'Round?'

'Yes, if you look at it under a big microscope.'

'A big microscope?'

The imprecise use of the word 'big' was jarring; all the same, he found it rather amusing. 'I mean,' he corrected himself, 'under a powerful microscope.'

The boy knew his father was pulling his leg and broke into uncertain laughter. Again he grabbed the man's arm and swung from it.

They were now walking on a narrow trail that cut through acre after lush acre of wheat fields. The dark green stalks came up to their knees. Their uniform height was proof that a rich soil had nourished them and that each seed-bearing clump of dirt had received plentiful and even watering. A profusion of supple wheat ears, gold-green and long-whiskered, was arrayed in neat lines and bent by the wind, reminiscent of rows of genuflecting worshippers at Eid prayers.

Whenever the season changed—he recalled—whenever the sun grew warmer and brighter and the roots of the wheat slowly turned a bright gold, the warm winds wafted in from God knows where and swept over the entire landscape like a spell, holding all creation, animate and inanimate, captive in their magical golden warmth. How they fired the sluggish blood in the veins and made it leap to the soundless melody that stirred the nameless emotions belonging, unmistakably, to the change of season, which made one neither sad nor happy, but only gave the sensation of being reborn, renewed. It was in just this season, he remembered, when as a seven-year-old he roamed with his father looking for game, his first air gun slung across his shoulder. His father would pluck off an ear of wheat, turn it upside down and quietly stick it inside the boy's trouser leg. The more he tried to pull the bristly thing out, the more it crawled up his trousers, while his father, feigning concern, would ask, 'What's the matter? Are you all right, son?' He would poke and prod and look him over, but do nothing to help his son dislodge the intruding bristle; instead, he just stood there snickering. Exasperated, the boy would lay his gun down on the trail and try with both his hands to somehow expel the source of his misery, but the wheat spike just hopped further up, like a bird. Although later, much later, upon growing up, he at last solved the mystery of the spear's upward locomotion, the knowledge did nothing to alter the image of the spear which his mind—or the part of it that is aware of the unknown, the truer than the true—had preserved in the shape of a bird or a grasshopper.

He stretched out his arm and plucked an ear of wheat, stuck the bristly whiskers between his teeth and looked back stealthily from the corner of his eye. His son was coming along behind him on the narrow trail, taking each step with extreme caution, his hands shoved into his shorts' pockets.

'History too is round—I mean circular,' he said.

'How?'

'It repeats itself.'

'How does it repeat itself?'

'Well,' he began, chewing on the wheat beard with his front teeth, 'it's like this: truly massive armies span out; they overrun country after country, allowing every single soldier to prove himself a gallant conqueror, his glories told in story and song. Precisely at this point, decline sets in. You know why? Because the vanquished is weak, and in weakness there is power. In the end the vanquished brings the victor down, by epic and panegyric, by feeding his ego, by pandering to his innate greed for domination. It just takes a little bit longer. That's the only difference. The victor finds out when it's too late, after he is lost beyond all hope of recovery. This is how history repeats itself. It is round—like any other thing that goes in circles, for instance, the moon, the sun, the stars, the earth, the sky, trees, plants, blood...'

'Blood?' the boy asked, confused.

'Very much so,' he replied. 'It circles in the body from the roots of one's hair down to one's toenails, and then back up, and down again, interminably, round and round and round...' he laughed.

The boy didn't. He was taking a serious interest in all this. 'Baaba,' he said, 'are people round too?'

That caught him off guard. Logic required that this should be the next question, didn't it? But like most people, he suffered from the illogical proclivity of the mind to shut out awareness of what is right before it. The question stunned him.

'Oh, yes,' he managed. 'Morning and evening, humans go through the same routine. Caught up in the same rut of habit, we move in the same circle, interminably, endlessly, and are therefore round.'

The boy laughed uncertainly.

'True brilliance,' the father concluded, 'is to somehow break free of this rut.'

They were passing through a field where sugarcane had been harvested sometime in early February. The weak, white soil had cracked and clotted into a bumpy terrain where dried cane roots jutted out menacingly. Minute, earth-coloured insects and worms crawled through the bare roots, and yellowed pieces of sugarcane peel skittered and rustled in the warm gusts of wind. A line of rust-coloured birds zoomed past above their heads.

'They should have ploughed the field by now,' he said.

'So why haven't they?' the boy asked.

'You see, if you leave them long enough the sugarcane roots sprout a second time,' the man explained, 'but don't yield half as much as the first time. Farmers who are lazy lie back and content themselves with that.'

'Baaba, farmers don't shirk at what they do,' the boy said.

'Whoever said that? They are no different from anyone, son,' he said. 'And so they are round too.'

The boy laughed uncertainly again and sprinted off, leaving his father far behind on the trail. As the father watched, the boy's momentum carried him a few steps into the freshly ploughed field ahead, and his feet, shoes and all, suddenly sank into the soft, crumbly dirt. This brought him back to the time when he had been a little boy who loved to frisk barefoot in a freshly ploughed field, his feet sinking up to his ankles as though inhaled into the cottony-soft earth, the peculiar moist dirt beneath the soles of his feet, at once cool and warm, producing a sensation quite out of this world. He broke his stride, squinted his eyes and looked over the shimmering surface of the field, inhaling the ancient, familiar smell wafting from its powerful, satiated black soil. His nostrils began to quiver.

'The farmer of this field is definitely hard-working,' he concluded.

'Baaba, is he round too?' the boy asked, a mischievous glint playing in his eyes.

'You rascal!' he shouted and ran after the boy to grab him.

Running one behind the other on narrow trails and laughing now and then, father and son passed many fields. The boy, much faster and lighter of tread, was running ahead as easily and swiftly as a hare, while his father stumbled numerous times off the trail into the fields, some wet, some dry, and his shoes became covered with mud and dirt. Whenever the trail ended in a T-intersection, the boy stopped, momentarily unable to decide which way to turn. Then he would look back, and finding his father quickly catching up with him, blindly turn left or right and take off again. But within that brief instant of indecision the older man would close the gap some more.

The two now chased each other along a relatively wide and straight trail through wheat fields which were being watered perhaps for the last time before harvesting. Scared by the sound of their footfalls, a couple of hares and a wildcat suddenly appeared out of the crop on one side of the path, jumped in front of them clear across the trail and disappeared into the crop on the other side. A flock of tiny ash-coloured birds took flight from a field nearby, skimming low over the wheat stalks. A gust of wind teased the wheat spikes on one side of the trail, brushed the man's face, ruffling his hair and making his blood jump in his veins, and disappeared into the spikes on the other side. He was now only a step behind his son. A strong desire to stretch out his arms and grab his son's soft, warm, vibrant body overwhelmed him. But just as he proceeded to attempt it, the trail abruptly came to a dead end. A well stood in the way. He stopped short.

The same trail!—he marvelled, as his mind returned to a fond memory—why, even the same season! He was a seven-year-old boy running ahead of his father when the trail had come to an end just as suddenly and, unable to control himself, he had jumped clear across the ditch that irrigated the fields. His father, who was unnerved by the very idea of a jump of any sort, no matter how short or small, had stopped dead in his tracks and started to fumble in the air, as if straining to retrieve a precious object. The same fields, the same crops, the same water running in the ditch, the same fresh, warm breeze that rustled sweetly through the green-gold profusion of wheat stalks, the same flock of tiny ash-coloured birds floating only inches above the wheat spikes as father and son chased after each other with a passion—father and son and earth! How events had a way of coming full circle! And with an economy, discipline and clockwork precision that were truly mind-boggling! He was amazed.

He bent his knees and sat down at the water's edge, then thrust his hand into the clear running stream and peered into it, feeling in his fingertips the simultaneous warmth and coolness he had experienced, at seven years old, as a uniquely mysterious attribute of deep earth, running water and the human body. He smelt the nameless fragrance of the moist, cool dirt and the half-ripe wheat crop. The familiar smell was indeed still there. Now, at thirty-five, he was discovering the awesome and timeless magic of life that ran in circles, and thought: water changes into blood and is transmitted through the earth from one generation to the next, from father to son. From father to son!

As he gazed at his own fine hand floating before him on the water, he recalled that back then an astrologer used to sit behind the well, where the interrupted trail picked up again, with odd-shaped coins and small brass cubes with numbers etched on them strewn on a rag spread out in front of him. He pulled his hand from the stream, ran it over his face, then wiped it dry on his hair and stood up. The well droned on dreamily, worked by a pair of oxen. His son had meanwhile jumped up and perched on the shaft and was tugging at the tail of one of the blinkered animals. In a grove of jamun and mulberry trees to the right stood the farmer's mud house, and in front of it the farmer was busily cutting fodder with his chopper. A water buffalo stood tethered to the manger by the mud wall. A pesky crow, perched on the animal's back, was pecking at it relentlessly. He took in the tranquil, shaded scene for a while and then strolled over to the back of the well. The place where the astrologer used to sit was empty.

The sounds of the squeaky well, the running water and the chopper, and the putrid odour of leaves left to rot in the shady spots, assailed him from behind; the shimmering spring colours and sweet rustle of wheat spikes, gently swaying in their lush profusion, flooded his senses from in front. Why, of all places, he wondered, had the astrologer picked out this particular spot? The only people who ever came along this trail were peasants, and as far as he could remember, he had never seen a single peasant visit the old astrologer. Why? One of those mysteries, he thought, that inhabited the landscape of childhood. Stranger still, as long as the astrologer occupied that spot, an aura of supreme contentment and serenity enveloped him. An antique black chest always sat next to him with a few crumbling old books piled on top of it; leaning against them was a rectangular piece of cardboard bearing the image of a human hand, the palm showing a network of crudely drawn lines, and at the bottom were the boldly inscribed words: jyotish, ramal, nujum, abjad.*

'Abjad?' he had asked his father one day. 'What does abjad mean?'

And his father knew about the abjad, just as he knew about everything else. His father, who wore a long, drooping, affectionate moustache and was an expert in practically all the sciences, had replied, 'It is the science of names, son.'

'Names?'

'Yes, names.'

'How so, Baaba?'

'A man's name profoundly affects his life. The science that studies those effects is called abjad.'

'How does a name affect one's life?' he asked.

His father sat down comfortably on the trail and placed his shotgun in his lap. Then he had his son sit beside him and answered, 'All this is part of the science of words. And words, son, are full of magic.'

'Magic?'

'Oh, yes.'

'How?'

'It's like this,' his father began, snipping off an ear of wheat, which he then put in his mouth and began to chew. 'Let's take your name for example. Morning, noon and night, your mother and your sister, your teachers and your classmates call you by that name hundreds of times, and you respond

*These words roughly stand for, respectively, 'spells', 'geomancy', 'astrology' and 'charms' devised by using the letters of the Arabic alphabet.

to them. Certainly that is one function, but not the only function of a name. It doesn't stop there. Every time your name is called out, it changes into a word—it even assumes a palpable shape, which is then released into the air by the speaker's mouth. And you may think it just peters out then, but actually it never does. Why? Well, because it is a living thing. It shoots back to your star, because they're connected together. Whenever it's called out, it takes off with sonic speed and heads automatically'—Father was rather fond of using this word, he recalled and laughed—'for your star, and bang! It collides with it. Every single time! And that's how it comes to have influence over your life.'

'Star—what do you mean, Baaba?'

'Each of us has a star under which we're born, live and die.'

They got up from the trail and started off again, one behind the other. When his father interrupted the discussion a little later to say, 'Well, it's about time you read the biography of Napoleon,' the image of the fat, three-columned foxed tome with small type, its red binding faded by time and much use, arose ineluctably before his eyes. The volume used to lie on a small, low table by his father's chair, and the older man would pick it up now and then to read or scribble something in the margins. As the boy thought of the book—which always exuded the peculiar strong odour of ageing paper, a smell he knew as well as, say, the smell of his shoes or his bed—he blurted out without thinking, 'You know what, Baaba? When I grow up, I'll become a writer.' His innocent declaration prompted the strangest reaction in the older man: his eyes widened and he looked at his son almost with sadness. He sat down on the trail once again, put the shotgun in his lap, sat his son down at his side and then said, 'Words are full of magic, son, but it is hard to use them properly.'

'Hard—why, Baaba?'

'I'll tell you why.' His father's eyes narrowed as he looked at the sky. 'Writing words is as hard as clouds...'

'Clouds?'

'Yes. You see these clouds: for the past hour or so they have stood in the sky like solid rock sculptures of fluffed, freshly laundered cotton—even ironed, you could say, perfectly still and unchanging. Right?'

'I guess so.'

'You also see how every single jutting point, each curve, indeed every single line is so sharp it seems to have been carved out of granite. Don't you agree?'

'Absolutely, Baaba.'

'And yet, despite their clarity and silence, they are packed with such fury and violence, vitality and power that they become indelibly etched on the mind, so that if you have seen them once you are not likely to forget them for years and years.' The older man's eyes suddenly lit up with an immense flash. 'You see that, don't you?'

'Yes, Baaba, I do.'

'But...' The brightness died out of his eyes as suddenly as it had come. He broke off another wheat spear, sniffed it sadly, and said, 'These clouds come only once a year...in spring, for a few days only, just a few days. The rest of the year it is the same old clouds—dirty, mud-coloured, fuzzy, drab as a cobweb. They drift in, rant and roar, and kill...' he tossed the spike into the field and abruptly stood up, 'the wonderful colours of the sunlight.'

They started down the dirt trail again in single file. He understood very little of the import of his father's impassioned discourse, and didn't especially care. Soon he let it seep out of his mind. He hadn't been serious about becoming a writer anyway. He had burst out with the words spontaneously, without forethought. Much later, as a grown man, when he did try to write books, the essence of what his father had tried to communicate falteringly that afternoon had suddenly become absolutely clear. Whenever he was struck by the magic of a thought and tried to capture it in words, the magic faded away. He would look with mounting displeasure at the words he had scribbled—a disgusting pile of dead worms which could scarcely stir anyone—and then lapse into a daze. He searched the sky for the spring clouds, but they were still some time away; he wondered how his father, a man who had never in his life written a book, happened to know all those things. How could he?

Those clouds never returned. And neither did he find the exact word he was seeking. The impeccable word—honed of steel, crisp, precise and powerful, which breathed if you looked at it and throbbed like a heart with a life of its own if you uttered it—kept him enthralled with its silent magic but never emerged from the confines of his mind. He always knew that words possessed magical power, but how impossibly difficult it was to write them he learned only now. Yet write he did, strewing enormous quantities of squiggly worms, and even achieved a measure of fame, but in the end he failed like every other writer, even the greats.

'Baaba!' The boy threw his arms around the man's legs and asked, 'What are you doing?'

'I'm thinking, son.'

'What?'

'What am I thinking?' he squinted into the air above the field, straining his memory. 'Nothing in particular,' he said.

'Nothing?'

He abruptly plumped down on the ground and invited the boy to do the same. He picked up a dry, broken stick and drew a circle with it in the soil of the freshly ploughed field. 'Let me draw it for you,' he said. 'This circle, here, represents the human being's basic attitude. All our thoughts fall within it. The world outside the circle is the realm of the unknown, the dark.' He made two marks close together on the circumference. 'This tiny slice between the marks represents the realm of pure goodness. And this,' he guided the stick along the rim to the right of the slice, 'is where the domain of iniquity begins, and here,' he moved the stick to the left of the slice this time, 'begins negative goodness. The lines separating the three areas are very fine, indeed they are almost invisible. Even from up close, you'll have a hard time telling the three apart; they appear to be seamless. And yet they share one thing in common: people's basic attitude. Whether we try to do pure good, evil or something on the spectrum of iniquity, the basic human attitude remains inevitably aggressive. Now then, even when we appear to be thinking, we are scarcely thinking anything at all.'

'Anything at all?'

'That's right. Unless this basic attitude changes, there is little hope of breaking out of this circle, and unless that happens, we cannot reach out to the vast unknown that lies outside the circle. And I mean truly vast, so vast that, by comparison, this circle is no more than a mere speck. True knowledge resides outside the circle, in the realm of the unknown. Understand?'

The boy laughed, unsure of himself.

The man threw the stick away and got up. He wrapped his arms lovingly around his son's neck, and the two turned back towards the city. He knew the boy had scarcely understood a word. All the same, the thought that someday, somewhere, his son would find himself face to face with these truths and would then understand everything and remember him, brought a smile of deep satisfaction to his lips.

On the return trek they took different trails that eventually led back to the same point where they had abandoned the highway for a stroll through the fields. The boy had broken free of his father's clasping arms and was now running ahead of him picking wild spring flowers. Along both edges of the trail a linseed field unfurled its dizzying profusion of screaming red flowers, broken by the occasional violet-streaked tulip rearing its hesitant head. There was also a wild rose bush. As the unsuspecting boy tried to pick a rose, a thorn pricked his finger and a drop of blood, shining brilliantly in the sun, oozed from the pierced skin. The boy let out a mild cry and quickly sucked up the blood. The older man rushed to the boy, examined the finger and advised him to keep sucking. He carefully removed the rose from the bush and offered it to the boy, who added it to his bouquet and started off again. The father, trailing behind the son, lifted his right hand to his nose and sniffed the fingers. Doesn't smell like a rose at all, he concluded. He remembered his own father, who had remained all his life something of a black sheep in the family, because he had pursued the carefree life of an idler with a passion, and without a care squandered stupendous sums on the rather expensive hobby of hunting. He often heard his own mother complain about his irresponsibility and shiftless ways. All he ever cared to do was live life as fully as possible and contemplate its mysteries. He did as he damned well pleased and loved as he thought best. In the end, perhaps it wasn't such a bad thing.

As he stood by the rose bush watching his son dart here and there collecting wild flowers, an irresistible thought occurred to him: To be grateful to them, sons don't need their fathers' wealth, respectability or social position, perhaps not even their achievements. A certain fragrance is enough, a fragrance left on the fingers by the merest touch of a perfect rose. A scent left so subtly one is scarcely aware of it, but which later, quite by accident, when the hand passes by the face, wafts to his nostrils. One is pleasantly surprised, searches for it everywhere on the body, only to locate it, finally, in the pores of one's fingers. And then, remembering that somewhere in the past he too had come upon a rose, the son feels infinitely thankful.

The boy stopped, seeing his father still standing behind on the trail. 'Baaba!' he called and raised his fingers to his nose involuntarily, and when the older man caught up with him, asked, 'Baaba, what were you doing there?'

'I was thinking, son.'

'What were you thinking?' the boy asked, and with a mischievous glint in his eyes, sprinted off.

Before chasing after his son down the trail, he let forth a deep and throaty sound of happiness, something like the resounding bellow of an ox. They passed through many fields, running now at a fast clip, now slowly. The present trail cut through numerous wheat and chickpea fields, and in one of them a bunch of village urchins was roasting a stalk of tender green chickpeas still in the pods. The warm, delicious smell of roasting pods rose into the air. The man broke his stride and halted on the trail for a while to observe, with mingled joy and sadness, the burning, crackling chickpea plants, the billowing smoke, and the band of eager-faced boys sitting on their toes peering into the fire. Meanwhile his son too had stopped and was looking at the boys, his hands on his hips. Soon he scampered off again.

They came upon many patches of wild land as well as fields, some cultivated, others fallow. The rising spring breeze caressed their faces and moved gently on. Finally they abandoned the fields for the open road. For a while they stood side by side, alternately gasping and laughing, then the boy drew back a little and punched the man's thigh with all his might a few times before wrapping himself around his legs.

The sun had started to climb down. The country road, shimmering in its radiant heat, was nearly deserted, except for a few peasants and their womenfolk returning from the town market. The men carried bundles tied to sticks slung across their shoulders; the women, slippers in hand, balanced big earthen pots stacked high on their heads as their small caravan moved rhythmically along the edge of the road and down the sloping bridge.

The man once again curved his arm around his son's shoulder and began climbing slowly up the steep slope. Coming to the bridge, he stopped. The city, his city, stood straight ahead, bathed by the sun which shone directly above it. Once again he planted his hands on his hips, as if to catch his breath, and turned around to look one last time, deep and far into the brilliant, crisp colours of the spring afternoon. The emerald green of wheat and chickpea, the flaming red of linseed, the deep yellow of the scentless wild flowers, the almond brown of freshly ploughed fields, the darkish green of fruit trees, the azure sky, the shimmering white spring clouds—one by one and then all together, the riotous feast of colours assembled in front of his eyes. He stood still, gazed at length at the strange landscape before him, and remembered the man he had seen die. In the instant before death, how his drained face had flushed with a sudden return of colour, his eyes gleaming with an unusual brilliance. In those brief moments before his body turned cold, how incredibly healthy he had looked...and how handsome! He shaded his eyes with his hand and concentrated on the scene until his eyes had absorbed it entirely. And then he proceeded to cross the bridge.

Like a migratory bird, he had alighted in this city early this morning. In the first light—when the bazaars and narrow lanes were still empty, except for a few devout worshippers returning after the dawn prayer or some strollers out to take the air, walking along as they quietly brushed their teeth with acacia twigs—he had stood at the door of his ancestral house, looking at it with the diffidence of a stranger, his son in tow, his suitcase dangling from his hand. The city sweepers, their backs eternally bent, went about their business sweeping the bazaars and cleaning the open sewers that flowed in the narrow lanes. A milkman cycled past bearing two large containers, swaying under their weight. A beggar cried for alms in his loud, dreamlike voice. He gently dropped the suitcase on the small brick platform in front of the door and waited awhile, taking in the old familiar sounds. Twenty years had passed, but these sounds, the first sounds of the day, were still the same. As a young boy he would squirm in his bed when they woke him up each morning. Or perhaps it was the other way around: he heard them only after his sleep had already broken. As he stood before the door with his head drooping, he experienced again briefly that pleasing though oddly unreal state of drowsiness in which the acts of sleeping, waking and hearing all merge indistinguishably. Nowhere, not in any other bed or bedroom, could he recall experiencing that state after he had left here. He raised his hand and gently rapped on the door—once, twice and a third time, while his son, stupefied by it all, just gawked at the tall houses around him. Two pigeons huddled under the eaves of a house suddenly took flight into the dim sky. The window of a top-floor room opened.

'Who is it?' a girl's head poked out of the window, her voice groggy. 'It's me,' the man answered dumbly, raising his head.

The girl's face disappeared behind the closing window. He looked around him nervously. There was the sound of feet descending a staircase, and shortly thereafter the door was flung open. 'Uncle!' the girl whispered, holding her breath.

He looked at the girl, scrutinizing her whole body, tall and slim and young, and realized the inevitable passage of time. He put the suitcase down inside the entranceway and hugged the young stranger. The muffled sound of a door opening and then closing came from the upper floor. He stepped onto the staircase. One look at the stone stairs and the colour of the walls, scarcely changed or even aged, seemed to transport him back twenty years into the world of his childhood. As he climbed the stairs slowly with his head bent low, a strange feeling overcame him, a feeling of familiarity and foreignness, the lot of every exile returning home after a long absence. It is something that is not just the perceptions of the eye and ear, but is sensed all over the skin and vibrates beneath it in the rhythms of the blood, making the body break out in goose bumps and time stand still.

He looked up. At the top of the stairs, leaning against the ledge, his sister stood waiting for him. More than half her hair had turned grey, the skin of her face was loose and sagging, and her large, gaping eyes bore the emptiness found only in the eyes of suffering women. He stopped a few steps from where she was standing and just stared at her quietly in the gathering daylight. She was only five years older than he. Graceful, tall, slim and vibrant with the nervous energy of first youth when he had left. For the second time, the flight of years gave him a rude jolt.

'Saeed...' her weak, quivering voice rose, and he didn't know when he moved, clambered up the remaining steps, came close to her and hugged her madly like a child, his heart drained of blood at the feel of a skeleton beneath her baggy clothing. He was only aware of holding against him a bag of bones, rocking perilously with each escaping breath, and of a smell as ancient, familiar and pleasing as the dreamy, half-asleep, half-awake inarticulate noises of first light, a smell that wafted from suckling babies and from sisters with whom one has cuddled and played in childhood. Raising his head for a moment, with no particular thought in mind, he saw his son and the tall, slim girl looking at him and his sister in wide-eyed worry, and a pair of golden pigeons cavorting joyously across the patch of sky visible above the corner of the courtyard. Thus without any great desire for the awareness, he realized that the sun had risen and the heart was but a scrap of wet rag being mercilessly wrung out. In another sense he had realized nothing, for time had lost itself in two bodies long exiled from each other, but of identical colour and smell.

Later he found himself eating breakfast in the big room, listening to his sister, who sat opposite him with his son in her lap. 'I got your letter,' she was saying, while he ran his eyes over every detail in the room between sips of tea. Out of all the furnishings he recognized only the massive walnut chest that stood in a corner. Everything else looked totally unfamiliar. The day the gigantic chest had been hauled into the house was still vivid in his memory. It was so large and unwieldy that it had gotten stuck midway up the narrow staircase. His father, towering at the top of the stairs like some decorated general on the battlefield, rained a barrage of instructions on the eight labourers who now pushed, now pulled the piece with all their strength, sweating profusely from the effort. He had just returned from school, a bit late, and was famished; he wanted to rush up to the upper floor. But there it was, stuck midway, unbudging, affording not the slightest space to crawl through as the eight stout, hardy men—in threadbare loincloths, their throbbing muscles glistening in the half-light, their bodies reeking of the strong odour of labour and poverty—fumbled dumbly with the improbably heavy piece, four in front and four in the back, his father's angry, crisp voice cracking like a whip above them. He smiled vaguely. The wooden chest, whose dark, wavy grain showed through the varnish on the surface, was used for many years to store an assortment of damask, cotton carpets and lightweight comforters, while its lowest drawer housed the extra bedposts and an old broken banjo. Whenever it was opened, a gust of its odour filled the air, the mingled smell of walnut and raw jute, wholly unlike any other odour in the world outside the chest.

As he took the last sip of tea, he felt an overwhelming desire to walk over to the chest and open it to see what kinds of things were stored in it and what kind of smell burst forth from it now.

'You didn't bring your wife along?' his sister was asking him, and he rambled on in answer. He was scarcely aware of the words spilling out of his mouth. His age seemed to have coiled back into his senses of smell, hearing and sight, and his eyes sought his sister in the form of the delicate, trim, tall girl who was now moving about in the room that had been his for many long years, bending over to stare at him and his son with a look that bespoke closeness and distance in equal measure.

One of the walls of his room, made entirely of wood, separated the bathroom. It shook violently whenever one tapped it. In a recess in another wall stood a wardrobe with a mirror. The mirror was so tall that one could see one's whole body in it. One of the upper shelves inside the wardrobe was always occupied by a copy of the Holy Quran, and one of the lower ones by a broken rosary belonging to someone—God knows whom. The third wall had two windows that opened into the alleyway. The windows used to be covered with a delicate mesh through which the slow, sleepy noises of dawn filtered in. Once, very early, before daybreak, guests had arrived in the house opposite, which sent their little boy scampering out in the alleyway, singing away jubilantly 'Dilwale...' He had heard that snatch of song dimly through his sleep; he had slowly awakened to it and found himself repeating it over and over again until the sound condensed into a body and acquired a colour—a rich golden colour that had lost none of its brilliance even after the inexorable passage of time. And it was thus that he discovered that if the past had a colour, it had to be a dazzling gold.

A violent desire arose in him to overturn the breakfast tray, dash off to his room, and peek in through the door to see what it looked like now and what sort of things it contained.

'You were wild in the head, Saeed,' his sister was saying wistfully. 'You take after our father so much.'

He got up. Large framed photographs of his long-dead parents, their smiles etched eternally on their faces, adorned the mantle above the fireplace. He also recognized his sister's husband, whom he had never met and probably never would. What could he have said to her—what? He yawned and quietly walked over to the bed and stretched out on it. Minutes later, he was fast asleep, his feet still in his shoes.

When he got up, his shoes were lying neatly beside the bed and all the doors were closed. He could hear the faint shuffle of tiptoeing feet—his sister, his niece and the maid, outside on the porch and in the kitchen—and the cackling laughter of his son rising above it.

After lunch he took leave of his sister for a couple of hours and went out with his son. On the way to the bazaar they came across four men who peered at them closely and then quietly moved along. Finding himself a stranger in a once familiar setting, he was gripped by embarrassment as he entered the bazaar. Hurriedly he raised his collar, pulled his felt hat quite low over his eyes, and with hands jammed in his pant pockets walked the entire length of the bazaar, indeed the whole city, as invisibly as though he were wearing King Solomon's magic cap. No one recognized him. This made him feel strangely sad and at the same time quite relieved. Returning now from his long afternoon stroll through the fields, before re-entering the city he once again lowered his hat, raised his jacket collar, and began his climb down the bridge with hands stuffed into his pockets.

Shielded by his newly acquired anonymity he covered half the city's length along the Circular Road before finally entering the bazaar. The dust kicked up by horse-driven carriages and automobiles had settled on his hat and shoulders and glinted in the last rays of the sun. Clouds had begun to gather around the sun. In the bazaar he recognized Rahim, who sold sweet iced drinks. He sported a dazzling white beard now. He was perched on his seat in the same old way, fanning away the pesky flies that buzzed incessantly above an assortment of bottles of homemade syrups, each a different colour. Once, at this very spot, Rahim had single-handedly taken on a band of seven robbers. But that was a different time, when Rahim used to wear a fine muslin shirt which generously revealed the firm grace of his form, his gently sloping shoulder blades and his taut, muscular arms. Now, though, the face buried in the thick white beard was recognizable only with the greatest difficulty.

He also recognized a number of other shopkeepers who sat behind the counter, each in his own timeless way. A few pedestrians probed and prodded him with inquisitive eyes and moved on, then turned to look back at him again, as if straining to place him by his gait, to remember something—but in vain. Twenty years is a long time, long enough to change childhood into youth, youth into old age, and to blur the memory. Instead of returning straight home, he turned into a lane on the right.

The lane, lumpily paved with bricks, embodied the whole of his carefree past, bearing traces of numberless ancient footfalls left strangely unaffected by time. The narrow street was almost empty at this hour; he took heart, pushed his hat up over his eyes and ran his fingers through his son's hair. The rising and falling hum of the bazaar was receding now, giving way to the noises peculiar to the lane: the languorous, hushed voices of women as they sat behind their porch windows chatting across the lane, cooking vegetables and peering at the passers-by; the suggestive squeak of a door opening behind them somewhere in the house, then closing; the mysterious, rhythmic sound of bodies meeting in the act of love in the cool comfort of darkened rooms, or simply lying at rest; the droning stillness of the afternoon.

He felt a powerful urge to spread out his arms and run down the lane making wild noises as he used to long ago, as a little boy, but the lingering feeling of estrangement quenched it; instead, he curved an arm around his son's shoulder and strode on through the lane with the stiff, purposeful gait of a middle-aged man or a pilgrim, yet supremely attentive not to disturb the patterns left on the brick path by his youthful feet in an ancient time. The women craned their necks to look at the pair, then their thoughts drifted off to other things. And countless men and women, inaudibly mumbling in their sleep after making love in the dark coolness of their rooms, didn't even notice the two.

This house, there, was where his friend Om lived; his sister, Pushpa, used to tie a rakhi around his wrist every year. Where might they be now? he wondered. Back then they all went to the same primary school and at least twice a week Pushpa would say to him, 'You know what? We've cooked a vegetable dish today.' Without further thought he would walk over to their house with them. They would settle down in the cool outer hall and eat puffy, round, paper-light chapattis with a vegetable dish served in tiny, glittering brass bowls. Later they would play on the steps of Pushpa and Om's porch, and no one in his family would worry as to his whereabouts. For in those days he had not just one house but two, his own, of course, and this other belonging to Pushpa and Om.

He broke his stride and peeked through the open door of the house—the outer hall, the courtyard, the storeroom, the staircase on the right—everything was the same, except a different family lived here now. The grey-haired old woman who sat in the outer hall working the spinning wheel lifted her dull eyes to look at him.

'What do you want, brother?' she said.

His eyes played over the beams supporting the hall ceiling.

'Who are you looking for, brother?' the old woman asked again.

'No one, Bibi,' he said in a low voice. His eyes fell upon the heap of cotton lying next to the old woman, and he wondered whether it came from this year's harvest. He ran his fingers through his son's hair once more and started off again.

The house exuded a strange, cool smell, he recalled, which also emanated from the bodies of Om and Pushpa. On waking up from an afternoon nap, his eyes still closed, it was this smell that would tell him that he had been sleeping in their house. He would open his eyes, catch the glitter of brass pots and pans on the walls of the dark room and sit up. Today, without that familiar smell, this house which as a child he had considered his own, had become a perfect stranger. Everything else was the same, only that smell had vanished—a smell which had no fixed domicile yet possessed a body, passed easily from place to place and also succumbed to death.

He was now passing by his old school. The good thing about the school was that it was located right in the neighbourhood and all the children went to it. This was the back of the school building, whose gate and several windows were crossed by horizontal iron bars, just like the doors of prisons and strongholds for treasure. The main gate faced the Circular Road. He removed his hand from his son's shoulder, walked over to the gate, and grabbing the iron bars, pressed his face against them like a prisoner and peered inside. School had ended a short while before and the janitors were closing up the classrooms. A few teachers stood leaning on their bikes on the veranda, chatting. The classroom directly across from him was for the fourth graders. He peered into it from behind the bars. He could see a chaotic jumble of desks smudged with ink stains, and on the blackboard was a division problem, solved but half erased. A framed picture of Allama Iqbal hung skewed on the wall facing him. It was the fourth-grade classroom, he repeated in his heart, where he had spent a whole year. He remembered how the boy who used to sit next to him reeked of old ink rags, and the boy next to that one always gave off an odour of the moist clay used on writing tablets and the dry, crisp smell of freshly sharpened reed pens, which he found infinitely pleasing. His true friendship, though, was only with Om and Pushpa, who sat in the second row, along with their own friends. During lunch break they would all scramble to the tap to apply a thick emulsion of clay over their writing tablets. Whenever one of them, while smoothing the freshly applied clay with the hand, left their clod of clay unattended, another would stealthily pick it up, quickly rub it on their own tablet, and return it to its place quite as stealthily, and in the confusion no one was the wiser.

He pulled back his face and gently rubbed his forehead where the iron bars had left their impression. Once again he ruffled his son's hair and laughed slowly. The two started off again.

Now, the house that stood next to the school held a great mystery for him. One look at it instantly brought to mind the man who had lived here, a tall, trim man of forty-five, maybe fifty, who always appeared clad in the outfit of the Khaksars, his pockets alwaya stuffed with Urdu newspapers and magazines. He owned a bicycle, from which dangled an odd assortment of old eyeglasses. Ostensibly he sold them, but nobody had ever actually seen him make a sale. All he would do was stop every few steps as he dragged his bicycle along in the bazaar, emit a deep, throaty cry: 'Chor uchakka chaudhri aur ghundi ran pardhan!' (Pickpockets and robbers for dignitaries! Common whores as honoured matrons!), and then eye the space around him with an air of childlike innocence and triumph. The shopkeepers would look at him tenderly, then laugh in embarrassment as if they were somehow implicated in the cry, even if they were not its target. After shouting his slogan, the man too would laugh light-heartedly and go on his way. His tone of voice and his face reflected no bitterness, only good cheer and a trace of harmless sarcasm. And his words were quite incongruous with his appearance and gait. He looked like everybody's friend, though no one had ever seen him stop for an amiable chat with anyone. Every morning, after he and his friends reached school, they would see the man emerge from the house with his bicycle and fix a padlock on the door. As they stood there and watched, he would step into the street, raise, without fail, his deep and throaty cry, 'Chor uchakka chaudhri aur ghundi ran pardhan!', dart his innocent, triumphant gaze over the faces of the schoolchildren gathered in the lane, and walk off towards the city.

No one even knew the day the man died. For three days his door remained latched from inside, he recalled, until the stench spilled out and hung in the air. The schoolteachers were the first to rush to the door. They pounded on it steadily. A few children who had scrambled to the scene, drawn by the noise, told them they hadn't seen the man come out of the house at all in the last three days. Neighbours gathered, the police arrived. They pounded on the door, called out his name, even tried to peek in through the cracks, and finally decided to break in. Inside, the man was found sitting in a chair, as casually as one sits at a meal, only his hand had slid off to one side. A scrap of paper and a writing pen lay in front of him on the table, with, he would find out much later, 'Chor uchakka chaudhri aur ghundi ran pardhan!' scribbled on the paper.

Through the legs of the grown-ups bursting into the room he had only had time to catch a glimpse of the man, and then a burst of stench hit him and sent him reeling outside vomiting into the open gutter. That day Pushpa told him not once but twice that vegetables had been prepared at her house, but he scarcely heard her and returned home straightaway. For the next few days he was unable to hold any food or drink.

He quickly turned and stepped into the street where, at the very end, his parental house was founded. Women ensconced behind their doorways or windows for an afternoon chat eyed him with interest, which made him feel self-conscious. Nervously he pulled up his collar, dropped his hat low over his forehead, jammed his hands into his coat pockets and walked on with his eyes fixed straight in front of him. Inside his pocket, his fingers counted out the change: five annas and three paise—his entire capital!

The clouds had now covered the sun completely, and a moist wind, bearing news of the coming rain, had started to blow. By the time he reached the door of his house, the first drops had already plopped down on his hat.

His son rushed to the stairs ahead of him, thumping up the steps. Raindrops fell, rapid and noisy, on the window eaves, and as they absorbed the moisture, the parched walls released a warm, soothing fragrance identified with raw earth. The precious smell that always came with the first rain showers and faded away quickly. He lingered briefly on the stairway, drew a few long breaths, and heard the joyous laughs of women somewhere in the house. Upstairs he saw his niece frantically running about the porch, pulling down the wet laundry from the clothesline, dragging the cots about and laughing. His sister, who had been sitting on the porch talking with a neighbour, quickly stood up, uttering a benedictory bismillah, as she saw him enter. The other woman turned around and looked at him with marked interest. But he crossed the porch and headed back to his room, his hands still stuffed in his pockets, his shoulders hunched. Then, just before crossing the threshold of his room, he froze.

His heart leapt violently, came halfway down, and remained, as it were, suspended in mid-air. He couldn't even turn around and look back; his head hung low as he stood at the door immobile, remembering, as the fat raindrops plopped down on his hat.

Nuri!—the canyons of his mind resonated—Nuri!

He began to breathe deeply, but couldn't retrieve that priceless fragrance that emanated from the walls with the first showers. It was gone. Very slowly he turned around and planted himself in full view of the portly middle-aged woman sitting on a cot on the porch.

'Nuri!' his lips moved but remained voiceless. The woman stared at him with a smile at once of recoiling modesty and welcoming familiarity. Rooted to the spot, he stared back at her as the raindrops tumbled over his blank, expressionless face like moments: drip-drop, drip-drop.

'Saeed!' his sister's voice rose, 'it's raining.'

He turned around as if in sleep, crossed the threshold and stood in the centre of the room. His son was comfortably settled in a chair, hands spread out on the armrests, staring blankly into the rain. He remained standing, immobile, his hands still in his pockets, as occasional drops of rain rolled over the brim of his hat and dripped from his shoulders and sleeves onto the floor: drip-drop, drip-drop. He was only eleven years old then and this portly woman, a lithe girl whose swaying body recalled the winding, upward motion and grace of a delicate vine. An impatient energy informed all her movements—she seemed scarcely to walk, but rather always to be running, thumping up and down the stairs and out into the lane; her skin was the colour of honey. The only solace of an eleven-year-old heart—he smiled distractedly and felt his heart return to its place. He breathed easily and lightly again. She was much older than he and wouldn't give him the time of day, of course. Still, for long hours, he would wait—glued to the door of his room or standing on the porch, at the window, in the street, at his house or at hers, anywhere and everywhere—to catch a glimpse of her, only to feel infinitely sad if he succeeded. This young woman exerted on that eleven-year-old boy a rich golden magic no one else could work, not his mother, his sister, his father or anyone. Every day, month and year, how he had waited for a glimpse of her, he remembered, and how she had remained oblivious of him the whole time, as if he didn't exist. Finally, when he had left home, he seemed to have brought her along—that golden image of the blossoming girl propelled with youthful energy; the first woman to steal his heart, whom he was never able to quite forget. He laughed again, as if trying to think away an unseen clap of thunder.

Afterwards many women had entered his life and gone out of it. Their fascination too disappeared with time, but not the fascination of that girl. It had endured. One image remained unalterably fixed in a corner of his heart. Its quiet rays guided him like a beacon, propelling him towards the next love after the last one had ended, keeping him eternally young with its endless reserve of warmth. He had never imagined in his wildest dreams that he would once again find himself face to face with his first love, and least of all in the present manner.

It was like a rock flying out of nowhere and striking a windowpane, causing the glass to crack into a web of lines but leaving the pane intact in its frame, each splinter reflecting a broken image: an eye here, a nose there, an ear here, a lip there—a frightening picture!

Still standing rooted in place, he craned his neck back to look out through the door. The cot was empty; there was only his sister, carrying a chair which she set down beside him.

'Nuri,' he heard her say, '…you recognized her, didn't you? Poor woman, her husband…'

He threw himself into the chair, unbuttoned his collar and ran his fingers slowly over his chest, as if trying to trace the lines of splintered glass. Outside the rain pelted down relentlessly, washing away the names and signs children had scribbled on the walls in chalk or clay. Just then, inexplicably, and suddenly, he remembered the splendid rooster—a bright golden-red one, wasn't it?—that they had slaughtered during a picnic at the beach. They had just killed the bird and laid it down when it suddenly sprang up and ran away, its throat slit, its half-severed head dangling to one side and bouncing like a flap as it violently fluttered away with its wings fanned out. Everyone took off after the rooster, but it fell into the river. The river was quite deep at that spot, and those of their party who could swim had all gone to fetch firewood. The rooster floated further and further downstream with the current. Their mouths gaping in disbelief, they gawked at the receding bird for a long moment like a pack of simpering fools, and afterwards laughed themselves silly as they puzzled over how the rooster, motionless once it had plopped into the river, had managed to spring up and sprint off.

All these years after the picnic, the memory of the rooster had come back to him once again. But this time he didn't find anything amusing in the scene. If anything, it appeared exceedingly tragic, and it saddened him greatly. And he asked himself with mild surprise: Where is the shoreline of these things that can take lifetimes to unearth?

He laughed again, but blankly, like the frightened laugh of a child walking, step by timid step, towards a pet animal. He got up again with a start.

Meanwhile his son had dozed off in the chair, his head lolling to one side. He was breathing deeply, his arms still on the armrests. Outside it was raining hard. The spell was breaking.

He pushed the brim of his hat high on his forehead, lowered his upturned collar, picked up the raincoat from the peg and slipped it on.

'Where to now?' his sister asked.

'I'm going out.'

'But Saeed, it's raining.'

'I'll be back soon. Don't you worry.'

'Saeed,' she raised her entreating eyes and asked timidly, 'you've come to stay, haven't you?'

'Yes.' He looked at his motherless child absent-mindedly and walked towards the door. Then suddenly remembering something, he turned around and looked boldly into his sister's eyes and laughed. 'Yes,' he said, 'I've come to stay.' He crossed the porch and began climbing down the stairs.

In the anteroom he met his niece, who had just stepped inside the house. She was drenched, carrying an empty pot in one hand and holding the bottoms of her shalwar in the other. He gently pinched her nose and asked, 'Where did you run off to, tabby cat?'

The girl twisted her body sharply and laughed, with a feeling of perfect closeness for the first time, and then said, 'I just stepped out for a minute, Uncle.'

He briefly stopped in the doorway, took off his hat and meticulously positioned it far back on his head. Then he stuck out his hand to feel the strength of the rain. A young boy leaning against the door of the house across from theirs was staring at him with eager but immensely sad eyes. The doors of the other houses in the neighbourhood were partly or entirely closed. Not a soul could be seen far and wide, except for a few birds that chirruped drowsily as they huddled under the eaves to avoid the rain. An unconscious smile broke on his lips as he stepped into the street paved with red bricks. With the unhurried gait of a cheerful man, he picked his way to the bazaar with the intention to seek out and visit his old acquaintances. The streets and neighbourhoods were almost empty in the pelting rain. Daylight was slowly ebbing away. Something—exceedingly delicate but ancient and powerful—had finally snapped and come loose inside him and was circulating freely in his blood. It had taken a lifetime to finally subdue his heart. During that time he had somehow managed to live. Today he was neither happy about it nor angry; he simply felt the beat of countless raindrops falling on his face. In his heart he knew that the raindrops had neither colour nor tone—only vitality and life.

OF FISTS AND RUBS

ISMAT CHUGHTAI

There was quite a crush of people at the polling station, as if it was the premiere of some movie. A long line stretched out to infinity. Five years ago, too, we'd formed such endless lines, as if we'd come to buy cheap grain, not to cast a vote. Wisps of hope flitted across our faces: regardless of how long the lines, our turn was bound to come sometime. And then you just watch, we'll be raking in piles and piles of money. He's our trusted man; the reins of good fortune will be in the hands of one of our own. All our miseries will vanish.

'Bai, O Bai! How are you?' The woman wrapped in a dirty-looking kashta bared her filthy, yellow teeth and grabbed my hand.

'Oh, it's you, Ganga Bai…'

'No, Ratti Bai. Ganga Bai was the other one. She died, poor woman.'

'What a pity! Poor woman…' And my mind zoomed back five years. 'Rubs or fists?' I asked.

'Rubs,' Ratti Bai winked. 'I kept telling her not to, but why would she listen, the blasted woman. Who are you voting for, Bai?'

'And you, who for?' we asked each other casually.

'Our caste-wallah, of course. He comes from our area.'

'Five years ago, too, you voted for a man of your own caste, didn't you?'

'Yes, Bai. But he turned out to be a real scrap. He did nothing for us,' she said, making a long face.

'And this one, he's also from your caste.'

'But he's really first class. Yes, Bai. You'll see, he'll get us our farmland.'

'And then you'll go back to your village and thrash rice.'

'Yes, Bai,' her eyes flashed.

Five years ago, when I was in the hospital giving birth to my Munni, Ratti Bai said that she was on her way to the polling station to vote for her caste-man. He'd made a solemn promise before a crowd of tens of thousands gathered at Chowpatty that the second he came into power he would change everything. Milk would flow in rivers, life would become as sweet as honey. Today, five years later, Ratti Bai's sari was even shabbier, her hair even more grey and her eyes twice as dazed. Hobbling on the crutches of promises made again today at Chowpatty, she'd come to cast her vote.

'Bai, why do you talk to that slut so much,' Ratti Bai opened her bundle of exhortations and advice as she pushed the bedpan under my cot.

'Why? What's the harm?' I asked, acting as though I didn't know.

'Haven't I told you? She's a very bad woman? Downright wicked, a slut.'

Before Ratti Bai came on her rounds, Ganga Bai had used exactly the same words to let me know her opinion of the former: 'Ratti Bai's a first-rate tramp.' The two hospital workers were always at loggerheads. Now and then they didn't even hesitate before coming to blows. I heartily enjoyed talking to them.

'That bum Shankar, he's not her brother.' Ganga Bai told me. 'He's her lover. Why, she sleeps with him!'

Ratti Bai's husband lived in a village near Sholapur. He had a small piece of land and was stuck to it. The entire yield was sucked up by debt and interest payments. Just a little bit was left; before long it too would be paid up. Then she would go and live with her children, happily ever after threshing rice to separate it from the husk. Both women dreamed with such longing of living happily pounding rice in their homes, the way a person dreams of Paris.

'But Ratti Bai, why did you come to Bombay to earn money? It would have made more sense to have your husband come instead.'

'Oh Bai, how could he? He works in the field. I couldn't have managed farming.'

'And who looks after the children?'

'Oh, there's a slut,' she said, calling her every bad name in the book.

'He hasn't married another woman, has he?'

'The bastard, he hasn't got the guts. No, she's a keep.'

'What if she becomes the mistress of the house in your absence?'

'How could she? Wouldn't I beat her hollow and stuff her with hay? Once we've repaid the debt, I'll go back.'

It turned out that Ratti Bai had herself chosen the poor, helpless woman left to care for her husband and children. Once the field became theirs, she would return home as a proper housewife and thresh rice. And what would become of the keep? Oh, she would find another man whose wife has gone to Bombay to earn money and who had no one to look after the kids.

'Doesn't she have a husband?' I asked.

'Why of course.'

'So why doesn't she live with him?'

'The little land he had owned was gobbled up. He works as a farm labourer, but for eight months of the year he steals and pilfers, or wanders into big cities and supports himself panhandling all day long.'

'Does she have children?'

'Of course she does. Four, at least she used to. One was lost right here in Bombay. Nobody ever found out what became of him. The two girls ran away and the youngest boy lives with him.'

'How much money do you send back to the village?'

'The full forty-one.'

'How do you get by?'

'My brother supports me.' The same brother Ganga Bai had said was her lover.

'Doesn't your brother have a family of his own?'

'Of course he does.'

'Where do they live? In the village?'

'Yes. It's a place near Poona. His elder brother takes care of the farming.'

'You mean *your* elder brother,' I said just to tease her.

'Come on now. Stop it! Why would he be *my* brother? Oh Bai, do you really take me for that kind of woman? I'm not like Ganga Bai. Do you know, hardly four days go by in a month that she doesn't receive a beating. Bai, if you've got any old, worn-out clothes, don't give them to that vile woman. Give them to me instead. Okay?'

'Ratti Bai.'

'Yes, Bai.'

'Does your "brother" whack you?'

'That tart Ganga Bai, she must have told you that. No, Bai, not very much. Just sometimes, when he's had too much to drink. But then he also shows affection.'

'He shows affection too?'

'Why wouldn't he?'

'But Ratti Bai, why do you call that scoundrel a brother?'

She started to laugh. 'Bai, that's just how we talk.'

'But Ratti Bai, when you earn forty rupees, why whore around?'

'How else would I manage? Three rupees for renting the kholi, the rathole where I live, and then I have to pay five to Lala.'

'To Lala, whatever for?'

'All the chawli women have to, otherwise he would throw us out.'

'Because you carry on this business?'

'Yes, Bai,' she seemed somewhat embarrassed.

'And your "brother", what does he do?'

'Bai, really I shouldn't say, but selling drugs is a nasty business. If someone doesn't bribe the police, they chase him out.'

'You mean throw him out of Bombay?'

'Yes, Bai.'

Meanwhile a nurse barged in and scolded her, 'What are you doing here jabbering away. Go, the bedpan needs to be removed in No. 10.' Ratti Bai promptly left the room, grinning, flashing her yellowed teeth.

'What's with you, you spend hours talking to these loose women. You need rest, otherwise you'll start bleeding all over again.' The nurse picked up my baby girl from the hammock and left the room.

Ganga Bai was on duty in the evening. She walked into my room without bothering to ring the bell first.

'Bai, I've come for the bedpan.'

'Oh no, Ganga Bai. Sit.'

'The sister will start hollering. The slut. What was she telling you?'

'Sister? Oh, she was telling me to rest.'

'No, not the sister. I mean that Ratti Bai.'

'Just that Popat Lal beats Ganga Bai black and blue,' I teased her.

'That son of a bitch, forget it. He wouldn't dare.' Ganga Bai started pounding slowly on my legs with her fists.

'Bai, you promised to give me your old chappals.'

'Okay, take them. But tell me whether you got a letter from your husband.'

'Of course.' Ganga Bai promptly pounced on the chappals. 'If that whore of a sister saw it, she would kick up a ruckus. She makes too much fuss.'

'Ganga Bai.'

'Yes, Bai.'

'When will you return to your village?'

Ganga's shining black eyes drifted off to the lush green haze of fields far away. She took a deep breath and said softly, 'May Ram give us an abundant crop this time. And then, Bai, I will go back. Last year the flood ruined all our rice paddy.'

'Ganga Bai, does your husband know about your "friends"?' I probed.

'What are you saying, Bai.' She became deathly quiet. I sensed she was feeling somewhat embarrassed. She immediately tried to change the subject, 'Bai, you had two girls in a row. The seth will be mighty angry, won't he?'

'Seth—who?' I asked, confused.

'Your husband. What if he got himself another wife?'

'If he did, I would also find myself another husband.'

'Your people do that? Bai, I thought you come from a high caste.' I couldn't help feeling that she was making fun of high-caste people. I tried my best to make her understand, but she firmly believed that by giving birth to a second girl I really would be thrashed. If my seth didn't beat me black and blue, then he must be an absolutely third-class seth.

Staying in a hospital is nothing less than solitary confinement. Friends and acquaintances visited me for two hours in the evening, the rest of the time I spent chatting and gossiping with Ganga Bai and Ratti Bai. Had it not been for them, I would probably have died long before then from boredom. A little bribe was all it took to get them to spill all kinds of things about each other, whether true or false. One day I asked Ratti Bai, 'You used to work in a mill, so why did you give that up?'

'Oh Bai, the blasted mill was a racket.'

'Racket?'

'Oh Bai, for one thing, it was awfully hard work. Still that would've been bearable, but the bastards kicked you out after a couple of months.'

'How so?'

'They would hire other bai log.'

'Why would they do that?'

'Why? Because if a person stayed for six full months, the Factory Law kicked in.'

'Oh, now I get it.'

In other words, the entire staff changed every few months. If any worker stayed longer in her job, she would be entitled to sick leave, maternity leave, the works, to comply with the Factory Law. So they kept switching workers every couple of months. That way a worker was employed for hardly four months a year. In between, women often returned to their villages. Those who couldn't afford to would run around to other factories looking for work. Some would roost along the sidewalks selling piles of rotten old vegetables. Swearing matches and fights broke out over turf. And since they carried on without a licence, they had to cough up some dough to 'feed' the policeman at the corner. Still, when an unfamiliar officer wandered that way now and then, there would be a veritable stampede. Some would quickly bag their merchandise and slither into a side street; some would get caught and start crying and wailing. But the police kept dragging them to the station. When the situation cleared up, they would swarm back, spread their tattered pieces of cloth and put their wares on display. The clever ones threw a few limes and ears of corn into a shoulder bag and walked along pretending to be shoppers themselves. When someone passed by, they would utter softly, 'Hey brother, buy some corn. Just one anna a piece.' Buying vegetables from one of them was to practically invite cholera.

The totally wretched ones resorted to begging, and if the opportunity presented itself they weren't above a quickie on the run. Perfectly primped, at least in their opinion, with a wad of paan stuffed in their mouths, they strolled up and down in the dimly lit area by the railway station. A customer walked in, glances were exchanged, and the deal was struck. The customers were mostly milkmen from Uttar Pradesh, or homeless labourers with wives back in villages, or eternal bachelors who only had these squalid streets and sidewalks to call home.

One morning a brawl broke out between the two bais on the veranda. Ratti Bai plucked out Ganga Bai's topknot. In return, Ganga Bai broke Ratti Bai's mangalsutra—her marriage necklace of black glass beads— an assurance that her husband was still alive. The poor woman started sobbing inconsolably as if she'd been widowed. The cause of the fight was the cotton pads that were used for cleaning wounds or for pregnant women and then discarded. According to the city ordinance, they had to be carefully burned, but it turned out that the two bais would remove the soiled cotton from the containers, wash it clean, roll it into a bundle and take it home. Since their relationship had become quite tense lately, Ganga Bai snitched about it to the supervisor. Ratti Bai started swearing at her, which quickly turned into fisticuffs. Both of them would have been fired but they whined and pleaded so much that the supervisor kept the matter under wraps.

Ratti Bai was a bit flabby and older. Ganga had really let her have it. When she came in to return the bedpan with a swollen nose, I asked, 'What do you do with the dirty cotton, Ratti Bai?'

'Wash it and dry it. It's perfectly clean.'

'And then?'

'Then we sell it to the cotton merchant.'

'Who would buy such germ-filled cotton from him?'

'The mattress man—the one who makes cushions for rich people's furniture.'

'Oh my God!' I bristled with revulsion. I remembered that when I had the cotton removed from a wicker sofa so that it could be re-fluffed, it had turned out to be completely dark. Oh no, was it the same cotton that was used for cleaning and dressing wounds! Is my daughter's mattress made from that too? My daughter, as delicate and fair as a flower, and this pile of germs! God curse you Ganga Bai! God take you away Ratti Bai!

Because they had gone after each other with their shoes today, Ratti Bai was writhing inside. And since Ganga was relatively younger, Ratti Bai considered her a greater sinner than herself. To add more fuel to the fire, a few days ago she'd managed to snatch Ratti Bai's standing customer. All those abortions Ganga Bai had had over time, and the live baby she had dumped in the gutter that still kept breathing even after she stuffed the umbilical cord in its mouth! A whole crowd had gathered near it. If Ratti Bai had wanted to, she could easily have spilled the beans and gotten her caught, but she buried the secret in her chest. And look at the cheek of that vile woman, the way she sits on the sidewalk selling piles of unripe jujube and guava, as though nothing had happened.

'Friendship is one thing, but what if something went wrong, Ratti Bai. Isn't it better to go to the hospital?'

'Why should we? We've got plenty of bais among us who are as good as any doctor. Absolutely first class.'

'Do they give you medicine to get rid of the foetus?'

'Of course they do. What did you think? Then there is this fists method, but rubs work best.'

'What is this "fists", "rubs"?'

'Bai, you won't understand.' Ratti Bai blushed a little and started to laugh. She had been eyeing my powder case for some days now. Whenever she dusted me with it, she would put a pinch on her palm and rub it on her own cheeks. I thought the box would be enough to get her to talk. When I offered it to her, she took fright.

'No Bai, the sister would kill me.'

'No, she won't. I'll tell her I didn't like the smell of the powder.'

'Why it smells fine, very fine. Oh Bai, you're crazy in the head.'

After a good deal of prodding she described the details of 'rubs' and 'fists':

'Rubs' work perfectly during early pregnancy—like a doctor, absolutely first class. The bai makes the woman lie down flat on the floor, then holding herself with a rope suspended from the ceiling or to a club, she stands on the woman's stomach and works it with her feet real well, until the 'operation' is performed. Or she makes the woman stand against the wall and after combing her own hair she ties it tightly into a topknot. Then, after dousing it with a fistful of mustard oil, she bangs it against the woman's legs like a ram. Certain young women, used to hard labour, don't respond to this. Then it's time for 'fists'. After dipping her unscrubbed hands with their grimy nails in oil, she just pulls out the throbbing life from the womb.

Most of the time the operation goes off without a hitch on the very first assault. If the performing bai happens to be a novice, sometimes one of the hands is broken off, or the neck comes out dangling, or even a part of the woman's own body that needed to stay inside spills out.

Not too many die from the 'rubs', but the woman generally falls prey to all kinds of disease. Different parts of her body swell up. Permanent wounds form and never heal, and if her time's up, she dies. 'Fists' are used sparingly—only when everything else fails. Those who survive aren't able to walk. Some drag on for a few years and then croak.

I threw up. Ratti Bai, who was describing all this with relish, panicked and ran off. I felt overwhelmed in the dreary silence of the hospital. Oh God, such a dreadful punishment for bringing life into this world—I thought, drifting off into a haze.

My throat was stinging from pure horror. My imagination began colouring in the pictures Ratti Bai had drawn for me and then breathed life into them. The shadow of the window curtain was trembling on the wall. Soon it began to flail like a blood-soaked corpse on which Ganga Bai had applied her 'rubs'. A horrific iron clamp in the shape of a fist with filthy nails sank its teeth deep into my brain. Tiny fingers, a drooping neck, in a sea of blood—the prize of the first assault. My heart sank, my mind felt dazed! I tried to scream, to call someone, anyone, but my throat jammed. I tried to reach for the bell, but my hand wouldn't move. Silent cries were stifled inside my breast.

It was as if the screams of someone murdered suddenly shot up in the impenetrable silence of the hospital. They rose from my own room, but I was unable to hear them, unable to hear anything that was spilling from my own mouth unconsciously.

'You must have had a dreadful nightmare,' said the nurse as she stabbed me with the syringe of morphine. I tried to tell her, 'Sister, please, don't. Look, there, the dead body covered with blood from Ganga Bai's rubs is writhing on the cross. Its cries are piercing my heart like a poker. The feeble sobs of the child dying in some gutter far away are pounding in my brain like a hammer. Don't give me morphine to dull my senses. Ratti Bai has to go to the polling booth. The newly elected minister is her caste-man. Her debt will be paid up with interest now. Ganga Bai will happily thresh rice. Please lift this mantle of sleep from my mind. Let me be awake. The spots left by Ganga Bai's blood are swelling on the white sheet. Let me be awake.'

I woke up when the man sitting behind the desk looking like a clerk stamped one of the fingers of my left hand with blue ink.

'Vote for *our* caste-man, okay,' Ratti Bai admonished me.

The ballot box of Ratti Bai's caste-man rose like a massive fist and came down with all its awesome power on my heart and mind. I didn't drop my vote into that box.

SUKHE SAAWAN[*]

ZAMIRUDDIN AHMAD

She woke up feeling embarrassed and sweaty. She quickly ran her fingers over her forehead, then her neck. Both were dry.

Through the door left ajar she looked out at the veranda shimmering with heat and light. She almost jumped out of bed, but realized it was Sunday. Languidly, then, she locked her hands and arched her arms, stretching them over her head. Then she extended one arm and unfastened the latch of the bedside window. A ferocious gust of hot air slapped her flush in the face. Outside in the alley, the sun lay stark naked. She was about to slam the window shut when the door of the house opposite hers opened. Out came the imam of the Jama Masjid, wearing a pair of pyjamas barely reaching down to his ankles, a kurta and a skull cap, both of some coarse material. A thin cotton towel, both ends tucked firmly between his teeth, not only covered his head but also his temples and the nape of his neck. The priest started off towards the alley's corner.

He must be going to conduct the noon prayer, she thought, as she closed the window.

Oh, no. She turned over to look at the clock ticking away on a side-table by the headboard. What? Only eleven-thirty. Not very late. Still, I should be up and about now.

But she didn't get up. She stretched out on her back instead and started counting the beams in the ceiling, wondering why, in this murderous heat, she had decided to sleep inside the room and not in the courtyard.

It was nearly two in the morning when I got back from the train station, that's why—she reasoned. If I'd slept in the open courtyard, the sun would have upset my sleep. Besides I didn't have to get up early today—did I?

Her eyes skidded off the sixth and the last beam and travelled on down to her legs. Her loose gharara, crumpled and bunched up in sleep, revealed a flash of calf, shapely and wheat-coloured, spotted here and there with traces of coarse black hair. She ran her hand over the stubble and then pulled the gharara leg a little way further up. The thigh was perfectly smooth and hairless. She bared the other leg. Again a hirsute calf but a perfectly hairless thigh. With a quick, nervous movement she pulled the gharara back down

---

[*]Literally, 'dry rainy seasons'; the rains, in the subcontinent, are associated with love, romance, and regeneration.

to her ankles, just as she had quickly covered her head and breasts with
her dupatta whenever she felt her father's presence.

Must shave!

She rolled over, belly down, and stretched her legs apart.

There was a knock at the front door. Bua will take care of it, she
thought. There was another knock. That's when she remembered that her
old maidservant had left for the day and wasn't expected back until late
the next evening.

Hurriedly, she got out of the bed, slipped on her chappals, and started
off towards the front door. Midway she hesitated, turned around and went
back over to her bed. She grabbed the dupatta from the headboard, threw
it round her neck, and started back. She crossed the hot-as-hell veranda
and still hotter dirt courtyard, came to the door, peeped out through a
rather wide crack and opened it.

Dulari, the sweeper woman, walked in, a large round basket with a
stumpish broom handle jutting out of it, balanced on one of her ample,
swaying hips. 'Salaam, Bibiji!' Dulari greeted her, walking straight towards
the latrine.

'Salaam,' she greeted back. Then she closed the door and went into the
kitchen and put the kettle on.

'Dulari!' she called the sweeper woman from the kitchen.

'Yes, Bibiji?'

'Don't forget to wash with phenyl.'

'I won't.'

Dulari—what an apt name! The mistress of the house wondered. She
really must have been a ravishing beauty in her prime! How fair her
complexion still is! And what lovely eyes!

She doesn't look like a sweeper woman at all. I wonder who told me
that it was a nobleman—a Saiyid, to be precise—from Amanabad who had
planted Dulari in her mother's womb. Oh, it was him all right, it was her
husband who had told her. She smiled.

She recalled how she had split her sides laughing when he had told
her that, back in those days. Dulari went by the nickname 'Platform' (for
everyone jumped on without paying), how every neighbourhood brat who
attained puberty tried her out first. No, I'd laughed because of something
else: he'd tickled me so. And he'd tickled me so because I'd teased him: 'So
did you hop on the platform too?' Oh, how he had loved to tickle me!

'Ram Dulari!'

'Yes, Bibiji?'

'Care for some tea?' And before the sweeper woman could speak her mind, she poured out some tea into a clay mug.

Dulari came over and installed herself in front of the kitchen door. 'Sure, why not?'

She picked up the mug by its rim between her thumb and index finger and gave it to Dulari, ever so careful not to let her hand come in contact with any part of the sweeper woman's body.

Dulari sat down, resting her back against the portion of the kitchen wall still in shade, and started slurping the steaming brew.

She stretched out her leg and pushed the small, low stool with lacquered red and yellow legs, towards the kitchen door and sat down on it. 'Any news?' she asked Dulari, pinching away from her ample bosom the gauze-like muslin shirt which the sweat had glued to her body; and took a sip of the tea.

'Who do you mean?' Dulari asked as she put her mug down on the floor.

'Ram Bharosay, who else?'

'What news could there be after so many days?' There was a note of despondence in the sweeper woman's voice. But the next moment saw her despondence change into palpable anger. 'The wretch, he must he hiding inside the slut he's run off with.'

But even this outburst failed to appease the sweeper woman. So she thought up an especially coarse invective to hurl at her runaway husband.

'No, don't!' the mistress cried, but to no avail. She was too late.

'Oh, I'm sorry,' Dulari said. She downed the remaining liquid in one giant gulp and got up. 'I must go now, Bibiji. I still have to do a few more houses.'

Dulari went back to the latrine, picked up her basket, balanced it deftly on her left hip and started walking towards the front door. Suddenly she stopped and asked, 'Has Bitiya left?'

'Yes.'

'When will she visit next?'

'Who knows,' she said, walking Dulari towards the door.

She closed the front door behind the sweeper woman and returned to her room.

She did her usual chores—dusting and cleaning—then took a bath and changed into fresh clothes. She went into the kitchen and from the basket hanging from the door frame took out two parathas and three kebabs, saved from the previous evening meal packed for her daughter and son-in-law for the train ride. She ate the meal and washed it down with two drinks of water from the fawn-coloured clay pitcher. Then she went up the stairs into the barsati.

It was sizzling hot inside the portico. Quickly she threw the windows wide open—the one overlooking the alley as well as the two facing the courtyard. The scorching wind, meeting with her sweat-soaked body, produced in it a sensation at once refreshingly cool and tickly. She began to hum, as her hands diligently and daintily returned the scattered objects to their familiar places. Finally, she turned to the twin beds set in the middle of the portico. One had not been slept in at all, but the other looked a mess: the thin cotton rug that served as the mattress had become so bunched up that on one side it exposed part of the frame and cotton-tape mesh, and on the other side fell all the way down to the floor, dragging the bed sheet along. A thin white sheet lay still folded at the foot of the bed: it hadn't been used. The embroidered pillow of the crumpled bed was where it should have been, but that of the other, also embroidered, had surreptitiously moved to the middle of its crumpled mate. The irregularity made her uneasy: so she grabbed the offending pillow and thumped it down where it belonged. But then, the very next moment, she was patting it ever so gently, the way elders affectionately stroke children's heads. She arched her body over the messy bed for a closer look, felt satisfied and began making it. Just then she noticed a rag way down under the bed. She reached in to pull it out with her foot, picked it up and examined it carefully. Oh! She murmured, disposing of it in the small tin basket under the back window, in which two garlands of bela flowers lay quietly withering away. She closed the window and, still humming, made her way downstairs.

That day there followed a stream of visitors and callers. Bua was the first and least expected; for she had herself said she wouldn't be back until Monday evening. The old lady removed her chadar, the wrap she wore when outdoors, dried her perspiring head and neck with it, lowered herself onto the foot of the bed, and made an attempt to explain why she'd been back early: because she had been worried sick that after the departure of Bitiya and her groom, my poor, little darling would be feeling miserably lonely, crushed by the dreary emptiness of the house.

And then Bua literally assaulted her with question after question. In answer, she told the old lady that 'the train was late, a full hour... Yes, it was very crowded. Still, the couple managed to get into a compartment... The rush should probably have eased a little after Kasganj, and they might even have found seats.'

'Poor children! They must've been awake the whole night.'

'Not really. They went upstairs into the portico right after dinner...to catch some sleep.' A glimmer of a smile danced in her eyes.

Now she asked Bua some questions of her own. And she was told that Fujloo, Bua's son-in-law, moaned and groaned the whole night long; the fever just wouldn't subside. What could she do? It was serious. So she had to take him to the doctor the next morning. 'He diagnosed typhoid and gave some red mixture...charged a whole rupee. Trouble never comes alone!... Yes, the fever's come down a bit... A good-for-nothing son-in-law! What a fine time he has chosen to fall ill, when Shubratan is hugely pregnant and about to deliver...'

She laughed. Bua is the limit! Does she really think Fujloo himself prayed to Allah to fall ill? Bua really shouldn't worry about the medical expenses. I'll take care of them... 'Employed or not, at least there's a man about the house.'

It was then that Bua told her she'd run into the vegetable vendor on her way back and decided to buy some vegetables. And since Adda Miyan's shop was still open, she thought she might buy a couple of pounds of meat as well. 'Fujloo'll be bed-ridden for Allah knows how long, so I thought I should do the shopping, or else you'd have nothing to eat.'

'You did the right thing,' she said, taking out her purse from under the pillow. 'How much?'

'What's the hurry,' Bua said, getting up from the bed.

But she insisted. Bua did some quick counting on her fingers. 'Seven-and-a-half annas for the greens and four-and-a-half annas for the meat—a total of eleven annas. No, twelve.'

She took out a rupee note and gave it to Bua. Bua undid the knot in the corner of her chadar, removed a four-anna coin and gave it to her to settle their account. Then she picked up the chadar and made for the dingy little room at the opposite end of the courtyard.

Next came Bulaqi, the water-carrier's son, a red cloth tied around his waist, supporting a skin full of water on one of his hips and part of his back. She asked him from behind the door of her room why Khairati, the boy's father, hadn't bothered to deliver the water himself.

'Father's thrown his back,' the boy explained, on his way out to the mosque to fill another skin.

'Why veil yourself from him?' Bua said. 'The boy's barely the age of our Bitiya.'

She disagreed. 'Quite the contrary. Looks like a full-grown man to me. Didn't you notice how tall and muscular he's become?'

The second time around the boy filled the bathroom tank and kitchen pitchers. Only after he'd left did Bua think she should have asked him for a third skin as well, to sprinkle on the scorched courtyard floor.

The mistress of the house was now standing in the courtyard freed from the oppressive sun, quietly cooling herself with a hand-held fan. 'Looks like it's going to rain,' she said, scanning the sky which was innocent of even a wisp of cloud. Only now, the leaves of the peepul tree in Lala Jeevan's compound no longer clapped wildly, and a scrap of paper lay listlessly for some time at the foot of the pitcher-stand in the niche under the stairs.

'So what are you cooking?' she asked, leaning against a courtyard pillar from where she could clearly see inside the kitchen.

Bua, who was diligently kneading dough in a flat clay bowl, answered, 'Meat-and-potato curry.'

'Do make some chapattis for Shubratan and the kids as well. And yes, there are some kebabs left over from last evening, take those along too.'

Bua gave her a look full of love and gratitude. 'Shall I fix you some tea?' she asked.

'Yes,' she said as she picked up the towel from the takht and made for the bathroom. 'You put the kettle on. In the meantime I'll have a quick bath, it's so muggy.'

When Puran, the flower vendor, came along and sang out, 'Bela garlands!,' she was still doing her hair. She stopped briefly and asked, 'Bua, didn't you tell him?'

'I did.'

'He must have forgotten then. Tell him again.'

'All right, if you say so.'

But Bua didn't tell Puran to stop delivering the garlands, Instead, she returned from the door with two strings of fragrant motia buds—pearly white and barely opened.

'Here,' she offered.

'Oh for heaven's sake! What will I do with them?'

Bua's ageing eyes perhaps failed to notice the change her offer had produced on her mistress's face. For if they had noticed, the old lady wouldn't have bothered to say, 'Tie them around your chignon. They'll look nice.'

She took the strings from Bua, who now returned to the kitchen, smelled them just once, and then nonchalantly threw them around the neck of the clay pitcher under the stairs.

When Suraiya came, she brought along a sweet, pungent smell that crowded and filled even the smallest space in the house. She put the basket with the tikari mangoes down on the takht and explained that her father had brought the mangoes from 'our Qaimganj orchard. He escorted me to the door. But he's already left. He has to see a lawyer. There's some urgent business.'

In the meantime Bua, after closing the front door, returned. 'It was Khan Sahib,' she said. 'He asked me to give you his greetings.'

She intoned walaikum and made for the sitting room with Suraiya in tow. There, she started giving the girl her lessons. Today's lesson included a ghazal. The girl listened attentively to her intricate explication of the different lines, but every now and then allowed her gaze to wander off to the older woman's face, fanning her own face once, then the teacher's, now with one hand, now with the other. When she came to the couplet:

> There is no strength left for speech, and even if there were,
> With what hope could I really tell my ardent wish

She couldn't stand the girl's silently intent gaze upon her. 'What's the matter? Why are you staring at me?'

Suraiya felt hugely embarrassed. The fan fell from her hand. She took the longest time picking it up. And then she said, rather timidly, 'Miss, promise you won't be offended.' She was speechless.

Taking her silence for an affirmative, the girl mustered all her courage and in one fell swoop got out the words. 'You really look very lovely today.'

She blushed. Unable to decide quite what to say, she blurted out the first thing that came to her mind, 'Stop. You shouldn't make fun of your elders.'

'Say what you will, Miss. Scold me as much as you want. But, by Allah, you do look very lovely today. Really. More than ever.'

'All right, all right,' she said, and resumed the lesson.

After the lesson both of them went out into the open courtyard. She instructed Bua to escort the girl back to her house. When Bua went into her room to fetch her chadar, leaving teacher and student alone, she abruptly hugged the girl, stroked her head, and said, 'Thanks for the mangoes.'

The sun hadn't gone down yet, but neither was it visible any more; only the top of the peepul in Lala Jeevan's compound still shimmered in the day's last amber light. The heat had relented, but it felt as oppressively close and humid as before. She pushed the takht from the veranda into the open courtyard, sat down on it and let her feet dangle.

When Bua returned, she told her to get going before it got dark.

Bua, packing the food to take along, asked her if she would have her dinner now.

'No, I'm not hungry,' she said. 'And listen, I won't be back from school until three-thirty tomorrow, so don't bother to come before then.' Then, as an afterthought, she added, 'Take some mangoes for the children.'

'These are from the Khan Sahib's own orchard,' Bua said, picking four of them from the basket.

'I know.'

'He's a very nice man.'

'That he is.'

'And so smashingly handsome.'

She made an inarticulate sound.

'His wife, too, was a very nice person. May God rest her soul in peace!'

'Yes.'

'He wants to marry again.'

'Oh,' she smiled. 'And just how do you know that?'

'Just now when I walked Suraiya back to her house, I went in to greet Khan Sahib's mother. She told me.'

'So fix him up with somebody. What are you waiting for?'

After a moment's hesitation Bua let out the words, 'For a certain somebody to just say "Yes".'

The younger woman realized that her joke had backfired; the thorn intended for Bua had pricked her instead. She hurriedly got up and withdrew to the kitchen, returning promptly with a box of matches. Even though it was still not quite dark enough, she lit the lantern hanging from the arch of the veranda. She was about to go back to the kitchen to return the matches when Saeen Baaba's voice assaulted her ears. At the corner of the alley, he was chanting in his deep, throaty voice:

For when the gypsy moves his tent
Pride and glory and the rest
Will not avail nor all your best?*

'He's mixed up his days! It isn't Thursday today, is it?' Bua mumbled as she got up and scooped up a bowlful of flour from the canister to give to the fakir as alms. As she was making towards the door, the younger woman quickly took the bowl from Bua's hands.

'Blessed be those who give; blessed too be those who do not,' chanted Saeen Baaba in front of the door.

The mistress of the house opened the door a crack and offered the bowl to the fakir. He emptied the contents in his own large, black begging bowl and returned the bowl to her. She nudged open the door a little further, and, still concealed behind it, asked, 'Do you like mangoes, Baaba?'

'Who doesn't, daughter?'

She went in and was back in no time with two ripe mangoes. She flung the door open all the way and emerged revealing all of herself to the full view of Saeen Baaba, the mangoes delicately balanced in her cupped palms. She offered them to the fakir, as if in tribute.

Trying his best not to look her in the face, Saeen Baaba picked the mangoes with such disciplined self-control that his fingers didn't even brush her hands. He then blessed her and moved on ahead, chanting away in his low, bass voice.

Planted in her door frame she just kept looking at how the fakir's broad shoulders, sturdy back, and tall frame mocked the alley's narrowness.

When she returned to the courtyard she found Bua sitting on the takht with the bundle of food set by her side. 'You don't intend to spend the night here, do you?'

Bua grabbed her wrist and made her sit down beside her. Then she said, 'I swear by the Holy Quran, my little darling, it is Khan Sahib's mother who brought it up.'

Only half-understanding Bua's intentions, she said somewhat confused, 'Brought what up?'

Still clutching her wrist, Bua said, 'She didn't actually say it, but she couldn't have been more explicit. She asked me to tell her if I had a

*This translation of a few lines from Nazir Akbarabadi's poem 'Banjaara-Naama' is by Ahmed Ali, for which see his *The Golden Tradition: An Anthology of Urdu Poetry* (New York: Columbia University Press, 1973), p. 187.

suitable match for Khan Sahib in mind.'

Gently she freed her wrist from Bua's grip and said very softly, 'Must you torment me, Bua?'

Bua was genuinely hurt. 'Torment you? I, who raised you, cherished you? How can I? My little darling, I say what I say because I care for you. Because I can't see you suffer so!'

'And yet you keep bringing it up. Time after time. You already know my answer, don't you? Now isn't that tormenting?'

'Back then I could understand your hesitation. You had Bitiya to worry about. Not any more. She's happily married.'

'Did I ever say she was a hindrance?'

'No, you didn't. But I'm not exactly a spring chicken either. I could see. I knew. I understand.'

'As a matter of fact, you don't. Not at all.'

'I may not be educated like you are, but I *do* understand. I know what it means to be a widow—I really do. I wasn't young when my husband died, but I wasn't old either. So you see, my darling. I do know.'

'Well, then, why didn't you remarry yourself?'

'I am sure I would have. Let's just say I wasn't lucky enough to find another man.'

She burst out laughing. 'Who could ever win an argument with you?', she said and looked at the almost darkened sky; the evening was falling over everything in a spray of fine mist. 'You'd better be leaving now, or the she-devil at the cremation grounds will get in your way!'

It was the twelfth day of the lunar month, the moon so full and bright it put the pale light of the lantern to shame. It was beginning to feel less and less stuffy. Leaves on the peepul trees in Lalaji's compound were wildly clapping. A cool, moist gust of wind had removed the fan from her hand. A recalcitrant curl, escaping from her topknot, dangled playfully over her cheek. Her soft, full body was spread over the takht, in a state midway between sleep and wakefulness.

A bolder gust of wind, saturated with moisture, came along: the lantern swayed, casting a maze of criss-crossing shadows on the veranda floor; the windows she had left open in the portico rattled; the little carved metal bowl lying upside down over the clay flask tumbled a little sideways like a tilted hat; and she lifted the hem of her kurta to wipe out the grit which the gust had swept up from the courtyard floor and sprinkled over her face. A bewitched moon luxuriated over the softness of her belly, planting kiss after impatient kiss, like a lover gone mad. Somewhere, far away, lightning flashed amid the thunderheads.

One, two, three... She counted up to fourteen. There was a second flash. She counted again. This time the thunder sounded at twelve, and the next time at only ten.

Oh, it's going to rain. And it's going to rain a lot, she thought to herself and sat up bolt upright on the takht.

A stray, translucent cloud passed over the moon.

She turned back to look eastwards: a veritable army of clouds was on the march. Within minutes it covered the sky from end to end, throwing the entire earth into darkness. Lightning flashed again; the smallest object in the house leapt out of the cave of darkness into full, blinding light and withdrew just as quickly back into the cave's dark bowels.

But she didn't so much as stir from her place.

She recalled:

'Aren't you afraid of lightning?'

'No.'

'That's something. Most women are so frightened they just pee in their pants.'

'Tut-tut!'

A few fat drops fell squarely on her smiling face. She heard the sound of many more fat drops pelt down on the takht and the floor. She got up and went over into the veranda.

The rain was now coming down hard in big, round drops. Meeting with the parched earth it released a warm, raw fragrance that rose to her nostrils and permeated her whole being. She quickly leaned her reeling head against a pillar for support.

Lightning flashed again, revealing bubbles in the collected water that formed and burst almost in the same instant. She pulled her shirtsleeve up to the elbow and stretched her hand out into the courtyard, like a beggar. The next instant her arm was drenched all the way to her elbow. She quickly pulled it back.

Her head still resting against the pillar, her glazed, dreamy eyes watched and watched how the lightning leapt naked out of its mantle of clouds and then, just as quickly, crawled back into it, how the bubbles danced downstream, only to melt into water the next instant.

After some time she took down the lantern, lowered the flame, and went into her room.

Some ten minutes later she emerged, hesitant and cringing with modesty, exactly as she had come out of this very room a good two decades ago in the first days of her marriage: the hem of her dupatta drawn low over her face, shy and blushing, avoiding the glances of her parents-in-law; and her husband—seeing how she had diligently smoothed every crease in her dress, had disentangled every curl, and had searched for telltale marks on her neck and cheeks—he had laughed noiselessly, his face buried in the pillow.

'What innocence! What naiveté!' he'd said. 'As if Father and Mother have no idea what we're up to!'

Carefully she closed the door behind her and padded back noiselessly to the middle of the veranda, as if afraid someone might see her.

A gust of cold, moist air slapped her across her naked body, making it shiver.

The thunder had ceased and there was no more lightning, only the rain coming down in a gentle, noiseless drizzle.

Gingerly she set one foot in the courtyard, then the other.

The rain showered its pearl-strings over her upright, self-possessed neck, her proud breasts, her bashful back, her exulting hips. Her arms came together in an embrace across her firm bosom. She raised her face up to the overcast sky and closed her eyes. Her ears heard a report of thunder as she saw the flash from behind her closed eyelids. Just then she opened her eyes.

It was raining heavily again.

Suddenly her hands shot up as if of their own volition, and her feet began to whirl over the muddied ground: round and round, faster and faster and faster. Several times the lightning flashed, the thunder clapped to stop her, but her undaunted body paid not the slightest heed: it kept turning round and round in a mad waltz, till the clouds, walls, roof, courtyard, veranda, pillars—everything began to whirl with her.

She tottered, stumbled to the takht, threw herself down on it, and covered her face with both hands.

The rain stopped, the clouds dispersed, and the moon came out again. The moon put a hand, full of caring warmth and tenderness on her shoulders, as if to say: Get up now!

She slowly got up and made it to her room—disoriented, looking lost.

When she came back out a quarter-of-an-hour later she was wearing the same gharara and kurta she had on when she woke up that morning. She crossed the courtyard and started clambering up the stairs. But she stopped midway and climbed down again. She removed those flower strings of half-opened motia buds, now a bit wet, from the water pitcher, went up the stairs, and came into the portico.

Then she gently tossed the flower strings into a heap by the pillow and facing them lay down on the same bed she had made around noon. But she took a very long time falling asleep.

BANISHED

JAMILA HASHMI

Birds flap away overhead. Daylight, turning a ripe shade of yellow, has descended to the steps of Achchal's large tank, and the ebbing rays have given the gurdwara's spire a golden-white tint. The fair beyond the vast field is beginning to wind down. Dussehra effigies will be set on fire before long. People will shout and scream, flee in mock dread, and the shower of sparks will look like fireworks in the bluish haze of the encroaching evening. The fire's embers will burn and jump for a long while, giving nearby faces a grotesque look, as if every last face, a veritable image of Ravan, has come to watch with glee Sita's ordeal of separation, her gruelling banishment all over again.

Banishment is a hard thing to endure. But does one have control over anything? Anything at all? Who wants to suffer knowingly?

Bhai used to say, 'What is it with you, Bibi? Always dreaming. This love lavished upon you today, the gaiety that engulfs you, all this will slowly end. Time diminishes everything, so slowly that we get used to it.'

Where is Bhai today? If the breeze, dipped in the scent of my homeland, which chases me like a spy, could somehow backtrack and find him, I would beg it, 'Go, ask him why the pain doesn't diminish. Toiling for years under oppressively heavy burdens and trudging along difficult paths, why does man still dream, longing for happiness? Why does he love light incurably'?

Why did Sitaji, after her exile had ended, pray for only one thing: to meet her Ramchandraji again? Doesn't misfortune harden the substance in man that longs for happier days? Why can't one come to love the dark? Yes, why not?

The pear tree has blossomed every year since Munni was born. When the seasons change, its branches are filled with flowers, the tree bends over heavy with fruit, deepening its bond with the earth. Its roots burrow deeper into the soil. No one can rupture that bond.

Munni has grown now. How quietly the years have padded past me!

Today Bari Ma asked Gurpal, 'Kaaka, take bahu and the children out to see the Dussehra fair. She hasn't stepped out of the village once in so many years.'

Gurpal snapped, 'When did you ever ask me to take her out, Ma? If she hasn't set foot outside the village, how am I to blame for it?'

Yes, how can anyone be blamed for that, really?

Whenever anyone calls me bahu, I feel insulted. I have been hearing this word for years, ever since the evening when Gurpal dumped me in this courtyard and cried to Bari Ma, who was sitting on a chauki, 'Look, Ma, I've brought you a bahu. A real beauty! The best of the lot!'

Bari Ma, raising the wick of the earthen oil lamp, strode over to me. My eyes were glazed over with hunger and dread. I had walked barefoot for miles and had no strength left even to raise my hand. I just collapsed at her feet. A single cow and a few buffaloes tethered in the courtyard stared at me for a while, then got up, leaving the fodder untouched. Bari Ma sized me up from head to toe, again and again, and then said to her son, 'If you had behaved like a responsible young man, I wouldn't have been in such straits today. I've practically gone blind from blowing into the fire to keep the hearth going. Even the kaharis, who helped out earlier, keep away from us, because we cannot give them any grain at harvest time. Just tell me, how much longer do you expect me to manage this house without any kind of help? If you could only put your heart back into farming, I could see some relief.'

Gurpal said, 'But at least look at her. You don't have to put up with the airs of the mahris and kaharis anymore. Here, I've brought you a bahu. She is your maid. She will do whatever you tell her to do—grind grain, fetch water, anything you want. I won't meddle.'

Many such 'brides' were brought to the village of Sangraon, but without the customary fanfare: no festive music, no racy songs to the beat of drums, no comic antics or spins or hip thrusts of nautch girls.

No one oiled my dust-coated hair. No na'in was sent for to make me up. I became a bride without a single piece of jewellery, without any sindoor for the parting of my hair.

Bari Ma heard Gurpal and looked at me as if I were some kind of calamity her grandson had picked up from the street. Still holding the lamp in her hand she quietly walked over into the kitchen. Nobody said a word to me. Oh, what a welcome this new bride was offered!

Since that day I too felt like Sita, enduring her exile, incarcerated in Sangraon.

At the fair the shopkeepers are taking down their wares, yelling obscenities at each other, puffing away at their beeris. They are dumping their gear on the pack donkeys with such cruel force, as if the animals were made of wood and had no feeling. The chariots used in the Ram Leela are standing at one side, and the boys who staged the performance are gobbling malai kulfis and pakoras with spicy hot sauce, unmindful of the stains the snacks have left on their colourful costumes, stains that look like a leper's open, ugly sores. Munni is so fascinated that she just stands and gawks at them. She doesn't even care that she could easily get lost. But what has care ever accomplished? One destined to be lost will be lost, even in a house full of people.

Gurpal tugs at her. My two boys are tired and grumpy. Every time they see a vendor, they tearfully insist on buying something from him. This is, after all, a fair. Here mothers, unmindful of their little ones, just forge ahead, carried forward by shoves and pushes. Their little lost children gaze in panic at every approaching face, and then bolt, crying. But when do those separated at a fair ever come together again? The separation stands like a wall between people who meant a world to each other once. Faces for which we are willing to sacrifice everything, in the faint hope that we might see them just once, vanish irretrievably. Paths, like the watery webs etched on the waves by minuscule crawling marine life, dissolve behind us. We can never backtrack on the paths we have already taken. Nothing ever returns. And the milling, jostling crowd at the fair can only move forward.

'Time lost is never regained,' Bhaiya would say, whenever he spotted me neglecting my studies or playing doll house with my girlfriends after school. 'Bibi, you must know that every moment past is erased. It turns to dust.'

That doll house was a gift from my Baaba, who had bought it at an exposition.

Munni is daintily holding her large rag doll with both her hands. Again and again she bends over and looks at it, while Gurpal is peering into the crowd above. The two boys, holding on to the clay replicas of Ravan, look at every passing face with astonished eyes. There is so much affection for her doll in Munni's eyes—a hideous face made of some rag over which the eyes and nose have been drawn with some odd colours, a ring in its nose. Her head covered with a gold-fringed chunri, holding on to her lehenga, this cheap little nautch girl would whirl into a dance any minute. So it seemed. The path back to Sangraon leads along the edge of Achchal's water tank and through some fields. Life's caravan moves along. Even if there is nowhere in particular to go as one meanders through life's straight or crooked paths, one still must go on, never stopping, on and on, even if one's feet are bruised, one's heart totally empty.

The bluish haze has descended still further over the landscape. Evenings make me sad; I wonder why. A solitary star throbs forlornly in the sky, like the flickering flame of an earthen lamp. In the blue, empty space its loneliness reminds me of my banishment. In this human wilderness I am like a lonely tree which neither blossoms nor bears fruit.

The star calls back to mind the ship in which Bhai had sailed across the seas to a far country. With his improbably large baggage, as he was getting ready to leave, my mother's voice was overcome by grief. And yet she held back her tears, as she took care of his things and prayed for him silently in her heart. Outside the house, Baaba was busy taking care of the arrangements. Bhaiya was visibly sad. And Aapa was padding back and forth in the courtyard as if in a stupor. Only I was chirping about everywhere in the house. After all, unless you're wounded yourself, you don't know how badly it hurts.

All of us went to the port to see Bhai off. While Bhaiya was busy going up and down the gangway taking care of the travel papers and personally overseeing the loading of Bhai's bags, I bent over the guard rail. Peering into the greenish, muddy waters below I fired one question after another at Bhai: 'What's wrong with this water? Why are there oil slicks all over it? Why are there boats? Oars? And doesn't one feel scared when a boat pitches on tall waves?' The barrage of questions exasperated him and he answered impatiently, 'All these things, Bibi, you will come to know on your own when you grow up.'

Today, I do know. I know how a boat without oars capsizes and sinks. But it doesn't always have to sink in the water. It can sink just as easily on the shore. Often a single wave is enough to send it to the ocean floor. Now that I'm grown up and have come to know things, Bhai is nowhere near me any more.

The ship's siren sounded. Baaba hugged Bhai, affectionately patted him on the head and said, 'Well then, may God be with you!' Bhaiya, overcome with emotion, threw his arms around Bhai. Aapa, sensitive and faint-hearted, broke down in sobs. Bhai comforted her, 'Just look at Bibi, how happy she is. What's there to cry about? I'll be back in two years. I'm not going away forever—am I?' And then he hugged me and said, 'Bibi, I'll bring you presents from—guess where?—Paris. Just keep writing to me—you will, won't you?' And I had nodded my head vigorously.

When the final whistle sounded, Bhai walked away so casually, as though he were only going somewhere nearby. We kept waving our handkerchiefs until the ship disappeared from view.

The port lights swayed on the waves, and the light of the receding ship flickered like a lonely star and then faded away. And with it, whatever light my life had known also faded away forever. Not even a stray gleam ever came up from the waves.

How I hugged Amma and sobbed. I heard somebody whisper into my heart, 'Never! You shall never see Bhai's face again!' My heart was throbbing fitfully, like the lonely star trembling with apprehension above the blue mist in the clear western sky.

The dark of the evening is spreading over the orchards in the distance. Gurpal has hoisted the two boys up on his shoulders, walking ahead of us on the white trails snaking through the fields. Munni is trailing along slowly. Ten fields up ahead, after crossing beyond the water ditches, he would wait until we caught up with him, meanwhile telling the boys the story of Ravan. But how would he ever know that Sita is trailing behind him, that he is Ravan himself?

Munni tells me: 'Ma, Swarup's Mama has sent her colourful clothes for Dussehra. All silk. They feel very nice. But, Ma, I don't have a Mama to give me such beautiful gifts. What's the matter with you, Ma? Why don't you say something? Didn't you like the fair? Are you tired?'

'Yes, Munni, I'm tired. I've grown old. I've had to walk far.'

'No, you're not old,' Munni said, full of youthful confidence, as she looked at me. 'You look just like the image of a goddess. Bari Ma says the same thing.'

How could Munni ever know how far I've had to walk? The immense distance from one life to another. When man's body shrinks and turns rigid, his heart is emptied of all hope. Then he's fit to be worshipped like a god. I've waited so long on the paths leading into Sangraon for those long separated from me that my eyes have glazed over. My heart is empty. I'm Lakshmi. And yet, the bonds of suffering endure. They are deep, strong, unbreakable.

Munni is asking again, 'Ma, don't I have a Mama?'

What shall I tell her? What answer shall I give? I just stand at the crossroads, lost in my thoughts.

How much I loved Bhaiya. But I also used to be so afraid of him. No sooner would he enter the house than the end of my chunri would slip automatically up over my head. My gait would become more measured and I'd find myself restraining my laughter. Standing next to him, it seemed nobody in the entire world was taller than him. How I loved my Bhaiya—who bore himself with restraint and dignity, who talked with an innate sense of decorum. He wrote in perfectly straight lines, never soiled the pages or smudged his fingers with ink. He'd say to me, 'Bibi! When you grow up, you too will write just as neatly.' What if he saw me today? What would he say? So much black ink has been spilled over my fate that you can't see a single straight line on the entire page! Oh, I never did learn to write neatly!

Back in those days I'd set up my doll house and think: we can all live in it—Amma and Baaba and I, Bhaiya and Bhabi and Aapa. All of us. In here. Life is a sweet song. We need nothing. We lack nothing.

When Bhaiya got married, I said, 'Our house is a paradise. A perfect heavenly abode.' If I were to have raised my hands back then in prayer, I wouldn't have known what to ask for. Today, too, I haven't asked God for anything. The end points of suffering and joy are not very far apart in this dizzying business called life.

Bhai sailed across the seas, and my dreams of paradise were shattered. The jagged splinters of my broken life have scattered like glass, wounding everyone who comes near me. So no one does. Nor is there anyone going over to the other side, as though the path runs through a cremation ground. It's desolate. Who has the time or inclination to listen to Sitaji's lament in this country? The pain of loneliness is hard to bear. And life so difficult.

Standing up ahead, Gurpal is calling me. He's calling Munni. Both of us are walking very slowly. Only dried stalks stand in the cotton fields now. People gather and walk away, as they always do, with the smiling flowers. The wheat fields are still too young, without ear or grain. Supple, soft plants bend over in the wind. One has to bow to the wind. Everyone does.

Bari Ma must be feeling very impatient. Anxious. An unknown fear on my account troubles her all the time. The pathway to the country she suspects I might flee to is fraught with incredible hardship. And besides, I've travelled with Gurpal far too long to have any strength left to strike out in another direction. After all, all walking must cease at some point. One just can't go on forever. Especially when there is nowhere to go. Where can I go—with my wounded heart, my darkened fate? Munni stands in my way. She is the great distance that separates me from my own family. How can I dare look beyond her, beyond that distance?

Bands of minstrels are coming behind us singing bhajans. The fair has wound down and the fair-goers have spilled out on the many paths leading out. Children cry and whimper and sulk as they walk. Labourers, talking loudly, walk past Munni and me, followed by fast-walking bare-foot women clad in bright clothes, holding back their veils just a little over their foreheads, packets of sweets bought at the fair in one hand, supporting their children on their shoulders with the other. Their slippers, tied to the ends of their dupattas, are dangling over their backs. An inexorable bond exists between the body and the earth. Nothing can come in between.

People are receding into the distance like a fading blur. A sadhu, strumming on his iktara, walks past us and turns onto the path to Sangraon. His song is so full of sadness. What he says is right: when hope for light persists... I don't hear the strum of his instrument. Only a snatch of the song itself, carried by the wind, reaches my ears.

'Why are you so quiet, Ma? Why don't you say something. I'm scared.' Munni, trying to clutch my hand in the thickening dark, is unable to hold on to her doll. She sobs; her voice is hoarse with tears. She can't think of anything else.

When she grows up, she will know it's useless to fear the dark. Once it has the upper hand, it is practically invincible. Bhai used to say, 'Bibi, there's incredible force in water. It makes its own way.' At the time I couldn't understand the secret of that force. Now I know how circumstances force us each to find our own way. Whenever Bari Ma calls me these days, I cover my head with my embroidered dupatta and answer softly, 'Yes.' I try to finish all my work efficiently, so that I can keep myself busy with more, just to spare myself the feeling of oldness, the assault of all these thoughts.

When I had the time, I had nothing to think about. Now there is something to think about, but I have no time. I feel something is lacking. Try as hard as I might, I can't shake this feeling. Things happen. Then there are days when nothing happens. Today, when I close my eyes, my heart whispers, 'My family will visit me any minute. The moment Bhaiya sees me, he will say, "What's this, Bibi? Embroidered dupatta? It doesn't become you at all. Come on, take it off. Here, look, what I've brought for you. Forget about your chores. Come, sit with us. Vacations are always too short. When I visit you, don't even think of going anywhere else, of doing anything. Just be with us."'

We would sit on sofas in the big sitting room, talk and look at the framed portraits of the family, sip tea, warm ourselves near the fireplace, and laugh. Amma would call out to us drowsily, 'You can talk in the morning, children. Now go to sleep.' At which Bhaiya would shout back, 'The whole year I live away from home. I always go to sleep feeling sad and nostalgic. What's the big hurry, Amma? Let's enjoy. We'll go to bed, don't worry.'

And I used to think: could all this crumble away like a dream one day? The little paradise we had fashioned from love and affection—would it be so covered over with dust that I'd look in vain for even a hint of freshness anywhere? Like photographs, are we merely shadows of reality? It was a crazy heart I had. A heart predisposed to think the oddest thoughts. An impossibly foolish, naïve heart!

I dream of impossible things and feel the excitement take hold of my heart. When I try to reason with it, it retorts, 'So what of it, Bibi? What have you got to lose? When did you ever hear of anyone having power over dreams? And besides, what's so wrong if the one you have been waiting for so long walks straight over to you one day?'

I reply, 'Only darkness is left for me.'

To which it says, 'Despair is the greatest sin.'

What can I possibly hope for? And from whom?

Munni tugs at the edge of my dupatta and asks, 'Ma, tell me, why doesn't Mama come to our house? Are we not going to his place on Diwali? All the other girls are going to see their uncles. Ma, I don't like it here any more. I didn't even like it at the fair. I'm sad. I want to go to my Mama's house.'

Who could tell me where her Mama lives? Outside Sangraon, all other villages look like doll houses to me, devoid of reality. Perhaps Sangraon too is unreal, a mere shadow. Perhaps everything is just a shadow.

And yet my soul keeps looking, for things that could never be found anywhere, hoping to hear voices that will never be heard again.

For some months now, as I carry the basketful of cowdung, churn milk, or pat and spread dung cakes on the ground, my heart beats in a peculiar way. A familiar fragrance wafts through the air, and I feel sweet melodies, played on different instruments, draw near me. All this makes me lose myself. Still, I know well enough now that those dear to me live in a country I cannot possibly hope to reach. Like the pathways leading to Sangraon, all other paths criss-cross each other so often that they confuse and make one lose one's way. Besides, what is to be gained from searching for a place which now exists only in stories?

Lights from earthen oil lamps flickering through the open doors of well-settled houses call to mind some fairyland picture.

Gurpal, the boys, Munni and I are now walking together, side by side.
Tall, soft reeds sway in the wind, and arch over to caress my hair with
their fuzzy, silken tops, as the breeze, holding the edge of its brocade veil,
begins to fall asleep.

It becomes easier if you have companions along the way.

Munni says, 'I'm tired, Ma. I can't walk anymore.' The boys too are
whimpering and crying. They're so groggy they can hardly keep their eyes
open, or even hold on to their toy Ravans. We leave the path and sit down
on the raised trail around a field to catch our breath. Munni drops her head
into my lap. Gurpal says, 'You know, lots of children were lost in the fair
today. And all because women are so stupid. They lose themselves, forget
to hold on to their children. They're so taken in by the Ram Leela, they
just gawk at the show and lose sight of their children.'

'Not just at fairs. Children become separated from their mothers even
outside fairs,' I say without looking at him, gently patting Munni on the head.

'Can't you ever bring yourself to forget that incident? That was a
different time.'

How can I make him understand that time never changes. Man suffers
because man cannot forget. That time lives on in my memory, just as it was.
Flames were going up everywhere. The country had gained its independence.
It had also been partitioned. Both Amma and Baaba said, 'All these people
who're afraid, they are mad. Look how they're fleeing to another country.
How can pain, how can suffering even touch you here among your own
people?' How naïve they were. Pain always comes from one's own people.
Sorrow caused by strangers mean nothing. Life, the whole of it, had lost
its beauty. The face of everything was covered with blood. The very people
who did charity in the name of Bhagwan, Guru, and Allah slaughtered
each other; those who readily laid down their lives to save the virtue of
their sisters and daughters considered a woman's honour no more than an
illusion. Independence and Partition broke our fetters, yes, but they also gave
the lie to the age-old words of brothers and compatriots—words trampled
in the dust under the feet of marauding bands of thugs.

Amma said to Baaba, 'Maybe we should take the girls and leave. I'm
terrified. It makes no sense to trust anyone these days.'

Baaba, as collected as ever, tried to comfort her, 'Bibi's mother, you're
worrying for no reason at all, just like everyone else. Nobody's going to
bother us. Partition was inevitable. All this commotion will die down in
a few days. Don't worry. Everything will be back to normal. Everything.'

In ordinary circumstances this would have been enough to reassure Amma. But not that day. She said, 'It's not just our lives that I fear for. Don't forget, we have grown-up girls. Listen to me, send us to my brother's.'

Baaba replied, 'Everywhere roads are infested with village hoodlums. They're butchering entire trains. This is not the time to leave. You just stay put in the house. God will protect us.'

Conditions had certainly made Baaba worried, but as time rolled on, he asked us to put our trust only in God. Little did he realize that it was already too late. He sought refuge in the old life and its values. That was his mistake, a mistake for which he paid dearly. As Gurpal was dragging me out of our house, I saw Baaba's body lying outside in the ditch, his face with its grey hair lying on the edge of the ditch. Forgetting his closed eyes and bloodied head, he was still praying, to whom only heaven knows. Could this be the time for any prayer to be heard? A shining spear had gone through Amma's chest and she fell on the spot where she had earlier prayed to God for the protection of her honour. And Aapa's screams—I can hear them even today sometimes in the howling gusts of wind. But I was just as helpless that day as I am now. What could I have done? Gurpal was dragging me away. My head was without its customary covering, but then I wasn't expecting to run into Bhaiya along the way, either. Had he been with me, who would have dared touch me? Drag me so dishonourably in the streets of my birthplace, every particle of which I loved with all my heart? Where is that country? My Baaba's blood was spilled over it. His grey head was dragged through its dust. If I could so much as snatch a glimpse of that dust, I'd touch it reverentially to my forehead. It certainly was more fortunate than I.

I had a slew of things I still wanted to say to Baaba. How much I had bothered Amma and teased Bhai and Bhaiya. And when my body was dragged all the way over to Sangraon, rather than ceremoniously borne in the bridal palanquin, I didn't have a brother there to complain, 'What, as I leave the parental home there isn't anyone even to say goodbye?'

Pain becomes easier to bear if there is hope—just a glimmer of hope—of better days ahead. I never was able to work through it all. What should I erase from my memory? And what should I retain? Gurpal! You never did allow me to look back.

Bari Ma's beatings, Gurpal's abuses, the pangs of hunger—I endured them all seeking strength from the dim light of a lamp flickering somewhere far away, in the hope that one day Bhai and Bhaiya would perhaps wander into

Sangraon looking for me. I'd smile at Bari Ma and without so much as looking at Gurpal I'd just walk away with Bhaiya. The wind would rustle through the neem leaves and sing and the entire village would celebrate and rejoice. Why does man consider himself the centre of the universe? Why, indeed? Unless the eye is used to darkness, one keeps straining for light, dreaming. Hopes keep circling the heart like vagrant thoughts.

Munni's birth loosened my ties with my dreams, and the assembly of hopes around the heart scattered. I learnt to wake up from dreams and take my present for real.

When the two countries made peace, sadness swept over Gurpal. Apprehension, anxiety burrowed inside him. Bari Ma and he would sit on chaukas and whisper God alone knows what between themselves. But they never felt the need to tell me anything. Munni had by now started to walk and stammer a few words. All kinds of rumours circulated around me and then subsided like a dust storm. No army ever came to reclaim me.

Subsequently I heard that soldiers from the other country visited a nearby village to seek repatriation of their abducted young women. Repatriate them to what country? Where? To whom? The thought crossed my mind that perhaps Bhai and Bhaiya too would come looking for me. They must have waited long for me outside the gates of the magic city. I must go. I really must. Everyday I'd tie my hopes into a bundle and peer with anticipation and longing at the bend in the lane.

That winter, soldiers did come to Sangraon to take me back home too. I thought: apart from being a sister to Bhai and Bhaiya, I was also a mother to Munni. I wondered: who were these soldiers? And what would that country be like? For the first time I felt unsure of myself. My dreamland turned into dust and vanished. I realized that my roots had sunk deep in Sangraon. Decimation, withering, and ruination—who likes them, after all? And besides, every girl must one day leave her parental home to join her in-laws. Well, maybe Bhai and Bhaiya weren't present at my wedding—so what? Hadn't Gurpal rolled out a carpet of corpses for me? Painted the roads red with blood? Provided illumination by burning down city after city? Didn't people celebrate my wedding as they stampeded, screaming and crying? It was a wedding, all right. Only the customs were new: celebration by fire, smoke, and blood. He had carried me to Sangraon. The rest of my life was to be spent here in the small dingy room of a mud house surrounded by grain fields. A house filled with the thick blue smoke of cowdung cakes.

Years later when Gurpal brought a book to teach Munni the alphabet, I kept staring at the letters. The words came alive for me. I remembered all the stories that both Bhaiya and Bhai would tell me, adding, 'Bibi, there are still more wondrous stories in books. You'll read them when you grow up.'

When the army did come to secure my release, I hid myself, just like the princess in the fairy tale. I wasn't about to leave with strangers. Why didn't Bhaiya and Bhai come to take me away? I felt hurt by both of them. And I've remained angry with them ever since.

Sometimes, when Munni lies down beside me, she asks, 'Ma, you don't visit Mama even on Diwali. Why doesn't anyone ever send us sweets?'

Your Mama never came looking for us, Munni. He never came to take me away. Nobody has so much time in life to go looking for someone. Love finds new crutches. Slowly. Bhaiya's children must be about as old as Munni now. They must ask their mother all about their Mama. And when they do, I'm sure she isn't forced to remain silent, or to so deftly evade talking about her brother. But there are times when the heart overflows with stories, and yet one remains tongue-tied. All these brides in the neighbourhood sit in the shade of the neem tree spinning their wheels and singing, but I remain quiet. What an aura of joy surrounds them! How sweet the songs of their parental homes sound! Seasons change. Every year a father or a brother comes to take one or another woman back home. You should see then how Asha, Rekha, Poroo, and Chandra seem to walk on air. They hug everyone before leaving. Their words sound like pure music.

When the young women climb to the rooftops to make the crows take wing so that they may judge from their flight the direction from which their dear brothers would come, my heart begins to pound in my throat, so violently that I feel it'll burst. When I raise my hand to make a crow fly away, it just falls back limply to my side.

With time, Bari Ma grew fond of me. Our bonds became stronger and deeper as I severed my last remaining links with my past. I'm her prized daughter-in-law now, her Lakshmi. She shows off the yarn spun by me to everyone she meets. When other women complain about their daughters-in-law, she praises me to high heaven just to rub it in.

What if the fragrance of grain and wheat mixed with the smoke rising all around turned into a sweet song! The sky arched over them slowly filling with stars; the water of the canal twisting in tiny waves—its notes! What if one day a young man coming along behind the peasants carrying bales of hay on their heads were suddenly to dismount from his horse right in front of my open doors, and I, dropping whatever I was doing, were to run up to him and hug him tightly, shouting 'Bhaiya!'

Oh, who do I wait for standing in the doorway? How long am I condemned to carry the corpses of my hopes, long since dead? Why have my eyes brimmed over with tears as I stand staring into these serpentine village pathways? If my tears were to fall on Munni she would wake up worried and surely ask, 'Ma, why are you crying?' How would I tell her what ails me? Suppose she asked: 'Ma, why are there tears in your eyes? You cry even on the night of Dussehra. Are you tired?'

Gurpal has put the two boys on his shoulders. Munni and I are bound for Sangraon. Rather than embrace a second exile, Sitaji has accepted a life with Ravan. Where would I find the strength to step out of the darkness with nothing but uncertainty for support?

All that was bright in my life has stayed behind, like the city. And yet, God knows why, I can't bring myself to love this darkness.

I must keep walking. Fatigue has spread throughout my body like pain. All the same, I must keep walking. Exile or not, one is compelled to move on in life's fair. As I move ahead, I cannot help wondering whether Bhai and Bhaiya too sometimes miss me.

It's Munni that I'm most afraid of. Tomorrow, she'll again ask that question. Of that I'm sure. But none of us will be able to answer it—not me, not Gurpal, not even, perhaps, Bari Ma.

Why are some questions so hard, so difficult, that nobody is able to answer them?

In the long wintry nights, suffering starts up a bonfire, summons old dreams, and listens to stories. How can stories ever be true! But the heart is very stubborn. It keeps remembering the past. Why?

I want to know: are there anxieties beyond Sangraon?

The stench of cowdung and urine, mixed with the fragrance of grain, flows on like the stream of life through the uneven village lanes.

Another day has ended. And days do get away from you, like gusts of wind. How far do I still have to go?

BEYOND THE FOG

QURRATULAIN HYDER

1

Throughout the day English sahibs, memsahibs, and their baaba log cross the bridge on mules and horses or riding in rickshaws and dandis. In the evening, the same bridge becomes the site of milling crowds of Indians. The swarm of rushing humanity going up and down the slopes huffing and puffing looks like the surge of a massive tidal wave. Movies starring Esther Williams, Joan Fontaine, Nur Jahan, and Khursheed are playing in the local cinemas. Skating continues in the rinks. In the ballroom of the Savoy the Anglo-Indian crooner and his band will soon start 'Enjoy yourself, it's later than you think.' Drums will be struck; maharaja and maharani log, nabob log, burra sahib and burra mem log will start dancing.

At this hour, while the whole of Mussourie is absorbed in merrymaking, a poor man stands quietly on this bridge near the bazaar—'*Kabira stands in the bazaar praying for everyone's well-being.*'

In his tattered khaki jacket, a cap coming down to his ears, he looks very much like a sweeper out of work. Holding a little English girl in his arms, he often wanders into the bazaar and stands there silently until dusk or sits on the low protective wall of the bridge.

Why does this sweeper Fazl Masih look so destitute and run down if he is entrusted with the care of some sahib's daughter? Strange!

And this fellow also looks a bit cuckoo. The likes of him were called holy fools in czarist Russia, and majzub in our culture. God knows whether this poor man is a majzub or was merely born an idiot. Anyway, most of the time he just stands quietly. The little girl with curly blonde hair is so incredibly pretty that she attracts the attention of passers-by who stop spontaneously to look at her. Now and then babu log will smile broadly and utter a 'Good evening, Missy Baaba' to her. Even recent English arrivals in Mussourie look at Fazl Masih with a smile, but the local English just pass by totally indifferent to his presence. The one-and-a-half-year-old girl, nestled in Fazl Masih's lap or riding on his shoulder, laughs, cries, or becomes absorbed in her teddy bear or her lollipop. Fazl Masih gazes at the Himalayas in the distance, beyond which lies the invisible 'valley of flowers'.

When it gets dark, he hoists the girl atop his shoulders and sets out for Vincent Hill with his head hung low. Just once, when some Lukhnavi passer-by stopped briefly and asked, 'Ama, whose daughter is she?' He replied with irritation, 'My sister's, sahib.'

'What do you think, Miyan, that Hindustan's Anglo-Indians just dropped from the sky?' another passer-by retorted with a resounding laugh. 'Well, this is just how they came into being.'

Perhaps the sound of that laugh reverberates in Fazl Masih's ears, but he never opens his mouth. He just plods along the uphill track to Vincent Hill with his head bent low, the little girl mounted on his shoulders.

The residents of the Vincent Hill area know that Katto ayah is the real mother of the little white girl whose father was a gora, a white man who played the drum in the army band, and that she is being brought up by Miss Celia Richmond, the white landlady of Richmond Guest House. Katto, a shapely and graceful sweeper woman with a delightfully sallow complexion, originally from Gorakhpur district, whose parents had been made Christians by Miss Celia's missionary father, was now Miss Sahib's nurse. Her real name was Martha, but she was called Katto because she went up and down the neighbouring hills with the speed and agility of a squirrel. Miss Richmond received the guest house as an inheritance from her uncle. The entire Richmond family is buried here in Mussourie's English cemetery. Miss Richmond has spent her whole life running this guest house. Circumstances have made her quite irritable, and because she makes a lot of noise, like a lapwing, the domestics and coolies of Vincent Hill have given her the nickname Chunchuniya Mem, the Rattle Ma'am. Hers is a second-class 'Europeans Only' facility where run-of-the-mill English, poor white missionaries, or fair-skinned Eurasians come to stay. With her keen, hawk-like sight, Miss Richmond can immediately see who has what percentage of English blood. If an Anglo-Indian with even the slightest trace of sallow shows up, she has Katto tell him that all the rooms are taken.

During the last days of World War II, a young Tommy came to stay at Richmond Guest House. He was in Mussourie on two months' leave recuperating from a recent illness. (During the war, out of sheer patriotism, Miss Celia Richmond had offered her guest house to the British government for the use of soldiers.) Before the war, Corporal Arthur Bolton, the white Tommy, used to be a drummer in the orchestra of an ordinary restaurant in London. He wanted to earn himself a name among world-class musicians, but lack of better opportunities, the fate of many artists, kept him anonymous and poor. When the war broke out he enlisted in the army as a drummer and was packed off to India. Like other soldiers in the British army, he was given instruction in romanized Urdu. But he also liked Indian music. In short, Arthur Bolton was an extraordinary Tommy, quite different from other whites of his ilk.

Because he wasn't a Sahib Bahadur of any consequence, that would allow him to stay at the Savoy, he flopped down at poor Chunchuniya Mem's. He strolled in the hills all day long or wrote poetry. He'd have Katto nanny sing kajris for him and keep time as she sang. When she sometimes swirled her bellowing white lehenga-skirt and jingled her bunch of keys with a jiggle of her hips singing, '*Mirjaapur men oaran-thhoran Kashi hamaaro ghaat*,' Arthur would become overjoyed, clap like a child, and start dancing with her. He liked Katto nanny a lot and had also struck up quite a close friendship with her crazy brother, Fazl Masih. The two would set out for the valleys at the crack of dawn to roam around and stare at the fog floating across the mountains. What lies beyond that fog?

2

When the time came for Arthur Bolton to return to the Meerut Cantonment he said, 'I'm used to speaking the truth, so I always end up losing. Our regiment will probably leave for Germany. A fierce battle is going on there. I may not be able to write to you at all, or if I do write a letter, I might not write any others. I'm pretty sloppy when it comes to correspondence. And what can a person write in a letter anyway?' But, as courtesy required, he did drop Miss Richmond a note of thanks from the Meerut Cantonment, in which he also sent his greetings to Katto and Fazl Masih and said that he was leaving for the European front in a few days.

When a daughter as white as snow and resembling Arthur Bolton in every last detail was born to poor Katto, Miss Richmond, unexpectedly, didn't grill Katto about the matter at all. She knew that Katto was not dissolute. And furthermore, she'd been born in her own house and had been a loyal domestic all along. With the birth of the child, Miss Richmond's otherwise quite dreary existence became somewhat animated and no longer felt so empty. She often wondered why on earth she was killing herself over the guest house. For whom was she piling up all this money? Now God had sent her such a lovely girl.

Miss Richmond also indulged in absurd fancies and theatrics now. And very much like her kind, ordinary middle-class English ladies, she was a perfect snob. She cooked up quite a story about the little girl to tell to the erstwhile residents of the guest house. 'Her father, Colonel Arthur Bolton, was lost in action on the Berlin front. Poor Arthur...' she would say heaving a deep sigh while serving guests their breakfast. 'Poor Arthur was my first cousin. Before coming to India he married the daughter of some Irish lord. Both of them were stationed at the Peshawar garrison. Soon after Arthur left for the front, poor Bridget died giving birth to the girl in the military hospital. Arthur had given my address as "next of kin" so the Red Cross sent the girl to me.'

Even at the girl's baptism at an English church in Mussourie, she had put down the name of the father as Colonel Arthur Bolton and crossing her heart with two fingers said under her breath, 'So help me God.'

India gained her freedom and suddenly Mussourie began to empty of its English, except for Miss Richmond, who was not about to return to Britain to work as a dishwashing and cleaning lady. Unexpectedly, her hotel, its 'European Only' sign now removed, picked up business, because Indians took great pride in staying in an 'English guest house'. Where earlier quite ordinary English stayed there, it now became the haunt of upper-class wealthy Indians.

Catherine Bolton, nicknamed Katy, who was now called 'little Katto' because of her frisky, coltish behaviour, went to a convent school. Here, they had started teaching Hindi and Sanskrit after Independence. The teacher was a wily young local man. Katy took Hindi lessons from him, and her fair colour left the free children of free India in a state of awe.

The English priest who had baptized Catherine left India and settled in Australia, but he kept up a correspondence with Miss Richmond. On Katy's fifteenth birthday he wrote about his concern for the girl. What kind of future would she have in India? Surely Miss Richmond didn't wish for her to marry some Hindu heathen? It would be far better if she brought the girl over to Australia.

Miss Richmond gave the matter serious thought: really, what future could such a beautiful Anglo-Indian girl have in India? Telephone operator, office secretary, or, God forbid, a call girl or cabaret dancer? Already Katy Bolton had become the talk of the town throughout Mussourie for her geniality. The day the shifty Hindi teacher tried to get fresh with her and, when she tried to fend off his advances, outright called her 'a coquette, a mongrel', she went home in a rage and told Miss Richmond everything that had transpired. There and then on that cold evening Miss Richmond made up her mind. She spent the whole night awake in her bed. It wasn't easy to leave home for good. What might become of her in a foreign land? But Catherine's future was at stake, it took precedence over everything. Come morning she sent for Katto and Fazl Masih. They came and stood in the doorway. Miss Celia sat by the fireplace busily knitting. Katy stood by the radiogram. In a grave tone of voice Miss Celia Richmond began, 'Katto, we're going to Australia. Katy Baaba will go with us. Start packing our stuff.'

Both Katto and Fazl Masih were stunned. The two white women before them seemed to have gone off their rockers. They burst out crying. After a while, Katto sniffled and said firmly, 'Memsahib, I gave birth to Katy; I won't let her go. My brother too, this girl is his entire life, Miss Sahib. The only reason I didn't marry was the fear of how a stepfather might treat her.'

'Be quiet!' the old hag yelled. 'Don't forget your place, Katto. What proof do you have that Katy is your child? How dare you say that?'

Katto was stupefied. She never expected that. Miss Sahib had never said such a cruel thing before. Falling to the floor, she cried her heart out.

Katy went into the other room. She could hardly wait to go to Australia. The prudent and far-sighted Miss Richmond had already told her a few days ago that Colonel Arthur Bolton was an imaginary being. Corporal Bolton and Katto were her real parents. But her entire well-being lay in keeping this secret under wraps. Katy, who had an instinctive understanding of the rules of survival, had taken this advice to heart.

In an attempt to reason calmly with the distraught woman, Miss Richmond now said, 'Katto, you're crazy, altogether crazy. You really ought to think a bit...with a cool head. What will be Katy's future after I die? A smattering of Mussourie natives still knows that she's your daughter. What if the news spreads all over? The caste system is rampant in India. Who will marry her? What is the value of an Anglo girl here after all? People regard her as no more than a tart. Do you really want your daughter to become a striptease dancer in some hotel? Or do you plan to marry her off to some municipality sweeper? Something to think about, isn't it?'

Katto was speechless.

Miss Richmond sold her establishment to a Sindhi who lost no time in expelling Jesus and Mary from the lounge, installing Guru Nanak and Shankar Parvati in their place, and replacing the 'Richmond's' sign outside with 'New Himalayas Vegetarian Hotel', but he let the old staff, Katto included, stay on. A bereft Fazl Masih and Katto came all the way to Dehra

Dun station to say goodbye to Miss Richmond and Katy. The train left the station, leaving behind a forlorn Fazl Masih in his kantop and a light brown quilted vest staring vacantly into space, as was his wont.

3

At the Sydney airport Miss Richmond swept her glance over the place and smiled with satisfaction. She had made it to a white country...finally. (Although she was pure white on both sides, she was born in Gorakhpur. Only once in her whole life had she been to England, and for no more than a few months.) Both she and Katy waited for some coolie to rush to pick up their baggage, but no one paid any attention to them. Finally, taking their cue from other travellers, they found themselves a trolley and started to load their bags. When Miss Richmond started to push the cart, her heart suddenly broke a little.

Reverend Sigmore was waiting outside in the hall and took them to his house. He helped Miss Richmond buy a small grocery shop in the market adjacent to his church and also a flat. Within two weeks, Miss Richmond found herself sitting in her shop by the scales. She had made her entry into Sydney's working class.

Catherine was enrolled in a school. It didn't take her long to unfurl her wings. She went on 'dates' now, returning late in the evening. Miss Celia Richmond, brought up on Victorian and Indian values, would admonish and rebuke her. Heated arguments would follow. The lives of both women had become miserable. A sixty-five-year-old uprooted English spinster and a sixteen-year-old girl of mixed blood with no clear background to speak of. A tragic pair of fake aunt and niece.

In Sydney, Miss Richmond couldn't cope with either her self-imposed exile or her loneliness for very long and died while Catherine was still in her eighteenth year. Reverend Sigmore assumed guardianship of the girl. He had her admitted into the school's boarding house. Within a few months she ran away. Not even in a blue moon did she deign to drop a letter to her mother or uncle. A few months later the priest also died. Catherine's boyfriends knew she had come into a lot of money. When she attained legal majority they started to play fast and loose with it. A ravishing beauty, her life's ambition was to become an actress, but back in those days Australia boasted neither a regular theatre scene nor a movie industry. Some rake advised her to take off for Hollywood, or if she wanted to enter London showbiz, the best place to start was the nightclubs there. She took cabaret lessons. In the meantime, she sold her grocery shop and had pretty much spent her entire inheritance. Money just slipped through her fingers like sand.

And so, wandering through Hong Kong and Singapore, she ended up in the Kuala Lumpur nightclub circuit, dancing cabaret here, working as a hostess there. But there she had to suffer the fierce competition of slant-eyed Anglo-Chinese prostitutes, and she was not, at any rate, a call girl, but the daughter of 'Colonel Arthur Bolton'. This imaginary colonel ensured, at every step, that she maintained her dignity. At times she remembered her overly strict, fake Aunt Celia Richmond and on occasion the image of her own mother and uncle sailed before her eyes. She would wipe her tears and light another cigarette wondering about all the upheavals her life had gone through. The Southeast Asia nightclub circuit had made her quite wise and equally melancholy. She had danced at the stag parties thrown by the high-living, pleasure-seeking sons of corrupt politicians and knew well enough the political and moral state of this part of the Third World. In every city in every country she found the same Bible on the side table in the hotel suites, and found the sacred text to be utterly useless. The mysterious old Chinese hags with incredibly small feet who sat in the back rooms of Chinese restaurants amid the blue haze of incense smoke and told fortunes were never able to solve even one of her problems.

In one Jakarta Chinese restaurant she ran into a delightful Dutchman, about forty, with a toupee pasted on his head and wearing something resembling a robe over his suit. He told her that he was a Dutch Sufi and a disciple of the Paris Sufi preceptor Inayat Khan. 'I've come from Amsterdam to gain knowledge of the mysteries of Indonesian Sufism,' he told her. 'I'm one of those who are referred to as "Dutch Sensitives". We possess a heightened sixth sense.'

'Your father is alive,' he abruptly said, digging into his chop suey.

She was jolted.

'You'll certainly meet him one day. He's a great man.'

'Really? What kind of great man?'

'I can't tell you. But he *is* a great man.'

Did this mean he really was a colonel and, by now, maybe a general in the British army? The thought made her incredibly happy. Half of her miseries vanished there and then. She felt herself quite safe.

The Dutch Sufi's nearness gave her a sense of profound comfort. Swept away by Sufism, ESP and her own desire for some sense of security in her life, she followed this mysterious man all the way to a mosque in Jakarta, where a slant-eyed, scraggly-bearded Indonesian 'Shaikh' had her recite the kalima. She was given the name Halima and she was married to the Dutch Muslim Muhammad Moeen Koot. As she signed her name 'Catherine Halimawati, daughter of Colonel Arthur Bolton' in the marriage register, she couldn't resist feeling an immense exhilaration flooding her soul.

That new Dutch Muslim was a staunch momin. He ordered Halimawati to cease her dancing and singing forthwith. But here was the problem: if she didn't dance in the Jakarta hotel where she did her floor show she would have to pay for her room and all her bills. Since Muhammad Moeen's money orders from Amsterdam wouldn't be in for quite a while yet, Catherine Koot was once again obliged to dip into her savings.

They had been living in the hotel for a fortnight when one morning she woke up and found that her Dutch Sufi was clean gone. And gone too were the diamond rings, the genuine pearl necklace and the earrings Celia Richmond had left for her, along with her remaining cash. The lofty Bible on the side table still remained, untouched, with an empty plastic cup on top of it. Just last night, her Dutch literature-loving spiritualist had repeated a line from some American short story writer, which went something like: You may wander through the whole world but a day comes when you realize that the world is full of Holiday Inns and plastic cups and that you must go back home. So Catherine Koot, stumbling about, returned from Jakarta to her home in Sydney. She was getting along in years, her ravishing beauty dangling precariously on the edge of evanescence. All she could find there was a job as a bus conductor.

A peculiar feature of the struggle for survival is that humans never admit defeat. Distributing tickets to the bus riders, she still daydreamed. Maybe at the next stop she would find the prince of her dreams, for who knows what lies beyond the fog?

4

Raja Sir Narendranath's great grandfather was a poor Brahmin fortune-telling astrologer from Kannauj. Pleased by some of his auspicious predictions, Shahenshah Jahangir bestowed on him a jagir by the edge of the Kali River. The present Raja Sahib is a staunchly religious man who firmly believes in sadhus and sants. After the government abolished princely states he moved into a gorgeous mansion in New Delhi and started a big business. It was in this connection that his eldest son (who earlier went by the name of Yuvraj Shailendranathji, but now is merely Mr S. N. Bajpai) took a business trip to Japan, Singapore, and Australia. This was the first trip out of the country for this rather naïve youth, so he was left quite dazed and fazed in Australia.

It was the Christmas season and a boisterous hustle and bustle had gripped Sydney. That day, as he was getting ready to go to the Opera House, he suddenly remembered the test match that was to take place in the afternoon between Australia and India, so he hopped aboard a bus for the cricket stadium instead and found himself a seat next to the window. The bus was a veritable portrait gallery of faces, one more beautiful than the next: Lebanese girls, Italian immigrants, round-faced Australians. When the bus conductor's hand came abreast of his face, he lifted his head and his eyes were dazzled: such a lustrous face, as beautiful as the full moon. Is such beauty possible! Seeing an Indian, the fairy-face smiled with a trace of fellowship.

The rajkumar had once heard someone say: if a white woman smiles at you, she's as good as hooked. He looked into her eyes a little less afraid and fell in love with her, heart and soul.

Those who visit a white country for the first time and fail to marry a mem within the first six months escape, otherwise not. Rajkumar Shailendra had been in Australia hardly ten days.

The conductor handed him his ticket and moved on smiling. Afterwards she gave him no more attention, but he was a man of firm resolve and nothing if not steadfast. The next day he boarded the bus at the same time. He succeeded, but only on the fourth attempt. He introduced himself: Prince Shailendranathji of India.

'Prince' did seem to make an impression on the earthly houri, because she had been watching princes and the sons of royalty all her life in Mussourie, right from childhood, and if someone on a bus in Sydney was introducing himself as a rajkumar, her experienced cabaret dancer's eyes could easily see that he was no fake.

The magic began to work on the fairy. Appointment for the evening, candlelight dinner, ballroom dancing, a leisurely stroll, shopping, high-placed family, English girl, a colonel's daughter, granddaughter of some lord—well, what's the harm?

It was a standing practice among our nabobs and raja log that they got themselves a junior begum or a junior rani of European blood, most of whom had been mere London barmaids in their earlier incarnations. But the headline news of free India was that all the rajwaras had been folded up, harems put paid to, and the law of single marriage had been slapped on the people. All the same, the snob value that an English or an American wife still had in free India was not something that Shailendranathji was unaware of. His first wife was a princess, a rajkumari, but the poor thing died within two years of marriage.

So when he proposed to Catherine she found herself in a Sydney ashram the very next day. Her nikah had been performed at a mosque in Jakarta. Here, the pundit recited Vedic mantras. She was given the name Shailaja Devi, to accord with Shailendra—the Bengali pundit explained with a smile.

'Akhand Sobhagyawati, Yuvrani Rajyalakshmi Shailaja Deviji—may she prosper and fructify!' Her nitwit of a husband, several years her junior, shook hands with her, beaming. On the marriage register her father's name was inscribed as 'Colonel Arthur Bolton of London and Peshawar Cantonment'.

5

From Meerut Cantonment, Corporal Arthur Bolton had straightaway headed to Berlin. The war ended shortly thereafter and he played his drum in the army band to celebrate the victory in different parts of England. Later, he was let go of his temporary employment in the army.

Arthur Bolton's father, a shoeshiner who worked in Piccadilly Circus, had died during the bombardment of London. His mother had died too. Arthur found himself a job with a dance band in the West End. He didn't marry. Why get into that mess? Years passed. After paralysis disabled one of his arms, he had to give up drumming. When he got out of the hospital he started working as a doorman. By now age had caught up with him. He still wrote poetry, which never got printed. He attended church regularly—churches, that is, that had somehow escaped being turned into Sikh gurdwaras. Since he knew Urdu he was able to hit it off quite well with Pakistani and Hindustani labourers. Actually, it was a Sikh watchman friend who had got him his present job in one of the stores of a major Punjabi businessman, Mr Khosla. It was a gorgeous showroom in Knightsbridge. There, everyone liked this soft-spoken, loveable, slightly eccentric old man.

That day, after arriving at the showroom, he did his cleaning and dusting in the hall. As he was arranging the scattered periodicals on the table his eyes fell on the cover of a women's magazine published from Bombay.

The face of the girl on the cover caught his attention. Inside there was a photo essay on the interior decoration of this beauty's house. Arthur Bolton plopped down on the sofa, took out his eyeglasses, and began reading it:

Yuvrani Shailaja Deviji is English and a member of British aristocracy. Her father, Colonel Arthur Bolton, was lost in action in the last World War. Her grandfather was an Irish lord. Rajkumariji has spent her childhood in Mussourie. Later she left for Australia with her aunt, Lady Richmond, where she trained in ballet dancing, piano, and interior decoration.

Old man Arthur was dumbstruck. He closed his eyes and remained in a state of quiet immobility for some time. Then he got up, walked over to a corner, dropped down on his knees and immersed himself in prayer.

For some strange reason he felt certain that Katto was still in Mussourie and that if he wrote to her at the same old address, she would reply.

And so she did. When he got her letter he asked the manager of the showroom for a month's leave which was granted. He went to India House to obtain a visa. Next he withdrew his life's savings from the bank, bought himself a return plane ticket, and spent the rest on gifts for Katto and Catherine. Carrying the heavy bag of gifts in his working hand, he would get tired, catch a brief rest in some doorway, and start walking again. With the money saved by walking, he bought a tie for his son-in-law.

Exactly a week later he found himself standing in front of the servants' quarters at the New Himalayas Vegetarian Hotel.

Katto nanny told him plainly, 'Sahib, my daughter didn't send me a letter and got herself married. What does this mean? Just one thing: she doesn't want me to ruin her new life.'

Katto was sitting on a rock outside the quarters working mustard oil into her hair. As ever, Fazl Masih sat under a pine tree staring quietly at the Himalayas. The valleys in the distance had become filled with purplish fog.

Old man Arthur lit his pipe with his working hand and pondered how incredibly peaceful this poor, illiterate, and heartbroken woman was.

'Katto, you're not angry at all?' he said, in a voice genuinely surprised.

'Angry—whatever for, Sahib?' she said. 'In whatever I had to go through, I lived up to the fate assigned by Chhati Ma.'

'Chhati Ma? Who is this lady?'

'A Bohri memsahib of Bombay once came here. When she heard how angry I was, she told me, "Katto Bai, the sixth day after a child is born, Chhati Ma appears at midnight and inscribes its fate on its forehead". Here we call it the "karm ke lachhann", the signs of fate.'

Arthur listened attentively. Raising his eyebrows, he rubbed his forehead and started laughing.

Katto continued, 'In the front room of these very servants' quarters, Chhati Ma came at night and inscribed on my Katy Baaba's forehead that she would become a queen. Listen to me, please, Sahib. Don't go to meet her.'

'Why?'

'Because I'm telling you.'

'No, Katto. Chhati Ma has also written down that both you and I will go to Delhi to visit her. I've brought so many gifts for her from England.' Arthur sat down beside her on the rock and started to open the bags with longing and eagerness.

6

A small, nicely manicured lawn was visible at the front of the grand mansion and right across from the gate stood the window of the bedroom which was featured in that English-language women's magazine. It was a pleasant Sunday morning in early spring. Out on the lawn Raja Sahib, his middle son, and a few European men and women were immersed in listening to the discourse of a Swamiji. This was some relatively new Swamiji who had just recently joined the international guru circuit and was now staying at Mouriya, having returned only a few days ago from France with a slew of his millionaire French and German disciples. After breakfast with Raja Sahib, he was holding forth on sat and a-sat when a taxicab pulled in at the gate and a threesome got out: a grubby old Englishman holding a Selfridges shopping bag, a poor native woman in an ordinary sari, and a crazy-looking man in a kantop and faded quilted vest with a matted salt-and-pepper beard who cringed and huddled behind one of the columns of the gate. The shabby Englishman held the hand of the boggled, fearful woman and started walking towards the lawn.

Raja Sahib lifted his eyes and looked at the new arrivals with extreme annoyance and wondered: how in the world did his Gurkha gatekeepers ever allow this riffraff in!

Maybe this clumsy bunch was from the horde of Jehovah's Witnesses, harmless, crazy missionaries. Early on Sunday mornings they just descend on the homes of decent people and tell them doomsday is right around the corner. Oh, how they make life miserable!

Coming near the chairs, the old Englishman stopped. When the Swamiji raised a silver glass to drink some water, the Englishman said cheerfully, 'Good morning friends!' Both he and the native woman stood there for some time. Everyone remained absolutely silent. The Swamiji was apparently quite irritated by this intrusion in the middle of his bhashan. In utter disgust he picked up a flower and started inhaling its sweet aroma. The Maharaja signalled with his eyebrows for them to sit down, and both promptly did.

'Maharaj, please go on,' Raja Sahib, a staunch believer in sadhus and sants entreated by humbly joining his hands.

Swamiji picked up where he had left off in his discourse on sat and a-sat. Old man Arthur craned his head and started to listen carefully. After a few minutes Swamiji paused to allow his French female disciple to change the cassette.

The old Englisman addressed him, 'Mister Guru! Your thoughts about truth and nontruth have affected me greatly. I too have come from England to make manifest a truth.' Then turning to the Raja Sahib he said, 'Your Highness, I'm the father of your dear daughter-in-law Catherine...' he took out the clipping from the women's magazine, 'Akhand Sobhagyawati Rajyalakshmi Shailaja Deviji.'

'Oh, what a pleasant surprise, Colonel!' The Raja quickly thrust his hand forward for a handshake smiling warmly. 'Colonel Bolton! Why didn't you inform us that you were coming? Ahead of time?'

'Your Highness,' old man Arthur cleared his throat, glanced around, and said with an angelic smile, 'there hasn't been a single colonel in my family in the past seven generations. My father was a shoeshiner, my mother a cook; I joined the army as a drummer. Now I'm just a doorman.'

Everyone present had turned into statues of solid ice. Arthur threw a sweeping glance around him and shook his head regretfully. 'All my life this has been my problem. I've always spoken the truth, nothing but the truth. And when I arrive here, what do I see but that Swamiji is talking about the essence of truth. This made me very happy. I've spent my entire life's savings just to see my daughter. I'm a poor man. All the same I've brought her some things as a dowry.' He bent over, picked up the Selfridges shopping bag from the lawn and then put it back down. The people remained as frozen as before.

Arthur started again, 'I'm sure Catherine would be delighted to meet her mother too. After all, she's been away since she was fifteen years old.'

Arthur stopped to catch his breath. Katto just looked at him, aghast, dumbfounded. Suddenly the atmosphere had turned entirely surreal. Such episodes don't happen in real life. Arthur started again, 'This foolish woman was afraid to come here. I told her, "Martha, are you afraid of the light? Don't be afraid of the light of truth. Truth is God. And we are His children. Aren't you eager to see your lovely child? So let's go to Delhi and meet our daughter. How could it be that parents and their children would hesitate to meet each other? How can they go against the law of nature? There's nothing to fear." And Your Highness, it is mentioned in your mythology that when Lord Shiva arrived at his in-laws, his arrogant and haughty father-in-law scorned him...' Arthur paused and cleared his throat, 'Forgive me, I gave the wrong example. What I meant was...'

The old coot, he's really insane, Raja Sahib thought. He was gaping at this weird stranger with wide eyes and his face was quickly changing colours but Arthur Bolton went on with his introductory harangue with perfect calm.

'So Your Highness, just now as I arrived at the gate I thought for a minute you might turn out to be as arrogant and haughty as Lord Shiva's father-in-law, but then your words struck my hearing. You were expressing your agreement with Mister Guru's utterance that man must speak the truth in all circumstances and have the courage to face it. Indeed it is siddhant and gyan. And Raja Sahib, you'll be pleased to know that my Saviour Jesus Christ has also said exactly the same thing. Actually, it is His truth-speaking that brought Him to the cross—quite a well-known event, you must surely have heard of it.'

The middle prince sensed that Raja Sahib, an irascible man, was just about ready to lose his temper and God knows what he might do. To smooth things over, he quickly asked, 'Would you like coffee or tea?'

Arthur looked at him with a smile. 'Martha, coffee?'

Meanwhile Swamiji had started to stroll on the grass. The middle prince poured some coffee and offered it to Katto nanny. Old man Arthur shook his head and said excitedly in Urdu, 'I'm very pleased to see that you don't practise untouchability. We are all children of God the Father. Jesus said that there is room for everyone in My Father's palace. Your Highness, my daughter's mother was never married to me. I didn't even know that Martha had given birth to Catherine. Thirty-five years later I saw her picture in a magazine. This is all God's work. Martha is a very courageous woman; she still works as a nanny in Mussourie. She is a righteous woman, a true Christian. Her mother and father were also true Christians, and they were also very poor. They worked as sweepers, cleaned bathrooms. Jesus said that the poor shall truly inherit the Kingdom of God. Your Mister Gandhi says the same thing too. He used to live in the Bongi Colony in Delhi. My Katto is also a bongi. She will also inherit the Kingdom of God, no doubt about it.'

Raja Sahib, who was glaring at the old man, dropped his head between his hands and bellowed at the top of his voice. Raja Sahib was ill tempered but no one had ever seen him shout like that before. Everyone stood up and rushed to him. He felt dizzy and closed his eyes, letting his head droop. He was beginning to faint. He had a weak heart.

7

Catherine, standing by the bedroom window, was watching this whole scene, which looked like a stage set from that distance. Life couldn't be more unbelievable! In the morning, when she was introduced to Swamiji at breakfast, both had instantly recognized each other. Swamiji was none other than the former Hindi and Sanskrit schoolteacher at Mussourie who had tried to get fresh with her, leading to Miss Richmond's sudden decision to leave for Australia. Just as they were about to leave it had come to light that he had siphoned off a considerable amount of school funds and dropped out of sight with some girl from the hill country. Back then too he was quite engaging and a sweet-talker.

After breakfast, when the opportunity offered itself, he told his former student, 'Now look here Katto Junior, it has taken me twenty long years and a lot of hard work to fashion this career for myself in the West, which is teeming with swamis nowadays and a cut-throat competition is raging among them. Even so, I've got no less than eighteen ashrams in Europe and America, not to mention disciples numbering in the thousands, so don't you go spilling the beans! In the bargain, I'll keep mum to your in-laws, conservative royal family that they are, about your being the daughter of Mussourie's Katto nanny.' The blood had drained from Catherine's face and her colour faded when she heard those words whispered to her. She'd left right away and hidden herself in her bedroom.

Meanwhile Swamiji had returned to the lawn and resumed his bhashan, but what had to happen, happened. A taxi stopped at the gate and she saw her mother getting out, followed by her half-crazy uncle, and an eccentric-looking English codger. They walked in and sat down on the lawn, and Catherine heard every word of this unbelievable father of hers.

One time a Delhi Begum Sahib had taught Miss Celia Richmond how to cook 'baoli handia'—crazy dish. Life too was a crazy handia which, having simmered for some time, now suddenly came to a boil.

Shaking from sheer terror, she looked at what was in front of her. Her uncle stood like a pillar by the gate staring into space, while on the lawn her insane father diligently went about destroying her life. How fervently and how much she had always yearned to meet him. How many stories of this man's innate goodness and innocence her mother and her aunt Celia had recounted—the man who had stayed barely two months in the guest house and left after winning everyone's heart. Perhaps God had created him just for that: wander in suddenly from somewhere, change the course of lives, and wander out just as swiftly. Unbelievable! Impossible! Are goodness and truth in their essence destructive forces?

Transfixed, she watched the players on the stage in front of her in what might well have been a scene from some comic opera had it not been so horrific: discovering that his oldest daughter-in-law was the child of a sweeper woman caused the Brahmin Raja Sahib to faint on the spot; the four Europeans, in order to escape the tentacles of the arch swindler Maya, had walked straight into the trap of the arch swindler Swami; the bogus holy man was now mouthing mantras to revive the unconscious Raja Sahib; her poor mother, who had shed tears all her life, still couldn't do anything but shed more; and her destitute father, paralysed in one arm, who had saved every penny with so much thrift to bring her something for her dowry from across the seven seas, was now looking at everyone, dumbfounded, like some foolish angel who had walked into the wrong place. A sudden wave of compassion and love washed over Catherine and she was overwhelmed by an instinctive desire to rush out and hug her half-mad, eccentric father, her suffering mother, and her dear uncle, to give up this palace, this aristocratic Brahmin family and her well-heeled husband, and leave with these loving, penniless, naïve, and crazy people, because her real home was where they lived, because ultimately the world is filled with Holiday Inns and plastic cups, three-storeyed Heinz-style houses with red sloping roofs, and nowhere had she found her place, her home. Was she really Akhand Sobhagyawati Rajyalakshmi Shailaja Deviji? Inside her skin she was just plain Catherine Bolton, and the conflict between Colonel Bolton and Corporal Bolton that had always left her exhausted and worn out was finally over. She would go outside and announce: Daddy, Mummy, here, I'm back. I'm coming with you.

She summoned up her courage and made for the door. Just as she was opening it, her eyes fell on her diamond bracelet. Her personal Mercedes gleamed in the sunlight up ahead in the driveway, and she suddenly recalled that she was expected at the golf club at eleven o'clock. Would all this disappear in the blink of an eye?

The sound of the shower rose from the marble bathroom and another thought crossed her mind: might her husband throw her out after this dreadful denouement? Much better if I leave honourably with these people on my own.

Her head swirled, as though she was standing on a sinking ship. She tried to grab on to the door. She must do everything to save herself. Such was the law of survival. Her nitwit husband emerged from the bathroom in his robe. 'What's all this noise outside?' he asked, walking towards the window.

Catherine heaved a deep sigh and said in a clear, firm voice, 'Darling, that magazine which had a pictorial essay about our interior decorations, remember? It seems to have created havoc. Some wicked gang has barged in to blackmail us. They're claiming to be my parents. Your father is running for election. I wonder whether this has something to do with that. Looks like your father's opponents have sent an untouchable woman with some English geezer to say that she is my mother, just to turn the Brahmin vote against your father. The old coot might just as well be a CIA agent. You must call the police...right now.'

Rajkumar Shailendra was a moron all right, but perhaps not an absolute moron. He lifted his face and looked at his fairy-faced yuvrani somewhat suspiciously. Catherine turned pale. She was shaking from fear. Pushing her out of his way, Rajkumar Shailendra rushed to the door and out to his father who had by now regained consciousness. Catherine ran straight to the bathroom and locked the door.

Outside at the gate her crazy uncle was asking after the well-being of everyone with his hands raised in prayer.

Kabira stands long wishing everyone well.

THE WAGON

KHALIDA ASGHAR

In a rush to get back to the city, I quickly crossed the dirt road and walked onto the Ravi bridge, looking indifferently at the blazing edge of the sun steadily falling into the marsh. I had a queer feeling, as though I had seen something. I spun around. There they were, three of them, leaning over the guard rails and gazing straight into the sunset. The deathly concentration made me look at the sunset myself, but I found nothing extraordinary in the scene; so I looked back at them instead. Their faces, though not at all similar, looked eerily alike. Their outfits suggested that they were well-to-do villagers, and their dust coated shoes that they had trudged for miles just to watch the sun as it set over the marshes of the receding Ravi. Impervious to the traffic on the bridge, they continued to stare at the marshes which were turning a dull, deep red in the sun's last glow.

I edged closer to them. The sun had gone down completely now; only a dark red stripe remained on the far horizon. Suddenly the three looked at each other, lowered their heads, and silently walked away, towards the villages outside the city. For some time I stood watching their tired figures recede into the distance. Soon the sounds of the night coming to life in the city reminded me that it was getting rather late and I'd better rush home. I quickened my pace and walked on under the blue haze of the night sky, pierced here and there by the blinking lights of the city ahead.

The next evening when I reached the bridge, the sunset was a few minutes away. I suddenly recalled the three men and stopped to watch the sunset, even though I knew Munna would be waiting on the front porch for sweets and Zakia, my wife, would be ready for us to go to the movies. I couldn't budge. An inexorable force seemed to have bound me to the ground. Through almost all the previous night I'd wondered what it was about the marsh and the sunset that had engrossed those strange men so entirely.

And then, just as the blazing orange disc of the sun tumbled into the marsh, I saw the three walk up the road. They were coming from villages beyond the city. They wore identical clothes and resembled each other a lot in their height and gait. Again they walked up to the bridge, stood at the same spot they had the previous evening and peered into the sunset with their flaming eyes, filled with a mute sadness. I watched them and wondered why, despite their diverse features, they looked so alike. One of them, who was very old, had a long, bushy snow-white beard. The second, somewhat lighter in complexion than the others, had a face that shone like gold in the orange glow of the sunset. His hair hung down to his shoulders like a fringe, and he had a scar on his forehead. The third was dark and snub-nosed.

The sun sank all the way into the marsh. As on the previous day, the men glanced at each other, let their heads drop and, without exchanging a word, went their way.

That evening I felt terribly ill at ease. In a way I regretted not asking them about their fascination with the sunset. What could they be looking for in the sun's fading light?—I wondered. I told Zakia about the strange threesome. She just laughed and said, 'Must be peasants, on their way to the city to have a good time.'

An air of mystery surrounded these men. Zakia, of course, couldn't have known it. One really had to look at them to appreciate it.

The next day I waited impatiently for the evening. I walked to the bridge, expecting them to show up. And they did, just as daylight was ebbing away. They leaned over the bridge and watched the sun go down, indifferent to the traffic around them. Their absorption in the scene made it impossible to talk to them. I waited until the sun had gone down completely and the men had started to return. This would be the time to ask them what it was they expected to find in the vanishing sun and the marshes of the receding river.

When the sun had sunk all the way, the men gave one another a sad, mute look, lowered their heads and started off. But, instead of returning to the village, they took the road to the city. Their shoes were covered with dust and their feet moved on rhythmically together.

I gathered my fading courage and asked them, 'Brothers! What village do you come from?'

The man with the snub nose turned around and stared at me for a while. Then the three exchanged glances, but none of them bothered to answer my question.

'What do you see over there, on the bridge?' I asked. The mystery about the three men was beginning to weigh heavily on me now. I felt as though molten lead had seeped into my legs—indeed into my whole body, and that it was only a matter of time before I would crumble to the ground reeling from a spell of dizziness.

Again they did not answer. I shouted at them in a choking voice, 'Why are you always staring at the sunset?'

No answer.

We reached the heavily congested city road. The evening sounds grew closer. It was late October, and the air felt pleasantly cool. The sweet scent of jasmine wafted in, borne on the breeze. As we passed the octroi post, the old man with snow-white hair suddenly spoke, 'Didn't you see? Has nobody in the city seen?'

'Seen what?'

'When the sun sets, when it goes down all the way?' asked the hoary old man, rearranging his mantle over his shoulders.

'When the sun goes down all the way?' I repeated. 'What about it? That happens every day.'

I said that very quickly, afraid that the slightest pause might force them back into their impenetrable silence.

'We knew that, we knew it would be that way. That's why we came. That other village there too,' he pointed towards the east and lowered his head.

'From there we come...' said the snub-nosed man.

'From where?' I asked, growing impatient. 'Please tell me clearly.'

The third man peered back at me over his shoulder. The scar on his forehead suddenly seemed deeper than before. He said, 'We didn't notice, nor, I believe, did you. Perhaps nobody did. Because, as you say, the sun rises and sets every day. Why bother to look? And we didn't, when day after day, there, over there,' he pointed to the east, 'the sky became blood red and so bright it blazed like fire even at nightfall. We just failed to notice...' He stopped abruptly, as if choking over his words. 'And now this redness,' he resumed after a pause, 'it keeps spreading from place to place. I'd never seen such a phenomenon before. Nor my elders. Nor, I believe, did they hear their elders mention anything quite like this ever happening.'

Meanwhile, the darkness had deepened. All I could see of my companions were their white flowing robes; their faces became visible only when they came directly under the pale, dim light of the lamp posts. I turned around to look at the stretch of sky over the distant Ravi. I was stunned: it was glowing red despite the darkness.

'You are right,' I said, to hide my puzzlement, 'we really did fail to notice that.' Then I asked, 'Where are you going?'

'To the city, of course. What would be the point of arriving there afterwards?'

A sudden impulse made me want to stay with them, or to take them home with me. But abruptly, they headed off on another road, and I remembered I was expected home soon. Munna would be waiting on the front porch for his daily sweets and Zakia must be feeling irritated by my delay.

The next day I stopped at the bridge again to watch the sunset. I was hoping to see those three men. The sun went down completely, but they didn't appear. I waited impatiently for them to show up. Soon, however, I was entranced by the last magical glow of the sunset.

The entire sky seemed covered with a sheet soaked in blood, and it scared me that I was standing all alone underneath it. I felt an uncanny presence directly behind me. I spun around. There was nobody. I was wrong. I couldn't have looked behind my back. How can anyone? All the same, I felt sure there was someone, standing behind me, within me or, perhaps, somewhere near.

Vehicles, of all shapes and sizes, rumbled along in the light of the street lamps. Way back in the east, a stretch of evening sky still blazed like a winding sheet of fire, radiating heat and light far into the closing darkness. I was alarmed and hurried home. Hastily I told Zakia all I'd seen. But she laughed off the whole thing. I took her up to the balcony and showed her the red and its infernal bright glow against the dark night sky. That sobered her up a little. She thought for a while, then remarked, 'We're going to have a storm any minute, I'm sure.'

The next day in the office, as I worked, bent over my files, I heard Mujibullah ask Hafiz Ahmad, 'Say, did you see how the sky glows at sunset these days? Even after it gets dark? Amazing, isn't it?'

All at once I felt I was standing alone and defenceless under that blood-sheet of a sky. I was frightened. Small drops of sweat formed on my forehead. As the evening edged closer, a strange restlessness took hold of me. The receding Ravi, the bridge, the night sky and the sun frightened me; I just wanted to walk away from them. And yet, I also felt irresistibly drawn toward them.

I wanted to tell my colleagues about the three peasants who, in spite of their distinctly individual faces, somehow looked alike; about how they had come to the city accompanying this strange redness, had drawn my attention to it, and then dropped out of sight; and about how I'd searched in vain for them everywhere. But I couldn't. Mujibullah and Hafiz Ahmad, my colleagues, had each borrowed about twenty rupees from me some time ago, which they had conveniently forgotten to return. And, in the bargain, they had stopped talking to me, too.

On my way home, when I reached the bridge, a strange fear made me walk briskly, look away from the sun, and try to concentrate instead on the street before me. But the blood-red evening kept coming right along. I could feel its presence everywhere. A flock of birds flew overhead in a 'V' formation. Like the birds, I too was returning home. Home, yes, but no longer my haven against the outside world; for the flame-coloured evening came pouring in from its windows, doors, even through its walls of solid brick.

I now wandered late in the streets, looking for the three peasants. I wanted to ask them where that red came from. What was to follow? Why did they leave the last settlement? What shape was it in? But I couldn't find them anywhere. Nobody seemed to care. Life moved on as usual.

A few days later I saw some men pointing up to the unusual red colour of the evening. Before long, the whole city was talking about it. I hadn't told a soul except Zakia. How they had found out about it was a puzzle to me. Those three peasants must be in the city, I concluded. They have to be. The red of the evening had now become the talk of the town.

Chaudhri Sahib, who owned a small bookshop in Mozang Plaza, was an old acquaintance of mine. People got together at his shop for a chat every evening. So did I, regularly. But for some time now, since my first encounter with those mantle-wrapped oracular figures, I had been too preoccupied with my own thoughts to go there. No matter where I went, home or outside, I felt restless. At home, an inexorable urge drove me outdoors; outdoors, an equally strong urge sent me scrambling back home, where I felt comparatively safe. I became very confused about where I wanted to be. I began to feel heavy and listless.

All the same, I did go back to the bookshop once again that evening. Most of the regulars had already gathered. Chaudhri Sahib asked, 'What do you think about it, fellows? Is it all due to the atomic explosions, as they say? Rumour also has it that pretty soon the earth's cold regions will turn hot and the hot ones cold, and the cycle of seasons will be upset.'

I wanted to tell them about my encounter with the three villagers but felt too shy to talk before so many people. Just then that ominous moment arrived.

A pungent smell, the likes of which I'd never smelled before, wafted in from God knows where. My heart sank and a strange, sweet sort of pain stabbed at my body. I felt nauseous; unable to decide whether it was a stench, a pungent aroma, or even a wave of bittersweet pain. I threw the newspaper down and got up to leave.

'What's the matter?' asked Chaudhri Sahib.

'I must go. God knows what sort of smell that is.'

'Smell? What smell?' Chaudhri Sahib sniffed the air.

I didn't care to reply and walked away. That offensive smell, the terrifying wave of pain, followed me all the way home. It made me giddy. I thought I might fall any minute. My condition frightened Zakia, who asked, 'What's the matter? You look so pale.'

'I'm all right. God knows what that smell is.' I said, wiping the sweat off my brow, even though it was November.

Zakia also sniffed the air, then said, 'Must be coming from the house of Hakim Sahib. Heaven knows what strange herb concoctions they keep making day and night. Or else it's from burnt food. I burnt some today accidentally.'

'But it seems to be everywhere—in every street and lane, throughout the city.'

'Why, of course. The season's changed. It must be the smell of winter flowers,' she said inattentively, and became absorbed in her knitting.

With great trepidation I sniffed the air again, but couldn't decide whether the sickening odour still lingered on or had subsided. Perhaps it had subsided. The thought relieved me a bit. But there was no escape from its memory, which remained fresh in my mind, like the itching that continues for some time even after the wound has healed. The very thought that it might return gave me the chills.

By the next morning I'd forgotten all about that rotten, suffocating smell. In the office, I found a mountain of files waiting for me. But Mujibullah and Hafiz Ahmad were noisily discussing some movie. I couldn't concentrate on the work and felt irritated. So I decided to take a break. I called our office boy and sent him to the cafeteria for a cup of tea. Meanwhile I pulled out a pack of cigarettes from my pocket and lit up.

Just then I felt a cracking blow on my head, as if I had fallen off a cliff and landed on my head, which fused everything before my eyes in a swirling blue and yellow stream. It took my numbed senses some time to realize that I was being assaulted once again by the same pain, the same terrible stench. It kept coming at me in waves, and it was impossible to know its source. I found myself frantically shutting every window in the office, while both Mujibullah and Hafiz Ahmad gawked at me uncomprehendingly.

'Let the sun in! Why are you closing the windows?' asked Hafiz Ahmad.

'The stench, the stench! My God, it's unbearable! Don't you smell it?'

Both of them raised their noses to the air and sniffed. Then Hafiz Ahmad remarked, 'That's right! What sort of stench...or fragrance is that? It makes my heart sink.'

Soon, many people were talking about the waves of stench that came in quick succession and then receded, only to renew their assault a little while later. At sundown the stench became especially unbearable.

Within a few weeks the odour had become so oppressive that I often found it difficult to breathe. People's faces, usually lively and fresh, now looked drained and wilted. Many complained of constant palpitation and headaches. The doctors cashed in. Intellectuals hypothesized that it must be due to nuclear blasts, which were producing strange effects throughout the world, including this foul odour in our city, which attacked peoples' nerves and left them in a mess. People scrambled to buy tranquillizers, which quickly sold out. Not that the supply was inadequate, but a sudden frenzy to stock up and hoard had seized people. Even sleeping pills fetched the price of rare diamonds.

I found both tranquillizers and sleeping pills useless. The stench cut sharper than a sword and penetrated the body like a dagger. The only way to guard against it was to get used to it, I thought; and people would do well to remember that. But I was too depressed to tell them myself. Within a few weeks, however, they themselves came to live with the stench.

Just the same, the odour struck terror in the city. People were loath to admit it, but they could not have looked more tense; their faces contorted from the fear of some terrible thing happening at any moment. Nor was their fear unreasonable, as a subsequent event showed a few weeks later.

On a cold mid–December evening, I was returning home from Chaudhri Sahib's. The street was full of traffic and jostling crowds. The stores glittered with bright lights, and people went about their business as usual. Every now and then a wave of stench swept in, made me giddy, and receded. I would freeze in my stride the instant it assailed my senses and would start moving again as soon as it had subsided. It was the same with others. An outsider would surely have wondered why we suddenly froze, closed our eyes, stopped breathing, then took a deep breath and got started again. But that was our custom now.

That evening I'd just walked across the bridge when I felt as if a lance had hit me on the head. My head whirled and my legs buckled. Reeling, I clung to a lamp post and tried to support my head with my hands. There was no lance, nor was there a hand to wield it. It was that smell—that same rotten smell—I realized with terror. In fact, it seemed that the source of the oppressive stench had suddenly moved very close to me, between my shoulder blades, near my back, immediately behind me—so close that it was impossible to think of it as separate from me.

It was then that my eyes fell on the strange carriage, rambling along in front of me. It was an oversized wagon pulled by a pair of scrawny white oxen with leather blinders over their eyes and thick ropes strung through their steaming nostrils. A ribbed wooden cage sat atop the base of the wagon, its interior hidden behind black curtains. Or were they just swaying walls of darkness?

Two men, sitting outside the cage enclosure in the front of the wagon, drove the two emaciated animals. I couldn't make out their faces, partly because of the darkness, but partly also because they were buried in folds of cloth thrown loosely around them. Their heads drooped forward and they seemed to have dozed off, as if overcome by fatigue and sleep.

Behind them the interior of the curtained wagon swelled with darkness, and from the heart of that darkness emanated the nauseating stench that cut sharper than a sword. Before I knew it, the wagon had moved past me, flooding my senses with its cargo of stench. My head swirled. I jumped off the main road onto the dirt sidewalk, and vomited.

I had no idea whether the people in the city had also seen the eerie wagon. If they had, what must have they endured? I had the hardest time getting home after what I had seen. Once inside the house, I ran to my bed and threw myself on it. Zakia kept asking me what had happened, but a blind terror sealed my lips.

A few days later a small news item appeared in the local papers. It railed against the local Municipal Office for allowing garbage carts to pass through busy streets in the evening. Not only did muck-wagons pollute the air, they also hurt the fine olfactory sense of the citizenry.

I took a whole week off from work. During those seven days, though hardly fit to go out and observe first-hand the plight of the city, I was nonetheless kept posted of developments by the local newspapers. Groups of concerned citizens demanded that the municipal authorities keep the city clear of muck-wagons or, if that was impossible, assign them routes along less busy streets.

On the seventh day I ventured out. A change was already visible. Wrecked by insomnia and exhaustion, people strained themselves to appear carefree and cheerful, but managed only to look painfully silly. Suddenly I recalled that in the morning I had myself looked no different in the mirror.

About this time, the number of entertainment programmes and movies shot up as never before. People swarmed to the movie halls—often hours before a show—formed long lines, and patiently waited to be let in, only to file out later looking still more pale and ridiculous.

In the office, no matter how hard I tried, I couldn't concentrate on my work. Intermittently, the image of the muck-wagon lumbering down the streets flashed across my mind. Was it really one of those municipal dump-carts? No. It couldn't be. Municipal dump-carts never looked like that eerie wagon, with its sleepy drivers, a pair of blindfolded, bony oxen, black curtains and the outrageously nauseating smell. What on earth gives off such an odd smell, at once fragrant and foul?

An insane desire suddenly overwhelmed me: to rush up to the wagon, lift up those swaying curtains, and peek inside. I must discover the source of the stench!

Coming to the bridge, my feet involuntarily slowed down. There was still time before sunset, before waves of the pain-filled odour began to come faster and stronger. I leaned over the bridge, an unknown fear slowly rising in my throat. The bottomless swamp, its arms ominously outstretched, seemed to be dragging me down towards it. I was afraid I might jump into the swamp, sink with the sun and become buried forever in that sprawling sheet of blood.

I became aware of something approaching me—or was I myself drawing closer to something? Something awaited by all men, those before and those after us. My whole body felt as though it were turning into a piece of granite, with no escape from the bridge, the miasma, the sun. For now they all seemed inseparable from my being. Helplessly, I looked around myself and almost froze.

The three men were coming towards me from the direction of the countryside. As before, they were wrapped in their flowing white robes and walked with their identical gait. I kept staring at them with glassy eyes until they walked right up to me and stopped. The hoary old man was crying, and his snow-white beard was drenched with tears. The other two couldn't look up; their eyes were lowered mournfully, their teeth clenched and their faces withered by a deathly pallor.

'Where were you hiding all these days?' I said between gasps and stammers. 'I searched for you everywhere. Tell me, please, what's happening to the city?'

'We were waiting. Trying to hold ourselves back. We had tied ourselves with ropes. Here, look!' They spread their arms before me and bared their shoulders and backs, revealing the deep marks of the rope.

'We did not want to come,' the old man said, drowned out by a fit of sobs.

'But there was no choice,' the second man said. Before he had finished, he doubled over. His companions also doubled over, as if unable to control a sudden surge of pain. The same wave of pain-filled stench stabbed the air about us, cutting us into halves, flooding our senses as it scrambled past us.

'There! Look!' said the old man, pointing in the direction of the distant villages and turning deathly pale.

In the distance, I saw the wagon come up the road from behind a cloud of dust. The drowsing coachmen had wrapped their faces because of their proximity to the cutting stench.

A cold shiver ran up my spine. The eyes of the three men suddenly became dull. They were approaching their end, perhaps.

The wagon rumbled close—the stench from it draining the blood from our bodies—and then passed us. Its sinister, jet-black curtains, fluttering in the gentle breeze, appeared, oddly enough, entirely motionless.

The three men ran after the wagon, caught up with it and lifted the curtains. A split second later, a non-human scream burst from their gaping mouths. They spun around and bolted towards the distant fields.

'What was it? What did you see?' I called, running after them. But they did not reply and kept running madly. Their eyes had frozen in a glassy stare.

I followed them until we had left the city several miles behind us, then grabbed the old man's robe and implored, 'Tell me! Please tell me!'

He turned his deathly gaze upon me and threw open his mouth. His tongue had got stuck to his palate.

All three had become mute.

My head whirled, and I collapsed. The three men continued to run, soon disappearing in the distance behind a whirling cloud of dust. Slowly the dust settled and I returned home.

For months now I have searched in vain for those men. They have vanished without a trace. And the wagon—from that fateful evening, it too has changed its route. It no longer passes through the city. After crossing the bridge, it now descends onto the dirt trail leading to the villages in the countryside.

The cityfolk are no longer bothered by the cutting stench. They have become immune to it and think it has died, like an old, forgotten tale.

But it continues to torment my body, and day and night a voice keeps telling me, 'Now, your turn! Now you shall see!' And this evening I find myself on the bridge, waiting for the wagon...waiting.

THE BACK ROOM

INTIZAR HUSAIN

The threshold of the back room appeared to her to be a boundary to a dark land. As she stepped across the dust-coated sill, her heart began pounding. With deliberate slowness, she moved into the dark room, always apprehensive and on the verge of turning back. Her perception of this room had changed many times. Out there, on the other side of the sill, was another world: dark but comforting and familiar. Often after playing in the scorching sun in the lane or courtyard, she entered the back room to hide behind its doors or slip behind the dirty, tarnished cauldron in one of the corners. The cooling darkness quenched her flushed, warm body. Her feet luxuriated in the chill of the soft soil. Mother was alive then. Whenever she saw her going in or out of the back room she chided her, 'Hey, you little pack rat! What are you doing rummaging around in all that junk? It's dark in there...what if a bug bites you?'

But her childhood had departed, her mother too, and with them, even that comforting darkness. The existence of the back room had become dulled in her memory—besides the house's many rooms, porticos and courtyards, she rarely even considered any more that it also had a back room.

The back room had remained closed for many years except when the change of a season required its opening. Sometimes particular seasonal supplies were needed. Occasionally it was also opened to store a broken charpoy or to take out a broken water-pot or a bucket splitting at the seams for repair.

This year, with the arrival of summer, the back room was opened again. The advent of this summer signalled another change in her perception of the room. She entered and arranged the winter quilts and mattresses on the upper shelf. As she descended she noticed a braided hairpiece hanging on a peg in front of her. She began thinking how oily and soiled her own had become. This one had a much nicer sheen, she was convinced. 'Why not take it?'

Suddenly her glance fell to the dusty floor below. God knows how many years had passed since it had been last swept. A broad, undulating line extended in the dirt from one corner where an old dusty chest of pots was stored and disappeared behind the tarnished cauldron in the corner near the door. She stared at it intently. Her feelings balanced between surprise and trepidation. She suspected something and contemplated calling Apaji. Then she noticed the ropes of the charpoy were lying loose and felt she had concluded hastily: 'It was probably only the imprint of the open charpoy lacings.'

Whenever she passed by the back room while sweeping the main rooms and courtyard, she thought of its dirt floor; a place where the dust was so deep that if she were to step inside, her bare feet were certain to be enveloped by the soft powdery earth. No matter how many times it was swept, there would always be more dirt. And that wavy line was there too, undulating across from the big chest to the copper cauldron. Its image billowed up in her mind and she tried to suppress it. But after a while her determination weakened and the coiling track-like line in the dark soil emerged in her imagination and swayed on into the darkness of the past...

'No, daughter, no! Don't ever call it out loud by its name!' Mother admonished Apaji. 'It has extra-sensitive ears and hears its name the moment it is spoken. I'll tell you about the experience I had once. I got up after my nap one afternoon and put on my slippers, and right in front of me in the courtyard was the cursed thing lying there, looking half-dead. I called for your husband. But curses! As soon as I uttered its name it went slithering off.'

Apaji was speechless, huddled up with her chin on her knee, her eyes fixed on mother's face. Mother started again:

'It is a very ancient one. We've heard tales about it ever since we first settled in this house. Our dear old mother-in-law—God rest her soul—used to go into the back room to get things without ever bothering to take a lamp. The poor old woman was nearsighted and tottered haphazardly into the room. There were a few times when it heard her footsteps and quickly slithered under the chest. But once she escaped by just a hair's breadth. She entered the room and began mumbling, "Hey, who threw this hairpiece on the ground?" She reached down to pick it up and, God preserve us, it was that snake!'

Apaji sat motionless. A shiver ran through her. 'Personally,' she said, 'I'd have never thought of such a thing. But now I remember a similar thing happened to your son. One day at high noon I went into the room to get the cot with the canvas strappings which I knew were grimy and needed washing. I didn't realize it at the time but he had followed right after me.

I was busy tugging at the cot when I heard him begin to mutter, "Who threw this cane on the ground? It was ordered specially from Naini Tal and they're hard to come by. Once it's broken that'll be the end of it." He was about to put his hand on it when, I tell you, it suddenly recoiled and slithered instantly out of sight.'

Mother confirmed, 'It's true. One moment he shows himself and the next he's disappeared... I pray to Allah that we be spared from all evil spirits.'

Apaji drifted off into her thoughts. Shuddering, she returned to her senses. 'Yes, may Allah protect us from every evil, and especially from that dreadful thing whose very name gives me gooseflesh.'

'But, Daughter,' Mother responded, 'each has his own fate. Those destined for good fortune will receive it even from their enemies. God bless our mother-in-law, she used to tell us this story: Once a prince was tricked by the family of his bride-to-be. They put a common old hag in the marriage palanquin instead of the princess. She was toothless and grey-haired. Her body was listless and her skin was as wrinkled as a prune. On the wedding night, she sat waiting on the nuptial bed, covered by a beautiful red mantle. She trembled, fearing the prince's arrival and the disastrous moment when he would lift her veil. Then suddenly a very strange thing happened. A black snake hung by his tail from the rafters just over her head. His mouth was gaping. He glided down, and then a little more until his mouth touched her hair. The pitiful thing froze stiff with fear. Then the most bizarre thing happened. He drew a strand of her hair into his mouth and then dropped it. The strand had turned completely black and was so long that it extended all the way down to her waist. He took another and another until all of her hair had turned completely black and was so long that it extended all the way down to her waist. When the prince entered, he was overwhelmed. He thought he had entered the boudoir of a fairy princess rather than an ordinary bridal suite. The fairy princess was his bride; her face shone like the moon, her body was supple and fair as flour, her tresses were luxuriant and serpentine. His heart and soul were captured by her beauty.'

Apaji fixed her gaze on Mother's face. She was astounded by the story. 'Mother,' she asked, 'how could she turn into a princess?'

'My dear, when fate is set in motion, even the physical body can change.'

'But Mother, a change like that?' Apaji exclaimed incredulously.

Wrinkles formed on Mother's brows. 'Do you think I would tell you a lie and wager my chances for heaven?' she said. 'If it's a lie, then the punishment goes to the one who first told the story. I told you just what I heard. But, Daughter, the crucial point is that every person lives according to the decrees of his fate. Normally that creature wouldn't hesitate to harm anyone. Snakes are poisonous enemies of mankind. They are such stubborn things that neither disease nor death can subdue them.'

'Oh, Mother! What are you saying?' Apaji couldn't contain her words of wonder and disbelief.

'Girl, you doubt everything. You may not believe this either, but it's said that snakes only begin to age after a thousand years. He sheds his skin a hundred times and just like that he's rejuvenated. He never dies a natural death. If someone were to bash his head in, well, that's a different matter.'

Apaji thought for a while, then asked, 'Mother, why doesn't he die?'

'Because he's eaten a charmed herb, that's why,' Mother replied and went on. 'Long, long ago—and you may doubt this too, if you like—there lived a king in Babylonia. He had a minister—a very chivalrous minister, it is said. Together, the king and his minister conquered one territory after another. Then one day the minister died unexpectedly. That shook the king's spirit but he bore the loss courageously and solemnly pledged to conquer death itself. A wise old dervish told him about one of the Seven Seas which contained a special herb. The king followed his directions and journeyed heedlessly, without thought of food or water, until at last he reached his destination. As soon as he arrived at the spot he plunged into the water and brought the charmed herb up from the bottom. Had he but eaten it, he would have rid himself of death, once for all. But as luck would have it, on his return journey, the king came upon a river. He was exhausted and decided to bathe and cool his body in the river. Leaving his clothes on the bank he splashed into the river. Meanwhile, back on the bank a snake snatched the herb into his mouth and slithered away quickly. The king dashed out of the water and ran after the snake. He trampled the whole jungle, turning it upside down, searching every tree, examining every cave. But, girl, the creature had completely vanished.'

Again and again things appeared and vanished; lightning would flash before her eyes, then darkness. This elusiveness of things was a constant source of bewilderment. She recalled her childhood and her playmate Battu. They played together untroubled by the time of day or concerns outside of their own amusement. And Battu—so accomplished was he in his ability to disappear at any instant from her sight! Those days were merely a dream to her now. How he could hide in the back room when they played cops and robbers! The corner where the big cauldron was stored, the big chest of cooking pots, the charpoy standing up on end—all those things slowly, slowly began to emerge in the darkness...everything but Battu. 'Oh God, where's he disappeared to? Which cave is he hiding in? Has he been swallowed up by the earth or eaten by the sky?" And just then, as she would be thinking all that, a dark, black head would begin inching its way up from behind the chest of pots. She would spring forward and grab him. "Aha! The thief is caught!'

Sometimes when they played hide-and-seek the back room offered the ideal hiding place. They would both enter it and hide themselves in a corner. A long time would pass while they stood silently. Slowly, very slowly the darkness would begin its work. It seeped into their bodies and then departed, establishing a new relationship between the inner and the outer worlds. The world of sound and sight seemed to remain far in the distance as the world of darkness began. A journey of infinite leagues. No signs, no stopping points. With the sound of footsteps in the courtyard the world of darkness contracted... Or when they played blindman's buff. Battu, the blindman, entered the back room with such confidence, as if everything were visible to him. He neared the cauldron and suddenly clamped his hands on her, catching her braid so forcefully that she had to let out a scream.

Only recently had she started using a hairpiece. There was a time when her hair was so long that it was a nuisance to care for. It was long, lustrous hair that braided into a thick black whip. It waved over her back, far below her waist. Before taking a bath, she used to sit on the small bath stool and loosen her hair to wash it with the soapnut powder she had prepared. Her tresses bobbed against the wet floor. But a sudden, violent attack of cerebral meningitis had left her hair dull and spotty. During the severe days of the illness she was in a coma for three days. She lost all sense of who or where she was. Now she thought about those three days as a long journey into darkness. She passed from one black boundary to another, each opening into a new, dark land. And finally, into the ultimate black kingdom. Again and again she approached the limits and turned back, returning to the world of sound and light. The effects of that long, fearful journey were apparent: her body had degenerated and her hair had become thin and short, its lustre dulled. Now, only with the help of the hairpiece could her braid assume its former length.

While passing through the courtyard her feet often led her in the direction of the back room. She remembered the oily, matted hairpiece. God knows how many years it has hung there on the peg. 'Would it be worth the bother to weave it into my own braid?'

Repeatedly she abandoned the impulse to go in and take it down from the peg. But unconsciously her glance returned to the back room, spurring thoughts of the hairpiece and an impulse to go there. She approached the door, halted and retraced her steps. The thread of her imagination began to lengthen and wind into the nooks and corners of days past...

'Mother, there was plenty of oil! I shook the lantern at bedtime and checked it myself. I think the wick must have fallen inside.'

'Well then, why did you turn it down so low?' Mother demanded. 'These are uncertain times; God knows what may come up. The lantern must never be extinguished! Poor me, I didn't know what to do. It was so dark in here I couldn't tell one hand from the other. I heard a rustling sound but couldn't make out what it was. I thought maybe it was a snake but wasn't sure if I was just imagining things. All of a sudden, the chickens in the coop began cackling. As soon as I looked towards the coop I saw it...you can't imagine how long it was! I almost dropped dead. I couldn't utter a sound. Finally, I managed enough courage to call you.'

'Mother, I don't remember you calling me.'

'Dear girl, you sleep like a log. Even if this house were filled with the tumult of Judgement Day or kettledrums played right in your ear, they still wouldn't wake you up. A sleeping man's like a dead man; woe to such a sleep! Anyway, I then called Naseeban. I kept calling her but she seemed to have dropped dead too. What could I do? I sat stone-still the whole night and kept reciting verses from the Quran. I was afraid lest I should fall asleep and someone might get up to go to the toilet and...especially Safia—she has this terrible habit of getting out of bed and sleepwalking barefoot to the outhouse. I was in this predicament when the sun finally arose and it gradually became lighter...'

'Safia! What are you doing?' Apaji's voice shot up from the kitchen. Safia mumbled something and instantly her thoughts vanished. Then she became so immersed in her household chores that she lost consciousness of her mind and body. She spread the brassware and kitchen utensils out in front of her and taking fistfuls of ash from the plate, dropped some into each vessel. She scrubbed each one so vigorously with the jute pad that when she rinsed them in the tap water and lined them up on the brick platform they reflected the sunlight like mirrors. They appeared gilded rather than scoured. When her ash-covered hands brushed against the running water the light blue glass bangles on her wrists made delicate tinkling sounds. Her fair fingers and wrists glistened with the water and a ray of light danced across her forearm.

Soon afterwards her glimmering fingers became covered with dough and the breadboard began ringing unceasingly from the steady motion of her fists. The moist dough stuck to her wrists and even one or two of her bracelets. Safia kneaded it to the perfect consistency. She rolled out paper-thin rotis and put them on the griddle. Then she placed each one on the open coals to puff them up and stacked them in the bread basket.

In the dusky light of evening when she removed the griddle from the hearth and turned it upside down, the countless flying red sparks looked like so many stars floating in the black soot.

'Apaji, the griddle's laughing!'

'The laughing of a griddle is not a good omen,' Apaji answered in a concerned tone. 'Put some ash on it.'

Even while performing these household tasks her thoughts would stray elsewhere. Sweeping the courtyard or tightening the straps on the canvas-laced cot, or unknotting the skeins of silken thread, the cellar of her imagination would open into its own world, independently of the motion of her hands. The wavy line began to reach into the darkness of forgotten days. The thought of Mother brought with it the memory of her gossip sessions and stories. She remembered how calmly she could pass over the most astounding things and yet be so shocked at banal matters. Once when she was cleaning a cauldron stored in a corner of the back room, she uncovered a snake skin with her hand. She picked it up nonchalantly and tucked it carefully away, saying, 'Basheeran could use it to prepare a syrup for her daughter who's ill with whooping cough.' There was another time too when the stiff carcass of a white pigeon found in the pigeon hole one morning made Mother suddenly remember the hissing sound she had heard come from the vicinity of the dovecote in the middle of the night.

She envied Mother, a person to whom invisible things revealed themselves. As for herself, ever since childhood her path had been covered by markings and clues of the phenomenal world, but the substance always eluded her. Shadows crossed her path at every turn, but never the figure that cast the shadow. Sometimes the traces appeared so fresh she thought a step or two more and she would catch up. Such a thought invariably set her heart pounding and made her body tremble and her feet too heavy to move.

It rained that day when she and Battu arose at early dawn and left the house in search of rain bugs. At the edge of the black mango orchard a drenched neem tree lay fallen on the soggy earth. It was long, serpent-like, and its trunk was jet black. It looked like someone had just flayed it with an axe and the white fat lay scattered everywhere around. The scene froze them.

'Lightning struck last night.'

'Lightning?'

'Don't you know,' Battu began, 'it rained all night and the lightning struck real hard. It seemed like it landed right on our roof...' He babbled on, 'A black snake used to live in the hollow of this tree. He was a very ancient one. He must have come out in the night. Lightning strikes dark, black things, you know.'

'Where did he go then?' she asked fearfully.

'Where did he go!' He laughed at her ignorance. 'The lightning ripped him to pieces.'

The contemplation of these things elicited an overwhelming longing for those days to return; that someone might seize the spotted snake of the past by its head and reverse the direction of the meandering procession of names and relics. To once again hear Mother tell stories and pontificate, but to ignore all that and dart out early at dawn, barefoot, in the pelting rain, towards the jungle to search for rain bugs. If there were no rain bugs, there were always cuckoos; and if there were no cuckoos, then at least there were always toadstools.

The awning overhanging the front of the balcony was so old its wood had rotted and turned dark; when it rained it looked darker still. After a few showers a white pulp-like substance pushed through its cracks and joints. Gradually black and white umbrella-cap mushrooms began to unfold.

Some mushrooms were chalky white, some were black speckled and others were striped. Picking them was often an inviting challenge. The toadstools growing on the awning were within the reach of both, but the big fat ones growing directly below it on the wall even Battu could not reach, let alone she. Once, however, supporting himself with the lattice and bracing his foot on the ledge, Battu did manage to raise himself high enough to just touch the awning—the most giant ones remaining still beyond his reach. That did not bother him, for no matter how far a thing was from his grasp, Battu was sure to make a daring attempt, once at least.

On the path to the mango orchard lay an old abandoned well. It was so shaded over by the dense foliage of a sprawling banyan tree that unless she bent over and peered hard she scarcely believed it had any water at all. Battu would crawl out on one of the branches directly above the well and announce audaciously, 'I'm going to jump...'

The ground seemed to slip from underneath her feet and she would find herself entreating, 'No, Battu, no!' From Battu's expression it was evident that her ardent pleadings made no impression on him at all and that he would jump into the well any moment. But he would not; instead, he would slide down the trunk of the tree to the ground. One day he jumped, though— jumped or fell or what, she could never know. He had gone there alone that day. She only heard the commotion afterwards. Shabrati, the water-carrier, came running and began pounding on the door of Battu's house. Battu's father ran out, looking stunned and worried, and made straight for the well, followed by many other people from the neighbourhood. Those who stayed behind stood about in small groups, dumbfounded.

'Who? Battu?'

'He fell into the old well—how?'

'My God, that child's really wild!'

Apaji was saying, 'That boy's a real daredevil. Whenever he came here, all he did was hang from the awning or the edge of the roof. He'd make my heart flip. I scolded him a thousand times for performing his acrobatics here. I even spanked Safia once for being crazy right along with him. But, I'm sure the ghouls ride that boy's back. He never listened to a word I said, nor anyone else's for that matter.'

'He's the only son of his poor parents,' interjected Mother. 'May Allah have mercy on them.'

Apaji's tone of voice changed, 'Yes, may Allah have mercy on them. I pray that he be spared, but I want to make it perfectly clear that whatever happens our girl will never become his. How can one trust such a youngster? Who knows what he might do!'

'Well, this is a problem for another time.' Mother heaved a sigh. 'Right now, God have mercy on the poor fellow. There's evil in that dark well. Every year someone's sacrificed to it.'

Evening came and some people brought him home stretched out on a cot. His clothes were drenched from the water, his hair was matted, face pale and sallow, and body limp. He was lying unconscious. For some time deathly silence settled over the lane—the same silence which was to return once again many years later and, again, on account of Battu: the day the telegram came. God knows what had gotten into Battu's head that, without telling a word to anybody at home, he enlisted in the army and volunteered for front-line duty. For a year or two there was no news of him. When finally it did arrive it came in the form of the announcement of his death while serving in a foreign country.

'Good Lord, a telegram about Battu!'

'A telegram about Battu? Allah, be merciful!'

Apaji, who was making rotis, suddenly turned the griddle over and snuffed out the fire. For a short time the lane was hushed. People stood about in small groups, stunned, only communicating through their eyes. As Battu's father read the telegram his hands began to shake and without raising his head he went inside.

She shuddered back into the present. She had put soapnuts in a bowl to soak and placed the bowl itself outside in the sun on the brick ledge; the soapnuts had ballooned up by now. Hastily she loosened her hair. The grey suds in her hair made it look even more off-colour. She finished bathing and went out into the mid-afternoon sun and stood a moment near the brick ledge. She tossed her hair from side to side a couple of times and then walked into the room and stood before the mirror. Some of the body and softness had doubtless been revived, but the qualities it once had when it waved over her shoulders or when she made a bun which swung freely like a shining platter were gone. For hours Mother combed it, arranged it and braided it. Ritually she used to pull it back into coiled strands and blow on them while reciting auspicious Quranic verses. Then taking a small hank of hair she would tuck it away in a chink of the brick wall. Now—now her hair is lifeless and thin. Mother's comb and skilful fingers are gone too. She turned her focus from her hair to her face, a face which used to radiate the essence of beauty. The previous glow of her body had begun ebbing too. She remembered hearing the whispers exchanged between an elderly woman and Apaji in a gossip session just a few days ago.

'Apaji, how long do you people intend to keep this girl at your hearth? She is already past the age. She'll get impatient if you aren't careful.'

'Do you think I want to keep her around at home any longer? It's hardly the time for her to be sitting around here...but what can I do?'

'As soon as someone comes along, marry her off, I'd say.'

She shook herself again and began combing her hair somewhat energetically. Arranging her hair with her fingers she noticed that it was dry and brittle despite all the oil she applied. Dullness had overshadowed its lustrous shine. While braiding it, she picked up the hairpiece. It appeared thinner than her real hair, matted and greasier. She put it down and went out into the courtyard towards the back room. She walked hypnotically, as if in a dream, as if someone had caught her in a magic spell. She put her foot on the door sill and opened the latch. She gave the door panels a slight jerk and shoved them open. As she entered the back room she suddenly became aware she was stepping into that realm of darkness. She recalled the wavy line coiling from the large chest to the cauldron. Her heartbeat quickened. She moved further into the darkness, as if descending below, where the earth beckoned. Another wave of delirium rushed her senses. A state of intoxication, a vague fear that some great trial might confront her—the mystery unknown. Moving on into the darkness she felt the soft earth beneath her feet, the same powdery earth which she had walked on many times before, where the details of her footprints would appear as etchings in the dust. She looked at the floor coated with fine dust beneath her feet, where was that wavy line? Had it been rubbed out or was it never really here? She reached towards the peg and took the hairpiece down. It was oily, matted, coated with dust. She put it back. As she came out of the back room, the intoxication which had flooded her mind had already vanished. And a dullness like that of her dry pallid hair began settling over her body like a fine mist.

Co-translated by Caroline J. Beeson

VOICES

MUHAMMAD SALIM-UR-RAHMAN

'I want to keep dogs.'

'What for?' the woman's voice flickered in the darkness.

'I want to keep dogs.'

'What for? Because we are lonely? Come to think of it, Suraiya hasn't written in a long time. Good, she must be happy with her husband. And Nasim—well, he's practically forgotten us. He never writes. What's that place in America? Sannata? Sansanata? That picture postcard...it was so lovely, no? God knows where I put it away. He hasn't sent us anything since, has he? Tell me! You haven't been keeping his letters from me? God knows what time it is.'

It was pitch dark inside the room. There had been a power failure. A chilly October night, with jumbled sounds drifting in from afar, like faint lines appearing and dissolving on a thick, darkened screen. The man felt he was lying on an ocean floor, splayed out among a profusion of oysters, shells, corals, seaweed, smooth round pebbles, fish eggs—splayed out like a fish, with his fish-wife, his *fishette*—could there be such a word, he wondered—right beside him. He caressed her thigh. 'My fish.'

The woman laughed softly. 'My dog.'

The man smiled. The woman couldn't see him smiling.

'Dogs!' he said.

'Wouldn't one dog be enough?' she asked.

'This too is a dream. Many dogs, all kinds of dogs: black, brown, white, chocolate, black-and-white, brindled, pied—even perhaps green, yellow, colourless—as colourless as water. I'm out hunting with them. Evening. A green expanse rolling out as far as the eye can see, in which we are speeding along like splashes of so many colours, speeding along. I want to hunt down the moon.'

'You are mad,' the woman said.

There was a silence. 'Oh, still quite a while before daybreak,' the woman thought. 'The night is like a mountain. We are climbing down...or up. Must be down. There isn't strength any more to go up. Down and down and down. Perhaps that might help in falling asleep.' Thousands of stairs—black-and-white, black-white. A hurricane lantern's moving right along, as if by itself.

'I'd go mad if you weren't with me,' she said.

'You are with me, all the same I'm mad,' the man said.

She plunged her fingers in the man's hair. It used to be so bushy, she reminisced with a twinge of sadness. Outside, a car sped by, crushing the gravel. Someone whistled along.

'We could be mad, really. After all, who can tell? We've nothing. We are mad, really.'

'It isn't easy to be mad,' the man said. 'The likes of you and I can never be mad. We are too damn conscious of ourselves. Too self-absorbed. You are your own prisoner, and I my own. The mad are a free people. That's why the world fears them and puts them behind bars. Wants to forget them. You may shackle a mad man however you will, but he'll always be free. How strange: we who are captives walk around in the world unrestrained, and the truly free are put away!'

'Then what shall we do to become mad?'

'Keep dogs!' the man said. They laughed.

A long silence ensued.

'Can't sleep,' she said.

'Yes.'

'Power's out; can't even watch a movie on the VCR.'

'Yes. If we could just fall asleep, we may be able to have a dream.'

After a brief silence he said, 'Let's play.'

'In the dark?' she giggled like a teenage girl.

'I mean with words. I'll tell you a story, a short one, then you tell it back to me, changing it along.'

'Changing it along—how? When did I ever know any stories?'

'Just the day before yesterday after watching a TV play, you said it should rather have been written in such and such way—remember? Well, think of my story as that TV play.'

She lowered herself upon him, supporting herself on her elbows. 'Here we go,' she said.

'Where?'

'Tell your story. That's all.'

'All right. Listen. Once upon a time there lived a man in a rundown neighbourhood of Baghdad. He was a nice and pleasant man. He inherited a little money. Which soon ran out and he was reduced to dire straits. One night he had a dream in which he heard someone say: Get up and betake yourself to Cairo. There by the baker's on the western side of such and such bridge there lies buried a great treasure. Dig it up and make use of it. When the man woke up, he thought that a dream was, after all, a dream; it would be foolish to put one's trust in it.'

'Treasure reminds me to ask you to take out my jewellery from the bank locker day after tomorrow. I'm planning to attend the Friday wedding. So don't forget.'

'Don't interrupt! When the same message was repeated in a dream three nights in a row and the tone of the invisible interlocutor grew increasingly insistent and threatening, the man decided he could no longer ignore the matter. Then again, no compelling reason required him to stay on. So he left Baghdad and, after enduring great hardship, arrived in Cairo. There he found the bridge and, sure enough, the baker's shop on its western edge. However, there was a problem. The site was by a very busy thoroughfare. Traffic never let up on it, day or night. At night, with the rush over and only a few passers-by around, there was always an armed squad patrolling the place. How in the world was he to dig out the treasure? The man was annoyed and regretted having been talked into such a profitless venture merely by a voice in a dream. One day he sat by a corner on the edge of the bridge, his head hung low in disappointment. It had grown dark. A few pedestrians still trekked along. Here and there a shop was still open. All of a sudden, one of the guardsmen, who sported a handlebar moustache, and who often joked around with his fellow guardsmen, approached the man. For some time now this guard had been watching the man loiter in the vicinity of the bridge. The man's garb and demeanour further gave him away as a stranger. Naturally the guard was intrigued. He asked the man why he wandered in the area and why he looked so glum. The man told him the whole story. Whereupon the guard broke into a loud laughter and said, "You are an absolute idiot! You saw a dream and right away, without bothering to think twice, went dashing out. Now you sit moaning. Oh dear, I too had a dream last year and heard a similar voice urging me to set out for Baghdad. There, under the jujube tree in the courtyard of the house of so and so in such and such neighbourhood, I was told, lay buried the accumulated treasure of seven kings. Night after night the same voice frightened and threatened me, but I let the words drop in one ear and go out the other. So, man, listen to me and go back home. For nothing'll come of dreams." Saying this the guard moved along—but the man was left absolutely stunned. It was his own name which the guard had mentioned. The name of the neighbourhood was also correct. And to top it all off,

he had a jujube tree in the courtyard of his house. Right away he knew
the meaning of his dream. He immediately returned to Baghdad and lost
no time in digging out the treasure. All his problems were solved in one
fell swoop.'

'That's all?'

'"That's all"—whatever do you mean? This is mysticism, my dear. Quite
beyond you!'

'Maybe.'

The stillness around them deepened further. They could clearly hear
the clock ticking away in the adjoining room: as if a pair of tiny hands
were pounding away, softly but incessantly, in an effort to dig out and pry
open something from somewhere.

'You give up?' the man asked.

'No. Let me think,' she said. And the man tried to conjure up a face—a
familiar face, especially when it was absorbed by deep thought: forehead
creased with a couple of lines, dark, thick eyebrows, jet-black eyes, with a
faraway look, mouth a little contorted, as if from the exertion of thinking.
'Would there still be lines on her forehead?' the man thought. He groped
for the woman's hand and held it. Then locked his fingers into hers.

'No. The story didn't end that way,' the woman said, all of a sudden.

'Oh!'

'By the time the man returned to his home in the environs of Baghdad
it was already night. He was wiped out from fatigue. He had bought some
fried fish on his way home. He thought he'd warm it up, eat, and then rest.
The treasure wasn't running away, after all. He'd worry about it tomorrow.
He had warmed up the fish and barely taken the first morsel when there
was a knock at the door.'

'Wow!'

'He got up and opened the door. And who did he see? The same
moustachioed Cairene. They both were struck with amazement. Then the
guard said, "Oh I see, so you're the one who lives in this house. Well then,
my dream was a true one." When the man's amazement wore off, he said,
"I've got this fish, not a whole lot, but you're welcome." The moustachioed
guard didn't waste a minute. Promptly he sat down and began eating. When
they'd finished eating, the guard said, "After I spoke to you I was struck by
the thought that my dream might be a true one. Without further ado I set
out for Baghdad. I already knew where I was headed for. I just asked for
the address as I went along. The sight of the jujube tree in the courtyard

reassured me and as soon as you appeared at the door I knew the days of want and indigence were over."

'The two shot the breeze for quite awhile. The guard recounted with great gusto all he'd endured. Evidently, some of the episodes were pure fabrications. All the same, he knew the art of making a story sound interesting. When sleep overwhelmed them, they retired for the night.

'When they got up in the morning, the guard said, "The treasure's as good as ours. No rush. Let's go out and see a bit of the city. I've heard a lot about Baghdad. And don't you worry about the expenses. I've got ten gold pieces on me."

'Happily, they went sightseeing. Had it been a small place they might've tired of it in a couple of days. Not Baghdad. It was improbably large and full of attractions: carnivals, fairs, a hundred different amusements and entertainments, numerous promenades and recreation parks. Out before the crack of dawn, they never set foot in the house before dark: strolling in a park once, luxuriating in a meadow next. Or they went boat-riding on the river, or just wandered through the sprawling suburbs. They went through every neighbourhood. Old, dilapidated palaces seemed to attract them the most. They felt a particular fondness for them. The new ones, full of splendour and magnificence, these they only looked at from outside with a transient joy. The fellow, he knew Baghdad like the back of his hand. Who lived where, what happened where, he knew every last thing about the city by heart. The guard, on the other hand, had a thousand stories at the tip of his tongue. Their tongues knew not how to tire, nor did their feet. Every night they went to bed firmly resolved to dig out a little treasure the next day. But the next day they consoled themselves saying that the treasure was, after all, theirs, so why the rush. "We still haven't seen such and such part of the city," they would say. "So let's go there today." And that's how the days passed. Their clothes soon turned into rags. They'd make do by patching them up. When hunger overwhelmed them they headed for a soup kitchen. Hand in hand they combed the streets of Baghdad all day long, or wandered amidst its gardens and ruins.'

'And the treasure?'

'Well, if they didn't dig it up, what can I do?'

'You've screwed up the story beyond all recognition.'

'You asked me to alter it as I went along. And so I did. I don't know what's good or bad.'

Neither spoke for a while. At last, the man said, 'Go to sleep!'

'How?' the woman shot back irritably. 'I would if I could. Seems I can't.'

'Well then, let's go out. We'll watch the stars. That'll help us fall asleep—at least that's what they say.'

'Nonsense!'

'Come on. We'll watch the stars. No harm in watching.'

They put their slippers on and stepped out into the small backyard. They stood on the grass and looked at the sky strewn randomly with innumerable stars, some shining brightly, others twinkling faintly. Their arms strung across each other's waist, they stared at the sky. The universe looked chopped up into unbelievable distances. God knows across what distances the light had to travel before it reached them.

'Grandpa knew all their names by heart,' the man said.

'How far the stars are!' she observed.

'How far? You mean how close?' the man said.

'Close?'

'That's why they're visible.'

'How perfectly cool is their light!'

'That's because the night is cool. It makes their light feel cool too. Merely an illusion.'

'What if we found an abandoned child here—wouldn't that be fun?'

'What's the use? We'll bring him up, worry our heads over him, he'll grow up and one day leave us.'

'That's never stopped parents from bringing up kids.'

'A dog never leaves its master.'

'I'm feeling chilly.'

Slowly, they walked back in. The man felt as though some of the stillness of the sky, a deep, dark, far-reaching sky, had somehow become entangled with their bodies and crept in right along. Still the space outside looked brighter compared to the pitch darkness of the room.

They lay down next to each other, and it was as if they had just climbed down from a high place and, exhausted, had stretched out on a slope to catch their breath. 'Sleep, too, is a star,' the woman thought. A dog barked in the distance.

'This story…' she began.

'Which story?'

'Ours. What if we tried to change it?'

'How?'

'Like get up, and leave. Chuck everything. The house. The things in it. Everything. Just keep moving. On and on. Sleep where night overtook us. Eat with contentment whatever we could find. No particular place to go. Only a road to walk on. Walk on and on. Nothing to own. Absolutely nothing. And no regrets either.'

'We don't have the guts for that.'

'We don't?'

'Yes. It's all very well to ramble on like this. But when you get up in the morning, you'll be able to see this house clearly…the things in it—then? Yes, then? Tell me! What do we have to show for a lifetime of toil except this great pile of material things. We can't leave. We're much too sensible for that. We couldn't make such a terrible mistake. Neither you nor I.'

The woman drew a long breath and then placed both her palms on the man's cheeks, as though trying to hold a great big bowl.

'What a pity,' she said, 'that we can't even go… I mean, can't even become free.'

DO YOU SUPPOSE IT'S THE EAST WIND?

ALTAF FATIMA

The enormous weight of three hundred and sixty-five days once again slips from my hand and plops down into the dark cavern of the past. The windows in this desolate room are wide open. How improbably strange the sky, draped in a sheet of dense grey clouds, looks behind the luxuriant green trees. It seems someone has filled space itself with a sweet, melancholy beauty. A cool breeze has finally started to blow, after much heat and sun.

Could it be the east wind?

Papers and books lie in a disorderly pile before me on the desk. I suddenly stop writing, screw the cap back on the fountain pen and clip it to my collar—not because the weather is absolutely delightful and the grapevine maddeningly beautiful and one simply cannot write a book on dairy farming in a setting so entirely out of this world. One cannot discuss the significance of the chemical components of milk any more than one can expound on the proper proportion of corn husk and mustard oilcake in the cattle feed. All right, not another word about cows or water buffaloes.

My problem is that I'm very absent-minded. I search for my pen everywhere, while it's clipped to my collar all along. I look at faces I have seen so often and wonder who they might be—I have never seen them before. And my memory is so bad I can hardly remember who has hurt me and who I have decided to hold a grudge against. Worst of all, the day I'm supposed to take care of some enormously important matter, I seem to end up spending in some atrociously silly task. Well, that's what it's come to with me. My one abiding fear is that the landscapes of my memory might become a yawning wasteland—derelict, empty, pallid. That I may lose my grip on familiar things and no longer recognize them at all. That's why I have pushed aside the sheets of paper and clipped my pen back on. Just so that I may lean back and squint into the far horizon and not let my eyes waver—trekking back along the past's interminable highways, that time may twist around and look back. It just might.

What! It really has! There, look, the past is calling me. The scene before my eyes is beginning to dissolve, and a long-lost horizon is forming in space. This gigantic gate, here—it's the same gate whose wrought-iron bars we would hug tightly, and swing form for hours on end. Tickets would be improvised and sold; the guard would wave the green flag, and the passengers, planting their feet on the bottom railing and grabbing onto the grillwork, would enjoy the train ride, as the others energetically swung the gate out into the street. Directly across the street from the gate the ironsmith's furnace would be ablaze, the clank-clank of red-hot iron being beaten into shape resounding through the air. And inside the gate small and large gardens opened to view hedges of nirbisi and delicate trellises draped with rose vines. We would make believe that our train was chugging along beside jungle and farmland. To bring the train into a station, we would stick the thumb under the chin, run the index finger along the ridge of the nose all the way to the forehead, and cry with all the power our lungs could muster: Koo-ooo! It felt as if the train were actually entering the station.

The entire summer vacation was thus spent swinging from the gate and playing wild games filled with violence inside the summer house. There would be bloody skirmishes between robbers and cops, the robbers would be finally caught, they would repent, and right away set up stands where they would sell guavas and mulberries. Clay flowerpots would be broken, the shards then rubbed smooth into ser and half-ser weights and all kinds of coins. And suddenly, one day, the vacation would end and school would start the next day. But on that next day I would pretend I didn't know, and would manage to stay in bed until nine o'clock. The school bus would come and leave without me. But this couldn't go on. The very next day I would be violently shaken awake at four in the morning. Every time the school reopened, a fresh calamity awaited us. This time, though, it came in the form of a new teacher: a portly woman draped in a borderless sari and wearing eyeglasses. She put a Hindi primer in the hands of each of the Muslim students, and ordered them to learn it on their own. When I saw the primer I was offended. We were in the fifth class, weren't we? Then why were we being forced to learn it? We had already been through a similar primer once before. All the pictures were exactly the same. Anyway, she informed us that Hindi was compulsory in the fifth class. I carefully put the primer away in my satchel, and it stayed right there. Two days later when she showed up, I easily rattled off the lesson: alif for anaar, be for bakri, he for hookah, and daal for dhol. Crazy! Idiot! She was beside herself with anger, and ordered me to learn it all over again.

What misery! But who could I ask for help? The rest of the girls were much older than me, and spent free class periods crocheting lace or knitting red and green woollen sweaters. I, who still played with marbles and broken glass bangles, felt shy in their presence. So I took the primer back and thought the teacher was crazy herself. There were pictures of hubble-bubble and she-goat all right. Bright and clear. Anybody could see that. Yet she must get angry. When she yelled at me over and over again, I had to ask Mother for help: the teacher doesn't teach but keeps telling me to learn from somebody at home.

'Go ask Robby Dutt. He'll teach you,' Mother suggested.

So I begged the boy whose father—whom we used to call Maharaj— lived in the quarters outside in the compound.

Robby Dutt—his big eyes smeared with a thick layer of kajal, wearing a gigantic black tika in the middle of his forehead to ward off the evil eye, and a gold amulet strung on a black thread around his neck—rolled his eyes and spelled out his terms:

'You won't pull my braid, right?'

'Right.'

'Let me swing on the swing?'

'Yes.'

'Push the swing twenty times for me?'

'Yes.'

'And give me gos-roti to eat?'

At this point I faltered. If I gave him meat to eat as he wished, Mother's displeasure was sure to follow. She had expressly warned me, 'Don't you ever give him meat—understand?'

'All right, don't,' he said. 'I won't teach you.'

'I will, I will. Okay, I'll give you meat.'

And when His Majesty came in to teach, he would straightaway crouch all of himself under a cot or a settee. I'd pull him out of there somehow, and then, in a voice calculated to overwhelm me, he would command: 'Read! Chhota "a"! Bara "uu"! "Ee"!' All those pages with pictures on them—he had made me learn in no time at all.

Then one day he taught me: 'Mohan accha larka hain. Bhor bha'e jagta hain aur ashnaan karta hain.' (Mohan is a good boy. He gets up early in the morning and takes a bath.) I couldn't believe that such familiar words could possibly come out of such a strange alphabet.

'You miserable ass! You aren't teaching me properly.'

'Parhaa'e to rahe hain. Aur kya tumra sar parhaa'en?' (But I *am*! What else did you think I was doing?)

'Liar! Fraud! English sounds come out of English letters. And here you are teaching me Urdu in Hindi!'

'Go to hell! I'm done teaching you!'

He would throw in the towel and flee, because the matter was beyond him. He himself couldn't figure out how Hindi letters managed to emit Urdu sounds.

It took me a long time to make my peace with the idea that the letters of this weird and totally unfamiliar alphabet produced exactly the same sounds as the Urdu script I was familiar with.

Now the writing drill got underway. 'And what's this—the silly squiggly thing stuck to it?' I'd ask, pointing at the maatra for the vowel 'o'.

This would throw him off once again. 'Yeh eme hi hai. Tum is se mat bolo. Apna kaam karo.' (It's just there. Don't meddle with it. Do your work.)

In short, he wasn't counting on explaining the vowel marks, and explain them he did not.

But something like anxiety nagged at my heart. Sheer deception, this! It didn't make sense that you read in the strange-looking Hindi script exactly what you read in the Urdu script. Surely it was a plot to confound the reader. Out of sheer stubbornness I took it to heart that there was no point in slaving over this. Robby Dutt too seemed to have become fed up with my daily bickering and nagging. So I put the Hindi qaa'ida to one side. There was another reason too: I was soon going to attend a school where there was no such nonsense. And so that was the end of his teachership and my discipleship.

He was now scarcely seen all day long. He'd go to school, and when he returned would dart out to wander around. Or else he would stay at home and talk like hoary old men. He had no siblings and all his close kin were back in his hometown.

Yep, Robby Dutt, you were really something. Even now I can see you vividly against the background. The truth is, you're never far from view. Whenever the rains come—and with them the thought that back at the old house dark rain clouds would be pouring down in a torrent, letting rivers of water gush noisily along the eaves, and people would be celebrating Saluno, the festival of Raksha Bandhan—how can I not remember you? When the ties of teacher and taught broke off between us, you quickly forged another bond. You stood behind the door and kept repeating in your muted voice: 'Tum kesi behni ho, tum hamre raakhi bhi nahin baandhat ho.' (What kind of sister are you? You don't even tie a raakhi on my wrist!) And yet again: 'Auron ki behnen to bhaiya logan ke raakhiyaan baandhat hain.' (Other sisters tie raakhis on their brothers.)

The whole day long you kept showing up behind the door, hurling taunt after taunt at me for not tying a raakhi, until Mother finally relented. She sent for a few raakhis from the bazaar and gave them to me. Next time when you sneaked behind the door, I grabbed your hand and tied the whole lot on your wrist. Seeing not one, not even two, but three separate raakhis on your wrist, you became overjoyed and sprinted off, reappearing only in the evening, clad in a sparkling white dhoti and lacework kurta, a Gandhi cap on your head, holding a brass tray, with rice, andarsas, bananas and coins amounting to about half a rupee. Then, extending your hand from behind the door, you set the tray down and said, 'This is your dacchana.'

Oh, you really were something. When did I have the mind to, when was I eager to tie raakhis? But every year, well before Saluno, you'd keep reminding me, 'Raakhi mangaali hamri?' (So, have you sent for my raakhi?)

Deep inside, how much you valued being made my brother. When Bibi came from Shimla for the first time after her marriage, you lugged her bedroll inside the house yourself, practically doubling over under the weight. When told that you didn't have to, that Jabbal could have just as easily carried it in, you replied quietly, 'Why Jabbal? After all, didn't Aapa's groom tease Aapa, saying what kind of brother you've got—he can't even carry your bedroll for you!'

And that wasn't all. You were pretty strange. You would fight over the swing, and when I gave it a push, you would say in your quivering voice, 'Not so fast! Easy! I'm scared!'

'Why are you scared? I'm not.'

You would say quietly, 'Tum gos-roti khaati ho, ham daal-roti khaate hain.' (Because you eat meat and bread and I eat daal and bread.)

And if anyone ever asked you whether you were Hindu or Muslim, you replied with great equanimity, 'Me? My clan and caste are the same as Begum Sahib's. Why, I'm Begum Sahib's son.'

This was, though, you were a Brahmin, and a Brahmin of the most elevated rank; indeed, so elevated that your doctor grandfather had no qualms about giving his daughter's hand in marriage to a confirmed idler such as your father.

Anyway, whenever a little free time came your way, you would quickly make wuzu, unroll Mother's prayer mat on the settee, and start performing one ruku after another, dropping your forehead in sijdah after sijdah, mumbling a prayer under your breath and quickly passing your open hands over your face. And if anyone laughed, you felt hugely offended.

If a Hindu reproached your mother, the Maharajan, saying that you always hung out with Muslims and mimicked their ways, she would just laugh off the matter good-naturedly, saying, 'Just as well. Let him live as a Muslim. This way at least he might live. My two other boys both died.'

Well, the high point of the story came when a craze to hold milaads swept through the entire neighbourhood. We did it too, and that did it. Nobody could reason with you. You fought with the Maharajan and kept insisting on holding a milaad too, and she, a simple woman, consented. She prepared the floor, spread cotton rugs and sparkling white sheets borrowed from our house; she sent for flower bouquets; she burnt incense sticks; and she begged Pathani Bua to come and perform the milaad, because 'my lallah wouldn't have it any other way'.

And guess who turned out to be the MC of the event? You, of course. Who else? You doled out paans to everyone gathered there, then daubed them with attar, sprinkling rose water from the dispenser every five minutes, worrying to death that you might have missed a detail that was part of the milaad ceremony at your Begum Sahib's.

On winter nights, when everyone tucked themselves quite early under heavy cotton quilts and sometimes listened to stories, you too would burrow into somebody's quilt and linger there.

And then it seemed the earth grew both weary of its weight and impatient with familiar faces and voices. It was like somebody had violently threshed the grain in a winnowing fan. One flew and landed here, another somewhere else. But grain and seed, no matter where they land, invariably set up fresh worlds for themselves, sending their slender roots, like leeches, deep into the earth. They cling to it, and in time tear open the earth's bosom and pop out.

Well, Robby Dutt, it's like this: I ended up here. You must be still there, grown into an honourable man, responsible and wise. Once again the rainy season has arrived. It must be pouring back where you are. Farmers, wearing folded gunnysack shells for raincoats, must be busy digging ditches and taking care of the fields. Flocks of herons and parrots must be zooming back and forth overhead. Brahmin women must still saunter out during Saluno carrying raakhis for their brothers, draped in snappy red and green saris, bindis on foreheads, feet stained with henna, black and green bangles strung up the length of their flashing white, plump arms.

Your arms must be covered with raakhis, and you must still offer dacchanas—but openly, not from behind the door.

So what? What do I care? I wasn't exactly dying to tie a raakhi, you practically forced me to. Then again, the time for those insignificant little nothings is well past now. Mankind now thinks only of big things, of things that matter, and despises everything that is small or looks diminished. And to tell you the truth, you or I or anyone who thinks about the past does wrong. Why must life stay fixed at one place? Life's ship must pitch and rock forever on the restless waves of time. What if we had gotten stuck on the beach?

On life's ocean one ship sails east, another west. Favourable winds push them on, and fate determines their destinations.

The ships of your life and mine also sailed to shores destined for us. And yet, why does this desire suddenly overwhelm me—to fly off quietly to where you are, sitting grand and dignified, to sneak up behind you and whack you and ask, 'Wanna have me tie a raakhi? And tell me, which tray of dacchana is for me?'

Why are all these long-lost memories returning to me, like an old pain suddenly come back to life? It's because after much smouldering heat and burning sun, a cool breeze has finally started to blow.

Do you suppose it's the east wind?

MA'I DADA—THE MAN WITH THREE NAMES

ASAD MUHAMMAD KHAN

Like the three names of maya*, 'Grandfather' Ma'i's names were also three: Majeeta, Majeed and Ma'i Dada. Those who called him Majeeta had given up the ghost during his lifetime. The few hoary old men who called him Majeed, or 'Arre Maan Majeed', lingered on for a while longer. To the rest—and this included the whole town—he was at all times Ma'i Dada.

His real name though, as he himself stated, was Abdul Mazid Khan Esoop Ja'i. Thus, in the police papers, ration cards, state hospital records and finally in the register of the cemetery, he was entered as Abdul Majid Khan Yusuf Zai—a name which would have been inscribed on his tombstone as well, had he left an heir, for that was his will. But the neighbourhood dhobis had spread the rumour that by caste he was a Hindu Teli who hadn't even been circumcised.

The reason Ma'i Dada gave for the absolutely disgraceful conduct of the dhobis was that as a strapping young man he had managed to offend them in the matter of their womenfolk, and this progeny of foul animals had had it in for him ever since.

All I know about his exploits in the dhobi quarters is that as a young man he was really something to behold, and that his last heart-throb, Jamrat Dhoban, died in 1965 at the ripe old age of seventy.

I have also seen a crumbly sepia photograph, shot from one of those old box cameras, in which an eighteen- or twenty-year-old Ma'i Dada is shown staring straight into the camera lens—holding an iron-tipped club reaching all the way up to his ear lobe, a gigantic paggar on his head, his eyes, glinting like stars, heavily lined with collyrium. The late Phupha Abba had taken this snapshot. He was the first in the whole town, in 1800 something, to have sent to a Parsi firm in Bombay for a camera, which had arrived cash on delivery. The scandal-loving gossips of the family had spread the rumour that Ma'i Dada used to kidnap women for Phupha Abba and his cronies and was their main contact with the local high-livers. But this was pure wickedness. Phupha Abba was a genuine Pathan who had memorized the entire Quran by heart. As for Ma'i Dada—well, wasn't he a Yusuf Zai after all? How could he even imagine stooping to such base

---

*The allusion is to the folk saying 'Maya ke teen naam—Parsa, Parsu, Paras Ram'.

things? It is said that Phupha Abba had bought him a tapancha, which he likely never even fired but which he nonetheless frequently used to put fear into people.

I remember Ma'i Dada making frequent references to this pistol. Long before Partition, some stinking bastard—or, as Dada put it, some 'azal giraphta, bhaan ka ghora'—had swiped it and the dhobis had spread the rumour that the thief had sold it to the junk-dealer for its weight in crispy sweet flats of gajak. Ma'i Dada was badly shaken by the incident, and was all set to report the theft to the police, but people talked him out of it saying, 'Are you looking for trouble? Don't you breathe a word to the police! An unlicensed weapon! Are you out of your mind? They'll just book you instead.'

Ma'i Dada felt utterly helpless. He stewed in his own juices and waited for years to find the son of a dog who had his tapancha, so he could rip out his guts and tie them around his neck. Or, as he put it, 'around the neck of that azal giraphta, bhaan ka ghora'.

To rip out someone's guts and hang them around his neck was his favourite threat. And the phrase 'azal giraphta' he had heard from my uncle who, back in those days, was particularly fond of reading the *Tilism-e Hosh-ruba* out loud to us.

It was Ma'i Dada's considered opinion that all these tomes—*Tilism-e Hosh-ruba*, *Qissa Tota-Maina*, *Anvaar Sohaili* and such like—were perfectly okay. But this English education, it turned a man into a 'naamard'—a sissy. He used this word for 'coward', and often regretted it tremendously: 'What an outrage! Ever since these Pathan bachchas have started to learn English, not one person in the family has managed to commit a single katal.'

One day Father overheard the comment and gave him such a tongue-lashing that Ma'i Dada remained out of sorts with everyone for a full four days. He didn't talk to anyone. Finally, on the fifth day, he signalled for me to approach him and confided in me that 'Aligarh has spoiled your father. He wasn't at all like this before. Now what is this? I say something perfectly proper and he flies off the handle. For no reason at all.'

But one thing was beyond dispute. Others didn't receive half as much love from him as Father and all of us brothers and sisters did. He was fond, though, of our entire clan—the 'kutamb-qabeela' in his words. He would tell me: 'I'm the mashtar of the saakh-sajar of your kutamb-qabeela.' And that 'nowhere else have I seen such a chaaron khoont saakh-sajar.'

By 'saakh-sajar' he meant 'shajara-e nasab'—the genealogical tree. But what 'chaaron khoont saakh-sajar' could possibly mean, I neither asked nor did he volunteer to explain.

And I can vouch for the fact that as far as my family and clan were concerned, Ma'i Dada was clearly an expert on its genealogical tree.

It was customary with the elders of this now-defunct line that as soon as a boy was competent enough to write his name, his dada, taya, chacha or father would hand him the genealogical tree and say, 'Here, now, son, make a hundred copies in a clear, neat hand.' Of course the genealogical trees could only be written with reed pens and the thickest, blackest ink. Writing the names of our ancestors with a pencil or a fountain pen was considered the height of indecency, indeed a veritable outrage against religion—a 'mudaakhalat fi'd-deen'. To draw the tables properly took whole months. But it was a non-negotiable matter, a determinism of birth which could not be escaped. After the tables had been completed, the family patriarch of the time would call in the boys to examine their handiwork. After he had had them recite the gamut of kalimas, the al-Hamdu Shareef and the four Quls, he would have a boy repeat his main and branch genealogical lines from memory and reward him with a machine-minted rupee. To miss a link anywhere in the chain was inconceivable, simply because So-and-So Muhammad Khan, son of So-and-So Muhammad Khan, and his own son, So-and-So Muhammad Khan, had for months roamed, swords unsheathed, in the boy's very dreams. How could *anyone* forget them?

My dada, though, contrary to the other family patriarchs, usually looked the other way if a boy turned in a poorly calligraphed work. Boys are human, after all. But if by mistake they entered, in place of So-and-So Muhammad Khan, son of So-and-So Muhammad Khan, the name of some other So-and-So Muhammad Khan, and Dada caught it, his wrath was sure to follow. The pens would practically be broken on the offender's fingers. 'You pig! What—you're turning my grandfather of the purest pedigree into a bastard!' Back then, we couldn't understand why Dada got so upset over this—all right, we'll correct the mistake, what's there to get so angry about?—but now I guess I dimly understand the reason for the severity that characterized our people. Separated from its native land by thousands of miles and several centuries, so that it had nearly forgotten its own native tongue, this Pashtun clan was fighting a losing battle to preserve its lineage, at least on paper.

For some of them also occasionally married into Sheikh and Mughal families, and a few miscreants didn't even hesitate to marry the daughter of a Syed. God forbid! To extract service from a woman of the Prophet's own family, even on occasion to scold her—the very thought of such disgraceful conduct was enough to send shivers down the spine.

So, like every other male offspring of the family, I too had to endure the torment of copying genealogical tables, a torment as mandatory as circumcision. On the face of it, managing eight generations between Alamgir Badshah and myself shouldn't have been particularly hard. But they were warriors, and didn't have much of a grasp of family planning. Well, I felt completely overmatched. For instance, So-and-So Muhammad Khan had sired five sons, who collectively sired twenty-eight or twenty-nine, of which only two were childless: the remaining twenty-six or twenty-seven had left X number of children, and they, in turn, Y number of children...and this only halfway down, to the fourth generation. Just then, an explanatory genealogical table would be thrown at us into the bargain: Okay, son, now figure out these four generations from their mothers' side.

Another misery, one even more complex and layered, would get underway at this point. Rarely, if ever, did they marry outside the clan. After all, purity of blood and bone had to be preserved. All this created a messy situation for me. A dada or nana by one genealogical reckoning turned out to be my chacha by another, and a mamun by still another somewhat remote computation. And no argument—period. How could it be otherwise! Several thousand sheets can't all be wrong. Now then, this gentleman, who is dead set on marrying my phuphi's daughter—he will become my brother-in-law; but if you look him up in column five of the branch-line of the table, then he'll be a brother, albeit by a somewhat circuitous computation.

The torment made me literally cry out. Just then, like a timely angel sent by God, Ma'i Dada would walk in to rescue me. Within seconds he would solve the knotty problem. He would stay with me for hours, unravelling knot after genealogical knot and giving a boost to my sagging spirit all the while.

It never even occurred to us to ask him about his own lineage. And if the thought ever did cross our minds, we probably refrained from asking out of deference to his sensitivity in the matter, made keener still by the dhobis' gossip. Once a venerable old lady good-naturedly asked him, 'Well, Majeed, you have crammed the genealogies of just about everyone, but do you know your own?' Ma'i Dada responded with the same good-naturedness, 'Yes, Biya, why not? Here: Samser, son of Samser, son of Samser, son of Abdul Mazid Khan Esoop Ja'i,' and then burst into roaring laughter. This historic joke of Nadir Shah Durrani had been related to him by none other than Uncle.

If a single two-word term could describe his ambition for us boys, it was 'Pashtuniyaat Expert'—one with full knowledge of the 'Pathan Saga'. Pashto, one of the grandest languages on earth, is spoken something like this: dagha da rora da pista da badaam rora da heeñg...It infinitely appealed to us that our ancestors had stormed the territory of the kafirs—the infidels—holding forth in such a grand language, and had stood in the midst of swarthy Bhils, Korkos and Gonds, fearlessly raising the cry 'God is One!'—and in this language no less! How this would have awed the locals!

Among my peers in the clan I perhaps had the most fertile imagination. I would take in every word that spilled from Ma'i Dada's mouth, my eyes wide and mouth open in sheer astonishment. While the other boys my age spent their time flying kites and playing hockey, I would sneak up to the rooftop of our baarah and to the small, dingy rooms there. Lying on the corrugated iron roof ten or fifteen hundred miles away from my clan's native Teerah, and two hundred and fifty or three hundred years distant from my Pashtun ancestors, I would fight tribal wars, or—after Ma'i Dada's favourite expression—throw myself with full fury into 'dandam danda aur talvaaram talvaar'.

My favourite game during summer vacations was to sneak into the dark storerooms chock-full of broken old furniture and other discarded odds and ends, or to underground vaults, and salvage a desirable piece of some corroded, half-broken weapon from the pile of arms covered over with cast-off farming tools. I would remove the rust and bring the metal underneath to a shine. Once in a while I would even find a whole sword or dagger, so disfigured by corrosion that it looked as heavy and artless as a plough, scythe or pasa. The piece would stir the strangest thought in my mind: this sword, which now looks no better than a plough, scythe or paasa, is perhaps our family—originally a soldier by profession, but now, as it lies cast off on the ground, reduced to farming by 'disuse' or 'misuse'. And so, in an effort to breathe some life into my corroded soldier, I would stage a performance before an audience of the young men and women of the family. Donning the torn farghul of embroidered brocade that belonged to my par-dada, half a sword bound to my waist, and spouting Pashto expletives (invented—you guessed it—by Ma'i Dada himself), I would sally forth and challenge the kafirs, chanting Pashto martial cries. This theatre, this restoration of arms, greatly pleased Ma'i Dada. And he participated with us in this game for hours. He was, as he let it be known, born amid the clanking of arms and loved weaponry of every description.

In the tumult of 1946-1947 Muslims fleeing their homes in the neighbouring non-Muslim states were arriving in droves in our area, because ours was a Muslim-majority town (perhaps it still is) and the state had been settled by the Pathans. One day Ma'i Dada rounded up from the railway station a family of artisans who specialized in making and refurbishing weapons. He had them wait in the baarah and went looking for Father, whom he eventually found at the school. Only God knows how he convinced Father that they were homeless people who had nowhere to go, and as he had provided shelter for four such families already within the baarah, Ma'i Dada argued, 'Miyan, you really must find space for them as well.' Later, after much effort and the subtlest manoeuvring, he managed to get a room emptied for the immigrants. He hauled away empty wooden crates, took apart the boards, cleaned out a small space and set up a tiny enclosure within the baarah. Come next day the newcomers had dug a hole and set up a bellows, and started churning out knife after knife and sword after sword. The very first zanbiya was fashioned especially for Ma'i Dada, its sheath covered with brocade cut out from Mother's old quilted waistcoat. And thus, after the dear tapancha, Ma'i Dada became the proud owner of a thoroughbred zanbiya. Referring to the painful period between the pistol's disappearance and the acquisition of the zanbiya, Ma'i Dada, almost smiling for the first time, offered this explanation: 'Now this tapancha—you could say the Creator meant *some* good to result from its disappearance. It was meant to be. Who knows, I might have gotten angry and stuck it in the guts of some bhaan ka ghora. Which would've gotten me into trouble: the police, booking, courts—and all the rest of it.' When someone raised the doubt, 'Ma'i Dada, what possible *good* could the Creator have intended by taking away the tapancha and granting the zanbiya, for you could just as easily stick the zanbiya in the guts of the ill-fated ghora,' he laughed heartily and, patting the brocaded sheath gently, shot back, 'Rascal! Who do you think I am—the Khuji?'

My uncle had introduced him to Pundit Ratan Nath Sarshar's character Khuji, and I had introduced him to Cervantes' Don Quixote. But Don Quixote he couldn't grasp at all. He would say, 'White men—they're all plain lunatics!'

It was precisely at this time that the state government started to take a harder look at licences for firearms and at any weapon with a blade longer than a few inches. New licences were still issued, but only after much begging was done and influence wielded, and against an atrocious annual fee—a 'jiyaadti ki baat!' The initial problem, however, was to obtain the licence itself. Ma'i Dada had Mother plead with Mamun, a big-gun officer in the police department, to use his influence. Ma'i Dada got lucky. A licence for the zanbiya was issued against an annual fee of twelve annas, which Ma'i Dada hated to pay every time. But at least it gave him the peace that no 'bhaan ki ghori gormint', let alone anyone else, would dare confiscate his zanbiya now. Before using their good offices both Mother and Mamun had had Ma'i Dada swear by the Quran that he would never ever threaten anyone with his zanbiya. 'No, Miyan, no. I'll swear by anything you want, no azal giraphta bhaan ka ghora will ever...' and so on.

Once every year Ma'i Dada would gather together the licences for his own weapon as well as for the myriad guns, rifles, scimitars, swords, daggers and dirks registered under the names of my father, mother, tayas, chachas, phuphas and khalus, and get in line to pay the renewal fee. When he returned he would start babbling straight from the men's dyorhi: 'What injustice! We have seen and heard of the time when not one, not two, but a full half-dozen cannons used to stand ready at the palace of So-and-So Muhammad Khan, even though he was no prince regent himself. No azal giraphta bhaan ka ghora would dare cast even the slightest disapproving glance at him. And that other So-and-So Muhammad Khan, although no prince regent either, had sixteen hundred swords...and those other weapons—all the sarohis, tighazes, khaandas, kirchis, zanbiyas, kataars, khukris and pesh-qabzes one ever saw.'

Father used to say Majeed should have been the custodian of the state's armoury. The sight of weapons increased the flow of his blood. Then one day the government issued an order for all arms to be deposited forthwith in the state storehouse. Ma'i Dada heard the news with a sinking heart. For the next two days he spat insults and indecencies. After the anger had subsided somewhat, he prevailed upon some of my elders, and they collectively suggested to Father that if a deposit had to be made, let it be only of the weapons licensed to the family, but not those others that lay safely hidden away here and there in the underground vaults, storerooms and inside the walls, as a trust we bore of our ancestors. They had never been entered in any register, so it was prudent to have them refurbished and kept ready, for times were bad. And besides, Pathan bachchas kept themselves ready even when times were good.

Father was a strict Aligarhian—a man of principles. Under no circumstances would he want to go against the government's express orders. Besides, he said, what good were weapons stashed away a hundred years ago? Why court unnecessary headaches? Let's just drop the matter right here. A disappointed Ma'i Dada gave in, but only outwardly. We boys could well see that some mysterious activity was going on all around him—in our courtyards, in the dhaadas—the subterranean vaults, and in the staircases—which Father knew nothing about.

Anyway, the licensed weapons were turned in. A few of the family elders and Ma'i Dada loaded the whole lot into two tongas and hauled them over to the police storehouse, had them write out deposit receipts and returned home empty-handed.

When I got back from school I saw Ma'i Dada squatting in the dyorhi, leaning against the wall, head bent low over his knees, as if he'd just returned from burying a blood relative. The pain had penetrated so deep that he wasn't even hurling obscenities at anyone today. A few days later, when he once again had to go to the storehouse, this time to turn in the arms of one of my tayas, Ma'i Dada didn't come back.

News arrived that he had been arrested and was cooling his heels in the main police lock-up, treating everybody to the choicest profanities. Within minutes the entire clan stormed out to mount a rescue operation. Though just an ordinary retainer in the household, he had nonetheless been raised at the dyorhis of the Mirza'i Khails. Most importantly, even if an outsider, he was, after all, still a Pathan—how could we abandon Ma'i Dada as a circle of menacing uniforms drew tightly around him?

Mother right away got into a tonga and went to the home of her brother who worked in the police. Banging her sarota on the table over and over again, she ordered her brother to have Ma'i Dada returned home 'right this minute'. And: 'Miyan, you have locked up one of our own ancestral workers, today an old man; tomorrow you won't hesitate to tie up our own sons. Was it just for this that our forebears cleared away the jungles with nothing but their swords and set up this state—eh?' My mother's majestic wrath was a sight to behold that day. She rambled on and on. After all, she was the paternal granddaughter of Ghalib's disciple Nawab Yar Muhammad Khan Shaukat. The caring nature of a thoroughbred nawabzada, the linguistic power of a robust poet was in full display.

Mamun was totally flabbergasted. 'But Manjhli Aapa, at least we should first find out why he's been locked up. Please listen, I'm sending someone to look into the matter this minute. Please do go inside. At least have something to eat with us. I urge you...' But Mother, like a rock, stood her ground, right there in the man's sitting room, dicing betel nuts with the sarota, possessed with a grandeur that inspired only awe. Mamun's entire household sat around her in a reverential hush, without stirring, each content with a single biscuit and a cup of tea, until Mamun simply had to slip into his uniform and go take care of the matter himself.

Less than two hours later Ma'i Dada was safely back in our dyorhi, going over his tale for the benefit of some two dozen illustrious Mirza'i Khails.

Aside from the abusive volleys of 'azal giraphta' and that other expression, all I was able to understand was this: when he arrived at the storehouse to turn in Taya's weapons, he found that Head Constable Sukhia Ram—a Teli by caste who 'in spite of his police uniform didn't look like a cop at all'—was in charge of the deposits that day. Ma'i Dada's and Sukhia Ram's first mutual misfortune was just that: the latter happened to be on duty. Had Bela Singh Thakur or Head Constable Gulab Khan been on duty instead, none of what transpired would have taken place at all.

Sukhia Ram's first offence was that he smiled at Ma'i Dada. He then topped it off with a series of other egregious mistakes, such as calling him a bare miyan—an old man—and offering him the peon's stool to sit on. Ma'i Dada stood to one side and just stared at the man, a volcano rising inside him. The final—unforgivable—wickedness that blew the volcano's top was that 'that Teli ka bachcha had the audacity to pick up a blade from our weapons' pile and, puffing away on his stinking beeri, start nonchalantly sharpening his pencil with it.'

It happened to be the pesh-qabz of none other than Nawab Ghaus Muhammad Khan Fateh Jang Bahadur. Its grip was made of agate with a delicate floral design so skilfully carved that it looked as though it had been moulded from wax. The blade bore the distinguished name of that jannat-dwelling ancestor in gold, and an inscription in Persian to the effect that it was crafted by an Iranian artisan especially for Nawab Bahadur, who used to hunt lions unmounted, fighting them face to face.

Well, it boiled down to this: first, Sukhia Ram was a Teli by caste, and second, smoking his beeri, he used the dagger of paradise-dwelling Nawab Ghaus Bahadur to sharpen his pencil.

Shouting 'azal giraphta', or maybe 'bhaan ka ghora', Ma'i Dada gave Head Constable Sukhia Ram such a whack that it sent his beeri as well as his pencil flying. Only then did he condescend to inform that son of a Teli:

'That weapon is the legacy of sher-bachchas, not your vegetable-chopping knife,' and 'It had already become polluted when your hand first touched it, and I kept my peace; but now that you bhaan ka ghora are sharpening your pencil with it, I'm not going to let you live,' and so on.

Obviously Ma'i Dada had to be taken to the lock-up.

The police chief was in a fix. A civilian had beaten up a minor three-ribboned police officer in uniform and obstructed him in discharging his duties. On the other hand the state had not yet been merged into the Indian Union. A Pathan nawab, in the shadow of maahi-maraatib—rank and insignia—still ruled as absolutely as he wished from his cosy seat on the state throne. It was his name that resounded from the pulpits of a thousand mosques in the Friday sermon: *May God perpetuate his dominion and his power!*—even as his grip on the staff of the state flag had begun to slip, and the ball of state annexation had been set rolling in Delhi.

Several hundred noble and not-so-noble Pathans—all from the nawab's prosperous and not-so-prosperous, educated and not-so-educated, cultured and not-so-cultured, but nevertheless influential, clan—stood surrounding the main police station when Mamun arrived on the scene. It wasn't for nothing that he had graduated from Aligarh with a major in Psychology. In less than twenty minutes, without once referring to his privilege or power, he smoothly persuaded his subordinate officer that what had happened was not motivated by criminal intent or by hooliganism, but rather by irritation and the wounded ego of a proud tribe losing out to history. The station chief was a Chauhan Rajput by caste, who perhaps could empathize with the agony of defeated hands accustomed only to brandishing swords. Moreover, he had no wish to create complications for his superior officers on account of a silly pencil-pushing head constable.

And so Havaldar Sukhia Ram received a summons stating: 'It has come to our attention that as a rare and priceless weapon of tremendous historical importance to the State was being handed over to your care...' and so on. Sukhia Ram was dragged in to explain.

Father sent Ma'i Dada away to the family estate to rest awhile. This was made necessary partly by the fact that Ma'i Dada had now taken to narrating, before anyone and everyone, the story of how the former chief of the state storehouse, Havaldar Sukhia Ram, fell from grace.

Who could have known that we boys would be obliged to witness Ma'i Dada's own near fall from grace. On some particular matter Father became hugely displeased with him. Right away he had a room cleared out for him elsewhere in the baarah. And so, for the first time ever, Ma'i Dada was forced to make a home for himself far from our dyorhi.

What happened was this: After Grandfather's death, one of our sisters married outside the clan, perhaps the first time this had ever occurred. The groom was highly educated but a civilian to the core. He came from a family that knew nothing of warring and fighting. After the wedding, as was our custom, he was taken to Ma'i Dada for the rite of salaami—to receive the customary gift of two rupees from him, for, of course, he was his elder. Since no elders were present at the moment, we boys were charged with helping him out through the ritual. Ma'i Dada hadn't been feeling well at the time. He saw the new daamaad and smiled, then mustered enough strength to sit up. We put pillows on either side of him to prop him up. He received the salaam from the groom and passed his hand over his head by way of benediction, and conferred the salaami gift of two rupees. And then he unrolled before him a veritable register of 'Pashtuniyaat'—that is, Pashtun lore.

For a full two hours the young man sat with his mouth gaping open as he took in Ma'i Dada's revelations. After an exhaustive harangue on the 'saakh-sajar' business, Ma'i Dada next told him that 'these Mirza'i Khails are a very gutsy clan, and so ferocious that one dare not even look at them askance. And these forty-odd houses in the mohalla, set up one next to the other, happen to be interconnected. Each house has a window opening into the adjacent house large enough to allow a man along with his sword or rafil (rifle) to pass through easily. So if one of the Mirza'i Khail houses on this side of the mohalla is attacked, a hundred or more armed Pathan bachchas can scramble from both sides in less than ten minutes to bring the situation under control and annihilate the attacker. For instance, in such-and-such year, So-and-So Muhammad Khan, after cutting down the naa'ib kotvaal—and his horse along with him—over some trifling matter, made a clean escape by passing from window to window, house to house. So then, this is the advantage of having the interconnected houses.' And these connected dwellings also fostered brotherhood and closeness among the relatives, which Ma'i Dada illustrated thus: 'There was a certain Bachchu Miyan of ours, and so-and-so par-dada of his had murdered so-and-so par-nana of his on a matter no more significant than this: They had both been invited to a valima banquet. The par-dada was already there when the par-nana arrived. At the time there was a lawsuit over some property going on between them. Nothing serious, though. Litigation, criminal assault and

such like were common among them. Dandam-danda aur talvaaram-talvaar
was also a common enough occurrence. And why not? They were sher-
bachchas after all. They had to occupy themselves somehow. Well, anyway,
when the par-nana started to remove his shoes—since the guests at the
valima were to be seated on the carpet—one of the shoes sort of fell on
the shoes of the par-dada, who was already there and closely observing the
movements of the newcomer. Just as the shoe of the arriving purkha fell
on the shoes of the other purkha, the latter flew into a rage. He got up,
shouted "Beware!" and with a single savage stroke of his sword completely
severed the offender's head, which rolled away like a corncob.'

The collars of the groom's new wedding sherwaani-coat were soaking
up the beads of sweat that kept dripping from his face. He had had three
drinks of water already and was totally ill at ease. Since it was getting quite
late, we escorted him to the women's quarters.

The next day a storm exploded. Ma'i Dada was ill. Father didn't say
anything to him, but he kept thundering to Mother:'Majeed's gone absolutely
mad! He scared the daamaad practically out of his wits. The poor boy
went home and lay down in a daze, asking the girl over and over if all he
had heard was true, if she wasn't the progeny of bloodthirsty murderers, if
swords weren't drawn at her home on the slightest of pretexts, if her people
didn't still attend valima banquets wearing swords so they could kill each
other all the more easily. This is really the limit! Why did he have to dig
up all these dead bodies? No family is free of some measure of craziness,
but do they run around advertising it? For heaven's sake!...'

A week later a room was prepared in the baarah and Ma'i Dada was
obliged to have his belongings moved there.

Away from the dyorhi his illness worsened. So even though we didn't
leave him alone for a minute, the truth is he felt quite lonely there. He
had somehow found out that Manjhle Miyan had become upset over the
incident with the daamaad, which is why he had been removed from the
dyorhi. A feeling of despondency had settled all over the baarah. One
day he started to say: 'These days Mazid Khan Esoop Ja'i has become a
burden on the earth. You could say it's his time to leave.' He wanted to
send for Father and make up with him. So I went to Father and told
him that Ma'i Dada was gravely ill, so would he please go and see him.
When Father arrived Ma'i Dada practically lit up. He chatted about the
'nukhson'—meaning the prescriptions—written out by the hakims and vaids;
the inevitable 'azal giraphtas' and 'bhaan ka ghoras', etc. also got going; and

then, clear out of the blue, he said in a chipper voice, as if telling Father a joke, 'Manjhle Miyan, perhaps I offended you in the matter of the daamaad and maybe that's why you've had me thrown out here.' Father jovially said something or the other. I was watching how Ma'i Dada's illness, his grief, his joking manner—which was obviously a pitiable attempt to patch things up with Father—had all affected Father. Ma'i Dada continued, 'Miyan, as it is, mashallah, you are a father yourself now, but you were a mere toddler before me once. You *cannot* understand the wisdom underlying my plans. As the saying goes—better to err on the side of caution—I have cautioned the lad, "Take heed, you don't know who you're dealing with. We're Pathans." And so, inshallah, the boy will stay in line.'

That very same day Father gave orders for the repatriation of Ma'i Dada back to his old quarters in the dyorhi, which brightened him up like the rains after a long drought. His condition began to improve somewhat. But he had become very old, and it didn't seem as though he'd last much longer. Mother relented and allowed his old flame Jamrat to look after him. She'd come and wash his face, help him change his clothes, feed him cracked-wheat porridge with her own hands, pour tea into the saucer and hold it as he gulped it down. The routine continued for months. Father had him seen by several doctors, different treatments were tried, but Ma'i Dada's condition kept steadily deteriorating. As he had no strength left to go to the toilet, half of his bedding had been folded up and the rope meshing of the charpoy pulled to either side to form a hole, an enamelled copper basin placed directly beneath it. Jamrat had willingly taken on the responsibility of cleaning him after the toilet, etc. But she was a family woman and couldn't stay at night. During the night I'd often see Father walking over to the dyorhi carrying potfuls of warm water, and hear the ensuing frail protests and cries of Ma'i Dada. He couldn't stand the thought of Father taking care of him. When Mother offered to send for a servant from her maika to take care of him, Ma'i Dada vehemently said he would have none of that. My father was at least acceptable, because he had been a child before Ma'i Dada once. So he was like a son; it's different with sons. 'I cannot allow my person to be exposed or otherwise seen in a compromising condition before ghairs—outsiders,' he told her. 'Biya, you'd better send me to the hospital before doing anything like that.' But everyone knew that he wouldn't last even two hours in a hospital. He had let it be known that 'I want to die in this very house.' He frequently slipped into semiconsciousness and remained so for hours on end. Jamrat and we boys during the day, and Father during the night, tried to keep him as comfortable as we could, but we were all exhausted.

It was this exhaustion and confusion that led Jamrat to overlook an express command of Ma'i Dada's. As he lay comatose, I happened to see him 'in a compromising position': He hadn't been circumcised.

I returned from the dyorhi quietly, my tiny head full of questions. The continuous hum set off in my head by this new and bizarre discovery would not let me be. I went up to the rooftop, strolled in the baarah, sat by Mother, and traipsed about. But Ma'i Dada was very sick and he truly loved us a lot. Before long I was back in the dyorhi. I heard him yelling at Jamrat in a frail halting voice and cry. She'd probably told him what had happened.

'Bhaan ki ghori, you've disgraced me just as I'm about to die…What will the boys think?' I heard him break down in sobs. A brief silence. And then: 'Oh, well—a Teli's son will always be a Teli's son. He doesn't become a Pathan even if the Pathans have reared him.'

It was impossible to remain there in the dyorhi any more. So I strode out to the baarah again.

Is it really true, then, that Ma'i Dada had been lying to us all his life? All those neighbourhood dhobis—they were telling the truth all along? I felt cheated, as though somebody had sold me a fistful of sand as sugar. But the matter was such that I couldn't even tell anyone about it.

He lived on for another three or four days, shuttling between unconsciousness and wakefulness.

Several months after his death I dropped the question on Father—the one that had remained my constant companion ever since the day the humming started in my head, giving me no peace. He was passing by the dyorhi on his way to the mosque when he saw me standing quietly by Ma'i Dada's room and stopped. He put his hand on my shoulder ever so gently and said, 'What's the matter?'

I told him what I had seen that day.

He stood there for a while in silence, and then said softly, 'Whoever he was, he loved you and wanted you to learn to live with honour and dignity like your forebears. And that's what you should remember. Understand? Now, go play.'

Then, just as he had started to move, he broke his stride, turned around and snapped angrily, 'And listen, don't let any son-of-a-bitch tell you he wasn't a Muslim! Don't let anyone say he wasn't a Pathan!'

THE OLD MANSION

IKRAMULLAH

The three lived in a single room. There was a room above it and another below. Every time the tenant in the upper room dumped out some water, it was these three whom the occupant of the room beneath them shouted and cursed at. Only after they told him they were not the ones who had emptied the water would he go after the real culprit. Likewise, when the man below turned on the faucet, which cut off the supply to the man on top, it was the three in the middle whom the latter called to account. They would point at the door of the offender, and the man would fall on him like a maniac. The three were quite fed up with the location of their room. A couple of times they even brought up among themselves the idea of moving out, but stopped short, for they were not likely to find another room with such cheap rent and, more importantly, right in the heart of the city. Moreover, the man above and the one below weren't exactly living in paradise either, so why should they try to find a room on the top or the ground floor? No place came without its peculiar problems. Why court new troubles? Why not quietly endure the ones they had? They'd gotten used to them after all, hadn't they? Let it be. No harm done.

The three had identical names. Then again they didn't. Only the first names were the same, the rest different. People called them Chhota (the youngest), Manjhla (the middle one), and Bara (the oldest) for convenience. I guess that'll do for us too. No compelling reason to use the names their respective parents had given them in the hopes they would turn out to have the qualities the names implied. But wishes are like flowers. By the end of the day only the stem remains, the petals fall off or are plucked out and scatter away. The men looked no different from a naked stem—dried up, shrivelled, scrawny. So people dropped the formality of calling them by their names.

Bara had been around for the last sixty, maybe seventy years. 'Around' in a manner of speaking—he seemed to merely roll in whatever direction he was pushed in this noisy and crowded world. When the massacres started in Bihar and his people fled, he fled with them. Some were killed on the way, others made it to the safety of East Pakistan in dire straits, and he with them. When death sentences were doled out to people for the sole crime of being Pakistanis, they fled East Pakistan, and he with them. He boarded a ship and, buffeted by the waves of the inner and outer sea alike, made it to Karachi. When Biharis became the target of frequent arrests and other punishments in Karachi, he moved to Lahore. The frequent divisions and partitions had taught him that the most effective strategy for survival in such situations lay in making a run for one's life. Groups would round up members of the opposite group and make short work of them, fully convinced that this was the easiest, most expeditious way of ridding society of impurities. After all, it was entirely possible that one of his own group might confuse him with the opponent and kill him. He had seen that happen, though for his part Bara was neither a staunch Muslim nor Pakistani nor even Bihari Muhajir. All he had ever wanted from the world was to be able to make ends meet, or if that was too much, then perhaps to have a meal a day. One could see just by looking at his face that he was still ashamed of the event of his birth sixty or seventy years ago. The shame simply wouldn't wash away, even though he had not been a participant in this crime, only its result. It was as though he were trying to hang his own dead body for murder. If anything, his embarrassment grew worse with time. It seemed he'd never die. In the end, he would simply liquefy from shame and flow like water into the sewer, careful not to bubble out of the gutter and get in anybody's way. He exuded his sense of shame before one and all—except for his two companions—as if he were guilty of some misdeed. Had it occurred to him that his life was the constant source of his shame, he would have certainly ended it. His mother had died when he was still a child living in his village. People would commiserate, 'How sad, your mother died,' and he would feel it was his fault that she died. He fled Bihar as a young man, made his escape from East Pakistan in his middle age, and took flight from Karachi as an oldster, and throughout these vicissitudes remained steadfastly shame-ridden; there was no need for his mother to die each time.

Manjhla found him sitting at Data Sahib's durbar one day, immersed as usual in shame. It seemed he had no one to look after him. Afraid that without proper care or protection the old man might die at the shrine, Manjhla had brought him along to the room with smoke-blackened walls and chipping plaster where he and Chhota had been tenants for the past several years.

Bara told Manjhla his name and stuck Azimabadi at the end. Azimabad was a good 200 miles from his village and he had never been there in his life. Why did he always indulge in this totally unnecessary misrepresentation? Oddly, it never caused him any shame. After all, one needed a bit of pride to live, never mind how you got it, otherwise there would be no difference between a human being and dirt.

Manjhla was a frightened man. Frightened of what? He couldn't tell. But he was up to his ears in fear. Anything that entered his mind instantaneously transformed into fear. He was even afraid of himself. Anybody might do anything, at any time, like a loaded shotgun. And so could he.

He came from a small village in Gilgit in the foothills of a large mountain two days' journey from Skardu. A trip either way required a night's stay en route. He didn't like living in Lahore. But he liked having his old father stay alive, along with his two young orphaned nephews and himself. He had to accept his 'like' and 'dislike' together, because his native Gilgit had no jobs to offer. At the end of each trip to the village he would return more convinced than ever that next time he went back, the mountain would have vanished, and so would the orchards, the river, even his village. If he couldn't go home one summer, fear instead of blood ran in his veins for the rest of that year. Two fears especially plagued his life, and due to them he would never step out of the house without wrapping a piece of cloth around his head and face. He feared that his eyes might accidentally fall on a woman he did not know, and in punishment, he might have to burn in Hell in the afterlife. That he was already in Hell in this life, without eyeing a strange woman, meant nothing to him. His other fear was the feeling that his face and bearing somehow looked different from the general population of Lahore. God knew what this might prompt the locals to do to him. In reality, nothing untoward had ever happened to him. Fears, however, follow their own paths, and past experiences rarely manage to hold them back.

One reason why he took a liking to Bara was that his short, sparse beard (never mind that it had turned grey) and the features of his face resembled his own, except that his complexion was darker. It was entirely possible that at some point in the distant past people from Gilgit had ventured forth to Bihar and settled there, or maybe it was the other way around. The human breed is like the wind: it can strike out in any direction and end up anywhere at all. Whether this had actually happened or not, the fact is that both had started out from faraway regions and ended up together in Lahore looking for work. Manjhla was mortally afraid of dying in Lahore and being buried there. Bara, on the other hand, couldn't care less. He no longer had a native place to feel passionate about. Sure he remembered now and then the streets and lanes in which he and his little friends had played together naked. What of it? One remembers a lot of things, does one die over each and every memory?

Chhota, too, was blissfully free of such hang-ups. He was a native of Punjab, and enjoyed the rare distinction of being homeless in his own home. He wore a perpetual smile on his face, which bore a scar from a cut about a half-inch wide, extending from the left corner of his lips across the jaw, past the ear, and all the way to the base of his neck. Since the facial muscles had been pulled taut to the left, it gave him a permanently smiling expression. When wracked by worry over some matter, he appeared rather to be smiling; when he cried, he seemed to be laughing, and when laughing, crying. He had obliterated the difference between the two acts in one fell swoop. Whether he laughed or cried, the sounds that came out of his mouth resembled those of a toothless hyena staring with hunger and longing at the half-eaten carcass of an animal and laughing—or crying (your guess). His grandfather had owned four acres of land and made do with the yield all his life. He had adopted two sons and a daughter and married them off. When he died, Chhota's father and uncle worried that two acres apiece wouldn't be enough to feed their families. The uncle sold his share to Chhota's father in instalments and struck out for Karachi in search of work, taking his family along. He never returned or had any further contact with the village. When Chhota's phupha died without leaving an heir, his wife inherited four acres of land from him. And when she too died, Chhota's father went to claim it for himself and his younger brother as their sister's heirs. But the deceased sister's devar confronted him with, 'When your father died, did you remember to give your sister, my sister-in-law, her share of the land? Instead, you dragged her to the tehsildar and had her relinquish her claim in your favour. Some cheek you've got now to come and claim her share of the inheritance according to the shariat.'

Chhota's father wouldn't budge and insisted on taking possession of the land then and there. In the ensuing scuffle, he was murdered on the spot, and the murderer went after Chhota to finish him off too, since he was the last surviving heir. His mother was hacked to death with swords as she tried to shield him, her only child, from the attackers. He received several wounds, and the attackers left him for dead. His maternal grandfather brought him to his village. He was fifteen when this grandfather died, and his maternal uncle drove him out of the house. He drifted off to Lahore looking for work and started living with Manjhla in a room in this crumbling mansion which some Hindu had built at the beginning of the twentieth century. Chhota owned six acres of land—on paper, that is. In reality, he could neither take possession of it nor raise any crops there. Indeed he couldn't even set foot in his native village without risking death at the hands of his enemies, one of whom had now become an MPA to boot.

This mansion constructed from outsize bricks laid with red lime mortar had a dyorhi tall enough to allow an elephant, howdah and all, to pass through it easily. At the time it was built, the days of travelling on elephants had long been over, but humans usually take their time perceiving change, adjusting to it, and freeing themselves of old habits of thought. The dyorhi led to a spacious courtyard bordered by verandas on three sides with rooms directly behind them. The same floor plan was repeated on the second (but only partially on the top) floor which had galleries roofed with corrugated metal in place of verandas. Drainage ditches ran along the edge of the courtyard and the walls of the dyorhi and emptied into the main gutter outside, into which the garbage from the upper floors was channelled through steel drainpipes. Where the pipes had ruptured, the broken or missing portions had been repaired by nailing metal foil to the walls. Thanks to this novel solution, all day long filthy, stinking water dribbled down the walls along which the pipes ran and emptied into the ditches. If a careless tenant upstairs dumped a large amount of water all at once, the half-clogged pipes overflowed into the courtyard. Stepping inside the dyorhi, one felt one had walked into the middle of an open sewer. The red lime mixture continually filtered down from between the bricks of the ceiling and walls in a fine powdery shower. During the British period the dyorhi had had a massive main gate that was regularly closed every night. Now, however, it gaped open at the street night and day like a sleepless eye. Most likely, rioters had smashed the gate in 1947, or the immigrants had used it for fuel. Something had happened to the gate, but no one knew exactly what.

There were about as many families living in the mansion as it had rooms. Some were the children of former allottees—those who were allotted these rooms in settlement of property left behind in India—some were tenants of the heirs of allottees who had made their way out of the cycle of poverty and moved to better places. The women carried out their household chores or work—mostly handicrafts, which they made on commission for local merchants—perched on charpoys laid out across their rooms, in the verandas or courtyard. Their filthy-looking children frisked about in the courtyard without a scrap of clothing to cover their bodies. A woman dared not intrude upon even an inch of space in the room of another, for this and numberless other trifles could land them in fights lasting the entire day. Sometimes the men would be dragged in as well. Perhaps these rows acted as a safety valve, releasing the pressures accumulated in the mind due to such hardships as cramped space, an overabundance of children, the crush of tenants, poverty, and disease. The number of hearths in the verandas and courtyard matched the number of rooms. A few old women worked as domestics in the homes of families in the neighbourhood, for wages and for meals. The men sold all kinds of wares on pushcarts, pulled rickshaws, did odd jobs, ran shops, or worked for hire.

The despondency, dissatisfaction, and uncertainty about the future that had haunted the emigrants who were settled in the mansion in 1947 still dogged its current occupants, the only difference being that now even people native to the city had begun to feel the sting of these worries. Like the emigrants who missed their former homes, the ill-fated crumbling mansion looked homeless, and seemed to miss its former occupants. Nobody took care of it, because they were all supposed to—collectively.

A large, octagonal bay window jutted out of the three men's room a couple of feet into the street like a miniature balcony. Seen from the street, it seemed to have four sides growing out of a large lotus flower made of stucco, a pattern repeated both above and below the window. The window had panels of stained glass and was permanently sealed from inside with wooden boards nailed in the shape of a cross, because it might, like any of the other bay windows in the building, come crashing down any time. If it could have been opened, it would have opened on the street like a royal enclosure of exquisite latticework from which a king might give audience. And if it had been the old times, one could even imagine the three men giving audience to their subjects: Bara shyly, Manjhla terrified, and Chhota smiling. After all, Bara and Manjhla had something of the Mughals in their haggard faces.

A narrow walkway, no more than a couple of feet wide, its corroded metal roof supported by a wooden frame and thin, carved pillars, began at the side of the bay window and ran along the row of rooms. Its flooring was missing in many places and one could see the street below through the gaping holes. The metal roof had come undone in spots and flapped in the wind like a spring; the stronger the wind blew, the more it rattled.

The wooden frame and the delicately carved supports had turned white like desiccated bones strewn across a stretch of desert. The boards of the frame, too, had come loose and hung down or curved upward here and there. Above the dyorhi's arch, a pair of lions, carved in red stucco and only dimly visible through years of smoke and dirt, stood catlike on their hind legs; like two friends being photographed together, they looked helplessly into the camera lens with the portions of their eyes still intact. Their tails had chipped away almost entirely, and their manes partially. The artisan who fashioned them had given them bodies like that of a she-goat, so that they appeared, strangely and simultaneously, a little ridiculous, a little pitiable and a little mean. Nowadays one can see any number of such one-eyed, truncated lions roaming the streets of Lahore, some of them even called 'Lions of Punjab'.

The evening had deepened, and the encroaching darkness had hushed the bustle and noise of the day. The three sat in their room talking. Without the straw of their friendship, they would have drowned long ago in this sea of people called Lahore. Evening was the only time when each could forget about his defining traits and feel the taste of life on their tongues, bittersweet. And they liked it.

The heavy late-evening air pressed down the stench rising from the courtyard, packed with charpoys on which young and old, women, men, children, slept as though drugged, as the empty pushcarts, large upturned wicker baskets, ropes lying coiled like snakes, and cold hearths waited in immobility for their owners to rise. And under some cots, cats and dogs were seen lying side by side in peace, rooting for bread crumbs or bones from which the last fibre of meat had been sucked off.

'Bade Miyan,' Chhota began, 'you didn't marry?'

'I wanted to, yaar, but it just didn't happen,' Bara cooed like one of the pigeons that roosted in the balcony for the night.

' "Didn't happen"—how so?' Manjhla asked.

'Well, you see, when I'd just arrived in Dhaka, I found myself a place in the area where a lot of Bihari immigrants had set up homes. There was this girl there. She too had come from Bihar. I liked her a lot. Whenever we ran into each other in the lane, we would stare at each other. This went on for quite some time. One evening, when the lane was deserted, I saw her coming along and accosted her. "Listen," I said.

'"Go on," she said.

'"I will die without you."

'She drew back from modesty, gave a little smile, scratched the ground with her big toe, and said, "Well then, talk to my Baaba."

'In that single instant the scent of her body permeated my whole being.'

'So did you go see her father?' Chhota asked impatiently.

'Yes, sir, I did. He asked me what I did. I told him that I pulled rickshaws. "Do you own the rickshaw?" he asked.

'"No. I rent it."

'"All together, how much money do you have?"

'"Forty, maybe fifty rupees."

'He said, "Come back when you have your own rickshaw and a thousand rupees in your pocket."

'Well, I left. Soon she got married and I gradually forgot about the matter. Not her scent though. That stayed with me.'

Chhota was smiling as he sighed. A sudden commotion in the veranda interrupted them just as they were about to break into hearty laughs. It sounded like a woman being murdered and screaming for help. They hurriedly pasted their dominant traits back on their faces. Chhota opened the door, smiling as usual, and peeked out. 'Nothing!' he said. 'Some cats are having a fight.' Then, sitting down, he said, 'Is that all, Bade Miyan? Just once in seventy years? You didn't try again to get married?'

'As a matter of fact, I did. One more time. But never mind. It's getting late and tomorrow is a working day. Go to sleep!'

'No, Bade Miyan, finish your story.'

'Well then, in Karachi I met up with a woman, an immigrant from Bihar like myself. Her husband had been murdered in East Pakistan. She had three children, the oldest about ten years old. I started to frequent her hut. She was extremely poor. Well, who wasn't? But she showed me great hospitality. I was sort of leaning towards it, and a couple of friends encouraged me besides, but this one had no scent. I refused.'

Once again there was noise outside, but this time it sounded muffled, like the moan of a child, followed by the sobs and cries of a woman. The three perked up their ears again, but Chhota tried to put their minds at ease. 'No call for fear or shame,' he said. 'That's just the way cats wail at night. They'll move on. Sleep now.'

The three fell asleep. In the morning they found out that an eight-month-old infant had died in the room next door for lack of medical attention, in the arms of his teenage mother, recently arrived from Swat. The mother kept crying, while the father, who must have been in his mid-twenties, lay in a drugged sleep on the adjoining cot after a shot of heroin. So it had not been cats after all.

The three men had no worries. But that didn't mean that they were a happy lot, either. Happiness doesn't really exist in the world. Let's just say they did not or could not indulge their misery. Their ability to feel anything at all had been snuffed out. Driven from pillar to post the whole day long like pack donkeys, they had come to look upon life as an arduous journey through very rough terrain. Hardship was a necessary component of the journey. A crumbling, filth-ridden mansion, hunger, disease, drugs, children dying like flies, the life-squeezing suffocation of cramped space, fights over trifles, and worse yet, daily visits by the police, the obscenities they shouted at the tenants and the way they humiliated every man, woman and child—through it all, the three would just sit, with their differentiating traits plastered across their faces, and look on in total indifference. So did the others, as though it were all happening to someone else, in some other city, while they were merely reading an account of it in the newspaper.

Fifty years had gone by; the country had passed through several governments, but the mansion and its residents remained without a home, without a country. It seemed that the rulers, all of them, were identical siblings in every respect, and these residents of the mansion were their stepbrothers. But why the jealous mistreatment? The mansion dwellers weren't exactly Yusuf in beauty: Here, even a twenty-year-old woman looked like an old hag and a prepubescent boy of ten, a mature young adult. The stepbrothers had robbed them of their innocence, beauty, youth—everything!

The night felt close and stuffy. The light from the street lamps filtered in through the remaining window panes and reached their eyes in shades of red, blue, and green, which irritated them. They cursed the man who had thought of putting in stained glass, to make it all look fetching, no doubt. Bara said edgily, 'I feel like smashing the panes that are left. That would let in some breeze at least.'

'If you feel so hot, we can go and stand on the veranda,' Chhota offered.

But the usual glut of charpoys greeted their eyes down below in the courtyard. A child would ask for water, the mother would get up cursing, walk over to the pitcher, drink a glass herself first, then give some to the child and fan him to cool him off. Slowly she'd succumb to sleep and her hand would stop moving. The child would start crying again, and she would hurriedly resume fanning. Meanwhile the Swati youth returned from somewhere, removed the padlock from the door and went in. Chhota remarked, 'When he left here in the evening he had his wife with him. How come he's returning alone?'

'Maybe she wanted to go back home and he went to put her on the bus or something,' Manjhla ventured in explanation.

Chhota began, 'This Moti Begum...'

'Moti Begum, who?'

'Oh, the fat one. You know her. The one who sometimes comes here in the afternoon all powdered and rouged to visit the women in the courtyard when they do their embroidery and needlework? I know she's lured two or three women into going out with her for six, seven hours at a time.'

'So?'

'Don't you understand? She takes them out to turn tricks. All the other women know that too. But they keep quiet. They're afraid that if they spill the beans, all hell will break loose. Or maybe as a precaution: what if they themselves needed her help at some point?' Chhota laughed in his peculiar way.

'Their men don't know about it?' Manjhla asked.

'God knows. But if they see a hint of prosperity suddenly appear in their homes and want to keep quiet, well, that's their business.'

'Chhota, you're in on all the gossip!' Manjhla said.

'Of course. You know why? Because I socialize with everyone. All you ever do is tremble from fear, and you, Bade Miyan, can never have enough of feeling ashamed.'

'And what do you do—smile?'

Chhota laughed his hyena laugh, then he said, 'You can buy anything in the mansion—liquor, heroin, hemp, women, labour, you name it.'

'You're too suspicious, Chhota,' Manjhla said. 'You *will* go to Hell. That's enough. Go to sleep.'

'Don't get angry,' Bara said. 'Maybe Chhota is telling the truth. I've seen this happen before. First in Dhaka, then in Karachi, maybe here too. Misery and helplessness always drive people to sell themselves.'

A few days later, when the three returned from work in the evening they found the residents standing in small groups and talking on the street outside the mansion, inside in the courtyard, and in the verandas. Manjhla, quaking with fear, said, 'It looks like something terrible's happened.'

Chhota, smiling, joined one of the groups and promptly returned to fill in his companions: 'Rumour has it that the city has declared the mansion dangerous and ordered its demolition.'

'These rumours always turn out to be true in the end,' Bara remarked, in deep shame.

Chhota continued, 'Someone was saying it will be torn down tomorrow, but another man said nothing of the sort was about to happen, that it was all a lie. Somebody else said that Sardar Rustam Khan's qabza men had met some of the allottees and offered to buy their rooms at a thousand rupees apiece, plus permission to live rent-free for six months. They refused, saying the offer wasn't good enough. The men taunted, "Okay, wait until tomorrow. When the City pulls it down, you won't get even a penny, and you and your families will have to sleep on the pavement, in the bargain. Only Sardar Sahib can stop the demolition. He's already bought up the shares of other allottees." Only God knows whether this was some kind of ploy or was true. Anyway, they left asking them to think it over, and promised to return at midnight to get their answer.'

Just then the Swati girl, lovely as a doll, came daintily down the stairs, alone, clip-clopping in her fancy sandals. Draped from head to toe in her chadar and looking straight with her clever black-bee eyes, she sped past them to the dyorhi and then out onto the street, where she waved down a rickshaw. She had a brief exchange with the rickshaw-puller. Both smiled, and she hopped in and left.

The three looked at each other. Was this the same mother who had sat the whole night long holding her dying child, too frightened even to cry in a loud voice? Or walk out onto the veranda and shout for help in her native Pashto, because she was a stranger here? Or muster the courage to kick her drugged husband awake? Bara said, 'If only hands meant to fan babies weren't lifted to hail rickshaws for such purposes!' And the three went back to their room.

A commotion continued inside the mansion throughout the night. People kept coming and going, talking among themselves. Schemes were hatched. The three couldn't sleep well. When they set out for work in the morning they saw armed police and city forces standing outside the mansion, ready to move in with their pickaxes, bulldozers, trucks and bobcats. An officer from the city was in charge of the operation. Some of the residents of the mansion were talking with him, thrashing their arms about and beating on their chests.

'Why weren't we given advance notice?'

'We posted the notice three times on the mansion.'

'It's plastered with notices. How did you expect us to see it there?'

'Well that's not our fault, is it?'

'If Sardar Rustam Khan had bought out the mansion, you'd go back quietly. But you won't listen to us.'

'That's not true. Anyway, you have three hours to clear out. After that, I'm not responsible for any damage.'

The three immediately returned to their room and started packing. Just then the man who lived in the room above them came stomping down the stairs and straight into their room, and asked, 'No water and electricity again today?'

'That's right,' Chhota answered, smiling.

'That fellow below you is a real bastard. He isn't going to give up until we give it to him.'

'He didn't cut them off. Not today. It's the city. They're tearing down the mansion.'

'Why?'

'It's dangerous.'

'So what? If it fell, it would have crushed us. Maybe a few cats and dogs as well. The pigeons roosting on the balcony wouldn't have gotten hurt; they'd have flown away. If the mansion collapsed, it wouldn't have done those stinking city bastards any harm, just like the pigeons.'

The three went on packing their belongings.

'This mansion is rock solid. It'll last another hundred years. You hear me? All it needs is a little bit of repair. Where will we go? The city doesn't understand.'

The man stomped down the stairs. The three picked up their belongings and strode out of the mansion—Bara shyly, Manjhla fearfully, Chhota smiling. Once again they stood on the street, wondering where to go next.

TWO OLD KIPPERS

SIDDIQ AALAM

'...sleeping as quiet as death, side by wrinkled side, toothless, salt and brown, like two old kippers in a box'.

—Dylan Thomas, 'Under Milk Wood'

Recently two pensioned old men in Calcutta met by chance in a public park. Six years ago, but on different dates, they had both retired from government service. Ever since, providence had been preparing for the day when they would be found sitting side by side on a single bench. Apparently they had each lived their lives and were now trying to invest their remaining days in something useful. Having arrived at this point, they were still poles apart.

Since retirement, one of them could be seen every evening without fail—every evening, that is, unless he was out of town—on one of the wooden or concrete benches at the edge of the grassy patch in the park. He spoke very little and when he settled down on a bench he stuck his umbrella vertically between his legs and rested his chin on its handle. Usually he preferred a bench that was remote and empty, but sometimes, when all of the benches were taken, he deigned to choose the one that had the least number of people and sat crouching in a corner so that if anyone tried to accost him he could pick up his umbrella and leave without wasting a second. During these six years he had surgery on his right eye, and most of his brow had turned grey. The crown of his head was bald and in the last light of the evening he often looked like a corpse that had escaped from the morgue of the nearby medical college and crossed the street to come here. All in all, his face seemed to be that of the ideal government pensioner who'd left everything that was his inside the walls of his office building.

The other old geezer, because he'd retired from the railway service, was able to get two free travel passes, which he used to visit places within the country. His addiction to gambling, acquired in his youth, had nearly ruined him. But now, at the tail end of his life, he mostly went to see religious sites, such as those at Varanasi, Puri, Tarkeshwar, etc. He'd also bought a little hut in a hermitage at Puri so he could spend his last days in peace. But mentally he wasn't yet ready for that, so, instead, he spent his days leafing through newspapers, or sitting idly and dozing on the terrace outside his building, or going to the public park. Now and then while dozing, he unconsciously found himself standing in the Antipodes with the waves of the Pacific swelling up around him. But all he could see, even on the waves, were racehorses swimming, or playing-card jokers rowing boats, or whirlpools circling around him like a roulette wheel. These Antipodes had stuck in his mind since his school days when his geography teacher had resorted to using a globe to explain the true shape of the earth.

One evening when a tired sun was breathing its last on the kadamb and karanj trees planted outside the park's perimeter wall, a chubby-cheeked boy was seen crossing the grassy patch escorted by his nanny. Noticing the two old coots sitting side by side, the boy, for some strange reason, began laughing and kept on laughing for quite a while as he repeatedly turned around to look at them. The first old man was still trying to figure out what might have made the boy laugh when he heard the sound of another laugh. Without thinking he turned sideways to look. It was another man, about his own age, perched on the other end of the bench.

'Why was the kid laughing?' he asked the other man in spite of himself, although it was the laugh of his own peer that was bothering him more than the boy's.

'Perhaps because he thought we're so old,' the other replied and started to laugh again.

'Well now, that's not so strange that you should laugh about it. At his age, I'd have laughed too.' He came to the boy's defence for no reason at all. 'And anyway what are old-timers for?' He was pleasantly surprised at his own magnanimity.

'What for? To burn in the Nimtala crematorium—what else!' The second man tittered heartily. Then he stopped, leaned towards the first and asked, 'Tell me a secret: would you allow them to perform an autopsy on you when you're dead?'

'What kind of question is that? And if they did, would I be there to stop them?'

'But you can. You can tell them in your will, I mean if you die a normal death.'

To get off the subject the first man said, 'Oh well. We'll worry about it when we cross that bridge,' but deep inside the question had rattled him. For a while he gazed at the immense field where giant tents and canopies were set up during the winter for the circus. The buildings outside the park rose high into the air like so many cardboard boxes, which some tiny hand might reach up and send crumbling to the ground any instant.

'But why was the kid laughing—really?' he wondered to himself.

Later he was surprised to realize he'd blurted out a whole lot of things to that stranger—that didn't jibe at all with his reticent nature. Then, in quite a mysterious way, the two old men ran into each other the next evening, and again the following evening, and then every evening. Neither had asked for the other's name. They also avoided talking about personal matters, which was good; it helps prevent discussing many painful subjects.

One day the second old man asked, 'Why do you always have an umbrella? Especially now when the weather is perfectly fine?'

'I feel defenceless without it,' the other replied unpleasantly. 'I've been lugging it around all my life. I can't give it up now. Impossible!'

'What kind of protection do you expect from an umbrella?'

'Why?' the other said irritably. 'There are many advantages, not counting the sun and rain. Suppose we're sitting on this bench and a snake slithers out of the grass right between our legs. We can at least defend ourselves with the umbrella. Or suppose you're late getting home one night and you take the Carmichael Hospital route where you find a body on the pavement. You can at least poke it with the umbrella tip to see whether it's alive or dead. And to tell you the truth, I can't even remember how many times I've used it to fend off attacks from stray dogs.'

'Wow! But you're forgetting one other advantage.' The other old coot was having a hard time suppressing his laughter. 'Say you're sitting on a bench and you're afraid you might have to face this man you really don't want to see, so you snap your umbrella open and hide comfortably behind it. Isn't that something? Ha-ha-ha!' He was laughing heartily, as usual.

'Have you ever been a circus clown?'

'No. But I've wallowed enough in the Hoogly mud to be a turtle,' the old man retorted.

There was a fence on three sides of the area of the park earmarked for the circus, and a row of dense and not-so-dense almond, kadamb, ashok, chatiyan and karanj trees ran along it. Beneath the trees, at suitable intervals, wooden or concrete benches had been placed haphazardly. Around this huge area a blacktop path had been laid out for strollers. When the lights came on in the buildings outside the park, the area was submerged in a kind of semi-darkness in spite of a few halogen lamps installed by the city. Many couples came here to take advantage of the semi-darkness. They sat on the thick carpet of grass and spent time enjoying the nice cool breeze. The two old coots just looked at them indifferently, as if they had no interest in whatever strange acrobatics were going on in that darkened spot. They had stopped holding forth critically on society's many different ills a long time ago anyway.

'Life's an awfully tiring game,' the second old man said philosophically one day. 'That fellow above,' he pointed at the sky, 'is a mighty dangerous scorekeeper. No matter how many goals you score, he cancels them out in the end and you're left with a big zero.'

'Have you started thinking about dying?'

'What good would dying do? Even if a tree stops flowering or bearing fruit, even if no leaves sprout on it, it's still better that it stays put. If nothing else, at least snakes and squirrels can find refuge in it.'

In the fading daylight their eyeglasses would light up as if somebody had carried off two mannequins from the show window at the Grand Hotel and set them down next to each other. The first old man was used to wearing a dhoti and kurta, so he appeared much older than his companion, who wore old-fashioned pants and a shirt.

'Judging by your clothes, you still look quite fit. Perhaps you'll live longer than me.'

'Don't curse me,' said the second man. 'My grandfather was already bedridden at fifty, but he dragged on for another thirty years. The old coot made life miserable for everyone. So, it's kind of difficult to say.'

Then he came up with an idea: 'Why don't we toss a coin. Heads you'll live longer, tails I will.'

Before the first old man could say anything, the other had pulled out a five-rupee coin and was holding it between his thumb and index finger looking at him expectantly.

For a moment, the first old man stared at the other. His pupils didn't move and he appeared to be immersed in thought. Suddenly he leaned towards his companion and said, 'You take heads and leave the tails for me.'

A derisive grin splashed across the lips of the second man. He tossed the coin in the air. It went up, spiralled down in front of the bench, rolled and then disappeared into the tall grass. They both got up from the bench and started looking for it. The second man stretched his hand out under the bench and ran his fingers through the grass. The first one thought it was his duty to provide moral support and joined in. They went on searching under the bench, behind it, and on either side, but the grass was so thick and the daylight penetrating that thickness so weak it seemed impossible to ever find the coin. Even so, the two old codgers went on rummaging through the grass until their fingers became soiled. Strollers passing by gawked at the two with wonder and amusement. Some even stopped to watch awhile.

'Looks like those old geezers have lost their dentures,' a teenager mockingly commented. The two stopped searching and quickly sat up. They were holding on to the edge of the bench, panting as if they had travelled a long distance. Suddenly their eyes met and they both realized the disappearance of the coin was in perfect accord with their wishes. Suppose they *had* found it? At least they were happy now.

But the second old man wasn't satisfied. 'We can think of some other way, can't we?' he said.

'For instance?'

'You see that fellow coming towards us. We can ask him his name. If he turns out to be a Muslim you'll live long, and if he's a Hindu I will.'

'What if he's a Christian? Quite a few of them live in this part of town.'

The second old man shook his head, disappointed.

'In that case, we'll need a third party to play this game. But what's the use. This world is so divided on every issue there aren't enough coins in it to suffice.'

In spite of himself, the first oldster had started to take an interest in this game, all the while conscious that what was happening didn't sit right with him. But their meeting every second day had acquired the force of destiny. Every time he traversed the distance from his home to the park, supporting himself on his weak, spindly legs and his umbrella, he was always overwhelmed by a compelling desire to go back, but some invisible force kept pushing him to the other man and that familiar corner in the park.

'Do you realize,' the second old man brought it up again, 'we can still do a lot to make our remaining time meaningful.'

'What do you want me to do? Start working again? Or join some social movement?'

'Of course not!' the second man smiled. 'Old men like us aren't good for anything. We have to stay the way we are. I do feel, though, that a hermit's life, the fourth state in which old men live in the wilderness and practise renunciation, is about right for us. This will cure the world of many ills. The new world will belong to new people. What do you think? I've gone so far as to buy a small hut in a hermitage. All it needs is a bathroom, which will be built soon. It's right on the edge of the sea.'

'I lost my faith during the Hindu-Muslim riots of 1947, or rather, I threw it into the fire.'

'That's strange.'

'Isn't it though?'

'And you think this will bring peace to your soul?'

'Well, at least it's made me rise above these filthy events and look at them dispassionately.'

For some reason the second old man started grinning again. 'You know what?' he whispered. 'We should try again. Maybe this time we'll succeed.'

'What difference would that make? Whoever dies first, it will be the same for the other. Sooner or later we'll all be on our pyres. But if you insist, all right…'

'Oh no, I wasn't joking. I'm quite serious. All right, let's just let it hang for a while. God knows I occasionally begin to fear you.'

Sometime during the afternoon it had rained and the smog had been cleared from the sky over Calcutta. The stars appeared large and bright in the sky. The second old man shifted uneasily on the bench. Perhaps he'd arrived at a fresh decision. He lifted his finger and pointed towards the pole star that had risen with the sunset.

'You see it, don't you, shining right between the two almond trees? It's my guess that in half an hour it'll be over the top of the tree on the right. Let's walk around the grounds once. If the star doesn't reach there by then, you'll live longer.'

'Who wants to live longer? Even so, if you must insist…'

The two old-timers started to walk along the edge of the blacktop path. The first man was intentionally walking fast, followed by the other, who was plodding along slowly on his long, spindly legs.

'You're walking fast,' the second old man said from behind laughing. 'Looks like you're hell-bent on living long.'

'That's nonsense,' said the first old man, slowing down because his heart was beating quite fast, which made it hard to breathe. 'This nonsense is not likely to alter the course of nature.'

'Then why are you practically running? You'll ruin your heart. Remember your age.'

'You're really a pest,' said the first old man as he continued walking. 'You should have been in politics. That kind of work suits your kind of dirty people.'

Without bothering to look behind him, he kept walking and covered half the distance in the dim light. The second old man had been left far behind and was shaking his head meaningfully. The first one stopped to catch his breath.

'If you walk so slowly, you'll miss the pole star.'

He heard the other shoot back from behind, 'Shut up! Can't you stop blabbering? Your mouth stinks, dirty old man.'

He started off again, but with each step his heart pumped so hard he felt as though a hefty hammer was pounding away inside his rib cage. Time and again he would stare up at the sky. He felt as though all the stars were rushing forward, as if they too were hell-bent on defeating him. He started to walk even faster, so fast that cold beads of sweat started to sprout on his skull. He could also feel traces of muted pain in his chest which quickly grew so intense that he promptly sat down on the ground, clutching his umbrella tightly. As he drew quick, deep breaths he felt as though the people and lights around him were fusing together in the cool atmosphere pervading the area.

The second old man was standing in front of him, grinning.

'If you run so fast, this is what you have to expect. It's not good for your health. So greedy and at such an age!'

Rubbing his chest he ignored his interlocutor. His chest pain was beginning to subside a bit. He got up, took a few steps on his wobbly legs and stopped again. The pain had returned.

'Let's drop this foolishness,' said the second old man, gently rubbing the other's back. 'Where in the world have you heard of a star moving? Why would it inch its way to the top of a tree? It's the earth that moves and gives this mistaken impression.'

The first old man was pissed off. Grabbing his umbrella, he pointed the tip at the other man, making a gesture, and mumbled something.

'Don't get mad,' the second old man said. 'Looks like you're not feeling well. Shall I take you to your house?'

'Go to hell!' the first one pushed the other's hand aside rudely. 'I don't need your help to get home. But I do feel we should rethink our acquaintance. Perhaps we're not meant for each other.'

And tap-tapping his umbrella, he started walking in the dim light of the field towards the park's southern gate. The second old man shook his head in disappointment.

'Strange! Why should it be my fault if the stars don't move?'

The next day he arrived at the park somewhat early, wondering how his companion was doing. But the old coot couldn't be seen anywhere. And he didn't appear for the next two weeks either, although the second old man went about methodically looking at every bench. A feeling of guilt began to stir in his heart: maybe the joke wasn't suitable for a man his age, he thought. One day, he simply couldn't stand it any more and set out to look for him. He'd always seen him come into the park through the southern gate, so he went out that gate and started walking along a fairly big street. He wandered in and out of the many small streets and alleys that branched off from it. He stared at the windows and balconies of buildings hoping to spot him somewhere, until night descended on Calcutta. Suddenly a dog materialized from somewhere, lifted one of its hind legs and started to pee on his shoes. By the time he realized what was happening, it was too late. The dog was already gone. Vanquished and unsuccessful he returned home with wet feet. He washed his socks and hung them on the line to dry in the balcony.

'Oh Lord, could he have died?' he wondered, pressing his eyes.

Three days later, he suddenly saw him, but on a different bench and in a different corner. He leapt towards him, but before he could reach him the first old man snapped open his umbrella and hid himself behind it. Stopping in front of the umbrella, he smiled, cleared his throat and said, 'I'm sorry for what happened that day.'

The umbrella didn't reply.

'Yesterday, I tried to look for you. But perhaps that was a foolish thing to do. To tell you the truth, I don't even know where you live, your street or your house number.'

The umbrella remained silent. The second old man gave a long, cold sigh.

'I've decided to go to the hermitage. That's all I'm good for now. I can give you the address if you like. It's a nice place. You would like it. You can stay as my guest for a week or two.'

The silence continued. Finally, he admitted defeat, turned around and left the park.

Three years later he returned to Calcutta. It was two o'clock and the park was deserted. On the grounds in front of him, a little boy was playing with a rubber ball under an almond tree. As soon as the second old man entered the park his feet carried him to the same old bench that stood in its place, somewhat skewed, as if it had all happened yesterday. He sat quietly on the bench for a long time. The trees' shadows grew longer, stretching across the field. It seemed as if the circus had just left a few days ago because potholes could be seen everywhere and there were animal droppings here and there. Remembering his old companion, the man smiled. Who knows, he might meet him again on this very bench. And if he did, he would tell him about life in the hermitage, about the tranquillity and peace he had found there. He would tell him how nice it felt to walk along the edge of the sea, with the land behind and nature's azure secret stretched out in front of his eyes. The sea from which Brahma and his progeny had emerged, from which every living creature had crawled like a fledgling just hatched from an egg. Look old fellow, if you're listening to me, if you want to live long, if you truly believe in living, you must consider abandoning the cares and noise of the city. The city's demands gnaw a man completely hollow from the inside. I wouldn't be surprised at all if one day people began withdrawing inside themselves. God knows what kind of ribs keep them from deflating or what strings help them walk.

He remembered all the wagers he'd put to the other man. And how, despite appearing indifferent on the outside, deep inside they were both anxious to win, as if their whole life depended on some insignificant coin or the movement of the polar star. What if his companion *had* won! The sky wouldn't have fallen. If one really takes stock of a man's entire life objectively, would it be so wrong to say that he has nothing to lose or gain?

His reverie broke to find the little boy standing before him.

'You want something? What are you looking for?'

'My ball,' the boy said hesitantly, pointing with his finger under the bench. The old man turned his head and looked behind the bench where a pink ball was waiting to be rescued from the small jungle of green grass. The man stretched out his hand to pick it up when something suddenly glittered on the wet ground beneath the grass.

'Good God!' Handing the ball to the boy, he stood his frail body up on its legs, went behind the bench and squatted in front of that shining object. It was a coin, a five-rupee coin, its Ashoka column side facing up. Wet from a recent rain, the coin was sending a shaft of cool, dim light towards him.

'Heads!' he screamed. His mind raced back to the time three years ago when the first old man had bet with him one evening about living a long life. 'So, *I* won the bet that day. What a miracle! How strange, this coin's been lying here all this time!'

He pried the coin from the wet dirt, returned to his place on the bench and started rubbing it between his thumb and index finger. The boy was kicking his ball under the almond tree. The jagged edges of tree shadows had advanced quite far and were touching the fence around the field. He realized time had flown by and he raised his slumped shoulders.

'Curse me! The one who said that in the end it's a man's character that counts was right. I'll probably remain a worthless old man till the day I die.'

He got up, wiping tears from his wrinkled face, and walked over to the grass behind the bench. He stuck the coin back in the wet dirt under the grass with its tail side pointing up.

FABLE OF A SEVERED HEAD

SAJID RASHID

5.40—Verar Local Express

Shifting his heavy red canvas bag from his left shoulder to his right, he looked up at the Churchgate Station monitor and scurried towards Platform 3. People were practically running to the platform to board the 5.40 local. Women office workers were scrambling into the ladies' compartment, pushing and shoving, being pushed and shoved in the wild crush, barely managing to keep their stride under the weight of their dangling purses and shoulder bags, as if this was the last train. Dog-tired from the day's gruelling work, he only wanted to plop down by some window and let the fatigue of the day, indeed of his whole life, slowly ooze out of his bones.

He spotted an empty seat almost as soon as he stepped into a first-class compartment. Before he could get to it, a young man who was lost in the music flowing from his MP3 player through the headphones pasted on his ears, practically lunged forward and grabbed it. He looked at the young man in disgust. 'All right, buddy, but you won't get to sit there long!' All the seats were taken now. With a quick, upward movement he thrust his shoulder bag onto the overhead rack, walked into the aisle, and stood holding the loop swaying just above his head. The train jerked softly and started to move. As it picked up speed, so did his heartbeat—thump…thump…thump…thump… Charni Road…Grant Road…thump…thump…thump…thump…Mumbai Central…Mahalakshmi…Dadar…thump…thump…thump…thump… The local was speeding along, people were getting off, climbing aboard, spilling into the compartment, a veritable coop packed with chickens. Yet they went on playing cards and chattering away. These were the regulars who sat in the same compartment of the same local train day after day and played cards or made small talk to kill the monotony of a few hours' commute. Bandra Station had already passed. The constant jostling and shoving of the crowd had pushed him into the narrow gap between two seats, close to the rack where his own red bag sat among an assortment of carry-ons. All of a sudden his cell phone started to ring. Putting it to his ear, he shouted something above the din, glanced at his watch, and hung up. He looked around the compartment and his eyes alighted on a flabby man sitting by the window looking outside, his jowls busily at work on a glob of paan masala stuffed inside his mouth. Thump…thump…thump…thump…Santa

Cruz was passing, the next station was Andheri. He quickly looked at his watch and just as he was dialling his phone an enormous explosion went off in his head...

For a split second he saw the crowd of riders, whether seated or standing, swirl in front of him a few times like photo frames. In less time than it took for his entire body to vault upwards with incredible force and fall back down, it disintegrated into big and small chunks of flesh and his severed head hit the ceiling like a ball squirting jets of blood everywhere before dropping onto the iron floor where it bounced once, rolled over to the frame of a seat, bumped into its leg, shook slightly, and settled. His stomach had ballooned for an instant and then exploded, followed by a long drawn out whistle, akin to the steam let out by a pressure cooker...*shooooon*.

In the thousandth part of a second, his eyes relayed this scene to his brain.

The sturdy ceiling made of metal sheets had been torn apart completely, as if some mammoth fist had come down on it with massive force; ceiling fans, twisted out of shape, dangled precariously by their cables; where before there was a window, now there was a gaping hole as large as a door; a blood-spattered shoe lay nearby; a wallet, its mouth gaping wide, revealed a few bank notes and a photograph of a little girl with pony-tails with drops of dried blood on her forehead and lips. Further away lay an open fist slightly curled around a broken pouch of paan masala. Blood from the ears of the young man listening to his MP3 had streaked all the way down to his jaws, his glazed eyes locked into vacant space, and nothing left below his stomach except a web of blood-drenched intestines. Screams of horror, shock, and terror were circling like a haunting echo. Feet clad in flip-flops, sandals, and heavy boots, were treading over blotches of clotted blood, stepping over torn bodies. Countless hands were hurriedly collecting shattered bodies, severed limbs and dead bodies on stretchers, and pieces of human flesh in sheets. The pair of frozen eyes saw this horrific devastation and a cold but exhilarating smile of immense satisfaction splashed across the lifeless lips for the thousandth part of an instant, an involuntary smile that appears after one has performed an impossible task.

The stench of rotting human flesh and gore pervaded the impenetrable darkness like some suffocating gas. Time itself seemed frozen inside this blood-chilling darkness—a darkness as terrifying as the gloom in the hollow of a grave. How long? He tried to calculate the time. Perhaps he had been waiting in the murky shadows of his grave for hundreds, indeed thousands of years for Judgement Day...

A shaft of milky white light suddenly lit up the intense darkness with a rumble, evoking the inevitable feeling that the impending hour of retribution had finally arrived. He saw a band of khaki-clad men standing in front of him, hands stuffed into white gloves and handkerchiefs tied tightly around their mouths. One man, somewhat more advanced in years, wearing a cap and uniform and a pair of rimless eyeglasses, appeared to be their chief.

'Mighty strange, wouldn't you say, Inspector Chauhan, more than three weeks and no one's come to claim it!' the chief said, touching him. His fingers had the steely grip of a vice. He was staring at the lifeless head that had swelled and now looked somewhat larger than ordinary heads because of the chemical process used to preserve it at four degrees Celsius for three straight weeks. His body was blown to pieces in such a way that not a single limb had been left intact. As soon as the head was dislodged from the body, all the blood had drained out and it had turned pale. His immobile eyes were open, the irises totally white. His jaw was shattered and turned sideways. The lifeless face, with its puffy nose slightly bent to one side, with its thick lips and broad forehead, had a deep scar in the corner of its upper lip from some old injury.

'How many dead bodies, would you say?' asked the chief in rimless glasses.

'Besides this severed head, there's just one other unclaimed body. The rest have already been picked up by relatives,' Inspector Chauhan replied.

'I see... The government has announced compensation of half a million rupees for the victims' survivors,' the chief said, his eyes riveted on the head. 'Someone or the other should have claimed it.'

'Sir, one woman is looking for her disabled husband. She shows up every morning with her child.'

'Did you show her the skull?'

'Yes, I did, but she said her husband's skin colour was dark. The head must be from someone with a lighter complexion. I even showed her the other unclaimed body, but that one is charred beyond recognition.'

'Until someone identifies this head, we'll have to keep it well preserved.'

'Sir, I've noticed something very peculiar,' the inspector hesitated.

'Go on, what is it?' the chief stared at him from behind his rimless glasses.

'Sir, look closely,' he pointed at the pale face of the severed head examining it carefully. 'It seems...like he was...smiling in his last moments.'

The chief first gave his subordinate a suspicious look: what in the world made him think the head was smiling! And then he examined the lifeless object with his own eyes. The lips were open a touch, revealing two lines of firmly pressed teeth over which the dried blood had taken on a darkish hue. He thought the lips were a bit stretched out, which Inspector Chauhan probably mistook for a smile.

'What rubbish!' the chief exclaimed jerking his head. 'Whoever smiles in their last moments! This is absolutely the first time I've heard such nonsense!'

He came from a village in Kanpur. His parents had died when he was just a child, the youngest of five. His eldest brother was some twelve or fifteen years his senior and had retired only a year ago after serving as an accountant in a sugar mill. He was the one who had looked after the whole family. Not for this reason alone, but partly because he was aware of his responsibility and had married quite late, the family too regarded him as their father. He had no children of his own; he treated his siblings as his children. The sister-in-law too was extremely kind and loving. The boy turned out to be quite intelligent from very early on, which led his eldest brother to get him enrolled in the Indian Institute of Technology at Kanpur. He did extremely well and stood first among the entire graduating class in Computer Science and Engineering, and he didn't have much difficulty landing a job with a multinational company in Mumbai. His dazzling achievement made his brother immensely happy and whenever they talked on the phone, he always advised him to be honest and hard-working, attributes that had won him the confidence of the management of the sugar mill. When his sister-in-law talked with him, she urged him to steer clear of the seductions of the city, its glitz and glamour, and never failed to ask him if he had found a suitable girl yet.

After he was settled in his job he felt that it was now his duty to live up to the expectations of his brother who, putting aside his own needs, had raised him and provided him with an absolutely first-rate education. Taking his brother's advice to heart, he was working with honesty and diligence—working, that is, until the day a fair, dreamy-eyed man with a long, light brownish beard that quite became him, unexpectedly appeared in his life and utterly changed its very meaning. A kameez that reached far below the knees and a shalwar that hesitated well above the ankles on his tallish frame gave him a sharp, keen look. This man raised so many questions about life's purpose and the value of death that he felt as shaken as the earth, indeed an entire population, following a seismic tremor. He had met him in some gathering of friends. On their very first encounter, it was obvious to him that a person simply could not look deeply into his large eyes for longer than a second. A conspicuous quality of his disposition was that he could say the crudest and most bitter thing with incredible softness. No matter how heated a discussion might be, he was never heard raising his voice or showing any sign of irritation or anger.

'A life bereft of the will to achieve something sublime and a death without the desire to accomplish something noble is only the destiny of animals. And such animals are found among humans too. If a person wants to truly live as a human, the first condition is to consider your people a single family and never hesitate to lay down your life, or even take life, for their protection and to obtain justice.'

'And did you? I mean, did you ever have to face such an ordeal?' asked someone.

He first stared at the man who had asked the question and then stretched out his right leg and pulled the bottom of his shalwar all the way up to his knee. Below his knee there was a stump fitted with a steel-and-fibreglass prosthesis. Almost everyone was taken aback because his gait never betrayed the fact that half of his leg was missing. He lit a cigarette and the room was filled with the pungent smell of an imported Rothmans. 'Every moment that follows another, I consider a new life; in other words, I can perceive death in every breath I take. Always ready to embrace it. Remember, only cowards are afraid of dying.'

Amazed, all he could do was gawk at this man with such a beautiful face and such indomitable courage.

'What makes life so precious to you—really?' he asked, looking at everyone in turn with a sweet smile. Then, after a pause, he proceeded to answer the question himself. 'Material satisfaction, sexual pleasure, blood relations—isn't that it? Is any one man able to achieve all this at once? And assuming he does, exactly how long do they last? Five, twenty-five, fifty years! But no more, do they? Worldly relationships are a deception. Relatives profess their love for you as long as you live, but forget you soon after you die. No one lives or dies for another. But just imagine a life that never ends, where time doesn't even exist, so plentifully supplied with goods and sexual prowess that youth's effervescence might never leave the body and one instant of pleasure might stretch over many centuries. So tell me now, which one is important: this ephemeral life or that other

—

one that never ends?' He was laying it all out, causing the eyes of his audience to shine with a brightness brought on by a concept of a life that transcended life itself.

'Isn't enduring inequity the same as giving more power to the tyrant? Isn't it the worst kind of cowardice? Are we not told that we must live like a ghazi, a warrior, and die like a shahid, a martyr?' He had said that haltingly, probing each face one by one. 'To defend the oppressed with force means the death of the oppressor. It isn't some kind of vengeance, it's simply the execution of justice.' He was talking softly but pointedly, though his face was blazing like red-hot copper.

The man's every word was teeming with numerous spearheads that invaded every single cell of his brain. For the first time he was overwhelmed by the feeling that like countless other men he, too, was yoked to a life that had no purpose, its centre occupied merely by his own family when, in fact, everyone among his people scattered throughout the world was a part of his family. Every time he looked at a newspaper or switched on a news channel, a slew of crying, inconsolable children, grieving women, and wounded, bleeding, frightened men stood before him. While surfing the net one evening, images of mutilated bodies and traumatized souls from all corners of the earth suddenly spilled out from the screen, formed a circle around him and stared at him silently. They looked at him helplessly, their despondent eyes brimming with questions, which made him panic and close his eyes. Their muted sobs, their painful groans made every hair on his body quiver.

He consulted his family doctor who listened and explained that those images had no reality. They were merely a reflection of his imagination. It was called hallucination. The doctor advised him not to dwell too much on melancholic events and depressing incidents and wrote a prescription for some tranquillizers. As long as he kept taking the medication, he didn't suffer from hallucinations, but if he neglected to pop a pill one day, those same shattered, bleeding images again poured out of the screen and stared at him, as if demanding: 'What have you done for us?' And then they would start to sob softly. Soon their anguished sighs shook the entire room like someone overwhelmed by a sense of guilt.

A thin, sallow-complexioned woman stood in the Anti-Terrorism Squad (ATS) room on the first floor of the Police Commission's hundred-year-old, black-stoned building, trying to appease the whimpering child in her lap. She looked pretty haggard, as if she hadn't oiled and combed her hair for days, although both the bindi in the middle of her forehead and the sindoor in the part of her hair seemed quite fresh. In the past three hours the police constable had asked her to leave countless times: the boss was out on inspection and would probably be returning late. She heard him out, but asked no questions and didn't budge. A while later, as Inspector Chauhan, wearing dark glasses, crossed the corridor swiftly and went over to his desk, he was slightly jolted to see the woman; he hesitated briefly and then went inside his cubicle. A swarthy, middle-aged man, his jaw constantly moving from the effort of chewing his paan and betel nut, followed him in.

The woman looked expectantly at the door swinging behind them.

'What's it like outside? Any news, Kala Babu?' asked the inspector, lighting a cigarette and offering the packet to the swarthy man.

'Eerily quiet...all over,' Kala Babu also lit a cigarette.

'Anyway, keep your eyes and ears open. It's been three weeks. We're under terrible pressure from the higher-ups,' said the inspector and rang the bell to ask the constable minding the door to send the woman in.

She entered, balancing the crying child on her waist.

'Have they found your husband?' the inspector asked.

'That's what I've come to find out from hujur,' the woman importuned.

'Well, look, there's just this one burnt body left. You've already seen it. You say your husband was crippled and very dark. And you think that unclaimed head isn't your husband's either?' Then, putting just the right amount of emphasis on each word, he said, 'I kind of feel that your husband...I mean in the blast...'

'No, please don't say that, sir,' the woman cried and shook her head refusing to believe.

'Did you have your breakfast?' the inspector asked.

She just stared at his face in silence. 'Will you have some tea and biscuits?' he asked.

'No, sir, I don't want anything. My husband...' and she burst into tears.

The inspector took off his dark glasses and put them on the table, opened a file and started reading. Kala Babu was looking at the woman intently. 'Don't cry, don't cry,' he said and subjected her to an enquiry of his own. Her husband hawked cheap Chinese stuff at the Andheri station. He hadn't returned home since the blast. His old deaf mother keeps remembering him and crying. It becomes impossible to reason with her or even ask her to stop crying because she can't hear.

'You have a ration card?' asked Kala Babu, staring into the woman's eyes that had by now turned red from crying.

'Yes, Brother,' the woman said quickly.

'The government has allocated altogether half a million in compensation, right? If no trace is found of your husband, you can also get...'

'No, Brother, no. I only want my husband.' The woman broke into a crying fit. Seeing his mother's state, the child also began bawling loudly.

The inspector briefly lifted his eyes from the file, gave her a look and then returned to reading. The Babu used every trick he knew to prepare the woman to accept the reality, but all she could do was keep sobbing.

'Come back two days from now,' the inspector said, without raising his eyes from the file.

The woman tarried a little with tears in her eyes and then said 'Namaste' and practically dragged herself out of the room. Kala Babu leaned towards the inspector and said softly, 'Sir, I'll be back in a minute,' and, following the woman, he too left the room. The woman was walking in the long corridor, taking small steps. Her child was still crying. Perhaps he was hungry... Kala Babu walked quickly and caught up with her. With a look of immense compassion he yanked out a hundred-rupee note from his pocket and held it out to her. When she refused to take it he tried to reason with her gently that it was meant for her to buy milk for the child. He stuffed the note in the child's fist. The woman burst into tears.

'Look, Bai, it's been a month, right? And not a trace of your husband, right? He might have perished in the blast, right? You have an infant and you need to take care of him, right? Weeping and crying isn't going to do much good, right?' He was talking like some nursery school teacher, stressing every word. 'The incident is still fresh, the government's still in a generous mood, right? This is the time to grab whatever you can. If time passes, the government will forget its promise. And then you'll knock about till your chappals wear out but you won't get a penny, understand? Let us know in two days, right? I'll speak to the boss and smooth things over for you, right?' Kala Babu's litany of 'right' was busy at work bridging the gulf between her mind and her heart. Her eyes were fixed in a daze on the face of this swarthy man who seemed like an angel in that moment. The child was gripping the note tightly.

'Believe me, I don't want anything from you,' Kala Babu blurted out impatiently, unable to withstand her vacant gaze. 'Of course there will be some expenses in getting the matter settled, but I'll pay that out of my own pocket. Just remember me when you receive your compensation, right?' He gently stroked the cheek of the child whose tiny hand was still clutching the note. He smiled broadly at the dazed woman, revealing his filthy brown teeth. The woman just stood there, as if her feet were nailed to the ground, lost in troublesome thoughts of the future. Pushing her into the vortex of a myriad questions and misgivings, Kala Babu walked with giant steps back towards the inspector's cubicle.

It was an unruly mob screaming slogans at the top of their lungs, holding saffron-coloured banners that were hundreds of years old, their foreheads smeared with saffron and red powder that was even more ancient. They were gathering around a dust-coloured, moss-covered, high-domed building like some rebellious tidal wave that surrounds a rock and slowly submerges it. The feral energy of madness had breached the ring of khaki uniforms without resistance. All at once frothing saffron waves swelled up ominously from the area surrounding the ancient building that stood like a formidable rock and caused it to crumble like a fragile, gritty sand dune, leaving no trace of either history or topographic feature, nor even the high-handedness of the law. There was only the wild uncontrollable mob that had smashed all the rules and regulations of law and nature, leaving in its wake a cloud of dust that was rising like their slogans...

The sun's red was dissolving into the saffron of deepening darkness like a wet cloth soaked in blood. Tridents, swords, spears and machetes blazed in the darkness and blood-splattered bodies fell to the ground amid muted screams and cries. As they ran for protection, children were pierced with the points of spears and swords and women's clothes were torn from their bodies. Hungry dogs mauled and gnawed at the naked bodies in the streets and alleyways. There was neither a place of refuge nor a protector anywhere in sight.

The DVD playing on the television ended, but each of its scenes kept playing in his mind like a horrific nightmare. The room was filled with a funereal silence. Whether this was due to some unpleasant incident or because of questions that had inevitably impinged on his consciousness after watching the film he couldn't decide. No one had argued that day. The cigarette pressed between the lips of the long-bearded man was glowing like suppressed anger. Searching their flushed faces with his piercing eyes, the man had communicated his message directly to their brains: 'If a person wants to truly live as a human, the first condition is to consider your people a single family and never hesitate to lay down your life, or even take life, for their protection and to obtain justice.'

He stayed up late that night, and only fell asleep after a lot of tossing and turning. In his sleep he had the sensation of his body touching someone. He felt around in the darkness until his hand touched something wet and clammy. Feeling alarmed, he got up and quickly turned on the lamp on the side table. He was astonished to see that the sheet covering him was sticking up in a strange shape. He extended his hand gingerly towards it and turned it over with one quick, precise movement. A scream escaped from his lips. A man soaked in blood was lying on his side. Both fists were pressed against his knees and he was moaning. With shaking hands, he grabbed the stranger's shoulder and turned him over. His heart dropped. He couldn't believe his eyes: it was he himself lying in bed, horribly wounded and mauled. No doubt it was he, same face, same height! His body was covered with deep cuts and bruises, as if it had been stabbed with some extremely sharp-edged weapon. He was sobbing and hissing: 'Save me! Please save me!...They're going to kill me!...'

Seeing himself in this state he began to shudder with fear. He felt the ceiling fan stopping, the ceiling itself beginning to cave in, the walls crumbling, the ground quaking...

In the morning he found himself lying on the floor with a nasty headache and a burning sensation in his eyes. Suddenly he remembered everything that had transpired during the night and stood up quickly, staring at the bed, his eyes wide with astonishment and a nameless fear. The sheet was crumpled but there was no sign of the wounded man who had been lying on the bed moaning from pain. And the sheet was spotless.

The long-bearded man listened intently to the description of his condition and then said with a peaceful smile, 'This is neither mental anxiety nor are you possessed by some evil spirit. All those grieving people you saw were your conscience. The wounded one lying on your bed was your soul.'

'What do they want from me? After all, what can I do for them?' he asked in a trembling voice.

The long-bearded man said with an affectionate smile, 'A lot. You can sacrifice your life for a noble purpose and thereby attain cosmic happiness in an unfulfilled life. This happiness begins as soon as a person is placed in his grave, which turns into a flower garden for martyrs.'

He felt very light and full of self-confidence after he shook hands with the man and came out onto the street. He felt a spring in his step, and all those buses and cars zipping by seemed like so many automatic toys in an expo, the passers-by like the lifeless creatures in computer graphics, and the skyscrapers like a pile of empty cigarette packs. Apparently he was prepared for that noble and grand purpose which promises a cosmic happiness in an unfulfilled life after death...

In the ATS office, the inspector with two sub-inspectors at his side was looking intently at the face of an elderly man in an old-fashioned shirt and trousers and with a closely cropped beard, who time and again, was comparing a picture of the severed head with the photo he had brought along. His hands were shaking from an unknown fear and anxiety, and his eyes were probing.

Yesterday, too, the man had come to the ATS office, but as he approached the staircase he noticed that some people who stood facing a bulletin board on the wall across were deeply absorbed in looking at a particular notice. A frail old woman in a Kolhapuri sari stood near the board resting her hand on the shoulder of a six- or seven-year-old girl. She would repeatedly interrupt, asking one of the readers in Marathi for something, but nobody paid attention to her. Her utter despondency caused the elderly man with the closely cropped beard to stop. Suddenly the eyes of the old woman fell upon him and she hobbled over to him. What she said to him in her Marathi-mixed-Hindi was that she was searching for the name of her son, Ganpat Tikkaram Gaikwar, on the list. Shaking his head, the man proceeded with her over to the bulletin board. A strange fear gripped him when he realized that the list contained the names of the dead and wounded from the train bomb blast. He took his glasses from his pocket and began reading the list:

1. Shivram Shantaram Moorey, 40 years
2. Ram Bachchan Yado, 53 years
3. Khatoon B. Ansari, 67 years
4. Dileep Ilhas Joshia, 45 years
5. Rita DeSoza, 18 years
6. Muhammad Ali Haidar Ali Pathan, 36 years
7. Vasant Jadhupovar, 28 years

8.   Tabassum Ayyub Shaikh 27 years
9.   Baby Shabana Muhammad Usman, 8 years...

He went on reading with slowly clouding eyes. Then, Number 112 appeared: 'Ganpat Tikkaram Gaikwar, 42 years.' The instant he read out the name the old woman collapsed on the floor wailing loudly. She was striking her face with her hands and the girl in tow tried her best to calm her. The man was overcome by the woman's inconsolable lamentation and a nameless misgiving seized his heart. He left the place and returned to the inn where he was staying. Today, when he explained to Inspector Chauhan why he couldn't come yesterday, the latter said, 'We see such lamentation every day, but what can we do? We can't turn back the way you did. We steel our hearts and perform our duty.'

The ATS investigating team had already examined the two pictures closely. They had the photo of a cheerful, smiling young man that had probably been taken for some identity card. Then there was this other picture of a swollen, severed head with terribly mutilated features.

'Yes, Darogha Sahib,' said the man, 'although the picture does not exactly look like my brother, the features do resemble his...somewhat. The face has become so distorted it is difficult to recognize.' Then in a trembling voice he added, 'I pray it isn't my brother.'

'And so do we. The fact is our team suspects that he was the same terrorist who planted the bomb in the train. But of course, it's just a suspicion. We'll have to investigate the matter thoroughly.'

A chill ran through the man's body and beads of perspiration appeared on his forehead...Chhotu? A terrorist? It just can't be, he thought. The question of whether he would give in to vice or go astray doesn't even arise given his upbringing. Besides, Chhotu wasn't argumentative or irascible. He couldn't be talked into doing anything perverse. A child who'd never killed a bird with a slingshot, how could he ever become a terrorist! They're police officers, after all. It's their job to suspect. It's not for no reason that people say, given the opportunity, they're not above suspecting their own fathers...

'When did you last see your brother?' a sub-inspector's query jolted him out of his thoughts.

'We haven't had a chance to see Chhotu in the last twelve months, but we did talk with him on the phone. We talked with him ten or twelve minutes before the bomb went off. We'd found a beautiful girl for him and I called him to discuss it.'

'What did he say?'

'Just that he was too preoccupied with a slew of important matters to even think about marriage.' As he said that, his eyes became moist. 'Darogha Sahib, may I look at the head?' He wanted to look at the unclaimed head in order to reassure himself that he wasn't wrong in placing his trust in his younger brother.

'Of course!' said the inspector and got up after instructing a sub-inspector to have the suspicious man who was in custody brought to the morgue of the J. J. Hospital in the other jeep. The elderly man walked out of the cubicle behind the inspector. Wiping away the tears he had so far managed to hold back in the inspector's presence, he proceeded towards the wooden staircase. As he was going down, steadying his trembling legs on the steps with difficulty, he couldn't believe what he was seeing: On the wall near the staircase some people were looking closely at a notice on the bulletin board. The old woman in the Kolhapuri sari whom he had seen yesterday was there again with her hand resting on the same girl's shoulder. She was making entreaties about something in Marathi to all and sundry but no one seemed to bother with her. He felt that she would soon see him and ask him to find out whether her son Ganpat Tikkaram Gaikwar's name appeared on the list... In great consternation he turned his face away and quickly left the building. He wanted to leave the place at once. He couldn't avoid feeling that the old woman was hobbling towards him as fast as she could, holding on to her granddaughter's shoulder for support.

His cell phone started to ring and kept ringing for quite a while, but he had no mind to take the call. As he sat in the rear seat of the jeep with the members of the ATS team, he was deeply immersed in thoughts of his youngest brother. Chhotu's innocent face dangled before him like a framed photograph. In a way, all of the siblings were deprived of parental love and were affected by its absence, but being the youngest, Chhotu seemed to have been affected the most. Perhaps that's why he never got into any mischief like most kids. For the first time he deeply regretted that he had been unable to buy nice clothes and toys for his younger brothers and sisters, especially Chhotu, the youngest—because he made so little money. He felt it even more strongly because now, earning a good salary, Chhotu was overly concerned with the needs of the whole household. On every festival he never failed to send clothes, toys, and shoes to his two married sisters and their children...The cell phone started to ring again. He was jolted from his thoughts. Quickly pulling the phone out of his pant pocket, he brought it to his ear. His wife was speaking on the other end.

'I heard it on the TV—the head might belong to some terrorist.'

There was a tremor of impatience and fear in her voice and she was having tremendous difficulty keeping herself under control.

'But the picture looks very different. Anyway, it will become clear after I've looked at the severed head that it's not our Chhotu's.' He said that in a deliberately loud voice and then hung up. He was amazed how easily and confidently he had lied. He didn't want to hurt his wife by telling her that although the picture of the unclaimed head didn't exactly resemble his brother's, the slightly curved nose and the scar above the upper lip were exactly like Chhotu's.

The J. J. Hospital morgue was about as old as the facility itself. With the man with the close-cropped beard in tow, the ATS inspector and his team entered the dreary morgue followed by two hospital sweepers who were pushing a gurney. The stench was so oppressive that just about everyone had put their handkerchiefs over their noses and mouths. Passing through a large hall where a few corpses lay stark naked on stone slabs, they stepped into the heavy, closed atmosphere of the refrigerated room. Here, dead bodies were kept on sliding shelves at near-freezing temperature. At a sign from the inspector one of the sweepers pulled out a shelf... The man with the close-cropped beard saw that it was the same head as in the picture, its frozen eyes fixed on him. His heart thumped loudly in his chest. He could recognize his brother behind seven screens, among a million people. In front of him was the head of his well-intentioned, dutiful youngest brother, the very sight of which rattled him to his very bones, the head of a man who had wasted his own life while taking the lives of innocent people.

'And here I am, left to wallow in the filth of an ephemeral world!' the thought occurred to him. 'Death is eternal sleep, they say. Amazing that one should say that without experiencing it! The fact is sleep vanishes with death, leaving protracted waiting in its wake...for one's salvation!'

The scene melted and became clear before the frozen eyes of the head. If it had a heart it would have fluttered wildly. His eldest brother was standing right in front of him, his face as lifeless as a piece of charcoal from which all the glow and heat had departed. He looked at him intently and saw him move his quaking hand towards him, then pull it back quickly. He was shaking his head...out of immense pain...anger...regret...denial...

'Look at it carefully.' It was the same voice he'd heard several times.

'No, Darogha Sahib, it's not my brother.' The words caught in his throat.
'Are you absolutely sure?' asked the inspector.
'Ye...ye...yes!' Bhai Sahib said with finality.

The head saw Bhai Sahib swivel quickly on his heels and make for the door. His neck bent down, his shoulders slouched, like an ox weighed down under the crushing weight of a yoke.

Once again the head found itself in nauseating darkness. Never in his life had he imagined for an instant that Bhai Sahib, who loved him like a father, would refuse to recognize him this way. A sentence echoed in the darkness: 'Worldly relationships are a deception. Relatives profess their love for you as long as you live, but forget you soon after you die. No one lives or dies for another.'

The feeling that he had really been living under the deception of relationships until now overwhelmed him. Thank God he had now not only extricated himself from the slush of this deception but was also witnessing its demise. If only he had freed himself from it sooner and devoted his life to the pursuit of his noble purpose. If only...

Was it only a few minutes or a few hours or a few years after Bhai Sahib left when there was again light in the darkness? This time quite a few people emerged from the dirty walls and came to stand before the head. The head's eyes first fell on the bunch of uniformed men, headed by the police officer who wore dark glasses. Then, somewhere in the midst of this throng he spotted the outline of someone in handcuffs, clad in white from head to toe. What the dead eyes saw after they had adjusted to this sudden flux of light was truly very surprising: his ideal, the Perfect Man was standing before him. His long beard was matted now. His face reflected apprehension and dread, his dreamy eyes the fatigue of many sleepless nights.

'Look at it and tell us whether you recognize him,' the inspector said in a commanding voice.

Why wouldn't he recognize me?—the head thought. He doesn't fear death like the worldly. He's a true ghazi, ready to sacrifice his life and take life any moment for the sake of his people. My relationship with him is not a blood relationship that material considerations or greed might rupture, as Bhai Sahib has done. Our relationship is based on unshakable belief, a solid ideal and a lofty purpose.

They all approached and bent over him, so close indeed that the head felt the long beard of the man literally poking into its eyes. For a moment he felt as though the other man was about to kiss his forehead. If only I could tell this man who has given me the true understanding of life—the head thought—that thanks to you I've accomplished the lofty purpose of my life.

The man straightened up, wiped the sweat off his brow, and then shook his head with a smile, 'No,' he said, 'I don't know who he is.'

There was a slight tremor in his voice.

Perhaps he didn't recognize me. How could he? After all, my face is so distorted... Had he recognized me he would surely have declared proudly: Yes, he's the young man who preferred martyrdom over a life of ignominy, who regarded his people as his own family and sacrificed himself for a great cause... That man's words were still reverberating in his mind: 'Live like a warrior and die like a martyr.'

'Don't lie! You do know him, don't you?' Inspector Chauhan's tone was quite severe. 'Wasn't this suicide bomber a member of your organization?'

Looking with contempt at his lifeless eyes, the man said, 'No. He was not one of us. We consider it a great sin to take the life of innocent people and the taking of one's own life is absolutely forbidden in our religion!'

Something exploded loudly in his head. His brain shattered and whistles started to blow in his ears as darkness fell before his eyes like a thick black curtain. Everything was instantly shut out from his eyes.

In the dimly lit morgue all of them were standing by the rack of the freezer with handkerchiefs over their noses. As always, Inspector Chauhan had on his dark glasses. Today, more than any other day, Kala Babu's jaw was working impatiently and doubly hard crushing the betel nut and paan stuffed into his mouth. The attendant and a clerk of the morgue stood holding a file and some forms. Behind them stood a terrified woman in a dirty sari with its hem drawn over her mouth. A chill brought on by some nameless fear was slowly spreading through her body. Perhaps she hadn't combed or oiled her hair for quite a few days, but the bindi mark in the middle of her forehead appeared quite fresh. However, today there was no sindoor in the part... The sound of a child crying nonstop outside could be heard in the room. The sweeper pulled the shelf out of the freezer with full force: the same unclaimed head was staring at them with its lifeless eyes. Kala Babu took out a small packet from his pocket, gave it to the woman in the sari and made a sign. The woman took a pinch of perfumed red dust and smeared it on the brow of the head with trembling hands. Joining her hands, she bowed to it reverentially, and then, God knows moved by what emotion, she burst into tears.

Kala Babu pulled out a length of virgin white cloth pressed between his underarm and thrust it towards the sweeper who extended his gloved hands, picked up the head, put it inside a polyethylene bag and wrapped it carefully in the cloth. The sweeper set this ball of white cloth on the gurney with the same reverence that one places a dead body before its survivors and then started to wheel the gurney towards the door. As soon as the woman emerged from the freezer room she took the crying child from the constable's lap and hugged it. Kala Babu took out several fifty- and hundred-rupee bills from his pocket and tipped the lower-rank workers of the hospital and morgue. After coming out of the building they walked towards a waiting taxi Kala Babu had engaged ahead of time. The woman and Kala Babu took the rear seat. The woman was holding the white-wrapped head in her lap as though it was not some dead object but a live bomb.

'Don't delay the last rites.' Despite its impenetrable polyethylene shroud and thick white-cloth wrap, the head heard the inspector instructing someone. 'Kala Babu, beware, it will begin to decompose very quickly now.'

'What a stench, Sahib. I can hardly bear it. We'll go straight to the Dadar electric crematorium.'

'Crematorium!' he protested with the full power of his lungs, but after the blast he had also lost his ability to speak. In his voiceless scream there was a protest that was unable to create the slightest vibration in the sensitive wireless waves floating in the air.

Before the taxi started the woman looked at Inspector Chauhan and joined her hands in a gesture of deep gratitude. Sitting next to her, Kala Babu was smiling broadly, puffing away on a cigarette pressed between his filthy brown teeth. Suddenly the inspector remembered something. He quickly ordered the taxi-driver to halt and said to the woman, 'Just pull the wrap and let me have a look at the face.'

The woman covered her mouth and nose with the hem of her sari, unwrapped the white cloth, picked up the head in its polyethylene bag and showed it to the inspector. The inspector removed his dark glasses, covered his mouth and nose with his handkerchief, and stuck his head in the window. He took a long hard look at the stinking, disfigured head, and started. He couldn't believe what he saw. The eyes of the severed head, which was melting away like hot wax, were shut tightly and its lips were pressed together so hard it seemed as if it was caught in a deathly struggle to arrest some unbearable anguish between its jaws.

THE POSE

ANWER KHAN

God knows what got into her head. She abruptly broke her stride and slipped into Shandar Cloth Store. Then she opened the door of the show window and, deftly, removing the lovely mannequin, stood herself in the plastic dummy's place and assumed its pose.

It was evening. The street was packed with people, but they were so preoccupied as they went their way that none of them noticed what she had just done.

Why did she do it? She probably didn't know herself. True, she was something of a daredevil in her childhood. But now she was a grown young woman, a college student, smart, sophisticated, urbane. Even the most audaciously bold boys at the college got cold feet walking with her. What she'd just done, well, it just happened. It was entirely unpremeditated.

Standing in the show window she felt a strange sense of comfort wash over her. She was now, after all, a part of this bustling marketplace. She could also look closely at the place, the whole of it, standing in just one spot, without having to move. Walking as one of the crowd or while shopping, she never felt herself a part of the life around her—the buoyant, strident life, full of vigour and excitement.

Her tense body gradually became unstrung, and an unbidden smile came to her lips. She quite liked it—standing with one foot slightly forward, the hem of her sari going over her head and then dropping down to wrap itself around the joint of her right elbow. She looked positively ravishing. She could stand in her new posture forever, she thought, overcome by a sudden impulse, although her knees had already begun to ache from the pressure.

She was just considering easing up on her heels a bit when her eyes caught sight of a peasant who suddenly cut through the crowd on the sidewalk and came over to the show window and began gawking at her with eyes at once full of lust and wonder. His eyes seemed to say—Incredible! These craftsmen can be so skilful! How they make statues that look like real people!

It was good the glass panel stood between them, otherwise the country bumpkin would certainly have ventured to touch her.

The peasant perhaps wanted to linger on for a bit, but the scouring glances of the passers-by forced him to move on. As soon as he had moved away, she relaxed her feet a little. Even shook them a bit. But now her lips began to feel dry. 'Just a little while longer,' she told her lips under her breath, 'and then I'll take you to a restaurant and treat you to a glass of ice water, followed by a steaming cup of some finely brewed tea.' Her thirst let up a bit and she slipped back into her former pose.

She certainly had no wish to exhibit herself like this to the pedestrians. Perhaps the thought had never even entered her mind. Rather, it pleased her to think that she was now a full participant in the teeming life around her. It was a strange feeling. She had never experienced it before.

'Oh God!'—the expression came from the lips of two college girls—'how lifelike!'

Their voices, travelling along the glass panels and filtering through the holes in the steel strips holding the frame, came upon her softly, as if from a great distance.

The two girls stared at her with admiration as they exchanged a few words among themselves, while she looked at them with tenderness. She was happy, incredibly happy. No one had looked at her with such appreciation before, at least not in her presence. Like a kind and caring queen receiving the adulation of her subjects, she sustained her regal pose until the girls had once again melted into the crowd and disappeared from view.

'Let's see who comes next?' she thought to herself.

Her feet had again started to protest. This time around, though, she sent them a warning, a rather stern one: scoundrels, stay put! Can't you wait even a little while? She wouldn't care a hoot about their protest, she decided.

She was still congratulating herself on her firm resolve when she caught sight of a cop who had just separated from the crowd and after taking a pinch of chewing tobacco from a box was rubbing it with his thumb. The moment he saw her, his hand stopped dead, his mouth fell open, and his eyes widened. She stared at the cop sweetly. The cop's eyelashes began to flap frantically; he rubbed the tobacco hastily and stuffing it between his lower lip and teeth practically stuck his eyes against the glass of the show window.

She was overcome by a powerful urge to laugh, but managed to stop herself with the greatest difficulty. Suddenly her feet began to itch uncontrollably. There was even a slight, involuntary tremble. But the cop thought it was a mere illusion, or the effect of the tobacco.

The cop stared at her for a long time. He would withdraw a little, then come back and inspect her closely. This went on for so long that she began to tire. Is the idiot going to leave at all, she wondered? She was feeling uncomfortable. She knew she couldn't go on standing in that pose. All the same, she also knew that she was safe inside the show window. Where would she find such a sanctuary outside?

Thank God the cop finally decided to leave, and she drew a breath of relief, loosened her hands and feet, straightened up her tense back, indeed even massaged it a bit. Night was approaching and the crowd had thinned down to a few swift-footed pedestrians.

Soon it will grow dark, she thought. She'd better get out of here while there was still some light. The fabric store must be emptying out. Somebody might see her getting out of the show window. She'd have to be very careful…and fast. And yet there was such comfort inside the show window! How she wallowed in that pleasure! Another ten minutes? Why not…

She was still mulling over this when she spotted her girlfriend Sheyama on the sidewalk. Right away she sprang into her former pose and held her breath. Sheyama threw an inattentive look in her direction and because her thoughts were elsewhere, the danger, luckily, was averted. The thought that some of her acquaintances might spot her here had not occurred to her until Sheyama came along. This was precisely the time when her older brother returned from work, she recalled with horror. He's already suffering from a heart ailment. What if he saw the family's 'honour' exposed so shamelessly out on the street? Wouldn't he drop dead?

Two boys appeared in her field of vision. They were returning from school, their satchels glued to their backs. They looked with zesty curiosity and pasted their faces—eyes and all—flat against the glass. 'Hey, she's real,' the voice of one of the boys entered her ear faintly. Once again she wanted to laugh.

'Idiot, it's plastic,' the other boy said. 'Whoever uses a live model?'

'But she looks so real. Seems she'd open her mouth and start speaking any second.'

'That's because of the evening. In proper light, you'd see.'

'Hi!' the boy said as he winked at her mischievously.

The other one broke into a gale of laughter. Then he too waved at her and said 'Bye!' and the two walked out of her field of vision.

As soon as they were gone, she suddenly began to laugh, but just as suddenly, became very nervous.

A young man was looking at her with perplexed eyes from across the glass. When their eyes met, he smiled. She smiled back, if only to hide her trepidation. She quickly grabbed the plastic dummy, and tried to install it, pretending to be one of the store clerks.

The youth's eyes were still riveted on her.

Arranging the sari around the mannequin she looked at the youth from the corner of her eye to see who he was looking at. His eyes lingered briefly at the plastic figure, then bounced off it and came to rest on her.

She backed up, supremely confident, opened the door to the show window and walked out.

None of the store attendants saw her leave, or if they did, she was so agile and so fast that they could hardly figure out what had happened. The doorman didn't notice, as he was busy talking to one of the sales clerks.

Confidently she strode away, briskly but lightly, happy and satisfied. As though she'd just unloaded the entire pestering weight of her body and soul. After she had walked away some distance, she turned around and looked back. The youth was still staring at her, perhaps with wonder.

She quickly turned down another street.

THE MAN

SYED MUHAMMAD ASHRAF

He peered down from the window and watched them go by. Suddenly he slammed the window shut, twisted around and turned on the ceiling fan. But, just as quickly, he turned it off. Then he slumped into the chair by the table and said in a hushed voice, 'More than yesterday—no doubt about it. They're getting bigger and bigger every day.'

Sarfaraz lifted his face from his palms and looked at Anwar. 'You've seen this only a couple of days. But me, I've been watching it for quite a while now. If I leave the window closed, it feels stuffy, if I leave it open, I feel even worse. I feel they are headed straight this way.' Sarfaraz became quiet. After a pause, he added, 'I was really feeling quite happy meeting you today after such a long time. But then, this mob ...'

'Not just a couple of days. I already told you about everything that happened on the trip. It's no different back in the village. Haven't got a clue what might still happen.'

Sarfaraz looked at his childhood friend fondly. He was meeting him today after a hiatus of fifteen long years.

They went back quite a ways and shared many memories...

Sarfaraz was still a teenager when his family sent him away to his maternal aunt's, so that he could study at the two-year college in a small town a couple of miles' walk from where she lived—a village larger than his own. The very first day at the college, a boy of about his age had helped himself to his eraser, as though the two had long been buddies. The boy had rubbed off the balloon-shaped flower from his art book, drawn in its place a duck-shaped lamp, and then handed the eraser back to him. At roll call, when the teacher called out 'Saiyid Anwar Ali,' this boy had answered, 'Here!'

'Saiyid Anwar Ali!' Sarfaraz intoned softly.

'Here! You're thinking of the good old days at the college, aren't you?'

'Yes. How did you know?'

'Just as dumb as ever. You haven't changed a bit, yaar. Who else ever called me by my full name at roll call except that art teacher?'

Sarfaraz smiled, though the bit about being 'dumb' didn't go down well with him. But he thought nothing of it, realizing that while he himself had risen to an important position, his childhood friend had remained merely an Urdu teacher in a primary school. Of course, he needed to say those things to overcome his insignificance.

But wasn't it Anwar though, he quickly recalled, who gave his sagging spirit the pluck needed to trudge back home through those eerie woods, haunting lonely orchards, and silent dreary fields on the stretch between the town and the village after school every day? How the countryside used to spook him! Sarfaraz leaned back in the chair, rested his head flush against the back, let his eyes gently close, and relived that dread of his early youth, and even savoured its memory.

The last bell at school rang at 4 o'clock during the winter and the boys shot out noisily to head home. They would walk with the swaying gait of drunks, their school bags hanging from their shoulders. Not even one boy from his village was enrolled in the college. Cringing from the dread that awaited him on the way, he would walk out of the school gate with steps that couldn't be slower or more heavy. Sometimes Anwar came out with him, sometimes not. When he did, he invariably accompanied him, but only as far as the pond. Beyond it even he wouldn't venture, because just ahead of the pond the unpaved country road veered sharply to the left making the town disappear from view altogether. But just as he said goodbye, he unfailingly tossed in a few words to give his friend's withering spirits a boost. 'Don't be afraid, Sarfaraz. There will be somebody around, just as soon as you've crossed the river and stepped into the orchard.'

He would look at Anwar feeling defenceless. But to avoid giving his friend an inkling of the dread churning his insides, he would reply with feigned bravado, 'Nothing to be afraid of. It's just that I feel a bit more at ease if there is someone around in the orchard. But if there isn't, I don't really panic.' Saying this he would set off for the village.

The two would look back at each other for some distance. As soon as Anwar dropped out of sight, Sarfaraz would touch the sacred amulet hanging from his neck and begin quickly to recite the 'Throne' verses from the Holy Quran. Before turning on the dirt path running along the river bank he would recite the four Quls from the Holy Book and blow on himself. Having thus braced himself with the protective powers of the Divine Words he would proceed towards the orchard with utmost caution. The sun would be going down at about this time. It became dark quite early during the winter. The sight of a few bicycle riders or passing bullock carts with their bells tinkling on the country road before the turn in the river path somehow emboldened him and gave him a sense of strength. But the moment he had stepped onto the path, an eerie hush fell all around him, made even more frightening when a buzzard suddenly shifted on its perch or spread out its wings overhead in the branches of a shisham tree. He would freeze and instantly forget the 'Throne' verses and recite instead Qul hu'l-Laah, managing a quick Profession of Faith in between.

The orchard now loomed into view—the old mango orchard, shrouded in a thick layer of fog in the fading orange daylight, whose interior remained as dark in the bright afternoon as it was at sunset. He could say this from experience: after all, he had seen it one Sunday afternoon. In the evening though, the orchard was a different reality. It seemed that the trees had somehow melded at the top to form a single continuous vault that could not be breached. Passing under a fajri mango he could practically hear his heartbeat. He would feel that Jinnaat Baaba (Father Goblin) was about to jump down from the tree any second.

Another fear gripped him just as soon as he emerged from the orchard and wound his way on the narrow raised trail along the sugarcane fields—the fear that a wolf might lunge out of the tall cane stalks and grab his leg. He would break into a sweat. Next the wheat fields entered into view, followed by the huge encroaching spread of the ancient pilkhun tree, above which loomed the minarets of the village mosque and the spires of the temple. Only then would his body, tensed by fear, begin to relax. He would feel a trace of strength return to his numbed legs and begin to hum loudly a bar or two of some film song.

Two or three times a month he was lucky enough to spot the man right away upon entering the orchard though invariably the man would be retreating towards his hut, a shovel in his hand. On such occasions Sarfaraz would begin to croon in the orchard itself, interrupting himself briefly to greet the man with ingratiating friendliness.

The man would stop, rest the tip of the shovel on the ground, look at him with blinking eyes and return the greeting, 'Ram, Ram, son. You're Patwaari Sahib's nephew, right? Do please give him my greetings.'

The hope that he might run into the man was what sustained him each day during his perilous trek home. Without that hope he might have long since dropped out of school and returned to his own village for good.

But he didn't meet the man every day. Once he was unusually late getting out of school. A volleyball match was on. He was so captivated by it that he lost all track of time. And when he did become conscious of it, he quickly looked at the sun, which, to his horror, had already turned a deep orange while he was still in the town. He shot out of the gate and set off for the village. Just as he turned on the river path the awareness that the man must have left the orchard by now hit him like a bullet, touching off a ripple of tingling through his entire body. He wiped the sweat from his forehead and entered the gloom under the shisham tree, emerging from it with the terrible feeling that somebody had just come down the tree and was following him. His throat locked. But he pushed on ahead slowly, his face blanched with fear, his body cowering. The sound of footsteps behind him suddenly stopped. The feeling that Jinnaat Baaba was about to take aim and hurl the magic ball at his back gripped him. He hurriedly recited the kalima in his heart and looked behind him from the corner of his eye. It was a huge monkey that had suddenly stopped in its tracks, dropped its front paws on the earth and was screeching at him menacingly. Monkeys too scared the hell out of him, but considerably less than Jinnaat Baaba. He clutched his school bag and halted in front of the orchard. He felt his path had been blocked both in front as well as in the back: in front was the desolate orchard, with no hope of seeing the man, and behind the monkey.

The sun had already gone down quite some time ago and the trees in the orchard had started their evening whispers. He stepped into the orchard. Passing by the old fajri up ahead, his heart fluttered fitfully: that's where he lived—Jinnaat Baaba.

Just then he heard a voice coming from some point to the right of him. 'You're very late today, son.'

What? So the man's still there! A ripple of joy rushed through him. He had never felt that happy, not even the day when the teacher gave him a *Very Good!* on his essay 'My Cow'. He lifted his eyes to look at the man. He was standing by the trees near the hut, buried in the fog. He looked at him closely. He had his shovel in one hand, the tip resting on the ground, and with his other hand he was trying to fix his all-purpose angocha-cloth over his ears. Draped in fog and clad in a dhoti and angocha, he appeared to Sarfaraz more a servant of Prophet Elias.

'Greetings, Man!' he said, chirping with exhilaration.

'May you live long, son. Don't forget to give my greetings to the Patwaari Sahib. And don't you hang about so late at night.'

He didn't respond. Later, after supper, he snuggled up to his aunt in the courtyard and told her all he had been through that day. He wanted her and her husband to know not just the incredible hardship his study at the college entailed, but also the horrendous perils that awaited him on the way to and from college each day. But when the aunt found out that a volleyball match had held him up, she scolded him instead of comforting him.

At bedtime, in the courtyard, he carefully wrapped himself in the comforter of thick cotton fluff, and speculated: 'What if the man died—how will I ever get back home from school?' But the thought that the man looked a whole lot younger than his uncle, and so was unlikely to give up the ghost any time soon, set his troubled mind at ease.

'Sarfaraz,' Anwar said, 'you know what? Your aunt's daughter Aisha is getting married. Your aunt sent for me the other day and complained that you have all but forgotten her. She also asked me to tell you that both she and her husband very much want to see you again, indeed they are quite anxious, and that you must attend the wedding.'

Sarfaraz felt terribly ashamed. But to hide it, he told Anwar in a solemn, nevertheless hollow, voice that his government job, which entailed tremendous responsibility, left him hardly any time to socialize. Then he remembered Aisha, his cousin, whom he used to carry around in his arms. How quickly she had grown!

'When is the wedding?'

'The bride's party will be arriving the day after tomorrow.'

'I'll be darned. How is it that Aunty went ahead and fixed the wedding date, in spite of what's happening all around? Haven't you seen how a total madness has seized these people? How they take out demonstration after demonstration on trucks and even tractors, laced with arms, faces flaming with rage, shouting slogans dripping with naked hate?...'

Anwar stared at him and then said, 'I too told Aunty that this was hardly the time for a wedding. Madness has spread down even to the villages. Why, the people in her own village have begun to feel differently. Their mood has changed. But what could she do? Aisha's engagement was fixed with the son of Uncle's own brother. The boy is due to return to Jedda in three days. Uncle has grown quite frail too. He'd sooner fulfil his responsibility towards Aisha while he's still living. Sarfaraz, you really must come along. Today. Call Bhabi on the phone and tell her to get ready.'

'Haven't you seen the newspaper, Anwar? Just the day before yesterday, they dragged the passengers out of the train and...' He halted.

Anwar was unable to say anything either. After some time, he ventured,

'All right then, let Bhabi and the children stay here at home.'

'Yes. I don't think I should let them come along.'

'It's one o'clock. If we start by twelve, we'll be able to make it there by six or seven in the evening.'

'Yes. It's a good 250 kilometre run—maybe 300.'

On the bridge across the river some people darted in front of the car and beckoned them to stop. Both friends had a sinking feeling. They had no weapon on them to defend themselves. An angry mob on trucks and tractors was coming along up ahead. Demonstrators were shouting nasty slogans, pushing ahead with a powerful emotion too complicated to name.

Both Sarfaraz and Anwar's minds went completely numb. They stayed inside the car, as the demonstrators filed past them on either side. The people who had beckoned them to halt remained standing, responding to the loud slogans. Sarfaraz immediately tried to remember the 'Throne' verses.

When the demonstration had passed by, those other people also caught up with it, all the while talking very loudly.

Sarfaraz, gripped by a terrible nervous tension, was unable to turn on the ignition right away. For a while both sat there in mute immobility, each experiencing the fear haunting the other.

When Sarfaraz did finally start the car, Anwar said, 'They don't mess around in the open with a few people. They've got specially trained men in every town and village for that. Last Friday, just as Ahmad left the city road for the orchard path... suddenly...from behind...'

A shudder ran down Sarfaraz's spine. He kept steering the car in total numbness. Anwar continued, 'Of course, if the demonstrators as a group attacked a few solitary individuals, they would get a terribly bad name for that. But, let me tell you, we're ready for them.' This last bit, he whispered in a tone of secrecy.

The sun was just setting as they took the turn to the path along the riverbank. Sarfaraz was reminded of his youth. How this silent river, the deserted path that ran along its bank, and the desolate orchards had appeared so improbably frightening to him then.

Suddenly he slammed on the brakes. A large monkey appeared in the headlights, its front paws resting on the ground, staring and screeching at them. Both broke into a smile. The monkey scurried off and clambered up a tree. A fluttering noise came from the top of the tree where a vulture shifted on its perch. Sarfaraz remembered how this flutter had scared the daylights out of him once.

'Just when did that happen? I mean this thing about shopkeeper Ahmad?'

'Four days ago, counting today.'

'Oh, no!...' Sarfaraz's fingers suddenly became moist on the wheel.

'What happened?' Anwar asked, although he knew precisely what had happened.

'No, nothing. I mean the incident is quite fresh. Were they able to find out...?'

'You've got to be kidding. Just as soon as the funeral was over the police chief scolded them instead. He said when they knew such incidents were on the rise, why did they let him stir out of doors after sundown in the first place. It's a lot easier for the attackers to kill and flee in the dark.'

'Stop! Back up and stop the car. We can't go any further.'

The orchard sailed into view as soon as the car got off the river path. Sarfaraz backed the car up and parked it. Then he walked and stood in front of the orchard.

He was looking at the fog-draped orchard for the first time in a long time. It didn't scare him at all today. All the same, a strange ringing stillness had quietly settled in both their hearts, a stillness so deep it could not be broken in spite of their conversation.

Just as the two friends passed under the ancient tree in which Jinnaat Baaba made his home, Sarfaraz suddenly stopped and squeezed Anwar's hand so hard that the pain penetrated clear down to his bones.

Anwar looked at Sarfaraz, who pointed with his eyes at a trail. Anwar was unable to see anything. In the darkness he couldn't even make out the place Sarfaraz was pointing to.

This time Sarfaraz pressed Anwar's hand even harder and turned back and dragged him along out of the orchard, stumbling and steadying himself all at once. He practically shoved Anwar into the car, quickly turned on the ignition, raced the engine full throttle on the raised river path, then across the bridge and down onto the country road. He was driving under a crushing nervous strain. His face was trembling and his whole body was drenched with sweat.

'All right, we've driven far enough, so tell me now.'

Sarfaraz pulled up the car and said, 'There was a man. He was standing bent over on the trail among the trees in the orchard. He had a weapon in his hand, and its tip was resting on the ground.'

A SHEET

SALAM BIN RAZZAQ

He was standing behind the window looking out onto the street, which one could see in the distance shimmering in the sun as if somebody had magically stopped a flowing river. It was the same street on which traffic flowed uninterrupted well into the night, where crowds of people milled about like crawling ants right up to midnight. Morning and evening, the noise from the traffic and the people gave the sidewalks the atmosphere of a carnival. But at the moment, both the street and its sidewalks were completely deserted. Not a soul anywhere, not even a sound.

His mind too was as empty as the street in front of him. Now and then, though, a whirlwind of some inarticulate anxiety or fear did sweep over him. Dread and despair had begun to thicken around him like gloom, and he felt smothered by it. He picked up the packet of cigarettes from the table near him, lit up, drew a deep breath, and exhaled the smoke out the window. There was no wind at all. The smoke dissolved slowly, like life ebbing away from a dying patient. He longed for home. The image of his beautiful wife Salma, the innocent pranks of his sons Sajid and Majid, and the deep affection in the eyes of his old, paralytic mother flashed before his eyes. Salma had told him as he was leaving, 'It doesn't look good at all in Bombay. I'm worried.'

But he had tried to allay her fears. 'Riots are common in big cities like Bombay. Nothing to get so worked up about. They usually don't affect business there at all.'

'But you said you were going to Dadar. Dadar is one of the places affected by riots. The newspaper said so.'

'Oh, come now. After all, Vidyacharan also lives there. I'll go to his house first. I'll meet the party with him.'

'What if you waited a few days?'

'You don't understand. Vidya told me that these people are absolutely genuine. The supermarket under construction there in Bhawani Peth belongs to them. Two or three local interior decorators are bending over backwards to clinch the deal for themselves, but Vidya wants me to get the contract. He's the chief engineer. It's a big contract, worth several lakhs. Such an opportunity's not likely to come my way again in a long time. I'll take the bus straight from Dadar after the deal and be back home in Pune by the evening. Don't you worry.'

Salma didn't say anything further, but the cloud of worry didn't quite leave her face.

He tossed the cigarette butt out through the window, stepped back and half-stretched out on the sofa. The ceiling fan was whirring away, making a muffled sound, like someone trying to let something out but held back by a nagging fear. Even though he was perfectly safe here, he still could feel fear surge up in him like a wave. Vidya, Vidya's father, Vidya's mother—they all tried to keep his spirits up with reassuring words. Vidyacharan's wife, Sushma, and his sister, Arti, kept piling more puris and servings of vegetable on his plate, and Vidyacharan's younger brother, Shyam, kept inviting him to games of carom. In short, the entire household was doing its best to draw his heart away from the thoughts that troubled him; still, anxiety weighed even more heavily with every passing moment.

It was around one o'clock in the afternoon when he got down from the Ashiyad bus at the Dadar terminal. He strode over to the sidewalk and stood there, his smallish briefcase in hand, looking for a taxi. But he spotted none. There was very little traffic on the street. Most of the stores had their shutters pulled down. The sidewalk had only a few pedestrians, who walked on swiftly with a purposeful gait, looking cautiously around, as though they were in a big rush to get somewhere. There was a strange but palpable tension in the air. He suddenly remembered what Salma had told him in the morning as he was leaving. An anxious thought reared up inside him, which he quickly shrugged off with a light jerk of his neck. Just then he saw a taxi approach from the right, carrying no fare. He stepped down from the sidewalk and waved, but the taxi just zoomed past him without stopping. The driver didn't so much as look at him. He was sitting behind the steering wheel like a statue, his hands frozen on the wheel. Afterwards a couple more taxis came along, but not one stopped. 'Okay,' he thought. 'I can just walk. Vidyacharan's house isn't all that far anyway. It'll take ten minutes at most to get there.'

He set out, briefcase in hand. After crossing the main street, he entered an underpass, and felt even more acutely the sense of gravity in the air. The entire passageway was infused with an eerie silence, and the sound of his footfalls was making his blood freeze in his veins. The passageway ended in a series of buildings, but most had their gates closed. Some four or five young men stood in a group in front of one of the buildings, heatedly discussing something or the other. Seeing him approach, one of the young men said something to his companions. They all fell silent and looked over their shoulders at him. He lowered his eyes and took long strides past them. He didn't turn around to look at them, but he could hear that they had resumed talking. He entered the gate of Building 11 and took the stairs to the third floor, where he pressed the bell to Vidyacharan's apartment.

Vidyacharan himself opened the door. The moment he saw him, he said, 'Arre, Anwar! Come on in. We were waiting for you.'

Inside, Vidyacharan's father was sitting in a wooden swing-seat poring over a fat tome. He closed the book as soon as he saw him and said, 'We were quite worried about you, son! You didn't have any problem on the way, did you?'

'No, Uncle. But I did feel a strange tension in the air. The streets are deserted, shops are closed, and I couldn't get a single taxi to stop.'

'Yes, it's been like this for the last two or three days. Today, though, the atmosphere appears to be even more grim.'

'I called your house this morning,' Vidyacharan said. 'Bhabi said that you'd already left about an hour earlier. If I'd caught you on the phone, I'd have told you not to come today.'

'What's the matter? Is it really serious?'

'Seems that way. Police cars are out patrolling. And there are rumours everywhere. About a hundred huts were torched last night in Dharavi. We could see the smoke even from here in the morning. I just heard on the telephone that several chawls have been set on fire in Jogeshwari as well.'

Now his heart began to sink even deeper, like a heavy stone in water. He could feel a faint restlessness squirm inside him. His silence prompted Vidyacharan to comfort him, 'There's no reason for you to worry. Everything is okay. Here, give me your briefcase.'

Vidyacharan took the briefcase from him and he sat down on the sofa. Meanwhile Sushma appeared with a glass and jug of water. After greeting him, she set the glass and the jug on the tea table, smiled and asked, 'How are Bhabi and the children?'

'They're fine,' he responded, smiling formally.

In the meantime both Vidyacharan's mother and sister walked in. 'Vidya!' the old lady said to her son, 'Take Anwar to wash his hands. Lunch is ready.'

Shortly thereafter low wooden stools were set on the floor and everybody took their seats. Thalis were placed in front of everyone, and Sushma and

Arti dutifully served the food. He took a look around and said, 'I don't see Shyam. Where is he?'

'He's gone to college. He'll be back soon.'

After the meal he picked up a piece of betel nut from the saucer and put it in his mouth. Then he said, 'Vidya, shouldn't we go now and take care of the job? I'll take the bus home right after.'

'But the office is closed today…because of the riots. I called you this morning to tell you just that.'

'Oh.' Anxiety deepened in the lines on his forehead. 'In that case, allow me to leave. I should return right away. Otherwise Salma and Mother will start worrying.'

'All right. But I think you should take the train instead. Let me walk you to the station.'

'Uncle, I'm leaving now,' he looked at Vidyacharan's father.

'Okay, son. Given the situation, we can't even ask you to stay over. But be careful. Give us a call as soon as you've arrived in Pune.' His voice was full of concern.

Just then the bell rang. Vidyacharan opened the door and in walked Shyam. The minute he saw him, he said, 'Arre, Anwar Bhaiya! When did you arrive?' He then came over and sat down right next to him.

'About an hour ago. Tell me, how are your studies?'

'Perfect. And I mean perfect…'

'How is it outside?' Vidyacharan inquired.

'Bhaiya, it isn't good. Somebody was knifed outside the railway station just a little while ago. Police cars are patrolling everywhere. A curfew's been declared in the area around the station.'

Abruptly everyone fell silent. He looked up, only to see that everyone else was looking at him. Vidyacharan cleared his throat and said, 'Let me call Inspector Rana and find out.'

Vidyacharan got up and dialled the number. He talked with someone briefly, hung up and returned to the sofa.

'What did the inspector say?' he asked, feeling impatient.

'He said that the trains are running all right, but the situation isn't at all good. A curfew is expected in the entire area any time. News has just come that a terrible riot's broken out in Mahim as well.'

'But, Vidya, I have to return today. If I don't, they'll be worried sick.'

Once again everybody fell silent. After a while, Vidyacharan's father said, 'Anwar, son, listen to me and stay here tonight. You can go back tomorrow after the work is done. Likely the situation will have become normal by tomorrow. Call Bahu and let her know that you'll be staying here tonight.'

'But, Uncle, if I start right away, I can make it to Pune by evening. If the situation doesn't improve by tomorrow…'

Just then a police siren blared outside. The police van was announcing the curfew.

'There, they've imposed the curfew. Didn't I say that they would, pretty soon?' Shyam said, suppressing his excitement. Then he got up, walked over to the window, and peered outside.

Vidya's father chided him: 'Shyam, shut the window and sit down quietly.' Then he ordered his elder son, 'Vidya, see to it that the windows in all the rooms are securely shut.'

Vidya got up and started to close the windows like a dutiful son, while his mother, Sushma, and Arti stood quietly inside the inner room.

Vidya's father got up and started to pace aimlessly. Shyam, somewhat miffed, went over to the sofa and plopped down on it. The room became dark with the closing of the windows. Vidya's seven-year-old boy, Pappu, asked his grandmother, 'Dadi, Dadi, what is a curfew?'

But nobody gave him a reply. In the semi-dark room they looked like so many quiet, immobile shadows. The only movement came from Vidya's father, who was still walking restlessly with his hands folded behind his back. He was bare-chested above the waist. The sacred thread hung over his shoulder. His head was clean-shaven except for a tuft of hair that hung over his back like a squirrel's tail. He had vibhuti painted between his eyebrows, and he was clad in a white dhoti.

Anwar had often seen him in just this garb. In fact, he had seen him like this for many, many years. A devout, religious man, he was nevertheless quite secular in his thinking. He was well read, not just in his own religion, but also in many others. Anwar respected him a lot, and the old man always treated Anwar with affection. Every time he met him, every time he spoke to him, he had the feeling of sitting in the shade of some ancient peepul and listening to an old, dreadlocked sadhu expound on the meaning of contemplative life.

Today, however, he appeared to be an altogether different man. A stranger, who never had anything to do with him at all, and not just the old man alone—even Vidya's mother, Sushma, Arti, Vidya himself, and Shyam, seemed strangers to him.

Anwar felt he would suffocate. His throat went dry and he longed for water. But, at this moment, asking for water would have amounted to an admission of his weakness. So he satisfied himself by running his tongue over his parched lips.

The darkness intensified the heaviness inside the room. Why didn't anyone turn on the light? Just then Vidyacharan, as if sensing his friend's wish in some occult way, got up and did just that. The moment the room lit up, a current of animation swept through it. Vidya's father resumed his place on the swing-seat, which began to sway gently like a houseboat. Shyam got up and turned on the TV. Pappu ran up to the rocking swing-seat and stood on it, clutching the bar for support. Sushma and Arti retreated to the inner room. Vidya's mother edged up to Anwar and said softly, 'Son, think of this as your own house. And don't let yourself worry too much. Nobody's going to harm you here. Now get up and call Bahu. She must be out of her wits with worry. Give her a few words of assurance. Tomorrow, as soon as the situation improves, you can return.'

He peered into the old lady's eyes: empathy and motherly affection was all he could see there. The unknown fear that had taken hold of his mind relaxed somewhat, and the feeling of being in the midst of strangers that had tormented him a while ago slowly began to disappear. Fear had raised a wall of suspicion. As the fear itself lessened, the wall too crumbled away. He took out his handkerchief from his pocket, wiped the sweat off his forehead, got up and went over to the phone. Sure enough, it was Salma who answered. The moment she heard his voice, she was overcome with emotion, on the verge of tears. 'How are you?' she enquired. 'Vidyacharan Bhai called right after you left. Where are you calling from? Come home quickly, please. I feel terribly afraid.' She said it all at one go, without seeming to take even a breath. Fighting back his own emotion, he tried to say in as normal a voice as he could possibly muster, 'Don't worry, Salma. I'll be back tomorrow. I'm calling you from Vidyacharan's house. Ordinary skirmishes, that's all. Nothing big. It'll all return to normal by tomorrow.'

'But why do you want to stay on overnight? Why not return this evening, if your work's finished?'

'That's just it. The work isn't finished. The office of the people we want to meet is closed today. I'll take care of the paperwork first thing tomorrow morning. I'll be back in Pune by the afternoon. Tell Mother not to worry. Vidyacharan is here with me. Kiss Sajid and Majid for me.'

'Give your mother my namaskar,' Vidya's mother instructed him in a loud voice.

'Aunt is sending Mother her greetings. I'll call you back again in the evening. And now I'll hang up. Khuda hafiz!'

Salma, too, from the other end said in a drained voice, 'Fi amani 'l-Lah!'

'It's good that you didn't tell Bhabi about the curfew,' Vidya said.

'All the same, she'll find out. Tomorrow. In the papers. She'll know everything. And she will feel miserable...'

He wiped the sweat off his forehead once again and sat down on the sofa. Then Vidyacharan grabbed his hand and brought him into the other room, with a bed, a couple of couches, a writing table and a few books. 'This is my room,' Vidyacharan said as he opened the window and slid the curtain to one side. 'I had it built only recently. You can rest here.'

He didn't reply.

'Pitaji worries too much. But really there's no need to close the window. You keep it open. Nothing will happen.'

He peered down from the window. It opened onto the main street. But the street was completely deserted at the moment.

'The bathroom's over there. Take a shower if you like. You'll feel fresh. But just rest now. We'll meet again over tea at four o'clock.'

He then stepped forward and put his hand on Anwar's shoulder. 'Don't think that I don't know what you're going through. But don't you worry. Everything will turn out okay. You'll get back to Pune in one piece—I promise.'

He looked at Vidya with a withered smile and stretched out on the sofa. 'I'm okay, Vidya. Don't worry about me.'

'Just yell if you need anything.' Vidyacharan left the room.

The evening news on TV showed a few glimpses of the riots in the city. The dreadful scenes left no doubt that rioting had spread through the entire city, and a curfew had been imposed in several areas. Towards the tail end of the news, the police commissioner was shown repeating the same asinine assurance: 'But the situation is under control.'

His restlessness grew worse. Even before the news had ended, he quickly got up and dialled his number at Pune, but couldn't get through. He tried again and again. Perhaps there was a problem with the line itself. A bit irritated, he returned to his seat.

'What happened?' Vidya's father asked.

'Looks like the line is out of order.'

Later, Vidyacharan himself tried a few times but had no luck. They'd already had their supper and were now commenting on the news.

Vidya's father said: 'What's gotten into people that they are slaughtering others just like them as though they were goats and sheep? I can't understand how a man can hate another so much.'

'God knows where these riots will take the country,' Vidyacharan wondered in a voice full of anxiety.

Vidya's mother joined both her hands against her forehead and said, 'May Ishwar protect us all.'

Suddenly they were all looking at him. He too wanted to say something, but just couldn't get it out. Not a single word. Thoughts were swirling in his mind like a whirlwind, but the corresponding words, before they so much as reached his tongue, perished like bubbles on the surface of water. The feeling that he had been caught in thorny brambles took hold of him. If he stirred even slightly, countless sharp needles would prick him all over his body. Never before had he felt himself so helpless. Just then Shyam got up, brought the carom board over, and said, 'Anwar Bhai, how about a game or two?'

A sense of relief washed over him, as if somebody had pulled him from the water just as he was drowning. He agreed right away.

The board was laid out. Arti and Vidyacharan sat opposite each other as partners, with Shyam and he as partners against them. The game began.

The round black and white pieces were arranged in the circle in the middle of the board and were then hit with the striker, which scattered them all over the board. For a long time, the striker kept hitting the pieces, sending them in the corner pockets.

He was playing well enough, but his thoughts were elsewhere, as scenes of the rioting played over in his mind—houses going up in flames, women running out screaming and crying, children weeping bitterly, old men stumbling along, young men brandishing swords and spears, and rising above them all the loud body-shaking cries of 'Allahu Akbar!' and 'Har-Har Mahadev!'

'What are you thinking about, Anwar Bhai?' Shyam alerted him. 'Take the queen! It's just within reach!'

'Where is it?' he asked, with a start.

The queen was within easy reach of him. He hit it with the striker. The piece banged against the edge and bounced back, fluttering on the board for a while before dropping dead.

Once, seven or eight years ago on Baqr Eid, he had sacrificed the goat with his own hands. But before the knife had completely slit the throat, the animal thrashed violently and got away from him, running to one side, blood gushing from the gaping wound. People ran after it and grabbed it. But he was unable to finish the job. Somebody else had to do it for him. Never again since that day was he able to slaughter an animal for sacrifice. Looking at the queen, now, as it wobbled on the board, he suddenly recalled that goat with its throat only half-slit.

'Come on, Anwar Bhai, what's this? You could've pocketed the piece so easily,' Shyam said, showing his regret.

'I'm sorry, Shyam. I'm just tired.' He leaned back in his chair and closed his eyes.

'Shyam, you play with Arti. Let Anwar rest.' Vidyacharan then grabbed Anwar's hand and made him get up.

'Let's try to call again,' Anwar said.

'Yes, sure.' Vidya dialled the number. He dialled again. And again. He shook his head in disappointment and said, 'I don't think it'll work. Looks like the line's dead.'

He quietly went into the other room and lay down on the bed face down. His heart was sinking. If only he had gotten some news of Salma and the children, perhaps it would have helped ease his worry. The thought of his helplessness hit him hard. He felt like breaking down in tears, crying his heart out. But even crying wasn't easy. What will these people think—people who were doing their best to comfort him? If he cried, not only would he humiliate himself, but he'd also hurt their confidence. Perhaps the limit of helplessness is the inability to cry when tears alone might help. Just then he heard a click and the light was turned off in his room. He turned over with a start.

'Nothing! It's just me. Go to sleep!' Vidyacharan said, closing the door gently behind him on his way out.

After his departure a deathly stillness swept over the room. Not even the sound of a dog barking anywhere. Perhaps even the dogs had withdrawn to their shelters, cringing with fear. Only the sound of some policeman's whistle rose now and then, or that of a siren. Meanwhile, he fell asleep.

God knows what hour of the night it was when a sound woke him. The same darkness and stillness was around him once again. But no, small cracks had begun to appear in the wall of silence. He heard the muffled screams of hundreds, no, thousands of people coming from afar. He got up from the bed, quietly opened the window and peered out. The street lay just as quiet and deserted as it had been earlier during the day. But he did see what he thought was smoke rising somewhere far on the western horizon. The sky, too, looked reddish. Perhaps there had been an immense conflagration there. The noise too seemed to be coming from there. Just then he heard the rumble of a truck on the street. It too was coming from the same direction. He couldn't see clearly because of the darkness, but could make out several people huddled inside the truck, with weapons flashing in the hands of at least a few of them. A tremor shot through his entire body. Just then he heard a faint clatter outside his room, which set his heart pounding. An unknown fear reared up in his mind like the hood of a cobra. God only knew what was about to happen! Could it be that the neighbours had found out that Vidya's family was harbouring an enemy, and so now were insisting, even this late at night, that they hand him over to them? He imagined himself being dragged out by a group of young men with saffron headbands. He would be gagged and, try hard as he might, just wouldn't be able to get a sound out. He groped for the light switch and turned it on. The room brightened. Shortly thereafter the door opened and Vidyacharan entered.

'You turned on the light—what's the matter?'

'Nothing. I just woke up suddenly.'

Vidyacharan stared and then said as he sat down on the sofa, 'I peeked in earlier, but you were sleeping.'

'How come you aren't in bed?'

'I can't fall asleep.'

'Why not?'

'I keep thinking that you don't feel safe here.'

'No, it isn't like that at all. You wouldn't let me be harmed in any way—I know that, Vidya. But given the conditions, it's hard not to feel at least a little bit alarmed.'

'I understand. But remember this: no matter how volatile it may be all around, all it'll take is a phone call, and a whole battalion of policemen will show up. The Police Commissioner is my friend. If you'd like to talk to him, I can arrange that right away.'

'No, no. There's no need. Vidya, please don't misunderstand me. I trust you completely.'

After a brief silence, Vidya abruptly asked, 'Want some coffee?'

'I suppose I could use a cup.'

'Wait. I'll go and fix some.'

The entire household came together again in the morning at breakfast.
The situation outside remained unchanged. The curfew, though, was lifted
for two hours. It was back in effect at ten o'clock.

Vidya called the railway station, police station, S.T. bus depot, Ashiyad
bus terminal, taxi-stand—just about everywhere to get some idea of the
situation. Everywhere he got the same answer: 'The situation doesn't look
good. Better not travel.'

The telephone line to Pune was still dead. Enquiries were made at the
telephone exchange, but no satisfactory explanation was offered. His anxiety
was growing worse by the minute. But deftly hiding what was eating away
at him inside, he kept talking to Vidya, his father, his mother, Shyam, and
Arti as normally as he possibly could. He had Pappu recite two poems
for him, and told him the story of the triple-horned demon, in which the
prince hacks off each of the three horns one after another with his sword.
Pappu was extremely pleased. He clapped and laughed for a long time.
For his own part, though, he wondered: how could a six-foot-tall prince
possibly exterminate a giant six times his size? But children are so gullible.
How easily they believe everything in a story. It's only when they grow
up that they sink into the quagmire of doubt, suspicion, scepticism, and
lack of trust. Seeing Pappu clap so joyously, he remembered his sons Sajid
and Majid. He quickly bent over Pappu and kissed him on the forehead.
Once again he started to feel anxiety tug at his heart. He got up and
returned to his room.

Standing at the window he gazed into the desolate street for the longest
time. All looked clear in the direction where he had seen that terrible smoke
rising last night. A few young men stood talking inside the compound wall
of the building directly in front. A police van drove in, moving at a snail's
pace, and slowly inched further and further away. Suddenly a noise erupted
to his left. He poked his head out to see. A scrawny young man ran out
of a narrow alley. His wrists were bound behind him and his clothes were
on fire. 'Help! Help!' he was shouting. 'Water! Water!' Perhaps his clothes
had been doused with kerosene, because the fire was spreading very fast.
His screams prompted the windows of the buildings around to open one

by one. A few people craned their necks to look at him. The emaciated young man was jerking his head, all the while screaming for help. 'Untie my hands! What will you get by killing me? Water!…Water!'

He ran towards the compound where the group of young men stood talking. But the moment he came near the gate, they quickly closed it. The man kept begging them for water. But they turned around and went inside the building.

By now the flames had completely enveloped the youth, who looked like a single flame in motion. Running, he fell, and started to roll in the middle of the street, still screaming in sheer torment.

The tied hands finally broke free. All at once, charged with a sudden surge of energy, he got up and started madly to tear off his burning clothes from his body. But once again he stumbled and fell down, and began to writhe and thrash on the ground. His screams subsided into moans, his convulsions getting progressively weaker. His clothes had turned to ashes that stuck to his body, which had itself become as charred as a piece of charcoal. His moans too subsided.

Only one or another part of his body twitched as the fire began to die down.

Anwar gazed into the scene like it was a frightening nightmare, his hands clutching the frame of the window. His temples pounded as though he had been stuffed into the belly of an endlessly beaten kettledrum. He was shaking…slowly.

Down below, the body of the youth had by now become completely charred. The fire too had died, giving off a few stray curls of smoke. Just then a police siren blared. People peering out quickly shut their windows, though some left just a crack from which to peek. He too backed up, closed the window with his tremulous hands, and looked out from the chink. The police van stopped a little way from the charred body. Four or five constables got down from the van, and the inspector from the front seat. The inspector walked over to the body with perfect composure. He had covered his mouth and nose with his handkerchief. The constables too held their noses between their thumbs and index fingers and followed him. They stood around the body. The corpse was now naked and had been rendered grotesque by the fire. The inspector said something, and one of the constables, still holding his nose, bent over and poked the corpse with his long stick. Then, shaking his head 'No,' he stood up straight. The inspector lifted his head and gave a sweeping look at the neighbouring buildings. Heads peering from behind the slim openings in the windows instantaneously withdrew like turtles.

The inspector thundered: 'Who burnt him? Tell me, who burnt him? Answer me!'

The openings in the windows further narrowed. Waving his stick the inspector walked to the corner of the alley on the left, peered into it, and then walked back to the corpse. Once again he raised his head to the windows and yelled, 'At least throw down a cloth to cover the body. Have you lost all sense of humanity?'

A painful silence swept over the scene for a while. Then a window on the first floor of the building in front opened and an old man, leaning halfway out, tossed a white bedsheet down to the street. Then another window opened. A woman poked her head out and she too threw a folded white bedsheet down to the street. And then another window opened, and then another. Seven sparkling white bedsheets were tossed out within a few minutes. The inspector shouted, 'That's enough charity! Now stop it!'

Two constables stepped forward. Picking up one of the sheets, they unfolded it and spread it over the corpse.

Anwar closed his window and sat down on the bed. Suddenly he felt the whirlwind of dread starting to subside in his mind, replaced by a terrible emptiness. Astonishingly, all at once, he had risen above every fear, every apprehension.

THE VULTURES OF THE PARSI CEMETERY

ALI IMAM NAQVI

I t was all so unexpected. They were stunned. They put the stretcher down abruptly, gawked at the dead body, then looked at each other with a million questions stirring in their eyes. Their eyeballs moved dumbly in their sockets for quite some time, and when they stopped, the two shrugged their shoulders uncomprehendingly. Then, simultaneously, they grimaced, severely straining their necks and letting their gaze hover over the dense trees of the Parsi cemetery. Not a single vulture! Not even as far as one could see! This was absolutely the first time that such a thing had happened. The bell had gone off two hours earlier to put them on alert. And sure enough, a quarter-of-an-hour later the attendants of Bagli No. 2 were handing the corpse over to them. The two had pulled the corpse into the bawli area and closed the doors behind them. Later Pheroze Bhatina, having opened the small window in the door and questioned the funeral attendants outside about the relatives of the deceased, asked one of them, 'How about the tips—did they give any?'

The attendant had smiled and flashed two ten-rupee notes at Bhatina, who promptly snatched them, stuffed one in the pocket of his dagla and gave the other to his companion, Hormoz. Then they shut the window.

'Good Lord,' Hormoz lifted his head and gratefully looked at the stretch of sky peeping in from the thick foliage of tall trees. Then he motioned to Bhatina with his eyes. The two bent over, picked up the stretcher, and started to walk towards the bawli.

'Pheroze,' Hormoz addressed his companion, walking along.

'Yes.'

'How long...I mean how long will we go on doing this sort of work?'

'Cut it out.'

'Yaar, is it the only thing we're good for?'

'So what do you think.'

'Nothing, really. I was merely asking.'

'That's all?'

'That's all. I swear by Zarathustra.' He looked up at the sky.

After a brief silence Bhatina said, 'Look, Hormoz. The Parsi Council took care of us, didn't it? Let's just say we were the unlucky ones. Right? What do you say?'

'Same story. Not much difference. But the truth is, I'm fed up. I'm just plain fed up.'

Their conversation was cut short, as they had reached the bawli enclosure. A single kick of Hormoz's foot opened the door and the very next instant they took their places by the corpse, one standing by the corpse's head, the other by its feet. The corpse's face, which had been smeared with yogurt, was absolutely white. Hormoz lifted the head a little and Bhatina quickly pulled the shroud clean out from under it. By turns they reverentially touched the corpse's feet, touched their hands to their eyes and chests as a sign of respect, and got up. A handkerchief had been put around the waist with the ritual kasti-string to cover the corpse's nakedness. They left it alone. Then they came to their quarters in the corner of the bawli compound and sat down at a table. After some time Hormoz set a wine bottle on the table and the two filled their glasses. Pheroze Bhatina popped a piece of arvi roll into his mouth and said, 'Hormoz.'

'Yes, what?'

'What a life!'

'What's the matter?'

'Bagli No. 1, 2, 4...the bell...son of a bitch...and...'

'And?'

'Yeah, and...'

'And—what?'

'Corpses...still more corpses...'

'I don't understand.'

'Just look. Look at the life of a Parsi.'

'Life?'

'Yes.'

'What about it?'

'His youth runs super fast but his old age merely crawls along like a freight train.'

'True, brother, absolutely true.'

'Yes, absolutely true.'

They kept up the litany of 'true, true' for quite a while as they continued to drink, breaking somewhat later into fits of sobs. After an hour or so the bell went off again. This time the corpse was coming from Bagli No. 4.

'There, Lord Zarathustra's provided for more wine.'

'Come on, yaar, let's get going.'

They made their way over to the bawli's main entrance. The door opened a second time. They slid the empty stretcher out. Moments later it was pushed back in with the corpse from Bagli No. 4. One of the attendants tossed two ten-rupee notes at them once again. But this time Hormoz stepped forward to grab the money. Then they closed the door, picked up the stretcher and started off toward the bawli.

'Hormoz?'

'Yes, what?'

'One day we too will end up dead, just like this, no?'

Hormoz stopped, turned his head to look at Pheroze Bhatina, and then asked him rather harshly, 'Now what makes you ask a question like that?'

'Everyone has to die.'

'True. But I'm not planning on dying quite yet.'

'Planning? What the hell do you mean?'

'Shut up, fool. What have we seen in life so far? Dead bodies, more dead bodies, and vultures. At the most, a little wine now and then from that fucking Sitara Road liquor store…crude, mixed with ammonium chloride… ten rupee notes. I ask: is this what you call life?'

Pheroze didn't answer, he just kept looking at Hormoz.

'Come on, brother, is it life?'

'What can I say. All I know is this: when the call comes, I must go. Somebody else will take my place. When you go, somebody else will take your place too.'

'Shut up, fool! Bastard! Pig!' Hormoz shouted.

'Don't make a racket. Stop talking about life. Look, we've got a corpse to take care of.'

They shut up. Walked over to the bawli in silence. And when they opened the door…

It was all so unexpected. They were stunned. They put the stretcher down abruptly, gawked at the dead body, and then looked at each other with a million questions stirring in their eyes. Their eyeballs moved dumbly in their sockets for quite some time, and when they stopped, the two shrugged their shoulders uncomprehendingly… And then they let their gaze hover over the dense trees of the Parsi cemetery. There was not a single vulture anywhere in sight.

This was absolutely the first time it had happened. Corpses, but no vultures in sight anywhere. Usually though, after Hormoz and Pheroze had dragged a corpse to the bawli, the vultures made short work of it within minutes. As they saw the vultures return, they would come back to the bawli, douse the skeleton with acid, which would then crumble like fine dust into the depths of the bawli—gone forever, who knows where? Sometimes no dead body was brought in for days on end. But on such occasions the Parsi Council would buy a goat and have it delivered to Hormoz and Bhatina who would then feed it to the vultures, lest hunger drive them away for ever. But this? Corpses—a shoal of them, so to speak—ready but no vultures around to finish them off!

Both gawked at each other with peeled eyes. After they had stood there dumbly for some time they put the second corpse on the mesh as well, then they covered the mouth of the bawli and gave each other a deep questioning look.

'What do you think? Shall I go and let Keqabad know?'

'Yes. Go!'

Bhatina went into his room and pressed the emergency button. The red bulb on the wall of the office of the Parsi cemetery began to blink. The clerks scampered out—confused, shocked. Similar bulbs also went on in the baglis. The clerics stopped the holy recitation from the Avesta. Dogs wandering about in the baglis were suddenly gripped by fear and slunk into corners. Mournful relatives accompanying their dear departed stepped out of the baglis in a state of prodigious nervousness. Everywhere there was a single question: What's happened?

Keqabad bounded out, looked at the sky closely and promptly went back in. People hemmed him in, noisily asking the same question, 'What's happened?' In response Keqabad announced, 'The vultures have gone away!'

'Vultures've gone away?'

'But why?'

'Something's bound to happen!'

'But what?'

The secretary of the Parsi Council received Keqabad's phone call. His forehead began to wrinkle. After he had heard it all he returned the receiver to the cradle, turned on the intercom and informed the director of the matter. Right away an emergency meeting was called. The matter was presented before the board of directors. But the question persisted: Where did the vultures disappear to?

'What did you say, the vultures have disappeared?' the police commissioner asked with a trace of surprise in his voice.

'Yes, our vultures have disappeared,' the chairman of the Parsi Council confirmed, stressing each syllable. In rapt attention he listened to all that the police commissioner had to say, his face turning one colour after another. He listened to him for a long time. After the commissioner had hung up, the chairman too had returned the receiver to the cradle and looked at the directors and found their gaze intent upon him with a single question. He apprised them of the substance of his talk with the commissioner. Each of the participants left the meeting with tremendous worry and only a slight feeling of reassurance. The secretary rang up the cemetery. Then Keqabad briefly summed up the substance of the exchange between the police commissioner and the chairman to the revered clerics and others present. From the clerics the news travelled down to the attendants of the baglis and from them ultimately to Pheroze Bhatina and Hormoz. Bhatina listened to the whole thing very carefully. He then looked at the sky, clearly visible from random openings in the dense foliage: there was not even a crow anywhere, or a kite, let alone a vulture!

All of a sudden they flinched. The bell had gone off again. A corpse was being sent from Bagli No. 3. Once again they were standing at the door. The corpse arrived. This time, though, the attendant thrust two fifty-rupee notes at Bhatina. After Bhatina and Hormoz had pulled the corpse inside, the latter grimaced and said 'Hormoz!'

'Yes, what is it?'

'Why in hell have all the Parsis decided to die only today?'

Hormoz didn't answer. He just went on looking at the sky.

'To start with, no vultures in sight; then corpse after corpse comes our way.'

'Where have the vultures disappeared to?'

'The police commissioner said the vultures, all of them, are flocking to the Kharki, Raviwar Peth and Somwar Peth neighbourhoods.'

'What for?'

'Oh these idiot Hindus and Muslims are at each other's throats again. There's been a riot. The bastards, they've torched everything: houses, shops, even ambulances and hearses, the whole lot. The street is littered with corpses. One right on top of the other. Piled high. Our vultures—well, they're having a feast there. And that police commissioner...he said that after the street's been cleaned up, the vultures will come back on their own accord.'

'Even if the street's cleaned up—so what? What makes you think the vultures will return? This fucking India...there is a riot every day here, every day a fire, every day people die. The vultures'll come back? The hell they will!'

THE TREE

TASSADUQ SOHAIL

I like solitude. Nobody visits me, nor I anyone. In the morning I set out for wherever fancy strikes me and stop wherever I feel like stopping. I go in whatever direction I please. I don't want anyone to reply to anything I say, nor expect a reply from me. This is why my acquaintances are not my neighbours but rather their cats. These houses, I know them by the cats that live in them: Suti lives in No. 9, Libi in No. 7 and Suzie in No. 2. I have never tried to find out who owns these cats. My only interaction is with the cats. Perhaps you wonder how anyone can possibly live like this? Surely one needs others at some point. Surely one must need to say something to someone. Of course such thoughts frequently assail me, especially during winters, when the sky is covered with dirty, drab-looking clouds and rows upon rows of gigantic leafless trees stand listlessly staring up into it. Then it becomes terribly difficult to stay indoors all alone. At such times I try to keep myself busy, very busy. Sometimes by painting, sometimes by reading books, or by listening to Mehdi Hasan or Musarrat Nazir on the radio. Sometimes I let myself be carried far away by the melody of their songs or ghazals to the narrow lanes of Pakistan, its neighbourhoods, villages and towns, thinking that it must be eleven in the morning there. Kites must be sailing in the crystal-blue sky; simple, ordinary folks must be on their way to work. Thinking thoughts like these and sipping wine, I often doze off. But that day I was feeling terribly depressed. The assault was particularly fierce. I felt that my mind would soon explode if I didn't find someone who would relieve my tension. I'd go mad, tear my clothes and jump in front of a bus. I sat holding my head between my hands for quite a while. When the tension inside me became unbearable, I grabbed my overcoat and dashed out to the park. The park was murderously quiet and a wretched silence hung in the atmosphere. I sat down on the roots of a tree, leaning against the trunk. I had a strange feeling that the tree hugged me, as if it were alive. This tree has been standing here for centuries. God knows how many people have come and sat down beside it like me. I have known this tree for the past thirty years. It's been a witness to my youth. I used to bring my girlfriends here. And today it's witnessing my old age. If only I could understand your tongue!—I said, looking wistfully at the tree in utter despair. Sher Khan, my tomcat—who used to listen to my ravings at such times, who was my intimate friend, my consoler and my comforter—had been dead for a month. He was a wise cat. We each knew every single habit and gesture of the other. I had seen smiles dance on his lips, and despair in his eyes. Cats talk, but they talk with their eyes. He and I used to talk through gestures for hours. The times when I'd be particularly down with melancholy, he'd sit near me and listen to me without blinking. Well, where Sher Khan is concerned, it's understandable that a person would talk to him because he was a living being, one who ate and drank and bounced around, and who was endowed with the faculty to observe, to listen and to understand. But talking to a tree?—that, surely, was madness, sheer madness. And although for years I had often sat down on its roots, I had scarcely ever imagined that a person could also talk to it. The tree is alive—I told myself—but is it also as full of life as Sher Khan? What difference does that make—I said to myself, feeling irritated. All I want, after all, is to vent a little. I'll leave after I've eased myself a bit, and nobody will be any the wiser. And even if the wiser, what do I care! I looked around. There was no one near or far. Grabbing the chance I draped myself around its trunk and broke into inconsolable sobs: God, at least give me enough courage to kill myself! I can no longer find the strength to go through life sobbing and crying. How long will I have to endure this torture? God only knows what else I spewed out in a single breath.

Surprised by the words 'Oh, sod off from here,' I flew and fell a few yards away from the tree. Who had spoken these words? I scanned the area with my eyes wide open. There was no one anywhere in the vicinity of the tree.

'You idiot!' the voice echoed again. It was the tree speaking.

'What? You're talking!' I said to the tree in a crackling voice.

'What did you think? That only you know how to speak? The noblest among creation? My foot!' he said angrily. 'Why, we have neither speech, nor feelings, nor do we understand. Right? All these, God has bestowed only upon you.'

I quickly withdrew my foot from the root.

'Thank you,' the tree said, and continued, 'It's true that we trees aren't in the habit of talking. You know why? Because talking breeds enmity. In bygone days, though, we did use to talk. But when these descendants of monkeys started to shoot off their mouths, and to consider themselves somebodies that could talk, we trees stopped talking. Let's see, we thought, what all man can achieve by blathering that we can't by keeping quiet. But now, today, after centuries, your utter stupidity has compelled me to break my silence. A few days of cold weather and there you go having fits of depression! A few clouds in the sky and you break into tears hugging the squirrels. For God's sake, have you ever bothered about anyone other than yourself? Your entire world is no bigger than the cocoon that surrounds you!'

The tree paused for a brief moment and resumed: 'You've no idea how fortunate you are. You can jump from a bridge and drown yourself if you like. Or put an end to your miserable life by hanging yourself with a rope. Or jump to your death from a window. But me, I can't die, even if I want to. I can't hang myself by a rope. God hasn't even given me the right to call it quits at a moment of my own choosing. Do you realize I've been stuck in the earth right here at this spot for the last five hundred years? Don't you think I sometimes feel like taking a stroll? To walk up to Golders Green Road? Or go to Brighton, strip off my leaves and loll about on the Nude Beach for a few hours. I long to have a suntan too. But I have never, I repeat never, allowed myself to shed a single tear. Think about it. From the day I was born till now I have never sat down to rest for a moment. Trees also have a desire to sit down and rest. Why do you humans think that we have no feelings? On cold wintry nights when you snuggle under the comfort of heavy quilts inside your homes and sleep a peaceful sleep, I stand out here, with my bare branches, shivering in the dark.'

'From the cold?'

'No, from fear,' he blurted out in a rage.

'What have you got to do with fear?'

'Why, indeed! Am I made of stone?' He paused, and then said, 'Well, I shouldn't say "stone". Because that stone, there…he too is afraid.'

'Why?'

'He's allergic to dogs. The other day he was saying that dog piss gives him rashes. But you wouldn't know about that. It's no fun standing here during dark icy-cold nights all alone.'

After that day I often went to the tree and talked to him. At least some of our thoughts were quite similar and we also enjoyed a kind of mental affinity. I'm not very religious, and he was not at all. He put absolutely no faith in religion. One day he said, 'The entire park is religious except me. All these tiny medicinal herbs you see are religious. And that weeping willow over there, he's the limit. In perpetual prostration. I've never seen him so much as lift his head a smidge. Maybe he'll do it only after he's had half of Paradise allotted to him.'

'So you think there's nothing after death?'

'At least I *think* there isn't, brother. And even if there *is* something, it certainly isn't what these trifling herbs imagine.'

By now the tree had become bored, so I said goodbye to him and left.

In the days that followed, I became ill and left for Pakistan. I had intended to stay there for a month, but I became so absorbed in setting up an exhibition of my paintings and in other matters that I scarcely felt the passage of time, until a whole year had rolled away. On the return flight to London, the passenger in the seat next to mine told me how a terrible wind storm in England had uprooted some half a million trees. I recalled having read something about it in the papers, but I was finding the number of fallen trees hard to believe. I remembered the 'Tree' with concern. How I wish I hadn't abandoned him! I thought about that for a while: even if I hadn't abandoned him, what could I have done? I couldn't have saved him. At most I could have spent a few more days under the shade of his thick foliage. Then again, it was possible that he hadn't been felled, that he still stood there swaying happily in the breeze.

When I approached the park, the tree was not there. His place was occupied by a flower patch in the middle of which gardeners had planted a spindly young tree and secured it with a thick bamboo prop so that it wouldn't bend over and break in an onslaught of ferocious winds. Overcome by sadness, I roamed aimlessly around in the park for quite a while, looking for all those trees the stormy winds had felled and obliterated. The entire park looked radically different. The soaring wall of stout white trees, which formerly stood behind the bandstand and seemed to pierce the clouds, had been completely wiped out.

One of the gardeners, whom I just barely knew, started telling me about the devastation caused by the storm as he turned over the earth with his shovel. He described how they had just removed the small, insignificant trees to one side and burned them, and how the really big trees had been bought by furniture-makers and hauled away to be stored. 'But *your* tree,' he said, 'I remember vividly, was purchased by a small Birmingham company. I remember that well because I myself had it loaded onto a truck. I doubt if anyone can locate it.'

I realized that the gardener was talking about something scarcely two months' old. I made a note of the company's Birmingham address and returned home. I thought about the matter for a few days. 'Look,' I tried to reason with myself, 'it's madness.' If anyone found out about it, they would surely think I'm crazy. But the madness didn't abate. On the contrary it became oppressive, until one day I found myself standing in front of that timber yard.

'Okay, sir, now what are you going to tell them?' I asked myself. 'That you want to look at the face of that dear departed tree? Well, you've managed to stay out of the loony bin so far, but don't count on it. They'll nab you and put you into one any day now. Suppose they asked you "Why?" What possible answer would you give them?' And then, as if in a flash, I seemed to stumble onto a suitable answer. 'I'm writing an article about that tree: the different stages it had to go through and how it ended.' The thought had barely hit me when I dashed into the office of the timber yard.

'Oh,' jerking back a golden curl, the blonde receptionist said after I told her that. She then opened a register. Her finger moved across the lines and stopped at one. 'Lot 17... We sold the biggest chunk of the tree to Mr Collin Turner, the sculptor.'

The next day I visited Mr Collin Turner in his studio. He was busy sculpting a nude. I asked him about the lot. He scratched his bald head and said, 'I think we made a Christ figure with Lot 17 and sold it to a church. But hold on, let me check.' After he checked, he scribbled the name and address of the church on scratch paper and handed it to me. I thanked him and left to look for the church.

It was a small, beautiful town. A lovely church stood some distance away from the residential area. The evening mass had already ended. Although the last of the sun's rays were still stretched out on the church roof, the shadows under the neighbouring trees had darkened. I walked slowly through the main door and entered the hall. I dipped my finger into the font of holy water, bent my leg ever so slightly and crossed my heart as my eyes looked straight ahead at the Christ. Picking my way along in silence, I approached the massive figure. Again I bent one leg and crossed my heart and then straightened up and stood next to an old woman. She was mumbling something. A little while later she tilted her head forward and bowed, and then she rose slowly and left. I raised my head for the first time and looked at the Christ. One of his hands was held out above my head and in his other hand he had a tall staff. With his half-opened eyes he seemed to be staring at the spot on the floor where I was standing.

The church was completely empty now except for the two of us. A dim light spread out around us. The glow of the lighted candles surrounding the Christ gave him an added aura of mystery. I extended my arm and placed my hand on his foot.

'So you've come,' he said.

A heavy bass voice crashed against the walls inside and then silence returned.

'Yes, my Tree.'

And as I said those words my eyes involuntarily spilled their cargo of tears. I grasped his foot tightly with my trembling hand. 'But, didn't you use to say that there was no hell or heaven after death?' I said.

After some time, when the tree didn't respond, I lifted my head up and looked at it. A strange, mysterious smile was breaking on his lips... the same as Mona Lisa's.

NOTES ON THE AUTHORS

ABDULLAH HUSSEIN (1936–2015) was the pen name of Muhammad Khan. He gave up a lucrative career in chemical engineering to devote his time to writing. He shot to fame with the publication of his debut novel, *Udaas Naslen,* for which he received Pakistan's highest literary award, the Adamjee Award, in 1963. He later translated it as *The Weary Generations* (London: Peter Owen, 1999) for the UNESCO Collection of Representative Works. His English novel, *Emigré Journeys,* a work set entirely in England, was published by Serpent's Tail, London, in 2000. It revisits the theme of his earlier Urdu novella *Waapsi ka Safar* (The Journey Back), and was filmed by Udayan Prasad as *Brothers in Trouble,* 1995. His Urdu work includes four novels, several novellas and short stories. He received from Pakistan Academy of Letters its prestigious Kamaal-e Fan Award in 2012. He lived in England for several decades but finally settled in Lahore. Before his death, he was working on a novel in English about Afghanistan.

ALI IMAM NAQVI was born in 1945 in Bombay, where he received his early education at Ismail Beg Muhammad High School. He has published two collections of short stories and a novel. He makes his home in Bombay, where he works for the Iran Council.

ALTAF FATIMA was born in Lucknow. On Partition in 1947 she migrated to Pakistan and settled in Lahore where she earned an MA and BEd from the University of Punjab. She is counted as a leading figure among women Urdu writers and has published several collections of short stories in addition to novels. Her second novel was translated into English as *The One Who Did Not Ask* (Oxford: Heinemann, 1993).

ANWER KHAN was born in Bombay. After his double MA degrees in Urdu and Persian he started working at the Bombay Port Trust. His first short story appeared in 1970, followed by a steady stream of fictional work. Before his premature death in 2001, he had published to critical acclaim four collections of short stories and a novel. His stories stand out for their keen observation of diverse facets of life in his native city, especially those of its minorities and subcultures.

ASAD MUHAMMAD KHAN was born in Bhopal, India, in 1932. He now lives in Karachi, Pakistan. A prolific writer, he has written a number of television plays; several of his short stories have appeared in the collection *Jo Kahaaniyaañ Likhiñ*. A selection of his stories in English translation, *The Harvest of Anger and Other Stories*, was published by Oxford University Press, Karachi in 2002 as part of its Pakistan Writers Series.

ASHFAQ AHMAD was born in Ferozepur district in 1925 and died at Lahore in 2005. He started writing fiction in the 1950s and quickly established himself as a major short story writer. *Ujle Phool*, from which the iconic short story 'The Shepherd' is taken, and *Ek Muhabbat, Sau Afsaane* are among his more famous collections. He also wrote a short novel and a volume of Punjabi plays. He was the editor of the tastefully produced literary magazine *Dastan-go* and the weekly *Lail-o-Nahaar*. Today his fame rests chiefly on his travelogues, radio features, and TV plays. He was Director General, Urdu Science Board, Lahore, for several years.

GHULAM ABBAS (1909–1982) edited the popular children's magazine *Phool* before joining All India Radio in the 1940s. He moved to Pakistan in 1947 and edited the Radio Pakistan magazine *Aahang* until his retirement in the late 1960s. He is considered one of the major writers of the Urdu short story, of which he published three collections. *Hotel Moenjodaro and Other Stories* is a selection of his stories in English translation.

IKRAMULLAH (CHAUDHRY) was born in 1930 in Jandiala, a small village in the Nawanshahr district of Jalandhar in India. He received his early education in Amritsar. His family moved to Multan after Partition. Here, he took a law degree and practised for a few years. Eventually, he switched to the insurance business, retiring in 1990. He has been writing fiction since 1962 and has published several collections of short stories and, more recently, a novel, *Sa'e ki Aavaaz*. His novella, *Gurg-e Shab*, was banned by the Pakistan government. In 2016, he received the President's Award for Pride of Performance. He lives in Lahore.

INTIZAR HUSAIN was born in Dibai near Bulandshahar in UP in 1925 and migrated to Pakistan in 1947. A writer, columnist, critic and translator, he published five volumes of short stories, three novels, and a novella. The *Journal of South Asian Literature* devoted an entire issue to him in 1983, and his second novel, *Basti* (Town), was nominated for the Man Booker Prize in 2013. Early in his writerly career, he wrote columns for the Urdu newspaper *Mashriq* and, much later, for the Karachi-based English newspaper *Dawn*. *The Seventh Door*, a collection of his short stories in English translation, was published by Lynne Rienner in 1997. In September 2014, he was made an Officer of the Order of Arts and Letters of the French Academy in recognition of his contributions to Urdu literature. He lived in Lahore and died there in 2016.

ISMAT CHUGHTAI, counted among the earliest and foremost women Urdu writers, was born in Badayun, UP, in 1915 and was educated at Agra, Aligarh, and Lucknow. She worked as a headmistress first in Jawra State and later at Bareilly. Her literary career started in 1938 with a play. Her short stories later appeared in the renowned literary magazines of the time, such as *Saaqi* and *Adabi Dunyaa*. A major voice of the Progressive Writers' Movement and an outspoken champion of women's causes, she moved to Bombay, married writer, producer, and director Shahid Lateef, and wrote for films and the radio. She died in Bombay in 1991. Her published work includes several collections of short stories, three novellas, and two novels, including *Terhi Lakir* (*The Crooked Line;* Heinemann, 1995). 'Lihaf' (The Quilt) is considered her most controversial short story, as it deals with the plight of a married woman thirsting for her husband's love and embrace which, when denied, drive her to the affections of another woman.

JAMEELA HASHMI (1929–1988) received her master's degree in English literature and taught in a school for several years. She is the author of several short story collections and novels. Her debut novel, *Talaash-e Bahaaraan,* was the recipient of Pakistan's Adamjee Award in 1960. Another novel, *Dasht-e Sus,* which brought her great critical acclaim, is based on the life of the tenth-century martyr-mystic, Mansur al-Hallaj.

KHALIDA ASGHAR was born in Lahore in 1938. She started writing fiction in 1963. After half a dozen brilliant short stories, she dropped out of the Urdu literary scene altogether. Married in 1965, she moved to Karachi in 1967. After a twelve-year silence, she staged a comeback in 1977—wiser, more experienced, somewhat less willing to take risks. The subconscious compulsions of a pained psyche, so powerfully captured in her earlier work, appear more muted in the stories spanning the second phase. She has published six volumes of short stories, some of which have been translated into Hindi, and a novel. She later settled in Islamabad where she taught English in a girls' college. 'The Wagon', which first appeared in *Savera* 35 (Lahore) in the early 1960s, is generally regarded as her crowning achievement and has been the staple of many English anthologies published overseas. She now writes under the name of Khalida Husain.

MUHAMMAD SALIM-UR-RAHMAN was born in India in 1934 and is an eminent Urdu poet and critic. He started his literary career with an Urdu translation of Homer's *Odyssey*. He is editor of one of the best modern Urdu literary journals, *Savera*, and was also an associate editor of the weekly *Nusrat*. Since 1963 he has been writing book reviews and literary columns for many English newspapers. He has published poems, half a dozen short stories, and numerous translations from English into Urdu. Three of his English poems appeared in *Poetry North West*. The first volume of his critical work on ancient Greek literature was published a few years ago.

MUNSHI PREMCHAND was one of the earliest writers of Urdu fiction. His phenomenal output was marked by his passionate belief in the transformative agency of literature in ridding society of its myriad social and religious ills. This consuming concern with society was already apparent in his short debut novel, *Asraar-e Ma'aabid*, (Secrets of Places of Worship), and most of what he wrote since revisited this theme in one form or another. The conditions of the country perhaps occupied his mind so completely that he couldn't imagine an autonomous role for literature. When the Progressive Movement came along, he blessed it with all his heart, because the Progressives, too, believed in using literature as a vehicle for bettering society. Premchand was born in the small village of Lamhi near Banaras in 1880. Here, he received his early education in Persian and Urdu under a maulvi in a madrasa. He first wrote in Urdu, but later switched to Hindi in view of the poor market for Urdu books, too small to support him. He has the author of more than a dozen novels, over two hundred short stories, several essays and translations of foreign literary works. Some of his novels and countless stories have been translated into English and other languages. His last novel, *Godaan* (The Offering of a Cow), finished just before his death in 1936, and the story 'Kafan' (The Shroud) rank among his most engaging and enduring works.

NAIYER MASUD (b. 1930, Lucknow) is considered the finest Urdu fiction writer today. He is a scholar of Urdu and Persian, a translator (notably of Kafka) and a short story writer. He started publishing stories only in the 1970s. He retired from Lucknow University as a professor of Persian and lives in the house his father built, appropriately called 'Adabistaan' (Abode of Literature). Besides his substantial research work, he has published four collections of stories, translations of Kafka and of contemporary Persian stories. More recently, his entire fictional corpus was published in a single volume (*Collected Stories;* Penguin, 2015). Masud was the recipient of the Saraswati Samman in 2007.

QURRATULAIN HYDER (1927–2007) ranked among the foremost women writers of Urdu fiction, produced seven novels, several collections of short stories, and translations into Urdu of such writers as Henry James, T. S. Eliot, and Truman Capote. Her critically acclaimed, but no less controversial, novel, *Aag kaa Daryaa,* has been translated into fifteen Indian languages, and was published in 1999 as *River of Fire,* transcreated by the author herself. She worked as one of the editors of *Imprint* magazine (Bombay) and later as a member of the editorial staff of the *Illustrated Weekly of India.* She spent a year as writer-in-residence in the International Writers Program at the University of Iowa. She was the recipient of many honours and awards, among them the Sahitya Akademi Award for her collection of short stories, *Patjhar ki Aavaaz,* and the Bharatiya Jnanpith Award. She was conferred the Padma Shri in 1984 and the Padma Bhushan in 2005 by the Government of India for her contribution to Urdu literature and education.

RAJINDER SINGH BEDI was born in Lahore in 1915. He first worked as a clerk in the postal department; later he joined the Lahore office of All India Radio and wrote many successful plays, having meanwhile established himself as a highly nuanced fiction writer, with the publication of *Daana-o-Daam,* his first collection of short stories. On Partition, he moved to India. After working briefly as Station Director, Radio Kashmir, he joined the Bombay film industry, producing and writing scripts for a number of successful films. His Urdu novel, *Ek Chaadar Maili Si,* translated into English by Khushwant Singh as *I Take This Woman,* received the Sahitya Akademi Award in 1965. Bedi, who died in 1984, is regarded as the second most prominent Urdu fiction writer after Saadat Hasan Manto. He received the Filmfare Best Dialogue Award for *Madhumati* (1958) and for *Satyakam* (1969).

SAADAT HASAN MANTO is generally regarded as the subcontinent's pre-eminent modern Urdu short fiction writer. He was a brilliant and prolific innovator. Born in Samrala (Ludhiana district) in 1912, he passed away in Lahore in 1955 at the age of forty-three. Of all Urdu fiction writers, he was the one who contributed the largest number of consistently high quality and equally controversial creative work to the Partition corpus. In pre-Partition India, he worked for a while at All India Radio, Delhi, and later moved to Bombay to work for the movie industry. On Partition, he emigrated to Pakistan. Manto's prolific writing, which includes plays, short stories, personality sketches, Partition vignettes, and articles have appeared in five huge volumes from Lahore. He was tried in court for his short story 'Thandaa Gosht', which is set against the rioting and bloodshed of 1947. Roshan Dhunjibhoy made a film on Manto for German TV in 1990 that includes the dramatizations of three of his stories. In 1987, another of his Partition stories, the all-time favourite 'Toba Tek Singh', was made into a feature film by Bandung Films, London. Manto was posthumously awarded the Nishaan-e Imtiaaz by the Government of Pakistan, and on 18 January 2005, the fiftieth anniversary of his death, Manto was commemorated on a Pakistani postage stamp.

SAJID RASHID was a noted writer and journalist and editor of the quarterly Urdu magazine *Nayaa Waraq*. A liberal Muslim intellectual and activist, he wrote columns for the Mumbai-based Hindi evening newspaper *Mahanagar* and also for the Pakistani publication *Akhbaar-e Jahaan*. He grew up in Mumbai, which is the locale of his stories in the collection *Ek Chhotaa Saa Jahannum* (A Small Hell), one of which is about his schoolmate Dawood Ibrahim, the don of the underworld. His Hindi novel, *Soney ke Daant* (Gold Teeth), for which he received an award from the Prime Minister of India, is based on the life of a prominent beef trader. He died in 2011.

SALAM BIN RAZZAQ is the pen name of Shaikh Abdussalam Abdurrazzaq who was born in 1941 in Panwel in Maharashtra. He finished high school in 1960 and published his first short story two years later in the literary magazine *Shaa'ir*. He is the author of three collections of short stories, two in Urdu and one in Hindi; he has also translated Marathi fiction into Urdu. Currently, he is putting together a two-volume selection of Marathi writing from the last twenty-five years, which he is also translating, for the Maharashtra State Urdu Academy. He lives in Bombay where he teaches in a school run by the Municipal Corporation.

SIDDIQ AALAM was born in 1952 in a small town, Purulia in West Bengal, and since 1983 has lived in Calcutta, a city which is the background of his first novel, *Charnock ki Kashti*. He holds an MA in English and a degree in law. Currently he is Senior Joint Commissioner in the Directorate of Commercial Taxes, Government of India. He has published three collections of short stories, *Aakhri Chhaa'on, Lamp Jaalaney Vaaley*, and *Bain*. He has also published poems, plays and critical essays in prominent literary magazines.

SYED MUHAMMAD ASHRAF, a prominent and well-regarded writer of fiction, was born into a Sufi family of UP. Educated at Aligarh Muslim University, he is now a commissioner of income tax in the Indian Revenue Service. He has published two collections of short stories, one of which has been translated into English as *Waiting for the Morning Breeze*; a novella, *Nambardaar ka Neelaa (The Beast)*; and a novel, *Aakhri Sawaariyaan*. His short story, 'The Man', was the recipient of the Katha Award for Creative Writing. 'The Man', together with the story 'The Rogue', portrays with engaging realism and sensitivity the collapse of mutual trust so essential for keeping a multi-religious society together, and powerfully evokes the paranoia that has gripped Indian Muslims following the resurgence of Hindu nationalism in recent times.

TASSADUQ SOHAIL (b. 1930, Jalandhar) is a Pakistani fiction writer and painter who returned to Pakistan in 2001 after living in London for forty years. He became famous following the screening in England of a TV documentary on his life and art produced by the well-known activist and author Tariq Ali. Sohail has regularly held exhibitions of his work in Europe and South Asia and is ranked among the foremost painters of Pakistan. He has also authored a collection of short stories, *Tanhaa'i ka Safar*. He lives in Karachi and is currently writing his autobiography.

ZAKIA MASHHADI took an advanced degree in Psychology from Lucknow University and worked in its Demographic Research Centre for some time and taught Psychology for six years at Loreto College. Her marriage to Shafi Mashhadi, a bureaucrat and a writer in his own right, and later the birth of their two children obliged her to put her writerly ambition on hold. She came to it much later in life but whatever fiction she wrote was received with critical acclaim. She has published five collections of short stories so far and has also published several books of translated fiction. She lives in Patna.

ZAMIRUDDIN AHMAD was born in Fatehgarh (India) in 1925 and emigrated to Pakistan in 1947. He worked as a journalist in India, Pakistan, the Middle East and the UK and as a broadcaster for the BBC, Voice of America, Radio Pakistan and Pakistan Television. He started writing fiction in the early 1950s. His writings include over three dozen short stories, numerous critical essays, radio plays, and TV serials. In his critical monograph, *Khaatir-e Ma'sum* (1990), he explores the dimension of female sexuality across the entire range of Urdu poetic genres. *Pahli Maut* (1985) is a Hindi translation of his selected stories. A selection of his short fiction was published posthumously by Oxford University Press (Karachi) under the title *The East Wind and Other Short Stories*. He had emigrated to the UK, where he died in 1990.

NOTES ON THE TRANSLATORS

CAROLINE J. BEESON studied Urdu at Cornell University, University of Minnesota, Minneapolis, and at Hyderabad (India).

FARUQ HASSAN (1939–2011) was a poet and translator of fiction and poetry into English and Urdu, including the poems of the celebrated Turkish poet Nazim Hikmet. He held degrees in English from the University of Punjab, Leeds, and New Brunswick. He taught in Pakistan and, after permanently settling in Canada in 1968, at Dawson College, Montreal. His published work includes, among others, collections of his Urdu poetry, and a volume of Pakistani Urdu short stories, *Versions of Truth*, which he co-edited with Khalid Hasan. *Regret*, a co-translated volume of two novellas of Ikramullah, was published by Penguin Books India, in 2014.

GRIFFITH A. CHAUSSÉE was born in Racine, Wisconsin, in 1963. After a BA from the University of Chicago, he moved to the University of Wisconsin, Madison, where he took a master's degree in South Asian Studies. He spent the 1989–1990 academic year in Lahore studying Urdu. He worked as Associate Editor of the *Annual of Urdu Studies* before moving to the University of Virginia, Charlottesville, where he teaches Hindi and Urdu.

JAVAID QAZI was born in Pakistan in 1947. He came to the United States in 1968 to study and finished a doctorate in English literature at Arizona State University in 1978. Over the last forty years, he has taught English literature in various universities in the US, at Manas University in Bishkek, Kyrghyz Republic, and at Girne American University in North Cyprus. He has also worked as a technical writer in the computer industry. He writes fiction and his work has appeared, among others, in *Kansas Quarterly*, *Sequoia*, *Chelsea*, *Toronto South Asian Review*, *Massachusetts Review* and the *Anais Nin: International Journal*. His collection, *Unlikely Stories*, was published by Oxford University Press in 1998. Late in life he developed a passion for painting and has produced admirable work. He lives in San Jose, California.

MUHAMMAD UMAR MEMON is professor emeritus of Urdu literature and Islamic studies at the University of Wisconsin-Madison. He is a critic, short story writer, and translator. He was editor of the *Annual of Urdu Studies* (1993–2014). He lives in Madison, Wisconsin.

ACKNOWLEDGEMENTS

Grateful acknowledgement is made to the following copyright holders for permission to reprint copyrighted material in this volume. While every effort has been made to locate and contact copyright holders and obtain permission, this has not always been possible; any inadvertent omissions brought to our attention will be remedied in future editions.

'Domains of Fear and Desire' by Naiyer Masud. Reprinted by permission of Timsal Masud.

'The Shepherd' by Ashfaq Ahmad. Reprinted by permission of Penguin India.

'Toba Tek Singh' by Saadat Hasan Manto. Reprinted by permission of Penguin India.

'Laajwanti' by Rajinder Singh Bedi. Reprinted by permission of Penguin India.

'Aanandi' by Ghulam Abbas. Reprinted by permission of the *Annual of Urdu Studies* 18. (2003).

'The Saga of Jaanki Raman Pandey' by Zakia Mashhadi. By permission of the author.

'Sunlight' by Abdullah Hussein. Reprinted by permission of the *Annual of Urdu Studies* 14 (1999).

'Of Fists and Rubs' by Ismat Chughtai. Appeared in the September 2010 issue of *Words Without Borders*. Reprinted by permission of Ashish Sawhny (The Estate of Ismat Chughtai).

'Sukhe Saawan' by Zamiruddin Ahmad. Reprinted by permission of the *Annual of Urdu Studies* 8 (1993).

'Banished' by Jamila Hashmi. Reprinted by permission of Penguin.

'Beyond the Fog' by Qurratulain Hyder. Appeared in the September 2010 issue of *Words Without Borders*.

'The Wagon' by Khalida Asghar. First appeared in *Indian Literature* Vol. 19, No. 6 (November-December 1976). Reprinted by permission of the author.

'The Back Room' by Intizar Husain. Reprinted by permission of *Sang-e-Meel*.

'Voices' by Muhammad Salim-ur-Rahman. Reprinted by permission of *Temenos* 12 (1991).

'Do You Suppose It's the East Wind?' by Altaf Fatima. Appeared in the June 2009 issue of *Words Without Borders*.

'Ma'i Dada—The Man With Three Names' by Asad Muhammad Khan. Appeared in the June 2009 issue of *Words Without Borders*.

'The Old Mansion' by Ikramullah. Reprinted by permission of the author.

'Two Old Kippers' by Siddiq Aalam. Reprinted by permission of the author.

'Fable of a Severed Head' by Sajid Rashid. Reprinted by permission of *Words Without Borders* (September 2010).

'The Pose' by Anwer Khan. Reprinted by permission of TSAR.

'The Man' by Syed Muhammad Ashraf. Reprinted by permission of the author.

'A Sheet' by Salam Bin Razzaq. Reprinted by permission of *Words Without Borders* (September 2010).

'The Vultures of the Parsi Cemetery' by Ali Imam Naqvi. Reprinted by permission of the author.

'The Tree' by Tassaduq Sohail. Reprinted by permission of *The Annual of Urdu Studies* 18 (2003).